KEY OF BEHLISETH

LOU HOFFMANN

Published by
HARMONY INK PRESS

5032 Capital Circle SW, Suite 2, PMB# 279, Tallahassee, FL 32305-7886 USA
publisher@harmonyinkpress.com • http://harmonyinkpress.com

ISBN: 978-1-63216-246-5
Library Edition ISBN: 978-1-63216-247-2
Digital ISBN: 978-1-63216-248-9
Library of Congress Control Number: 2014943594
First Edition September 2014
Library Edition December 2014

First Edition published as *Beyond the Wizard's Threshold* by Loretta Sylvestre, Marion Margaret Press, November 2010

Printed in the United States of America
♾
This paper meets the requirements of
ANSI/NISO Z39.48-1992 (Permanence of Paper).

To my mother Gerda Maria Hoffmann
because she loved adventure

and to Anna Jones
because she believes in magic.

ACKNOWLEDGMENTS

SO MANY gifts of time and perspective have influenced this novel that it isn't possible for me to name everyone who deserves my thanks. I am grateful to all equally, not only those few I'm able to name in this brief paragraph. I must thank my daughter, Kimberly Moore, who listened, read, and critiqued with appropriate heartlessness during the first draft of the novel—and who still loves the story and characters almost as much as I do. My papa, Roland Sylvestre, gets credit for making me, first of all, a reader, and thus a writer. Others include Stephen Mertz, Karla Lammers, Jason Rolfe, Anne Barwell, and Patricia Nelson. Very special thanks go to Catt Ford, whose talent produced a cover I consider no less than stunning. Paul Richmond, thank you for patience and positivity. Last, but in no way least, heartfelt thanks to Elizabeth North and Nessa Warin for believing in my book, and to Anne Regan and all the hard-working, skilled editors and staff at Harmony Ink.

"How queer everything is today! And yesterday things went on just as usual…. Let me think: was I the same when I got up this morning? … But if I'm not the same, the next question is, Who in the world am I?"

—Lewis Carroll, *Alice's Adventures in Wonderland*

TABLE OF CONTENTS

PROLOGUE: MIDSUMMER THREE YEARS AGO...

The Guardian

MIDSUMMER DAY had hardly begun to cool in Black Creek Ravine when Hank George took up his station outside the cavern known as the Doorway. His waist-length, iron gray braids fell heavy in the humid heat, but that didn't account for the way he felt, as though stones weighted his chest and shoulders.

Inside the rock, the luminous halls of the cavern led to a series of tunnels. The Road Between, it was called. Many generations past, the Others had come to Earth by that dark path. Decades later, they'd traveled the same route back to the world that was their home.

A Guardian had watched at the Doorway ever since.

Hank had been watching for more than fifty years. Countless days he'd listened to the ethereal song of the breeze sighing through the cavern. A strange sound always, but never before had it raised the hairs on the back of his neck. He sat down on his favorite stump just outside the cave's entrance; though he remained outwardly calm, tension thrummed through his muscles like voltage through power lines. He rose and took a step toward the entry. A blast of air colder than January cut through his thin shirt and blew back his braids. Perhaps anticipation seized him, maybe dread.

Something was coming. Something was about to begin.

The Wizard

ALONE IN his dilapidated wooden tower, gray-bearded wizard Thurlock leaned out the west window to survey the hundreds of partygoers making merry in the vale that dipped between the Sister Hills. He tried to laugh at toddlers' antics, dancing couples, and smiling old folks tapping arthritic feet to the music of fiddles and pipes. He watched Luccan run across the grassy North Rise, where he and L'Aria, his friend for life, endeavored to fly their new kites. He tried to enter into the prevailing Midsummer joy.

He failed miserably. This was Luccan's twelfth birthday, the day the boy should have received his cardinal name so he could begin to gather the strength it would impart. Knowing a little of what his fortune might hold, the wizard thought surely the youngster would soon need all the strength he could find.

Across the vale stood the neat, sunlit windows and varnished logs of Sisterhold Manor, Luccan's home. Beyond that, in the near distance, Oakridge rose from the hillside like a monument to history. When Luccan was only two hours old, Thurlock had brought him out into the summer dawn and fumbled him into his father's strong but equally fumbling hands. The man had carried his child to the sun-sparked granite on the ridge and whispered a name into his ear, a powerful name known only to them, witnessed solely by the wind.

Now, because of what Thurlock had not done then, disaster threatened—for Luccan, for Sunlands, perhaps for all the world of Ethra. The infant, of course, had forgotten the name. His father had become lost. And the Gods' Breath, fabled dawn wind of the Sunlands, kept its secrets.

The Witch-Mortaine

PRIVATELY, ISA thought it would be best to kill the boy and have done. Granted, the recent strange behavior of time brought opportunity. And true, the boy's unformed powers might boost her own—in the service of her master, of course—if she could subvert them.

Yes. She would bow to the wishes of the Ice-Lord, Mahl, and alter her course. The boy would live, long enough at least to determine if he could be put to use. If the costs in time and effort grew too vast, the boy's death would destroy the enemy's hopes, and Mahl would be appeased.

She took stock of her image in the looking glass. The light filtering through the icy walls of her keep lit her eyes with blue fire and emphasized her long bones and sharp angles. The reflection pleased her. Gone was the soft-faced girl of ages past, the girl who had been a fool.

Staring back from the silvered glass was a woman of power, a witch who could wait for reward.

Yes. She would sow seeds now for the Sunlands' defeat. Later, when she reaped vengeance against the one man who mattered, the fruit would be that much sweeter.

From glass shelves holding bottles, boxes, and vials, she gathered the bits she would need for the spell.

Midsummer stood on the cusp. The moment for cold, hard magic had come.

Part One:
Luccan Lost and Found

CHAPTER ONE:
PALE BLUE, WICKED COLD

In the present day....

WHEN LUCKY stepped off the asphalt at the end of Twelfth Street and into the weeds, it was twilight, a time of day that should have stretched at least an hour on June 21, which was, after all, Midsummer. But Lucky only made it halfway across the mile-wide strip of open land that separates Valley City from Black Creek Ravine when night took him by surprise. It had fallen way too fast.

He tried to laugh it off, even joking aloud with himself, "All I did was blink!" But the darkness had already taken him, and now it crept up his spine, cold like something witched from its grave. He tried to convince himself he could handle the eerie feeling. "It'll be okay, Lucky," he said. "It's been a creepy day, that's all—and it's almost over."

The day in question—which happened to be his fifteenth birthday—had staggered by, every hour weighted down by Lucky's sincere wish that it would move along and get itself over with. Now, as he made his way home, the wind moaned in the pines nearby, and the moon hung like a bloodred bubble in the sky between the rock spires known as Death of the Gods. Frogs and crickets went stone silent just ahead of his every step, and webs appeared out of nowhere, as if hungry spiders by the thousands rode in on moonlight to stretch traps in the grass.

Lucky stopped and leaned forward, hands on his knees, needing to catch his breath. He wasn't sure what had him so winded. Was it because he had to lift his long, bony legs so high to get through the tall grass? Or was he spooked by the sinister night?

After a moment, he pushed back his exasperatingly thick hair—it was *always* in his eyes—and marched on. Before he'd gone ten more steps, Maizie, the big yellow mongrel he'd raised from a pup into a best friend, started barking. Lucky slowed, scanning the field around him and the shadowed trees looming ahead. He felt sure Maizie had seen, heard, or smelled something that didn't belong. She never barked when he was coming home. She hardly ever barked at all.

"Chill," he told himself, and then he started walking again. Seconds later, Maizie bounced out of the trees like a big ball of animated sunshine and greeted Lucky with her whining, toothy grin, just like every night. He had to laugh despite his mood.

"Okay, girl." He dropped a bag of groceries so he could use a hand to fend off Maizie's sloppy tongue and rough up her thick yellow fur. Her tail wagged hard enough to mow the weeds flat in a circle around him, and for those few seconds he didn't feel quite so cursed.

But she bounded off toward home, and as he picked up his spilled groceries—mostly pouches of ramen noodles, precious even at three for a dollar—the shroud of unease dropped around him once more. He didn't even try to shake it off. Hefting his grocery bags, he forged ahead through the whispering weeds until he reached the edge of the wood.

In the pines, an owl called "who." In Lucky's strange state of mind, it sounded like some sort of challenge, so even though he felt completely silly doing it, he answered, "It's just me." He almost wanted to laugh again, but that feeling didn't last long. When he emerged from the trees and caught sight of the shack he called home, he stopped and stared while a chill prickled over his scalp like a tattoo needle made of ice.

Something wasn't right.

Could he have somehow come to the wrong place?

For the comfort the sound of his voice might offer, he spoke aloud again. "Don't be stupid, Lucky. You know your way home by now."

He'd been living there for nearly a year. After about that same length of time sleeping in alleys and doorways—only occasionally sleeping in a bed, which was even worse—he'd been raveled to within a hair's breadth of wanting to give up. Even now he didn't want to think of what that might have meant. But he'd been truly lucky, for once, and happened on this old shed while he was looking for a place to hide from truant officers who'd spotted him trying to panhandle. He'd slept better that night than he had in a long time, and the next morning he decided to make the place his own. He'd swept away bugs and spiders, pounded loose nails, and even mended split planks, and within a few weeks he'd patched it up. Ever since, he'd shared the ten-by-twelve space with Maizie and a family of finches in the eaves, and he'd come to think of it as the one secure place on Earth.

The shack might once have been in the center of a pasture or field, but the walls of Black Creek's infamous gorge had since crumbled, and now the structure squatted at the cliff's edge, at the end of the flats. Ordinarily, that precarious location didn't trouble Lucky. But tonight… tonight a mist rose from the ravine and pearled silver in the moonlight, twisting and twining like ghost flesh. The strange, swarming fog cut the cabin's hulk off from everything beyond, as if the place he counted on as refuge now hunkered at the edge of oblivion, the brink of the world.

He shoved his hair out of his face and sighed. "You think too much, Lucky," he said, trying to snap a leash on his imagination. He forced himself to take one step, then another, and strode to the door with Maizie close and quiet at his heels.

"See?" he said, glancing at Maizie as he pushed open the shed's door. "It's exactly the way we left it." Blankets, toothbrush, half-empty bag of kibble, everything remained in place. Nothing was moved, nothing mussed, nothing touched. "Nothing's wrong at all." It was a lie. Lucky knew that even as he said it, and like all lies, it hurt him like ice in his bones.

His sanctuary had ceased to be safe.

He sat down hard on the shelf he called his bed, hung his wearied head in bruised hands, and stared at his knees. Instead of seeing those scarred joints, though, he watched in his mind a replay of the day's events. He tried to pinpoint the moment when things had gone from bad to worse. He wanted to figure out why an ordinary day had become a nightmare. But then, it was Midsummer, it was his birthday, and his birthdays were never ordinary. Possibly this hadn't been his worst Midsummer ever, but it had been close.

The morning had started with a dream about a key he had in his possession, one of a handful of inexplicable objects that were all that remained of his childhood. And a woman with golden hair and eyes shaped like Lucky's but green rather than coppery brown—he'd dreamed about her before. She had pushed the key into his palm and flung him some cryptic advice he could no longer remember. Then she'd vanished, shrieking, and some cold, dark, horrible thing had taken her place. Lucky screamed himself awake and bolted upright, smacking his head on the shelf above his bed. He'd been left with a lump the size of a duck's egg on his forehead.

It throbbed, and it had turned purple by the time he reached the bus stop at Twelfth and Main an hour later.

He sat down to wait for the number sixty-eight bus, wishing for shade. With his arm draped over the back of the bench and his feet sprawled out nonchalantly, he hoped he looked cool despite the heat wafting from the asphalt. When an old man trundled up wearing gray sweats and combat boots, he ignored the fact that the stranger looked weird, even for downtown Valley City.

After waiting some time, Lucky wondered if maybe he was late and the bus had already come and gone. He turned to the old man, hesitated, but then said, “Excuse me, sir. Do you know the time?”

“Time? Excellent question.” He fished in a jacket pocket Lucky never would have guessed existed and brought out a pink paper bag, then opened it to show crullers with maple frosting melting in the heat. Lucky inhaled deeply but tactfully refused the implied offer. When the old man set the bag on the bench between them, it rolled itself up. That couldn’t possibly be true, of course, and briefly Lucky wondered if the bump on his head had affected him more than he’d thought.

Then the stranger said, “I’ve brought enough for both of us,” which seemed an unlikely thing for him to say, considering they’d never met. While Lucky debated whether to respond, the man brandished a huge yellow umbrella and flourished it open over their heads just in time for rain to begin falling from the *still cloudless* sky. “Eight forty-six.” Out of the same invisible pocket that had produced donuts, he’d pulled a large clock with a glass housing, gears whirring and clicking inside quite independently of each other, and hands, but no clock face.

Lucky fought the hypnotic effect of the device, forced his gaze away, leaned his elbows on his knees, and cradled his throbbing head.

The old man asked, “Not feeling quite yourself today?”

What the hell does he mean by that? Lucky didn’t answer the old man; instead he stared out into the street, which had gone strangely quiet. He ran a hand through his hair, as if getting his hair out of his eyes could clear the weirdness from his vision. One car, a hulking Ford Crown Victoria, idled at the stoplight. By some trick of the light, its white paint reflected bloodred, and the windows were tinted a blue so dark the driver looked like a ghost.

Without warning, the odd old man dropped the umbrella in front of Lucky's face. When he snapped it shut a moment later, the white car had vanished, the traffic had returned, and the rain had ceased.

LUCKY'S DAYS, generally, were built on routine. Unlike most fifteen-year-old people, he worked for a living—self-employed. Valley City was small, but he wasn't the only teen living on his own. For the first year, he'd done what the others did, namely live on the streets and find any way he could to get a few bucks for food and necessities. Except he couldn't lie or steal—not wouldn't, couldn't. He didn't want to be a thief, but he would have done it if he could—it seemed to work for other people, and sometimes he'd been really hungry. But the first time he tried to steal, he got horribly, stupidly, embarrassingly sick. That seemed a cruel blow by fate, all the more so because nobody could explain it. Maybe he would have an explanation if Hank had still been around. Hank had been the closest thing Lucky'd had to a grandfather, but he didn't like to think about Hank anymore. That was a sickening story all on its own.

Stealing was out, so he was left with panhandling or letting people pick him up and pay him to do things he didn't want to think about—not in that context. He got pretty good at panhandling—surprising what people will give you if you tell them the truth—but when he was desperate, he did what he had to do to stay fed and warm. The so-called adults who'd wanted to touch him made him sick too, but that was way easier to explain than vomiting every time he tried to lie.

After he settled in his shack, though, Lucky started to think he should try to find another way to make a living. The fact was, Lucky was different from the other teens on the street—even more lost if that were possible. Not because he was gay… or bi, probably, if he was being honest. Some of the friends he shared street corners and dumpster sandwiches with were straight, some were gay, some were too hungry or too messed up to care. It wasn't the most important thing. All of them were on the street because their families had put them there, one way or another. They all came from crap homes, and they all had crap choices for getting help or doing anything about their situation at all.

But all the others had one thing Lucky didn't have—an identity.

Someday, with luck, they would become adults. Their adult lives would surely be an upstream swim, but the possibilities remained: they could get an education, they could work, they could rent homes, they *might* have a future.

Lucky's circumstances were different. He didn't remember a crappy home or a mean parent; he didn't remember home and parents at all. He couldn't remember anything before his twelfth birthday. He had no ID, no school records, no birth certificate, no last name. He thought he had something in common with the migrant workers who came to the valley to work. Most worked on the farms, but some got jobs in private homes, and ultimately Lucky took his cue from them.

His first customer had been unintentional: Safianu, a man from Cameroon with a delightful, joyful accent and a history of drug addiction. No longer addicted, he was old—maybe sixty—and sick, so finally the state thought him worthy of food and shelter he didn't have to lie or steal for. Lucky hadn't been thinking of a job when he'd cleaned up Saf's apartment. He'd been thinking of helping an old friend. But Saf had been the kind of generous man who would share whatever he had, including both money and hard-won self-esteem.

"Lucky," he'd said, his accented speech musical in a way that commanded attention while at the same time tickling something inside, "you are a good person. I will pay you for your work."

"Saf! You don't have enough money to pay people. I'm doing this because I want you to be a little more comfortable. Anyway, you already fed me twice. That's plenty."

Saf slammed a hand down on the table, making Lucky jump and look up. "You will not disrespect me. You work, you will be paid—at least what little I can manage!" He took Lucky's hand and laid a crisp ten-dollar bill across his palm. "Finish here. Come back next week."

What Lucky liked about that first job was that it felt clean; it was work he could do and not wish at the end of every day that he could escape his life. Sure, not all his customers were as worthy as Safianu, nor as beautiful. Lucky had seen pictures of Saf as a young man—oh my! But lots of people made enough money through vice or petty crime to pay him a few bucks—and everybody likes clean clothes and made beds. In very little time, he'd set himself up in business as a chore boy to Valley City's low-level underworld, usually making at least enough money to feed himself and Maizie.

So Lucky wasn't aimlessly wandering the city on his fifteenth birthday, and he wasn't waiting idly for bus sixty-eight. He needed to get out and drum up some business. Getting up late and smacking his head on the shelf had already set him back, and he didn't need some crazy old loon with a strange clock and a yellow umbrella to screw things up even worse. He needed to get his day back on track—find some customers, and avoid police, social workers, and the truancy patrol. When the sixty-eight finally rolled to a stop and the doors popped open, Lucky practically leapt aboard and swung into his usual seat on the curb side and two back from the driver, whose name was Rob.

"Hey, Lucky," Rob said after pulling away from the curb.

"Rob," Lucky answered. "How's it going?"

"You don't look so good today. Who'd you get in a fight with?"

"A wooden shelf," Lucky answered and then smiled when Rob laughed.

Conversation went on hold while they waited at the next stop to pick up a mom with uncooperative twin toddlers and let off a beat-up looking man who smelled like sweat.

As they pulled back out into the street, Rob spoke over the engine's whine. "Cops pulled a vice crackdown last night, Lucky. Thought you might want to know. Streets are pretty empty today."

"Crap." Rob knew how Lucky made his living, and he knew downtown very well, having driven this same route for years. What it meant when Rob said the streets were empty was that apparently a bad dream, a crack on the head, and a strange old man hadn't been trouble enough; the day would also be tough, businesswise. Most of Lucky's usual employers would likely be eating cheese sandwiches and waiting to see the judge.

Lucky scraped for work most of the day, made no more than a few dollars, and finally in desperation went out to the Langdon brothers' uptown bungalow to see if they could use some help cleaning up after last night's party. The brothers, Benny and Johnny, were always flush with cash, and they partied every night. Lucky had no doubt they'd have a humongous mess. They always did, because they and all their friends used any drug they could lay their hands on and generally courted insanity. Lucky guessed there was no such thing as a quiet night at the Langdons' house.

Not long after he arrived, Lucky stood in the center of the cyclone-struck kitchen, waiting for any special instructions and preparing to wrangle for money. "There's barf in the green bathroom," Benny Langdon said, his eyes mostly closed against the sun beating down from the skylight. He riffled his blond hair, either trying to wake up or scratching some itch, and shook out a rain of blue glitter. "Did you bring gloves?"

Of course he had. After a year in the laundry-and-chores business, Lucky had certainly learned to come prepared for the gross and the yucky. He had other things on his mind. The Langdons' sprawling house was always sliding into chaos, and though Lucky was sure they had every intention to keep their word, working for them was risky business. Lucky had to be sure nothing came between him and his money.

"Pay me now."

"Half," Benny said, patting at his jeans pockets. "The other half later." His brow scrunched in a puzzled look and then cleared as he apparently clicked on a mental link. "Oh… yeah, my cash is in my jacket. Wait a minute and I'll find it." He started to work his way around the room, shifting bottles, cans, and pizza boxes on the counter and kicking at piles of litter on the floor.

Silent, dark-eyed Johnny—the other Langdon brother—had been standing by, looking a bit like a zombie. But now he picked up a Frisbee-shaped object, which was leaking ketchup and had pickles poking out the sides, and found a stash of limp bills on the table beneath it. He pinched a twenty and a ten in his fingernails and held them out. His stiff, sour face dared Lucky to object.

Lucky needed groceries. Maizie needed a flea collar. Cash was cash. He rinsed and blotted the bills, folded them in a paper towel, and stuck the packet in the hip pocket of his cutoff cargo pants.

Three hours later, he congratulated himself for having had the foresight to insist on the advance. The job had gone fine until he'd disturbed one of the Langdons' friends, a young, burly woman with a black Mohawk and serpent tattoos for bracelets. Lucky thought she was striking and even thought he could be attracted to a woman like her, but only if she wasn't crazy. She happened to be lurking behind a closed door doing… who knows what? She took offense when the vacuum cleaner bumped the door one time too many, yanked it open, and started yelling. When she stopped yelling and reached for him, Lucky ran.

He was blocks away and still running when his shoe broke and he fell down an embankment. At the dusty bottom of a dry wash, he lay low among litter and tumbleweeds and took the opportunity to catch his breath, hoping also to give the woman time to lose interest. Fifteen minutes later, give or take, he climbed up to street level and picked his way through a forest of sticker bushes and signs telling him who should get his vote and what herbal remedy could help him lose twenty-five pounds fast. His pursuer had gone, but his relief was short-lived. Beyond belief, the blue-glassed Crown Victoria that had been stopped at the light when the strange old man was messing around with his umbrella crept by just then.

Like an omen.

"I hate omens," Lucky said, talking to himself again. Omens were never normal, and he desperately sought normal. And that car! Everywhere he'd ventured all day, he'd encountered the big sedan with its bug-eye windows, through which he could just make out the driver's wild-haired, haggard, hook-nosed profile.

Later, as the sun began to sink, with his broken sole slapping annoyingly on the pavement, he trudged from the Twelfth and Main bus stop across the parking lot to the Quick-Shoppe on the same corner, calculating what he could buy and what he and Maizie would have to do without. He now sported enough bruises for the Guinness book, a headache thumping like the bass in a gangster's car, and a rare but heartfelt nasty mood that did not improve when he saw the Crown Victoria cooling in the market's parking lot.

Seriously, he thought. *Enough is enough.*

The store's sixties-vintage automatic doors tried his patience but eventually huffed open and admitted him to the familiar glow of fluorescents and the rattle, beep, and clink of the aging market's interior. He accepted a cart from a teenage bagger with a red pimple, a salon haircut, and brand-name cross-trainers. And a real job. And a future full of everything Lucky could not look forward to, such as a driver's license, high school graduation, and a scolding from a loving parent if he stayed out too late on Friday.

Envy began to smolder uncomfortably in his gut until it cut loose with a sharp jerk—strangely, he actually felt it happen, as if someone reached in and gave his personality a twist. Then he started feeling mean. Really mean. And for the first time ever, being mean felt good.

He almost ran down a little kid with his cart, and he didn't even say he was sorry. A lady reached for the best, juiciest apple, and he snatched it right out of her hand. He knocked down a rack of Cuddle Soft toilet paper and made a point not to feel bad as the rolls bounced under an old lady's bedroom slippers, tripping her up. While this was all going on, part of him stood back and wondered what was happening to him—he didn't even recognize himself. Still, he felt so alive, energized, and it lasted right up to the moment when a tall, horrid woman cut off his progress down the pasta aisle.

When he saw her beak nose and frayed hair, he knew instantly where he'd seen her before—she was the shadow behind the Ford's blue windows. He peered at her from the far end of the aisle, letting his thick hair fall forward to hide his gaze.

"Those have got to be the ugliest eyes I've ever seen," Lucky said but only under his breath. She couldn't have heard, yet suddenly she closed the distance between them and stopped, legs planted wide and hands on hips, less than two feet away. She stared, eyes wide, and Lucky drew back, horrified. What he'd said was true.

Her eyes were ugly, indescribably so: pale, pale blue, bloodshot, and wicked cold. Their chill bellied over his skin like snakes of ice and froze him to the spot. His throat closed as she slowly reached out a sharp-fingered hand toward his neck.

"Hate," she said in a voice that could have crushed stone. "Anger. It's good, isn't it? Powerful—that's how it feels." She laughed, a slithering sound, and then whispered, "Don't let anyone fool you, boy, and don't try to fool yourself. You love that feeling of power. Everyone does."

Her claw-fingered hand was an inch from his bare neck and creeping closer. That part of Lucky standing in the wings watching insisted *This is not really happening in the grocery store*, but the rest of him panicked. This woman seemed strong, immense, a giant, a glacier.

She could kill me with one squeeze, he thought and imagined the sound of his own neck bones snapping.

Her hand stopped. She leaned close to his face and whispered again, but this time softened her voice into something slick and glistening, a lure. "You know, boy, you could feel that kind of power all the time, every minute. Come with me, Luc—"

A crash and the shatter of glass cut off her words and broke the hold of her gaze. Lucky turned toward the sound and found the floor and his bare shins splattered with something red. The sight of glass shards poking through that shining liquid shifted his heart into high gear, and panic threatened to paralyze him. Finally, after a couple of time-warped seconds, the scent of garlic and basil got the message through to his brain. *Not blood, spaghetti sauce.*

He looked up from the mess on the floor and relief gave way to confusion. All he saw was a yellow disk. An open umbrella. *The* umbrella and the same old man he'd met that morning at the bus stop. Incredibly, the man stood there in the pasta aisle like a silver-haired swordsman, holding the umbrella by its round golden handle and thrusting its pointed end at the woman. Lucky stayed rooted to the spot, mouth open, staring while those two strange creatures sparred.

The old man lunged forward, back straight and arm outstretched, looking strong as iron. The umbrella fluttered and spun and, inexplicably, cool relief blew over Lucky like the west wind. In a flowing voice, steady and calm, the stranger said, "Isa, you shall not succeed."

"And you will stop me, I suppose?" She followed the flinty words with a laugh.

Silence rolled in. No one moved.

In a voice barely audible yet strong enough to bust that stretched silence wide open, the old man said, "A word has been spoken, Isa, a Command. I'm yet strong enough to enforce it."

The woman shrilled her response. "You will not keep him!"

Lights flashed, thunder cracked, and the air thickened with smoke and sulfur. Then the Quick-Shoppe went as dark as the back of the moon.

CHAPTER TWO: OLD THIEF, RHYMES WITH SHERLOCK

THE MORNING after his birthday, Lucky once again flopped on the bus bench next to a bottle in a brown paper bag and nudged a trio of cigarette butts from the curb to the gutter, moving them a few inches farther from his too long, too sensitive nose. Last night, after his dark walk home with the groceries—which he had managed to buy despite the impossible events at the Quick-Shoppe—he'd spent half the night sorting through his possessions, trying to figure out what had been taken and decode the reason why. He had discovered the what, but the why had left him mystified.

He'd slept three hours starting at dawn, a wearying ride on runaway nightmares. The exhaustion of his crazy day, the nightmares, and too little sleep left him feeling slow and moving like a slug on sand. By the time he got to the bus stop, ten o'clock had come and gone.

He stood, unfolding his tired limbs into long, straight lines, as Valley City Transit sixty-eight hissed to a stop and engulfed the gutter's trash fumes in a diesel cloud. The doors folded open, and he boarded, carrying his shoes. The left sole still hung loose from yesterday's chase, and he'd brought along some dollar store Power Glue to fix it. Rob frowned but let Lucky board with bare feet even though it was against the rules.

"Thanks," Lucky said and stepped down the corrugated rubber aisle to claim his seat.

The lumps and rips in the vinyl upholstery weren't comfortable, but they scratched at the backs of his knees the way they did every day—normal, and that was what he liked, what he needed. If he could, he would collect normal like some people his age collected Yu-Gi-Oh! Cards, but normal had a talent for avoiding him. He just knew this day would be no different. And when the bus door rattled open for someone to board a few blocks down the line, he had a solid premonition.

It's going to be him.

Sure enough, the bent-kneed old man he'd met twice yesterday clambered aboard. He waved at the fare counter, and the gears inside whirred and ticked while coins multiplied, and Rob said, "Thanks," just as if he got paid that way daily. In heavy black boots, the man tromped up the aisle, ignoring the numerous empty seats, and slid in smiling next to Lucky.

This time he carried a canvas bag. From it he produced—among less remarkable things—an amber-colored dinner plate, a hovering light with no visible housing, and his ever-present yellow umbrella. Lucky did his best to stare out the window, but when the old man proffered a crinkled pink bag filled with maple bars, his resolve broke. Silently cursing his bottomless stomach and passion for maple—which always reminded him of Hank and his year of better days—he accepted the pastry with sticky fingers and said, "Thanks."

But he hadn't even taken a bite when brakes hissed and the bus slowed so quickly that Lucky skidded off the seat, folded into the space in front of it, and slammed his still-sore head against the back of the next seat forward. He recovered his dignity and his seat to find Rob shaking a fist at a—by that point—way too familiar white Ford. Cutting across lanes, the car dodged suddenly in front of the bus and squealed into a right turn, barreling down on a young woman laboring to pull onto the curb a candy-striped stroller holding a baby in pink and a stuffed orange bear.

Lucky's seatmate, the strange old man, scowled. His eyes seemed to flash, and he jabbed his umbrella toward the corner and muttered some foreign words with lots of "th" and "s" sounds. A ray of light, which Lucky preferred not to notice, shot from the umbrella's tip. Stroller, teddy, baby, and mom vanished with a pop, reappearing in the same instant safe on the sand-and-dust-strewn sidewalk, and the speeding car mowed down only the plastic bags and dust it raised under its wheels.

Flushed and short of breath, Lucky said, "It's not real!"

The old man next to him said, "When will she learn? The high laws apply everywhere, even to her!" Then, as if just hearing what Lucky said, he shook his head and said, "Of course it's real, young man, and judging by your condition, you know that."

Lucky wanted to scream, but sudden pain in his stomach and a wave of nausea prevented him from saying anything for at least a full minute. When it had passed, he leaned back tiredly, looked again at the crazy old man, and asked, "Pardon?"

"Thurlock," the graybeard said, answering neither of Lucky's questions. "Rhymes with Sherlock." It took some time for Lucky to decipher what he meant. Then, when he figured it out and politely offered his own name, the old codger rolled his eyes and said, "I know who you are, boy. We've met."

Lucky had an inkling that Thurlock referred to some other time, some meeting more normal than yesterday's strange encounters, but if that was the case, he didn't remember the occasion. Of course, that came as no surprise. Lucky didn't remember the first twelve years of his life.

Beyond frustrated, he shoved both hands through his hair and winced as he made contact with the sore spots. Explaining the weirdness of his life to this nosy old man raised too great a challenge, so instead he closed his eyes, leaned his head against the cool window, and faked an out-like-a-light sleep. When the bus slowed for his stop in the city's low-end suburbs, he jumped off as it rolled, not caring that he didn't have anyplace in the area he wanted to be.

He landed on a square of dead grass outside a chain-link fence enclosing more of the same, in a blaze of hot sun. But shame overcame him—he'd been rude, he thought, and he didn't approve of that. When others failed to treat him with respect, he hated the powerless way he felt, and he'd long ago vowed not to do that to others. Strange as the old man seemed, troubling as everything about him was, he had shared his maple bars. Lucky turned quickly to wave belated thanks, but Thurlock wasn't looking at him; the bus window framed his profile.

A sharp light glanced off the chrome of a parked van and struck the old man's straw hat as he settled it on his silver head. There, the beam glinted off a small, metal object that Lucky recognized instantly. He owned it. As far as he knew, it had no value to anyone except himself. Yet last night, searching his burgled shack, he'd found that this little trinket was the only thing that had disappeared.

"My key!" He shouted as if the words would magically stop the bus. That didn't happen, so he dug his newly fixed shoes into the turf and took off after the old man, who seemed to be an old thief, at a dead run.

Less than an hour later, sweat trickled down his ribs, the late morning sun burned his neck, and a fat black fly buzzed his ear. He ignored it all and crouched behind a juniper shrub, spying on Thurlock. He had a nagging sense the old man didn't belong in Valley City, and neither did the equally unusual house into which he'd vanished.

Except for the wooden tower that jutted five stories or so skyward like a giant thumb, the building would have been ordinary if it had stood across town in the fields past the Martinez Bridge—just another rundown farmhouse. Here at the end of a road in a roomy neighborhood known for hired help, Land Rovers, and swimming pools, the tower appeared no more misfit than the rest of the ramshackle place.

Misfit—that was also a good description of the old man he'd chased into that hideout. But he had to smile. *As if I have room to talk.* He could count on his fingers the things that made him forever an outcast. Things like being the only kid in Valley City with no last name, like not knowing whether he had brothers or sisters or even parents, like living in an abandoned shed teetering on the brink of Black Creek Ravine, the spookiest place in at least three counties.

Probably, nobody else in town would have chased a weird old man three miles uphill to reclaim an odd bit of metal that served no purpose at all except to assure Lucky that, though he couldn't remember his childhood, he did have one. It had been quite a run too. Lucky laughed, despite his aching head and the sting of sweat in his eyes, remembering how Thurlock had sped through the suburbs on his crooked legs.

Definitely, he thought, *I'm the only one around fast enough to keep up.*

He hadn't yet caught his breath from the long uphill run, but already the silver-haired thief came back outside, looking refreshed. Again, the old man mumbled foreign words that seemed vaguely familiar, though Lucky couldn't think what language it might be. Thurlock held his hat in his hand, looking everywhere except at the shrub Lucky hid behind. He tugged at his grizzly beard for a moment, then stepped forward and placed the hat on the peeling porch rail. Bit by bit, he turned and tilted it until sudden sunlight flared like lightning from the stolen key.

Lucky felt sure the old man was manipulating him, though he couldn't imagine why. Thurlock had advertised that he had the key. It seemed he knew Lucky was watching—somehow. But Lucky felt the draw of that shiny metal trinket as strongly as if he needed it to stay alive. It commandeered his thinking, blocking out all considerations, including questions why and safety issues.

The broad porch sagged everywhere except where the steps held up a direct path to the door. There in the corner, on the once-white two-by-four that might or might not keep a person from falling into the unkempt but lush pansies below, Lucky's golden key shone, tied to Thurlock's hatband by its silken yellow cord. It drew Lucky like a magnet.

The slender key had an odd shape and fit perfectly in the palm of Lucky's hand. Lucky knew that because he'd palmed it every day for the last three years, studying the feel of it and imagining what it might do for him, the way Aladdin might have handled his lamp, the way Scrooge might have counted his coins.

Yes, the key was precious to him, but he had trouble holding on to the idea that anyone had stolen it—especially this old man, Thurlock. He tried to picture him creaking through the shack's plank door in the half light, stepping so lightly he disturbed not even dust, going straight to the cardboard box that held Lucky's few treasures—souvenirs of a life long gone—and taking the key.

Only the key.

Strange though it seemed, that had to mean he'd been searching for precisely that singular object. *Why?* Lucky asked himself. And, considering the fact that the old man had appeared three times in Lucky's life in the past two days, he had to ask another question, possibly more important. *Was he after the key, or was he after me?*

CHAPTER THREE: BEYOND THE THRESHOLD

ANOTHER HALF hour passed and still Lucky crouched behind the juniper, sun pounding his shoulders. His legs, which always seemed longer these days than the last time he looked, had turned themselves into two big cramps. He stood up, hoping for relief, and turned sideways to the sun, trying to make himself narrow enough to stay concealed behind the scraggly bush.

As lanky as he was, or "skinny" as some called it, hiding shouldn't have been tough to pull off, yet when Thurlock came out again, he looked right at Lucky's hiding place and picked up the hat—making sure once more that it flashed, catching the sunlight. Then another man came out of the house. In contrast to the gray-eyed, ruddy-faced old thief, he had brown skin like Lucky and dark hair. He wore a T-shirt and jeans but stood ramrod straight and moved easy, like a man used to being strong enough for any task. Broad-shouldered and fit, he stood so tall his head barely cleared the top of the doorjamb.

Thurlock, the bent, shrunken-seeming geezer, was even taller.

That's impossible. But maybe not. Lucky remembered the showdown at the Quick-Shoppe. Thurlock had seemed giant then. So which was real?

The two men stood together in the shade, speaking in low tones. Then Thurlock's volume rose and, in a voice as smooth as tacks in a blender, he said something that caught Lucky's attention because it included the word "boy" and ended with the word "stubborn."

"Blood pressure, sir," the younger man said, and he stepped off the porch in shiny boots that seemed altogether too hot for the day after Midsummer. He used one of those same boots to level the weeds in front of the door to a tool shed across the yard. While he worked the door open, he raised his voice and added, "Breathe."

"My blood pressure is fine, Han." Thurlock's face went tomato red, and he crossed his arms in a huff, but Lucky could clearly see his chest rise and fall through several deep breaths. When Thurlock passed through the door to go back inside, he must have ducked, because Lucky knew with absolute certainty that the beam couldn't really have arched itself up to let him pass.

Lucky blinked hard, trying to clear his eyes. "Too little sleep," he muttered. "Too much sun. I'm hungry, thirsty, tired, confused. Not crazy."

The sun threw even more heat as it began to drop toward the southwest. No true wind rose to cool the sweat trickling down Lucky's limbs, but skirls of hot air twisted over the foothills and dusted the tarred street. A gray cat ambled off the porch and hunched in a patch of milkweed just inside the once-white picket fence, staring out at Lucky through the slats. The man Thurlock had called Han, white T-shirt darkening with sweat, rode the back of an industrial-strength lawnmower, balancing left and right to steer it over the oversized lot—a charioteer slaying weeds.

The house, floating in a sea of unkempt lawn, didn't appear foreboding. It was large but loosely assembled, with one thing hooked to the next as if every room was an afterthought. And the skinny square tower poked up stories higher than the rest, looking ready to fall any minute.

The front door, on the other hand—a massive panel carved with unknown symbols, fitted with black iron hinges and a golden doorknob—did look foreboding. It no more fit on this decrepit house than the house fit in this posh neighborhood or than combat boots fit on an old man with gray sweats and weird clocks.

But there the door was, regardless, and if there was anything Lucky was sure of, standing there peeking through the juniper fronds, it was that he did not want to knock on it.

He stepped out from behind the juniper, no longer caring if he'd be seen by the people inside the house. With the hot sun beating on his shoulders, he stood staring at the door, wondering at it. Why would such a place exist? Why would he have been led to it?

I hate this damn world, he thought, not for the first time, and as always he wondered exactly what he meant by "this" world. But that was just it. At the moment, that metal trinket, that strange key the old man had taken from him, represented some other world—one where he'd spent the childhood he couldn't remember at all. He knew he was fooling himself to think of it that way; there were no other worlds. But still, he thought of that time and place with such longing, he couldn't help but think maybe it existed in a world he *wouldn't* hate, if only he could return.

And the key.... Well, it must mean something. What if it could open...?

Don't be stupid, Lucky. It's just a trinket—a toy.

But it's my toy, and that old man Thurlock took it.

I need to get it back.

He drew in a deep breath and with it sufficient courage to move. One step at a time, one foot in front of the other, not faltering, he crossed the pavement, entered the gate, navigated the crooked walk, and climbed the steps to stand in front of the door. Up close it was even more terrifying, the symbols and pictures almost alive.

He stepped closer, but stopped. Sunlight angled under the porch roof and brushed past his arm, illuminating the door—which, he saw now, stood open about six inches. Carved into the oak panel, a crowned horseman thrust a sword into an exploding sky. His fingers close but never quite touching the wood, Lucky traced the detail on the sword's hilt. He could have done it with his eyes closed.

Every day, he ran his fingers over this same strange symbol, a disc surrounded by twelve sharp rays to represent the sun. It was rendered in relief on some strange coins and etched into the hilt of a solid amber knife—things he kept hidden in the cardboard box of treasures where he also kept the key that had been stolen. Lucky had supposed the heavy coins might be valuable. When he'd found himself alone and broke, he'd squandered hours at Valley City Library searching reference books, checking Amazon and eBay, and following mazes of links, Googling every coin collector on the web. He'd found not so much as a single picture of a coin like the ones he had, no alphabet to match the runic lettering, and nothing on the twelve-rayed sun.

But in front of him, on the door of Thurlock's house, that symbol shone, drawing Lucky's gaze upward along the thrusting sword to the six-foot lintel. Pungent cedar, fresh cut. Droplets of sap wept from the runes inscribed across it.

This isn't right, he thought. *It's too... new. The rest of the house is practically falling down. Far from normal. Far from safe.*

If I step through this door, I'll never come back....

Uh-huh. Get real, Lucky.

He shook his head and his battered skull hurt, but he almost welcomed the pain. At least it felt normal, like the sweat trickling down the back of his knee and the blue-backed fly hurling itself against the windowpane. Everything else had gone strange and silent. No traffic, no birds, no children playing in the distance.

As if the world is waiting....

Right. Ridiculous.

Gravel crunched on the pavement down the block, loud in the silent afternoon, calling for Lucky's attention. The white Crown Victoria with its blind blue windows crept up the road, and the sight struck Lucky like an ice bullet, dead center in his chest.

He turned to face the doorway—a portal, he remembered, that had somehow reshaped itself to let Thurlock pass. No way could he ever step through any door that might do such a thing. Yet he balled his fists and straightened his shoulders. Fighting what felt like triple the usual gravity, he lifted his right foot and watched it travel across the threshold. He let it fall on the other side like an anchor, and then he followed it into Thurlock's house.

Beyond the threshold, in an ordinary living room, yellow afternoon sun bathed two overstuffed chairs and an oversized stone hearth. A worn, once-purple rug covered an equally worn wooden floor. The breeze billowed gauze curtains at the windows and wandered to the dining room. There it stirred music from the prisms of a massive chandelier, which in turn cast rainbows over the round, age-beaten table beneath it. In the middle of the scarred top rested a copper tray with glasses, spoons, sugar, and lemon so fragrant Lucky almost sneezed.

He couldn't have said what about the scene seemed so frightening, unless it was only that it was so unexpected. He could more easily have handled the dark he'd seen past the open door when he was standing outside. But this....

He pivoted on his heels, ready to flee.

Thurlock's voice came from some distance behind him and above, not loud, the tone flat. "Don't run," he said and then mumbled something unintelligible.

Lucky thought *Fat chance* but found himself standing stock-still, which was frightening—dumbfounding, even. It wasn't that he couldn't move, he just... *didn't*! He opened his mouth to castigate the old thief, demand the key, and ask to be left alone, but nothing more than strangled syllables came out. He spun in place, turning to face his stalker.

Thurlock stood on the stair, his expression grim, clad in long gray robes and Roman-style sandals that wound up his legs. He'd seemed ridiculous in sweats. Now he seemed magnificent. Powerful. Magical.

A wizard.

Thurlock raised one brow.

The panic that had dogged Lucky all morning, just a step behind at every turn, engulfed him there in Thurlock's house. His head was pounding and he felt sick to his stomach. The room began to spin, and he almost went down, but when he reached out blindly, he met something solid for support.

An arm. A well-muscled brown arm. *Han.*

He wanted to swat the man away from him, but it felt so good, even in this strange place with these strange people, in this small way, to have someone *for once* take care of him. Still, he needed to address the problem. When he'd steadied himself and gathered enough breath, he said, "You took my key! You… you…." His voice, which hadn't been more than a squeak though he'd wanted to sound bold, trailed off. There was too much that needed to be unraveled. He couldn't find the first stitch.

"You're right, of course." Thurlock's gray eyes peered over the top of silver-framed spectacles, studying Lucky, and he tugged at his gray beard.

Surprised that the old man had taken his weak protest seriously, Lucky stood perfectly still, willing his heart to stop pounding in his ears so he could listen—really listen—to what Thurlock had to say.

"You are absolutely right," Thurlock continued. "But believe me, I do not mean to harm you. It would be wrong, dangerous even, for me or Han Shieth, here—" He paused to gesture toward the younger man. "—to threaten you in any way. Fortunately, we know about that, even though you most likely don't remember."

He pulled his spectacles off, stuck them in a hidden pocket in his robes, and slumped into the closer of the two armchairs. "It's been a long couple of days," he said.

Feeling as spent as the old man looked, Lucky sighed and pushed his hair out of his eyes, then spoke quietly. "I'm sorry. I didn't mean to be rude. I meant to knock on your door and ask for my… the thing you have."

"A key," Thurlock interjected. "You're right to think of it as a key."

"Key," Lucky agreed, then continued. "Maybe you didn't even steal it. Maybe you found it." His legs started to shake, and a breath later Han took a firmer grip on his arm and helped him to the other armchair. Lucky sat but otherwise ignored the change. "Maybe I made a wrong assumption—never assume, right? But when I got off the bus, I looked back at you and saw that you had my key on your hat, and I *had* to get it back."

"Yes." Thurlock brightened. "Therein is the hope, young man."

After pondering that seeming non sequitur for a moment, Lucky dismissed it. "Listen," he said. "I don't know what's going on, and I don't know how you got the key, and I don't know why you or anyone else would want it. It's useless, as far as I can tell, so why it matters I can't say, and it probably doesn't make any sense to you, but it is important. It's important to me. I've had it since… a long time! So please, just give it back." Out of breath, he stopped.

Han stepped toward an arch leading to a large, old-fashioned kitchen. "Shall I make some tea, sir?"

"Yes, please. I'm absolutely parched." Thurlock still sagged deep into the armchair's cushions, but the idea of refreshment seemed to perk him up. "Iced and sweet?"

"Of course. And, sir, might I remind you that the lad is tired and bewildered, and though I don't think he knows, he's bleeding?"

"I'm bleeding?" Lucky took a quick inventory and found that indeed, the side of his leg had a sizeable scrape and steadily oozed blood.

"I think you scraped it when you were trying to hide in the juniper," Han responded, then looked back at Thurlock. "So, as I was saying, sir, perhaps it would be good to move things along." On silent feet he went into the kitchen with the gray cat following behind, just as silent.

"Well, then, Lucky," Thurlock started, "here's how I see it." He pulled himself up from the chair and began to pace in front of the giant stone hearth that took up an entire wall, hands clasped behind his back. "Certainly, the key is yours. And to clear up the mystery for you, I have it because Lemon Martinez stole it, on my orders." He broke off midpace, scratching his beard, and gave Lucky a direct stare. "He's very good at that sort of thing, you know."

"Lemon?"

"Martinez, yes, the cat. You'd be surprised at his skill. Of course Han trained him, and he's the best there is. At training animals, that is, not stealing. The stealing was more like a dormant talent. You see we found him under Martinez Bridge—"

"Master Thurlock." Han's voice carried from deep inside the house. "You might want to get to the point, sir?"

Thurlock looked at Lucky and rolled his eyes. "Thank you, Han." Pacing again, he said, "He's right. The point is definitely what I need to get to. I have a tendency to ramble on, you see—"

"The point, sir," Han reminded.

"The point is," said Thurlock, "well, the point is…." He stopped pacing and put both his hands on Lucky's tired shoulders. "I'm sorry you've been frightened. I took the key because it was important to bring you here, to this house. Kidnapping you wouldn't encourage you to feel comfortable, and you wouldn't have accepted an invitation. You probably would have dug an escape tunnel all the way to the South China Sea just to avoid me."

Thurlock gazed evenly at him. His cheek twitched; probably a tic, but to Lucky it looked like pain, a wince repeated over and over again. It made Thurlock's next words seem important, maybe even urgent.

"I have erred. I've hurt you and that was never my intent. I assure you neither I nor Han are serial killers or anything else that's ugly—we're not like any of the predators you've probably met in the last few years." Lucky didn't have to decide whether to try to deny he'd had such thoughts, because Thurlock kept talking. "You can leave, if you want, with your key. If you go, I'll watch over you as best I can, and—"

"Watch over me?"

"—and I'll never again force you or trick you into coming here. You never need come back, if you wish it that way. Or—" Thurlock shifted his gaze, and though he didn't move, his gray eyes closed in on Lucky's until it felt as if they stood nose to nose. "—or you can open your eyes, and look into mine, and let yourself see with that part of you that you trust even though you don't understand it, the part that knows when something is important, when something is true."

Lucky knew what Thurlock meant. He was aware of that extra sense; he used it often. When he was younger, he'd told Hank that it was like he had a special antenna, and they'd started calling it the Antenna of Truth as a joke. But how did Thurlock know?

"I'll tell you something, if you'll listen."

Lucky swallowed, feeling cold feet walking up his spine.

"I know that yesterday was the third anniversary of the first day in your life that you can clearly remember. I know precisely where, through a cave in Black Creek Ravine, you emerged from a past that has ever since been lost to you. I know what—or I should say who—put you there."

"Tell me!"

"I don't think I'd better, just yet."

"That's not fair."

"Never a truer word said, I'm afraid, but remembering is something you'll have to do yourself. If you want help, though, I'm your man."

Lucky was almost afraid to speak. He had a disturbing vision of Alice beleaguered in Wonderland. If he said anything at all, everything might get even crazier. But he had to ask: "What would happen if you told me?"

"Let's say it isn't a good gamble. The odds are against us, and what we would risk is too precious." Thurlock smiled—an expression at least as sad as any Lucky had seen. "What we would risk," he said, "is you. We might lose you, and that would be a tragedy far beyond our personal grief."

He stepped to where the straw hat rested on the fireplace mantel, detached the key with its silken yellow cord, and held it out to Lucky in his left hand, palm down. "This is the Key of Behliseth, and it's yours." He looked directly at Lucky, never blinking.

Lucky rose from the chair, stood in front of the old man—surely a wizard—and couldn't help staring back. He waited, knowing Thurlock had more to say, and he knew it must be important, though he would have preferred to deny it.

"In your heart," Thurlock said, "you know this world isn't your home. What was done to you three years ago upset a delicate balance. The aftermath of that event threatens our world and this one too. It's urgent that you unlock the mystery of your past. You have the power to do it, and the courage. Call upon it."

Lucky fixed his gaze on the small golden key, his mind awash in riddles. But one thing he understood: Thurlock offered him the prize he'd coveted for so long, the thing he wanted more than anything else—a chance to reclaim the memories of his lost childhood. The prospect frightened him, but when it came down to it, he had only one option.

He raised his hand and turned the palm up beneath Thurlock's, slow motion, like swimming through water thicker than blood. He recalled his Midsummer morning dream. This was how she had stood, the woman with green eyes, holding out the key. And this was how he had felt, reaching for it—like the whole world, even the air, was trying to keep him from it.

His skin quaked when Thurlock took hold of his hand, and he gasped, wide-eyed. The old man's grip was strong, warm, and unbelievably familiar. When Thurlock took his hand away, Lucky closed his palm around the Key of Behliseth.

It shivered like something alive.

"Please, stay for tea," Thurlock said and beckoned him farther into the house.

The invitation rang in Lucky's ears, and the idea of an ice-cold drink teased his dry throat.

Han came from the kitchen carrying a crystal pitcher of red-gold tea with chattering ice. Thurlock moved to stand beside him. His silver hair returned the sun's shine like white gold, and he smiled. The two men spoke, but Lucky heard a chorus of voices from every corner of the room.

"Welcome," they all said. "Welcome, Luccan."

CHAPTER FOUR: THE M.E.R.L.I.N. AND THE WIZARD'S JOB

HAN THOUGHT Luccan must be in shock of some sort—he stood rooted to the spot where he'd received the Key of Behliseth from Thurlock, so still it was hard to tell if he breathed. Han set the pitcher next to the tray, took the lad by the elbow, and led him to a chair at the old, weathered table in the dining room where sunlight and a cool breeze could reach him. Once seated, Luccan fidgeted, shaking his leg, popping his knuckles, and repeatedly shoving his hair back. That last gesture, Han remembered, had already been a habit by his fourth birthday.

While pouring Luccan a glass of tea, he covertly looked the boy over, cataloging changes. They were many and great—really *young man* was closer to right than *boy*. Han chewed his lip, wondering where Luccan's lofty stature had come from. Luccan had already grown taller than either of his parents. His eyes, they were like his mother, Liliana's, though Lili's were green instead of brown. Han smiled inside, noticing Luccan had inherited his mother's straight nose too, but about two sizes too large. It could be hoped the rest of him would catch up. In the meantime, thank the gods, it was offset by the coarse mane falling over his brow. His father had likely given him that thick hair, but Lohen's had been chestnut and curly, while Luccan's grew straight as string and had a red-brown, bloodstone color all its own.

Even as a toddler, he'd battled that heavy hair, which had refused to stay contained no matter how often it was tied. It used to fall in his eyes whenever he bent to study a rock or a bug. It blew wild in the breeze when he threw his head back, laughing—and he was always laughing then. But a lot had happened since Luccan was a carefree boy splashing through puddles, monkeying up trees, and racing over the fields around his home.

Presently, Han laid a hand on Luccan's shoulder, intending it as a gesture of comfort, but Luccan stiffened in alarm, so he took his hand away and went about preparing to offer comfort in other ways. In the kitchen, he filled a basin with warm water and scooped crushed ice into a checked-cloth ice bag. He collected soft cloths from the linen closet and then visited the medicine chest for Band-Aids and salve.

He returned to Luccan's side with the supplies, but as he set about tending to the boy's injuries the amazing truth of the situation struck him, almost stealing his breath.

Of course, Han already understood the facts. He'd served as the wizard's shield man—also gardener, cook, and housekeeper—long enough to know that time could not be counted on to move at the same rate, or even in the same direction, from one world or moment to the next. But for him, the past year spent with Thurlock in Earth had seemed only as swift or slow as any he'd lived in Ethra—and that was deceptive

Luccan had just turned twelve when the Witch-Mortaine Isa banished him. Now his fifteenth birthday had just passed, but thirty years had flown by in Ethra. Liliana had endured three decades clinging to hope for her only child, and Han had spent thirty years searching for him. He'd followed Thurlock from world to world, time to time, going stoically into the Vortices, never letting on that he shook inside every time they stepped across a Portal of Naught, never giving up.

At last the gamble had paid off. Here in the flesh sat Luccan. Han gave him the ice bag, and the lad tilted back his head, closed his eyes, rested the bag on his bruised forehead, and blew out a relieved-sounding sigh. Han smiled, knowing Luccan couldn't see the expression, and set to work bathing the scrapes on his leg and covering the area with salve.

He breathed a prayer to whoever might hear: *He's safe at last. Let him stay that way.*

Immediately, though, the chandelier over the table began to shake and spin, and the grind, whir, and clack of magical technology swelled until the whole room shook.

Oh thanks, Han thought, silent but sarcastic nevertheless. *It's always nice to know you gods are listening to my little prayers.*

Luccan started to stand, ready to flee. That wasn't a good idea. Lacking time for subtlety, Han put both hands on Luccan's shoulders and held him down. Luccan stared at the chaos spinning in the glass on the wall, which he'd probably thought was a window. Albeit a strange window—how many Earth houses had a six-foot-diameter round window looking out on a brick wall not more than inches away?

Truthfully, the M.E.R.L.I.N. device looked strange enough doing nothing at all. But it wasn't an ordinary window. The wizards in Research and Development at the University of Nedhra, in their home world, had done something new with magic, creating a device that mimicked Earth's technology. It could do some of the things computers and androids could do, and some things those devices couldn't even get close to.

When activated, the amber panes around the edge flashed, the central pane gyrated, and the whole thing pulsed and thrummed until one of its pre-enchanted functions locked in. Even someone with limited magical talent, someone like Han, could operate some of M.E.R.L.I.N.'s functions: retrieving messages, creating reminders, calling home. But this time, it was the vortex tool, the artificially produced Portal of Naught, that came to life.

Obviously, someone approached—either someone who wielded a wizard's power or some other kind of being entirely, uninvited and unannounced.

Han sent a mental call of alarm upstairs to the wizard and shifted into something like a fighting stance, but kept one big hand on Luccan's shoulder to hold him in the chair. But almost immediately the clashing sounds sorted themselves into a lilting melody, a magical song Han knew all too well. The soaking-wet, petite figure and sassy, slightly crooked features of a familiar face took shape—L'Aria, a completely uncontrollable girl nine months younger than Luccan.

Han stood up straight, rolled his eyes, and blew out an exaggerated breath. "What are you doing here?"

Han had to admit, her eye-rolling skills were far superior to his own, and when she'd finished demonstrating that, she flashed defiance out of her black irises in a way he never could have managed. He admired that ability, a little.

"I came to see him." She pointed at Luccan and gave her dripping sable hair a flippant toss.

Han shook his head and laughed, exasperated, but then he noticed Luccan seemed on the verge of wild panic, eyes all but bulging out of their sockets. L'Aria's right lower leg emerged into the dining room, water dripping off it and pooling on the floor. Han held Luccan in his chair with both hands now, by main force. At the same time, he donned his I-am-the-Captain-of-this-army look, and said, "Spitfire, go back. Get away from the M.E.R.L.I.N., now."

Though 99.9 percent of the Ethran population would have complied instantly, it was no safe bet that L'Aria would obey, instantly or ever.

She'd defied Han since her toddling days, mouthing off, fuming at him, and thoroughly earning the Spitfire nickname. Besides, it could be argued that the girl had every right to be in the middle of things where Luccan was concerned.

As L'Aria was the only child of the strangest, most enigmatic man in Ethra, everyone had always known she was unique. But on the night of Luccan's disappearance, it had become clear how important she was to Ethra's future and how closely her fate was tied to Luccan's. That night, she'd fallen into a stupor and couldn't be roused even by Thurlock. Finally, her father, the legendary Tiro, had carried her away to Greenwood Forest. Neither had been seen again for twenty-nine years.

Last year, the day after Thurlock and Han had come to Earth, she'd shown up alone at the Sisterhold, still a girl, only two years older than she had been the day of Luccan's disappearance. Every wizard, witch, and scholar in the Sunlands and beyond ran to the scrolls. Histories, prophecies, and theories papered walls and tables and even floors in studies and classrooms around the globe.

But it was Rosishan, the least scholarly of all the great witches, who'd figured it out. L'Aria's fate was inextricably tied to Luccan's. Luccan had aged in Earth years, and so had she. Born at spring equinox forty-one Ethran years ago, this year she'd turned fourteen.

Now, Rosishan showed up in the M.E.R.L.I.N.'s window, coming up behind L'Aria from the Ethran side. She grabbed hold of the girl's elbow and yanked her not-too-gently back out of the Portal. Usually, Rose only sparked Han's ire—her attitude was every bit as difficult as L'Aria's. At the moment, though, he could have given Rose a great big smooch (even though she wasn't at all his type). Regardless of whether the girl was linked to Luccan, this seemed an exceptionally inconvenient time for L'Aria's brand of trouble.

As he began to breathe easier, the M.E.R.L.I.N.'s glass cleared to show, once again, only the bricks outside. He experimented with lightening his hold on Luccan's shoulders, and when the lad stayed put, Han stepped around and peered into his face. Luccan's eyes were still a bit glazed, but he breathed evenly and healthy color had begun to replace the pallor of fright.

Moving only his eyes, Luccan glanced up. "Merlin?"

"M-E-R-L-I-N. It stands for Magic for the Evocation and Reorientation of the Ley-lines Interweaving Naught."

"Uh…."

"It's useful."

"Useful?"

"For instance, yesterday we used it to find you."

"Lucky me."

Han smiled at Luccan's nervous pun, but it made him wonder. Certainly, Thurlock's power and skill had brought them to Luccan, but maybe luck had worked in their favor too. Han was no expert, but converging time streams seemed beyond predicting, let alone controlling. He chewed his lip, remembering….

Two days earlier, Midsummer Eve

THURLOCK SEEMED excited, holding forth about some expected event, slipping into the language of Earth's sciences, which he'd been studying with all the admiration of one scholar for another since the moment they arrived. Unfortunately, Han had no idea what the wizard was rambling on about.

"It's an anomaly," Thurlock said, and his aged eyes sparkled.

"Anomaly?"

"A rare event, unexplainable. The time streams of Ethra and Earth will become, for a bit, isochronous, and they'll quadrate at Midsummer."

"Sir?"

"They'll flow together, and Midsummer will coincide, here and there."

But the next morning, when the coinciding Midsummer indeed arrived, along with Luccan's fifteenth birthday, Thurlock's excitement dissolved into pique. Simply put, the old wizard wasn't a morning person. He stood in a swath of early sunlight that cut across the dining room, blew out a surly breath, and muttered, "May as well begin."

He activated M.E.R.L.I.N. with a flick of his wrist, read his stored reminders, mumbled, let in the cat, yawned, and checked his M-mail for letters from home.

A tinny female voice said, "There are zero messages in your inbox."

"Of course." He scowled and yanked the belt of his robe tighter. Halfhearted sparks escaped from the tips of his gnarled fingers.

"Blood pressure, sir," Han called from the kitchen.

Thurlock took the prescribed deep breaths and washed down the aspirin Han supplied with a long swallow from his mug.

But then Thurlock said, "Good tea," and even if he hadn't palmed his eyes and leaned on the back of a chair, his quiet tone would have alarmed Han. The old man looked tired, and not the kind of tired that could be cured with a charmed forty winks. A tired wizard could make mistakes. Han worried—he considered it part of his job—but he did it silently while chewing his lip, watching the wizard out of the corner of his eye, and breaking eggs for breakfast.

Even fatigued, Thurlock could always make his job look easy. After another gulp of tea, he faced the M.E.R.L.I.N. and activated its locator function with a strong word and an almost invisible gesture. "Find," he Commanded, "Luccan Elieth Perdhro." It was as much of Luccan's whole name as anyone living knew, and for the last three years Thurlock had routinely invoked it to guide this spell. In his deep-chested baritone, he added, "Suth Chiell."

Those were old words, from a language long unused. A title, it meant "Sun Child," and it belonged to Luccan. Han understood Thurlock's purpose: including the title in the invocation would bring the search to the eyes of Behlishan, the god of light. The god who made the title more than words. The god who held the wizard Thurlock in service—and had for a thousand years.

Day after day since they'd arrived in Earth a year ago, the wizard had stood in that spot and repeated the routine. Day after day, the locator pane failed even to flicker. But yesterday, the wizard spoke and M.E.R.L.I.N. pulsed into brilliant life.

Thurlock's petulance vanished. He stood with straight spine, shoulders back, and suddenly everything about him transmitted a single message—power. Double-time, Han lifted the bacon from the pan and turned off the burners, clothed himself in his warrior strength, and stepped out to take up his watch at the wizard's left hand—his place in the scheme of things.

Just at the moment when Luccan's dilapidated shack had appeared in M.E.R.L.I.N.'s screen, a dark cloud mushroomed in the east of the viewer, and a brooding weight fell on Thurlock and Han.

Han broadened his stance, shifted his weight, and set his mind for a fight.

Thurlock held up an open hand to summon his staff. When the yellow umbrella slapped into his grasp, he blinked at it, confused, then said, "Oh, of course."

As deftly as if his staff had always worn an umbrella disguise, he swooshed it open, pointed it toward the east, and set it spinning so fast the blur of yellow silk became a second sun. The chandelier overhead responded with showers of tiny lights, and M.E.R.L.I.N.'s viewer flooded with golden brilliance. "By Behlishan's light," the wizard then intoned, "Witch-Mortaine, you may not follow here."

Instantly, the ominous cloud stilled, frozen in place.

The wizard added gently, "Be gone, Isa."

A crack of thunder had been her only answer. The pressure in the air lifted, and the roiling vapors in the cloud retreated toward the eastern end of Black Creek Ravine. With a final flash of blue fire, the dark cloud disappeared.

Shaking his head, Thurlock sighed. "My fault."

"We're still secure here, sir," Han reported, then smiled. "Nice move with the umbrella."

Thurlock chuckled, dipped his head in a mock bow, and set to work weaving a protection of guardian spells, misleaders, and wards. "Which," he said, "is what I should have done first."

They quickly found Luccan in the M.E.R.L.I.N.'s viewer, which showed him at home with a yellow dog curled at his feet. The shack's décor included two threadbare rugs, a frayed poster of horses galloping over grasslands, and a cracked mirror. Shelves housed books, trinkets, candles, and a single setting of chipped white dinnerware. A broad, low bench had been converted to a bed, made up with limp feather pillows and an old quilt of dim patchwork colors.

Order and cleanliness ruled the small space. Clothes were neatly folded, canned goods and dog food stowed. A broom and dustpan leaned in the corner. Hand and dish soaps, comb, toothpaste, toothbrush, and floss all marched in neat single file alongside a green plastic tub. A workbench ran the length of the wall opposite the bed, and Luccan sat there on a three-legged stool, bent over some task.

Han held his breath while taking in the scene, then let it out on the boy's name. "Luccan."

Thurlock gave him a sidelong look. No other person alive would have known Han well enough to hear the emotion behind that quietly spoken name, but Thurlock knew Han very well and made it clear he guessed exactly what was going on in his head. He reached over to pat Han's arm, saying, "Easy, my friend." It helped.

"It's amazing, sir," Han said, admiring Luccan. The boy had somehow made the shack into a home, by no means a fine place but well tended—and miraculously its threshold had wards of protection.

The boy's dog rose to her haunches and growled at the spot near the door where, so to speak, Han and Thurlock stood watching. When Luccan turned to see what the dog was growling at, he abruptly froze, eyes narrowed with suspicion.

Thurlock cursed. "Behl's teeth! I think he senses us." He shut the M.E.R.L.I.N. down quickly and turned to face Han, saying nothing for a moment. Then, with twinkling eyes, he smiled and said quietly, "As an Earthborn might put it, wow!"

Han laughed, and then Thurlock sank onto the nearest chair and picked up his teacup.

"Wait," Han said, gesturing. "I'll get you some hot water for a fresh cup."

While he waited, Thurlock started to talk. "We have to bring him here; it's the only way we can keep him safe. And we'd best do it quickly." By the time Han came from the kitchen with the kettle and his own coffee, the wizard's expression turned grave.

He didn't have to explain. Han, a military man, understood the danger of letting time pass while one's enemy advanced. They proceeded to toss ideas back and forth as to how it might be done, considering and dismissing everything from cookies to kidnapping. Other notions exhausted, Han went out on a limb. "It's a bit… shady, sir, but we could trick the lad."

A long silence stretched between them. When Han's nerves got the better of him, he went back to the kitchen to finish preparing breakfast. As he put down a final plate of toast and pulled out his chair, Thurlock locked eyes with him. Tugging thoughtfully at his beard, he asked, "Did you have something in mind?"

Han looked at Lemon Martinez, aiming a thought in the cat's direction. I may have a job for you. Are you willing?

Lemon returned the look from his sunny spot on the porch rail outside the east window. He flicked his tail in obvious irritation. What's in it for me?

The chance to serve the cause of justice—

Like I care!

—and possibly save a life—

Don't make me repeat myself.

—and ply your sticky-fingered trade, and play with something shiny.

Lemon yawned, curling his tongue, and flopped onto his side. Fun idea, warrior, but on the other hand, I could nap.

Han gave the cat a sly sideways look. He had an idea, something to offer he was pretty sure couldn't fail. Although Lemon Martinez loathed magic in general, he loved the wizard's things—slept on his pajamas, for instance. He sent the message: I'll sneak you into Thurlock's closet.

Lemon's eyes went wide and lit up with greed. Deal!

"Stop! That's enough cat-talk." Thurlock hated to be reminded that, powerful wizard though he was, he generally could not read minds, cat or otherwise. "Just tell me your plan," he said.

Han had to chew his lip to quench his smile. "Lemon has skills, sir. They might be useful."

"Thievery?"

"Well, breaking and entering...."

Another uncomfortable lull in the conversation ensued, during which Thurlock made a number of faces and spread blackberry jam on his toast. Finally, he said, "We wouldn't actually be stealing."

"No, sir."

He pursed his lips. "Whatever we take, we'd give it back."

"Yes, sir."

In minutes they worked out a simple plan. The cat would sneak into Luccan's shack and steal the Key of Behliseth. Thurlock favored that item as their target, explaining that of the things Luccan still had from his true home, the Key was the one that would trouble him the most if it were lost. "Even if he doesn't know why," he added, "he'll want it back."

For a moment, the wizard's eyes grew distant.

"There's jam in your beard, sir."

"Jam? Oh, jam, thank you." Dabbing absently, Thurlock smiled. "And the Key is made to order for a cat burglar—he can carry it easily by the cord. He can crawl under the eaves without breaking anything and perhaps avoid scaring Luccan unduly by tripping his wards—"

That reminded Han of what he'd seen. "Sir, how could Luccan have set wards?"

Thurlock laughed. "My best guess? Raw magic. He's done it with a wish, unaware."

"That would take considerable talent."

"Considerable at the least. And that talent bodes well for Luccan's future and ours, unless Isa gets to him first."

Stacking mugs and plates to clear the table, Han spoke loudly to be heard over the clatter. "Too bad we don't own a truck, sir. Lemon and I could be a stone's throw from the lad's shack in minutes."

As expected, Thurlock growled the pat answer he gave to every plug Han put in for embracing Earth's transportation technology. "No hang gliders, no motorcycles, no truck!" He shoved his chair in for emphasis and added, "Even that lawnmower of yours is dangerous."

"Sir, even Isa drives."

"Since when do we envy the Witch-Mortaine?"

"Speaking only for me, since the day she bought herself a big white Ford."

A short while later, Han donned manly running shorts and a pair of perfectly white shoes and lifted Lemon Martinez to his shoulders. He'd have to run the twelve miles to Luccan's shack, because Lemon wouldn't travel by any other available means. Just as they were stepping out the door, Thurlock approached.

"I'll also be going to that part of town," he said and stepped over to the M.E.R.L.I.N. "I'll make contact with Luccan—he's waiting for the bus at the moment. If he remembers me, it'll make everything easier. And if not.... Well, it just seems wise to contact him now. Isa has found him. She'll be after him too."

WIZARDING IS a tough job even for the very best, and at present, with Luccan safely inside Thurlock's door only one day after his birthday, exhaustion nearly knocked Thurlock off his feet. Han, looking out for the old man as always, had sent him upstairs to his tower, saying, "Rest, sir," with that ridiculous formality that didn't hide his concern. Thurlock had followed Han's instructions, but wizards recuperate quickly if they know what they're doing, and now, after ten minutes under the quilt and five more in the shower, he was up and ready.

To some, the room at the top of Thurlock's tower might have seemed strange and cluttered, but to him it was home, and he took it with him wherever he went—literally. In it was his four-poster bed, stacked with pillows and covered with the purple-and-gold quilt his sister had made for him centuries ago. The bookshelves and the two fat chairs before the stone hearth bespoke comfort and always beckoned. A rough wooden table shoved against the wall never failed to hold a cornucopia of oddments. At the moment, it bore stacks of clean and dirty dishes, three jigsaw puzzles in worn boxes, very small things, hidden devices, and five huge socks.

He sat at that crowded table and sighed in a not-so-very-wizardly manner. He was anxious to talk to Luccan, but first he *should* call the boy's mother.

He didn't want to do it.

He dreaded it.

She could be a difficult woman. He tried to think of a reason to put it off, but wizards, at least good ones and those of the bloodline, absolutely cannot lie—even to themselves—and he eventually came to admit that a reason to procrastinate did not exist.

He scooted his chair closer to the table and extracted from the heap a dinner-plate sized disk of amber and glass. No one would have known by looking, but this little portable thing was a cousin to the big M.E.R.L.I.N. downstairs. He held the disk up, watched his reflection scratch its beard, sighed again, and gave in to his mind's penchant for wandering and self-doubt.

If I'd spent more time wizarding and less time dragging Han through the Vortices, I could have found Luccan long ago.

He'd lately realized he should have focused his search on Earth from day one. Ethra and Earth had a common origin, were nearly parallel, and occupied roughly the same space, so they wandered in and out of each other's time streams. Far from stupid, the Witch-Mortaine had understood that relationship and exploited it on Luccan's twelfth birthday.

And what is it that makes twelve such a dangerous age?

On the day Thurlock turned twelve, he'd come home through Midwinter snow on leave from his apprenticeship. A scrawny boy with more power in his hands than he could safely handle, he nearly fried his mother meaning only to warm her a bit. From that day forward, her once-lustrous hair stuck out in a frizzled mass. A thousand years later, the shame still burned.

But his mother, Behl bless her, never held it against him, and he could look back and laugh. Not so in Luccan's case—his banishment wasn't laughable at all. And no one could find humor in the violence of Han's twelfth birthday.

Thurlock shook his head. A thousand years of wizardry hadn't been long enough for him to solve the puzzles and answer the why. What made him think he'd do it this afternoon?

Besides, one thing he had learned in the last ten centuries was that if a man has to make a phone call to the temperamental mother of a missing child—a mother who also happens to be a highly skilled witch, a captain of the cavalry, and a powerhouse politician—it was best all around just to do it.

CHAPTER FIVE:
THE STORY OF LUCKY'S DARKEST NIGHT

THURLOCK CAME downstairs before Lucky had a chance to fully recover from the shock of being held in the chair by Han while watching a girl come through the M.E.R.L.I.N.

"You have nothing to fear from Han," Thurlock boomed from the stairwell.

After Lucky picked himself up and reoccupied the chair he'd knocked over jumping at the sound of the wizard's voice, he noticed the old man seemed refreshed. He smelled of soap and his silver curls were brushed, gathered, and tied. His back was straight, his eyes were bright, and his step was spry. Once again in swirling robes and soft sandals, he looked magnificent.

"And, you have nothing to fear from me." He sat down at the table, two chairs from Lucky, and pointed at the window that wasn't a window. "The M.E.R.L.I.N., there, is a device, technology, a tool. As for L'Aria, she's willful and surprising, but when it comes down to it, she's just an ordinary girl."

Pouring Thurlock a fresh glass of tea, Han coughed. "Ordinary, sir?"

"Point taken. Still, a girl, nothing more frightening."

To Lucky, for whom everything not normal remained a bit frightening, that statement begged argument, but he said nothing and didn't move. Ever since he'd come into this house, his abs had been clenched so tight he could have done an infomercial for the latest fitness machine. He knew he would have to talk to Thurlock in order to get what the old man offered; he truly wanted his life back. But some caveman part of him preferred to crouch in a corner and hide, invisible. So after the tea and Band-Aids, he'd refused all Han's offers of further comfort. Even food. Even a chance to nap, though every bone and bruise begged him to accept.

Han loaded three spoons of sugar into Thurlock's tea and stirred it in, the ice in the glass tinkling like tiny bells. He handed the tea to the old man with an easy, familiar smile, and Thurlock accepted it with a nod, a sparkling eye, and a grin. Despite his reticence, watching the friendly exchange made Lucky feel lonely to be left out. When Thurlock turned and included him in his smile, Lucky's heart flipped with joy, even though that felt ridiculous.

Then Thurlock looked at Lucky and said, "I want—"

Though he spoke for some time and surely must have completed at least that first sentence, Lucky heard not another word. He'd tuned out. His briefly happy heart flopped down around his navel and cold dread took over, leaving him with just one question. What does Thurlock want?

"—I believe I speak for Han as well." As Thurlock finished his speech, he turned to Han with a questioning look.

Han didn't answer. He chewed his lip, watching Lucky, "What's the matter, lad?"

"What?"

The old man raised his eyebrows and then spoke slowly. "I was saying, Luccan, that I want you to know we're glad you're here."

"Oh, that's what you want. I mean, uh.... Thank you, sir. Thank you very much."

"Luccan," Thurlock said, "is there something you want to ask me?"

Yes, definitely. He had questions, one in particular that had been howling for an answer ever since Lucky stepped into this house. But "No," he said and then clutched his stomach against a sudden pain.

"Are you sure?" Thurlock seemed amused, not worried.

"Yes," he lied again and shielded his eyes from the stab of too-bright light from the chandelier.

"I think you have a question."

"No sir, really," he said, choking the words out despite the burning coal that seemed to be stuck in his throat.

With no sound but Lucky's labored breathing, the silence grew until Han sighed and broke the new-formed ice. "Are you hungry now, Luccan?"

Of course I am! I haven't eaten anything all day but a maple bar. "No, please," Lucky said and doubled over in his chair. Then he added, "I think I'm sick," which was true, the first thing he'd said in five minutes that wasn't a lie, so the pain eased up a bit.

Either Han's upper lip itched or else he was trying not to laugh. Fortunately for Lucky, he was able to answer all Han's next questions truthfully. He asked if Lucky would rest a while ("no"), if he wanted to borrow a fresh shirt ("no"), if there was something left undone in tending to his injuries ("no").

"Do you want an aspirin?"

Lucky's contrite glance met Han's golden-brown eyes for the smallest fraction of a second. He hoped Han could see the apology; he hated to be rude, but he couldn't bear the pain of another lie, and he couldn't accept anything from either of these men, at the moment. So he said nothing at all.

"I hate to do this, Luccan," Thurlock said, "but I think it's for the best." He mumbled something unintelligible to Lucky, and then, in precisely the tone he'd used that afternoon when Commanding Lucky not to run, he said, "Ask your question."

Lucky's own voice startled him. "Did you know Hank George?"

"Hank George? Why?"

"You know my name."

Thurlock smiled and nodded, clearly pleased. "Yes we do, though we weren't sure you remembered it. Pretty foxy of you, boy. You never gave a hint of recognition." He tilted his head sideways and pursed his lips. "Do you remember anything else?"

Lucky scratched his head rather violently, which he often did when he was trying to ignore an irritation. He noticed the bump wasn't quite so sensitive, thanks to Han's ice bag, he supposed. But Lucky was ticked. Thurlock had forced him to ask. Lucky knew he'd had no choice—the old man had used some kind of magic. Then, when he'd asked the question, Thurlock responded only with a question of his own.

Lucky answered anyway—not forced this time, but recognizing the futility of staying silent. But he couldn't help sounding curt. "I don't remember much, no. A big house, fields, and water, a lake or something. I try to think about when I was a little kid, and I can feel people around me, but I can't see their faces. I remembered my name, and I told Hank the day I met him. I've never told anyone else."

Lucky found it strange that Thurlock and Han knew his name, but it had become obvious they knew much more than that, much more than he himself knew. He picked absently at a scratch in the tabletop, a chill breath of fear prickling the back of his neck. These two men had power over him.

"Don't pick at that, Lucky, you're making it worse." Han had at last taken a seat at the table. "Why," he asked, "did you not tell anyone else?" His expression was thoughtful, as if he expected a certain answer, perhaps testing a theory.

Lucky looked back at Han and then dropped his head into his hands. Too much was happening, too fast. He'd survived through the last year alone, always at the edge of disaster. He'd gotten pretty good at sniffing out danger, and this situation reeked of it. But did the threat come from these men or from elsewhere? Or maybe both?

A year ago he wouldn't have had to worry. Hank had still been doing the worrying for him, as he had since the day Lucky had crawled out of the cave so shaken he could hardly stand. Hank George had been there, and he'd taken Lucky in. For two years, living in Hank's old log cabin, Lucky had a life that was perhaps eccentric, but almost normal.

Hank treated Lucky well and taught him about the world. Since boys with no identity couldn't go to school, Hank gave lessons at home. And when Lucky had finished chores and lessons, sometimes they'd watch TV on Hank's old set with the rabbit ears. Hank had paid Lucky to stand and hold the antenna, because that way they got channels they otherwise couldn't get—from other countries even, from across the ocean. Hank's nephew, Henry, would come sometimes from Sacramento, where he worked as a firefighter. On those days, they'd all swim in the creek, or read out loud by the fire, or maybe Henry would take Lucky for a ride on his black-and-chrome Harley.

Incredibly, after losing everything—parents, home, even the knowledge of who he was—Lucky had been happy. They'd laughed, Lucky and Hank, a lot. And every once in a while when Lucky was feeling down, Hank would sit with him and pat his shoulder, even though Lucky refused to cry. "There, now, Luccan, ease up," he'd whisper. "You'll feel better." And Lucky would feel better, like magic.

Since Lucky came out of the cave on Midsummer, they chose to call that day his birthday, and it felt right. Last year on that day, Lucky had stumbled out of the cool shade of his bedroom into the morning sun that streamed into the cabin's great room. He spotted Hank in the kitchen, tying his long steel-colored braids behind his back to keep them out of the gas flame while he cooked. "Morning," Lucky mumbled, and then sat down at the pine-slab table.

"Hey, Lucky," Hank said and then greeted him with the same words he used every morning. "What do you remember, today?" As usual, the question went unanswered—Lucky hadn't remembered anything. But that day was special. Hank had made Lucky a sort of birthday cake—a stack of pancakes, maple syrup, and a big glob of whipped cream, bristling with fourteen flaming candles. They'd sat at the table and Hank had read the Wizard of Id comic out loud from yesterday's Valley Independent, and they'd laughed and gotten sticky together eating the birthday breakfast.

Afterward Hank said, "Do your chores up early. Henry said he'd come down for your birthday. We'll go to the lake." Then Hank left to walk the high trails along the ravine, as he had each day for fifty years or more.

But this time he didn't come back.

Somehow, he'd fallen from the path he knew so well and smashed his brains on the rocks in Black Creek's bed. Lucky had heard helicopters but didn't connect them to Hank. He had only wondered what was taking Hank so long. He'd finally begun to worry, until he heard about Hank's accident on the television, but even then he hadn't believed the man had simply fallen. *He died because of me*, Lucky had thought, and although he had no idea why, he knew it was true.

He'd run away from the cabin before Henry had time to get there from the city. He never went back and never saw Henry again. He'd heard a few times about a tall Native man around town looking for him. But Lucky didn't want Henry close to him for the same reason he later rejected the one boy on the street who could have been special to him. He didn't want to be close to anyone. He wouldn't risk having another friend get hurt because of him.

Never again.

Yet at the moment, sitting in Thurlock's kitchen, he faced a different situation. *This time, I'm the one taking the risk; I'm the one that might get hurt.* Thurlock and Han scared him. Honestly, he didn't think they meant him harm, but at the heart of all the strangeness in the wizard's house, he sensed some unfathomable, undefinable, extraordinarily dangerous power.

His cautious mind and street-kid instincts screamed *Crap, Lucky, just cut and run!* But he couldn't; that inner knowledge, the one they'd given the silly title Antenna of Truth, was going crazy, and it told Lucky none of this was chance and not much was choice. This was deep water, swift current. Lucky—no, Luccan—was in it "fins and gills," as Hank George would have said, and he was going to have to swim.

Thurlock broke into Lucky's thoughts. "Will you answer, Luccan? I won't Command it."

"That's nice of you, sir." Lucky tried unsuccessfully not to sound sarcastic, but Thurlock only raised an eyebrow and chuckled. Annoyed, Lucky demanded, "How do you do that, anyway?"

"Well, as you mentioned, I know your name, at least enough of it to accomplish a Command."

It made no sense at all, but Lucky had a heart-racing feeling he'd been told something important. He stared. Thurlock scratched at his beard, donned spectacles as if about to read fine print, and looked at Lucky over the wire rims. "By the way," he said, apparently attempting to sound casual, "do you remember any more of them?"

"More of what?"

"Your names, of course."

Lucky didn't, but when he shook his head, he wasn't saying no; he was expressing bewilderment.

Nevertheless, Thurlock said, "Ah, too bad, then… or perhaps not."

Lucky decided to pretend the conversation had never jagged off on that whole tangent. He pointed his gaze at Han and answered the question he'd been asked. "Hank George…. I met him when… when I came… lost… well, the first day I can remember. He didn't ask my name, but I told him, and he said that I should keep it to myself. 'You never know,' he told me, 'who might be looking for your name, or what they might do with it.'"

"Smart man," Thurlock said.

"He started calling me Lucky. He said it sounded enough like my name that I would feel like me, but different enough someone else wouldn't recognize it. And he teased me." Lucky smiled. "He said I needed all the help I could get, and if everybody called me Lucky, maybe the spirits would believe it."

Thurlock and Han laughed, but then Han sobered, biting his lower lip into a serious line. The gold in his eyes shimmered, his gaze intense but not hard. "How did you come to meet this man?"

Lucky had never told the strange story of the day he met Hank. Even when Hank had still been alive, he'd tried not to think about it. Sitting at Thurlock's table, now, he felt a knot deep in his belly come undone and set that hard tale loose.

"I REMEMBER everything about that night," Lucky began. He knew right away that before the night was over he would tell Thurlock and Han all of it, tastes and smells and sounds, the brush of the breeze over his arm, the trickle of rain—not tears—down his cheeks. But first, he told them about Hank.

He recalled the sound of Hank George's drum, his knuckled hand holding the curved beater, the way the painted hide stretched over the drum's "bones." He told them about Hank's song, and about how he made him feel safe. The love and gratitude he harbored for the old man came together, glowing in the center of his chest. He took a deep breath and let his first-ever telling of the story of his darkest night pour straight from his heart.

"I don't know what would have happened," he began, "if Hank had not been there. Maybe I would have died. I told him once that him being there that first night was the only reason my name 'Lucky' might be true. He said that wasn't so, it wasn't luck. He'd been there because of a promise he'd made and a habit of keeping it. He called himself the Guardian."

As Lucky spoke, the last of the prism-scattered rainbows in Thurlock's house stretched thin, dimmed, and disappeared. Dark crept in. Their faces donned veils of shadow. They could have been anywhere. They could have been in that cave where, three years and one day ago, Lucky awoke.

"It was cold, dark, wet. At first I couldn't see anything at all, but then I realized that to one side there was a glow, so dim I had to stare to be sure it was there." He had heard water, waves on rocks, maybe, and something splashing.

"I pictured some horrible creature—it was the first thought that made enough sense to scare me. From then on, I was terrified every single minute, even after Hank had me safe. It only lasted one night, I know that now. But then it was all I knew, all I remembered of life. Forever.

"It scared me even to move, but finally I stood up and crept toward the glow. I found a passage, and I followed it." He'd clung to the walls even though they cut his hands, crawled where the ceiling dropped, slithered over slime that stank like rotten eggs.

He clenched his fists where they lay on Thurlock's scratched tabletop and raised his eyes to meet Han's. "The whole way, I kept saying, 'No, I can't do it.' Eventually, though, I did. I reached the end of the tightest, slimiest, smelliest stretch of tunnel, and I had to close my eyes, the light was so bright."

He'd expected to emerge into daylight, but found himself standing in a cavern. Its glimmering ceiling soared overhead, so high it did seem like starlight, but brighter than stars ever should be. The air moved like breath, carrying whispered chimes.

"It felt like I'd blundered into a giant's tomb." Hank waited there, and Lucky had been afraid of him too. "But as soon as he got me out, he started taking care of me. He never stopped until he died."

After a silence, Han rose and made a circuit of the three front rooms in Thurlock's house, turning on small lights over the mantelpiece, next to the sideboard, on the stove. Their allied glows pushed back the dark. He closed the windows too, shutting out a surprising chill, and drew down the shades. Thurlock went to the door to call in the cat, the sound of his voice rising warm above dampening night. Han gave Lemon some milk and Thurlock some tea—hot this time.

To Lucky he said, "Would you like a glass of milk, lad?" Perhaps he knew Lucky was set to refuse, because he quickly added, "Chocolate, if you like; Thurlock won't drink the white kind." Lucky accepted, returning Han's smile, and the sweet milk soothed and cooled him. Thurlock asked if he was too tired to go on, but he felt refreshed enough, and the rest of the tale pushed like something solid at the back of his teeth, wanting out.

It had not been quite dusk when Hank brought him out of the cave, and for a few minutes the sun had warmed him, but when night fell it turned cold despite the season. Lucky had shivered so hard he'd barely been able to stand. Suddenly, remembering it there in Thurlock's house, he laughed, and then explained when he saw Thurlock's questioning smile. "Hank got an ax, and I thought he was going to kill me, but he just used it to split some firewood."

He recalled the warmth of the fire and how completely lost he'd felt. He'd sat wrapped in Hank George's old quilt, quenched his awful thirst with the water Hank dipped for him from a barrel, and eaten the stew Hank had heated over the fire. But he'd still felt empty and confused, and the more Hank quizzed him, the more hopeless he became.

Hank had told him later that he'd hated having to question him, asking the same things over and over, hammering away. He'd done it, he said, to be absolutely sure he was right about who—and what—Lucky was.

"I couldn't answer anything except the one question he didn't ask. Finally I shouted it out. 'My name is Luccan, that's all I know.'"

As if borne on the memory, Lucky drew away from that room in Thurlock's house almost physically, fell back to that night three years ago and that bright fire in front of the cave. He was there, drowsing, watching the smoke as it tumbled and twisted up to the darkening sky, leaving holes for stars to peek through, coloring the moon like ink and filling that long, long night with fragrance. He heard Hank George speak, saying things that, for all the three years since, Lucky had tried hard to forget.

"You are one of the Others."

With those words echoing from the past, the story Lucky was telling took complete hold of him. Entranced, he walked to Thurlock's living room as if he were at home and sat in one of the two threadbare armchairs, bare feet digging into a soft, thick rug. Han followed, apparently in much the same mental state, said nothing, just stood until Thurlock gently pushed him into the other armchair. On the windowsill, Lemon Martinez made tiny movements of his paws and whiskers, dreaming.

Lucky saw those things at the edges of his vision as he stared into the grate, the cold, empty heart of a massive wall of river-rounded stone. He was only distantly astonished when, at a small gesture from Thurlock, flames sprang up in that hollow like sudden blooms. The old man then fetched a straight-backed chair from the table, set it facing the fire between Lucky and Han, and sat silent and wakeful, waiting as his strange glass clock ticked on the mantel. Lucky closed his eyes, feeling Thurlock's flames warm his face.

When he opened them, time had fallen away completely, and it was Hank George's wood fire three years past that he watched. Then, he'd been a child, bewildered and unable to believe. Now, digging the truths Hank George knew out of the past for the first time, telling the tale aloud in a house where magic happened, he began to believe.

"I'M WORRIED about you, boy. In the old stories, the Others came through that passage because there was something bad happening in their world, but they came of their own accord. You're alone. You seem to have lost yourself on the way. Someone sent you, and I'll bet dollars to donuts they didn't have your best interests at heart."

Hank put his back to the flames and faced Lucky. He said, "Listen, now," and his voice, soft as old leather until that moment, went sharp.

"You're lucky to be alive, I'd say. There's some kind of darkness following you. Until you know its nature, young cousin, you'd better hang on tight to your name and anything else you brought with you and be on your guard. As long as I'm alive, I'll do what I can to keep you safe.

"But I don't know," he said. "I don't know if that will be enough."

HAD HANK George truly spoken these words? Sometimes Lucky wondered, thought that perhaps he had only dreamed it, hypnotized by fire and food and the soft, safe night that wrapped him like a blanket. And now, this room in Thurlock's house enfolded him the same way, wizard's flame shielding him against harm. He glanced around the room, like coming up from deep sleep to the surface. *Strange but real*, he assured himself. Then he slid back down to the dream.

"EVER SINCE the Others came and stayed with us for a time, some children were born with this." Hank pulled his T-shirt back from his brown shoulder and turned it so Lucky could see. "The Mark of the Others," he called it. But in each generation, fewer and fewer newborns

were marked. "In my generation," Hank said, "only my sister and I bore the Mark. My nephew Henry is the last."

LUCKY OPENED his mouth to tell more but, suddenly exhausted, he only said, "I'm done." He leaned his head back, and his eyes fell closed.

Han took a deep breath and broke his silence. "It's as the prophecy says, isn't it, sir?"

Thurlock answered immediately, "Without question."

Lucky snapped his eyes open, feeling like he'd just awoken, oddly disoriented, like a goldfish dropped in the rum punch. He looked from Han to Thurlock. "Prophecy?"

"This time in the story of our two worlds was foretold a thousand years ago."

Lucky waited, sure the wizard would say more, but all Thurlock did was pull thoughtfully at his beard. Finally, he blurted, "What does it say you have to do?"

"Do?"

"The prophecy...."

"Oh," Thurlock chuckled. "Prophecies don't work that way. They tell you some of what will be or might be, but they never tell you what to do about it. Mostly useless, really."

"Then why did Han bring it up?"

"It's not important." Thurlock walked over and put his back to the fire as he spoke.

Han walked to the window. "Interesting, though," he said.

"What about the Mark, then?"

"The Mark, yes," said Thurlock, turning to the hearth to motion the flames higher. "That's interesting too, wouldn't you say, Han?"

"Very much so, sir," Han answered, opening the window to fan cool air into the room.

The wizard paced silently before the fire, hands clasped at his back. Then, decisively, he pivoted to face Han. "Would you be so good as to take your shirt off, please?"

"Certainly, sir."

Lucky's mouth flapped open, but he had no time to form a question or run from the room. Thurlock took two huge strides over to Han, mumbled "Pardon me," and pulled back Han's thin, ribbed undershirt to reveal a tawny, well-muscled shoulder branded with a mark as wide across as the length of a man's thumb. At its center burned an almost perfect disk; twelve rays exploded around it. As light as cream where Hank's had been almost black, it was the polar opposite of Hank's Mark of the Others.

"Our world is called Ethra, Luccan, Behlis Ethra." Thurlock's voice was a whisper, yet it echoed from the hearth and set flames dancing. "This," he said, "is the Mark of the Sun."

CHAPTER SIX:
A MAGIC HE'D BELIEVED FOREVER LOST

THE TOWER walls, glass colored blue like deep ice, stole the last of the day's light from dusk. A man with heavy chestnut curls and a scarred face limped along the crow's walk, circling round and round. His steps fell as listless as his greasy hair, and his mangled left hand dragged along the thin rail that separated the pinnacle from the clouds it speared. The cold steel burned, and he pulled the nearly useless limb against his body, trying to rub life into it with his better hand.

He stopped, facing the black stone columns the Earthborns called Death of the Gods. He swayed, feeling for a moment that if he stared long enough, he might fall through the empty space between those columns. Shaking his head, he turned to face west. He found the view of Valley City, sprawled across the dusty floor of Cirque Basin, much less disturbing.

The waking metropolis lay confined in a round valley, walled in by the ring of peaks known as the Noose, crags that jutted up like teeth to guard the basin that was once the fiery throat of a volcano. Black Creek Ravine, an uninhabited crack in the crater's floor, split the valley and its city into halves.

In places, cliffs bound the creek in a deep, narrow channel. Elsewhere the walls rose in crumbling slopes, or folds of smooth basalt, or bore shelves that supported groves and meadows. The deep, wide parts of the gorge taunted Hench with lush, living greens—stark contrast to the desert valley and bony peaks surrounding it.

At the dry, eastern end of the ravine, the creek gushed from underground caverns, tumbling between the pillars of Death of the Gods as if they were giant gateposts. On the north bank, time-chiseled palisades loomed forty feet above the watercourse, but on the south side, a low rise at the bank sloped into a sunken plain.

The Witch-Mortaine's tower rose from that boulder-strewn plain, rooted between high ridges and veiled in spells.

At this hour, the entire crater lay in shadow, but even in the half-light and with only one eye, Hench's vision was sharp. He could see cars sliding along the city's roads, trailing columns of red and white like snakes of light. He imagined the people piloting them, tired Earthborns who wished they'd already arrived wherever they were going.

He wondered about their lives. Did they have any kind of magic? Had they ever had it? Had any of them possessed magic and love and a good life and lost it all? He wondered whether their cars would pile up in a panicked crash if they but once saw through the magical veils and glimpsed the deadly crystal beauty of the spire from which he gazed.

He worked his shoulders into a painful shrug, wishing he could rid himself of the black shadow that weighed them down, a shadow he himself had created out of anger and hate. He shook his head in persistent disbelief that it had overtaken him so easily, so fast.

He'd committed himself to vengeance, and the shadow had been born, a larval vampire that fed on his spirit, consumed his strength and joy. It grew stronger with every cruel choice and every time he lashed out, burning with rage. It fouled his every step, turned even his best intentions to evil end, drained him of substance as surely as if it had torn his heart and bled him dry. The remains had become a joke, fool to a fiendish witch, tool in the hands of the person he most hated.

He leaned against the rail, half wishing the steel would vanish and let him go. The wind thrummed against the glass and steel of the spire, but he ignored it. Whatever shame Earth's night winds might hiss into his ear, they couldn't carry the single word he should not have forgotten. Only the Gods' Breath knew that name, and he had little hope ever to stand again in that sweet dawn wind of the Ethran Sunlands.

"Hench!" The witch Isa shrilled her summons into the darkling sky, and though it was not his name and thus had no real power over him, it was hard to ignore. She well knew that he would answer to that demeaning tag or any other slur she cared to impose.

"Hench," she growled again, "I want you in here now."

He held his feet to their places and stretched his small moment of defiance as far as it would go. Leaning out across the rail, he looked down past the once-living land that surrounded the tower's base, poisoned now to ash and ice and dust. A fathomless moat guarded the structure, empty and falling away to black death. It would be a long drop if a man were to jump.

"Hench," the screech came a third time, "*now*!"

He lingered a scant moment longer until a cloud came between him and the hope of silence with which that black abyss taunted. He sighed, clothed himself in servility, and bent to open the hatch leading into the Witch-Mortaine's lair.

Isa's chamber was as cold as polar ice. The caustic blue glass of the tower's shell, a foot and a half thick, formed the floor and one wall; white stone had been chiseled square and stacked to build the others. Hewn of blue-veined marble, the witch's bed remained hard and bare. Hench entered through a steel door and limped into the room. The sound of his steps returned in echoes from the dungeons below.

Isa spun on her blue-slippered heel, face twisted with anger. "You took your time, thrall."

Hench dropped his eyes lest they enrage her further but resisted the temptation to throw up a shielding arm and cower. With the intuition of a whipped hound, he gauged her mood. The crystal flash of her pale eyes made it plain she was at the end of her small patience, but he was safe enough for the moment. She held no weapon, wouldn't spend her other magic on him except in dire need, and she'd never touch him with her bare hands. After all, the same hallowed blood still ran in his veins.

Still, he used her formal title and bowed from the waist. "I'm sorry, Witch-Mortaine Isa." He wasn't pretending. He'd borne too much pain at the wrong end of her favorite weapon—a whip with myriad glass-tipped tails—to deliberately court her displeasure. His guide in every choice was knowledge, scarred into flesh and memory, of the agonies Isa was all too willing to inflict. He might risk a small, secret defiance but never open rebellion.

"Of course you're sorry, fool." Isa paced back and forth, sharp steps rattling the rows of bottles and vials on her worktable, shaky as it was on a slim pedestal of steel. She slammed a hand down on that table and turned her gaunt face toward Hench. He looked in her direction but kept his one-eyed gaze from meeting her eyes. He watched instead the shadows of her jewel-colored potions quaking after her blow. He concentrated on stillness, a hunter's skill he still owned.

These days, it often made no difference what he did or said. She was frustrated, and she took it out on him. She had spent a year, by Earth's time, searching for a boy she herself had banished to this world. Despite her powers and her foul god and her alliances with the evils of Earth, she had not been able to find the child.

Isa drew in a long breath, her bony chest heaving, and the dissatisfaction in it belied her words. “Your duties will change. The boy has been found.”

For one shred of a second, when she said “the boy,” Hench thought he heard another sound whispered around the edges. A name? He wanted to hold on to the moment, pursue the phantom memory, but he saw the witch narrow her eyes, studying him. His face must have registered the shock. Quickly, he buried the reaction and all emotion beyond her reach.

Except fear—he let that show. She liked to see it.

“Look at me,” she snapped, and he did, but by then his eye was as empty as death. She strode a step closer and leveled her deadly regard at him, snarling. “What is about to happen is the reason you’ve been kept alive, little man.” She pivoted abruptly to face the empty center of the chamber, raised her hands high, and lifted her voice in the visceral language of her god, the Ice-Lord Mahl.

Dark Chant threatened to bury his thoughts in ice, and the god’s presence, the void that was his essence, bore down on him. He fell to his knees.

When finally the sound stopped and the cold weight receded, he stayed down, head bowed to the floor, sucking in desperate breaths. Too late, he heard the whine of the witch’s scourge slicing air, and then barbed tails cut through the leather on his back, shredding his skin. That one blow, which channeled the Ice-Lord’s touch, drained all remaining warmth from his body, turned the beat of his heart to icy shivers, impaled his thoughts on blinding blue-white light.

Isa spat an order to rise, and he struggled to put his feet under him and obey, but strength refused to flow to his damaged left leg. He toppled.

“Stand, slave,” she snarled again. “Or perhaps you’d like a taste of real pain today?”

“Mortaine Isa,” he begged, buying time. “Please, no.” At last he found his feet. Cautiously, fleetingly, he raised his eye to hers.

A moment later—completely calm—she said, “Very well, Hench. Be thankful. Worthless as you are, Mahl has favored you.” Her thoughtful gaze felt strangely unthreatening. It was a face of the witch Hench had never seen, and apprehension gripped him like pincers. “Behold,” she said, “his gift.”

In the center of the chamber, where there had been nothing before Isa's Dark Chant, stood a bulky, irregular shape covered with a cloth of glowing graveyard blue. Isa pulled the cover away and revealed a granite stone. Hench chanced a look at the witch, not knowing what it meant.

"Put your hands on the rock," Isa said, more quietly than he had ever heard her speak.

"Mistress?"

"Do it."

"Yes," he said and limped toward it, afraid of what it might be, what new persecution the stone might hold, but certain about what the witch would do if he didn't obey. His weak, wasted left hand fell onto the rock, and he drew in a sharp, surprised breath. He felt a current there, the faint flow of magic. Did he recognize it?

Anxious, he placed his right hand deliberately, palm down over the curve of the stone. An instant later the magic hidden in the stone recognized him and the current grew strong. Tears threatened. This was a magic he had believed forever lost.

"You know what it is? You can feel it?"

"Yes, Mortaine."

She paced as she spoke, like a lecturing professor. "The Black Blade, sometimes called the Obsidian Knife or the Dark Twin. Fool! You had it in your hands. But you threw it away twenty-seven years ago, from the Heights of Gahabriohl into the depths of Mardhral." She stopped and spun to face him. "Why?"

He hedged. "The magic in it was no longer useful to me."

"Hah!" Her laugh was sharp, cut short, but it echoed against the glass and steel of the tower. "Well, be that as it may, Hench, I have reason to believe that you can still use it. My Master believes that makes you a person of interest, potentially useful in the upcoming struggle over our precious boy."

She smiled but looked as though she had swallowed something bitter. Hench had the unexpected notion that she was doing something not entirely of her own choosing. He guarded his face, keeping that realization, and a flare of hatred, secret.

She turned her gaze away and again raised her arms. "Hold fast to the stone, fool," she said flatly, and then she started Dark Chant once more.

This time he didn't fall. He knelt and embraced the stone, shivering as the magic of the Blade coursed through him, both dread and welcome. The blue granite in his arms grew icier with every repetition of the chant, but when the stone shattered, though pebbles battered his flesh, his arms wrapped around the Knife. Silence fell over the chamber like snow.

"Go, Hench, get to your place." The witch's voice trembled, breaking the stillness. "Take that thing from my presence."

"Mistress." He stood and bowed his head in her direction, his voice small but clear.

He exited the steel door and lurched down a flight of narrow stairs. Though they were musty and small—no more than a forgotten corner—Hench had furnished his quarters with cast-off comforts: torn mattress, lumpy pillow, worn gray rug. It wasn't a home, and the feeling it gave of safety was false, but it had become his den, and he inhaled its dusty air gratefully. He sank onto the mattress and pulled a frayed blanket over him, warm and soft against the cold, bloody wounds of the lash.

Curled around the Blade, he slept, unafraid of its edge.

CHAPTER SEVEN: THE LION, THE COOKIE, AND THE HEART'S DESIRE

THURLOCK SAT in the faded brocade of the armchair Lucky had deserted, his sandals flung aside. He glanced up from massaging his feet as Han stepped into the room from the stairwell. "He's sleeping?"

Han nodded and tossed a chunk of wood into the fireplace, then watched as the flames caught along its split edge. Magic flames were well and good, but the scent of cedar and the crackle of wood fire spoke to Han of home. He opened the damper to let the heat escape. It wasn't the season for a fire, but the air cooled enough in the foothills at night, and the flames calmed him.

"Thanks for making him comfortable," Thurlock said. "I'm relieved he chose to stay."

"It's not surprising. Once his belly was full of those burgers and fries of yours, he could hardly keep his eyes open." Han smiled, taking a seat in the other armchair. "But he did talk to me, sir, a little, and that surprised me."

"And pleased you, I see."

Han didn't miss the teasing twinkle in the old man's eyes. He smiled. "He's worried about his dog, and his things. I told him I'd go with him in the morning to get them. That's all right?"

Thurlock nodded but stroked his beard thoughtfully. "I wish we could just keep him here until we can get him home. I fear we've woken the sleeping lion."

"Lion, sir?"

"Earthborns have such wonderful sayings, don't you think? Lions disturbed from dreams get nasty. In this case the lion is the witch. She knows we've got him. She won't be slow to respond."

Han hesitated but then spoke his mind. "I think it might be a mistake, sir, to keep him here against his will." He drew in a breath to continue but then stopped to chew his lip, thinking how best to frame what he had observed in Luccan's character. "He's skittish as a colt," he said finally, "and he's used to being on his own, making his own choices."

"And he wants to think he can trust us, but he doesn't." Thurlock ran tired hands through his gray hair, freeing it of its leather band. "So we'll take the path of least peril. Better to have you go with him than have him leave on his own. Perhaps I'll follow, if I don't have to go home tomorrow. We'll need to take steps for his safety in case he gets separated from us both."

Han nodded. "I thought of that, sir. I gave him our phone number."

Thurlock studied his attaché with a worried frown. "We don't have a phone, Han."

Han lit up with a jack-o'-lantern grin. "Luccan doesn't know that."

After a few seconds, Thurlock's puzzled frown disappeared and he nodded, laughing. "Oh, I see. Good thinking, then." He chuckled some more and added, "Yes, that'll do for now. I'll throw what protection I can on him too. He won't be safe, but he'll be safer, at least."

The topic having turned to safety, Han confided something that had troubled him since yesterday morning. "Sir, Luccan's shack.... He was living right on the edge of that ravine."

"And?"

"Well, it's a troubling place. I mean, I know there's the Portal down there in the cave, but it's more than that."

Han recalled the day, soon after they'd arrived in Earth, when Thurlock brought home an armload of books from a local library and dumped them on the table. "A little history," he'd said. "A little geography. It never hurts to be informed."

Han preferred to get information firsthand, but the wizard was the boss. He'd cracked the books, and he'd found tales about the ravine that he wasn't likely to forget. Now he asked, "You remember those stories about what happened when this place was settled? Unexplained deaths, disappearances, and... uh... the homesteads...." He was having trouble getting the words out. They threatened to launch his most horrible memories.

Thurlock understood his distress. He leaned forward and patted Han's arm. "They were burned, yes," he said.

The plain words blunted the spear of memory, and Han relaxed, letting the tension ease out of his shoulders.

"The place has a bad reputation," Thurlock was saying. "And you're right. There's more to that ravine than meets the eye. It's more than the presence of the Portal entrance; the worlds are closely intertwined there. It's my guess that the place has been targeted off and on for centuries by Ethrans with less than neighborly motives and enough power to make it count."

Lost in thought for several seconds, he tugged at his beard. "That's why the locals stay away as far as they can," he said. "I'd lay odds they don't even look down when they drive over one of the bridges." He gave his beard a couple more pats and then turned to Han. "Why did you bring it up?"

"Why would he choose to live there?"

Thurlock smiled. "Because he's a smart cookie."

"Sir?"

"It's another figure of speech, Han. What I mean is that I imagine he felt quite safe in that shack and near the ravine in general. It gave him what he needed most—a place where people wouldn't notice him. He couldn't afford the attention of the authorities. He wouldn't be able to tell them even his name; who knows where he would land? And, he wouldn't want to be noticed by the criminal element either—"

"But he works for them."

Thurlock cocked an inquiring eyebrow.

"That's what he talked about, sir, while we were putting sheets on the bed. He told me how he's been getting by since Hank George died. He watched the other people on the streets, especially the kids. He saw the things they did to survive—stealing, panhandling, and, well, other things." Han looked up to meet the wizard's steady gray gaze. "He did some things—things he wouldn't name, but I can imagine—when he had to, at first, after he realized stealing was out."

"Yes, it would be, for Luccan."

Han shook his head, thinking about the crazy life the boy had led for the past year. Then he smiled. "He said at first, of the possibilities, stealing was the only one he figured he might be able to do. So he tried it."

Thurlock grimaced and shook his head. "It didn't go well, I presume?"

"Every time he laid his hand on something that belonged to someone else he heard a horrible ringing in his ears and his head hurt. It wouldn't stop until he put the thing down. And then, once, somebody caught him trying."

"He tried to lie about it?"

"That's right."

"Sick?"

"Vomited on the man's boots."

"Oh," said Thurlock, rolling his eyes and getting suddenly to his feet. "That's worse than what happened to me the time I tried it. At least I made it outside." At this Han burst out laughing. Thurlock put an indignant hand on his hip, glowered at Han, and said, "It wasn't funny at all."

After a renewed bout of laughter died down enough for Han to speak, he said, still chortling, "You tried to lie, sir?"

"Don't act so surprised. Everyone lies at least once; it's only that a person with the old blood doesn't try it a second time. Or at least most of us don't. By the Lights of Heaven, I worried the boy was going to kill himself with half-truths tonight."

"He's willful, isn't he?"

"A bit of an understatement, I'd say. But considering who his mother is—"

"Some can lie, though." The statement silenced them both. There were important exceptions.

"Yes, of course," Thurlock acknowledged, "if they've turned away from the light."

Han moved closer to the hearth. "I'm sorry, sir. You're right—you trying to lie, that isn't funny."

"Nonsense, my friend. It wasn't funny then, but—case in point—I have to be honest. Thinking about it now, it's hilarious."

Han smiled again. "In any event, sir, Luccan's experiment turned out to be a good thing. The man made him clean up the mess, and his whole house, and he did such a good job the guy hired him to do his laundry. Later, when Luccan decided he could do chores for money, he paid the guy a visit. The man not only had work for him but also referred him to his friends. Most of them made their living running small-time cons, so that's how Luccan has been getting by—doing laundry and whatnot for criminals." Han gave Thurlock a puzzled look. "He said they were almost always honest with him, sir, paid him as much as they said they would or sometimes more."

"Ah, well there you go. That's one of the supreme puzzles. It's easy—sometimes, at least—to tell whether something someone has done is right or wrong. It's not so easy, though, to judge a person good or bad. But at least the story shows us Luccan is resourceful."

"And honest."

Thurlock reclaimed his chair and laid his head back. Letting his eyes close, he added almost in a whisper, "Poor kid." He heaved a sigh and changed the subject. "I suppose I'd better try again to call his mother."

"Be brave, sir."

"Cut it out."

Han fought down the corners of his mouth, "Seriously, what can she do from a world away?"

Thurlock shot a look at Han, eyebrows arched. "You call her, then."

"Not my job, sir. Good night." Han exited the front door, straightened the welcome mat one last time, and closed the door behind him.

"Coward," Thurlock accused.

Han's only response was to laugh.

BY THE time the door clicked shut, Thurlock had moved to the dining room and set the M.E.R.L.I.N. spinning, and he smiled despite his mood as a soft Sunlands night settled into view. Moonlight cast a silver sheen on the log-and-thatch bulk of Sisterhold Manor, and a few of the windows in its broad face winked with yellow light. He froze the viewer with a raised hand, wishing he could linger.

"Get on with it, old man," he said, laughing at himself, and directed the viewer forward.

When it showed him the gold-varnished door, he imagined knocking with the brass stag knocker and lifting the latch, and then watched as it happened in the viewer. He stepped into the familiar old house, or at least that was how it felt. The Lady Grace Liliana sat at her dressing table in a room painted summer-sky blue, with white lace panels at the window that fluttered in the breeze. A candle's flame cast gold on the polished floor and set Lili's pale complexion aglow, but her eyelids drooped over tired eyes. Her golden hair hung loose, shining, and her fingers toyed with the smooth-worn handle of her boar-bristle hairbrush.

"Just finished your nightly one hundred beauty strokes?"

Liliana eyed him through the M.E.R.L.I.N. that doubled as her mirror. "He's with you," she said. "I'm coming tonight."

"That's not wise, Liliana." Thurlock slumped in his chair at the dining table. "I know you're anxious, you've waited thirty years." He looked away from the M.E.R.L.I.N. to avoid her gaze and poked his yellow-umbrella staff listlessly at the chandelier.

"Yet he's still a boy."

Thurlock nodded. "More or less. For him it's been three years. He's fifteen—nearly a young man."

"He needs his mother."

"He needs his mother—as we all need his mother—to stay put where she is and keep things in order in his home world. Which reminds me, what happened with L'Aria this afternoon?"

"I wasn't here." She wore a look of distaste, but as she turned her attention away from the girl, her expression changed to a worried frown. "I went up to Northvale. Strange things are happening again. I was going to ask you to come home tomorrow. A lot of people are upset." She paused and the frown changed again to displeasure. "And L'Aria's run off again."

Thurlock ignored Lili's well-known dislike for her ward. "Strange things?"

"Deaths. And no, I didn't find out anything useful. The circumstances are very much like the Greenwood incidents a few years ago, dead trees and missing blood. Of course, we all know who the likely culprit was then."

"Likely, but not convicted."

"True, and he's dead now, so they say. But then, we haven't found his corpse."

"Nor shall we, if what we surmise is true. Mardhral Canyon makes a deep grave."

She was quiet, methodically rearranging the creams, lotions, and scents on her dressing table. Bringing a bottle down with a sharp crack on the hard wood, she said, "But that's not what this call is about. How soon will you be bringing Luccan home?"

"When he's ready, and I've determined that it's safe." Thurlock, annoyed, batted the chandelier with his umbrella, and the fixture started to swing.

"Put that staff down, uncle, you're making me nervous. Why can't Luccan come home? You said he has the Key and the Amber Knife. And he has enough magic! I'm sure of it."

"It's highly likely that he does, considering his birthright." Thurlock abruptly dropped the umbrella on the table. It set loose a shower of sparks. "Nix," he said, arresting the accidental magic.

He sat up straight and scowled into the M.E.R.L.I.N. "Whether he has magic or not, he can't use it. Yes, he has the Key of Behliseth and the Amber Blade, but those are only tools. He'll get into trouble if he tries to use them with neither skill nor knowledge." He saw scorn in Lili's green eyes. "And don't call me 'uncle,' niece. You only do that when you want something."

"Why can't he use his magic? He was born to it."

"I've told you this before, Liliana, but I'll tell you again." His words were terse. "If he tries to travel through the Vortices—or even if we try to bring him through—when he doesn't have a clear idea who he is or where he's going, he could end up anywhere in a thousand worlds. Or worse, everywhere in a thousand worlds."

He pressed the heels of his hands to his eyes, leaning on his elbows. "For Behl's sake," he said, frustration leading him to take that sacred name in vain. "He only remembers one of his names. Worst-case scenario, he could end up nowhere at all."

"And why is it that he only has one of his names, uncle?" She drummed her long nails on the golden wood and didn't bother to keep the accusation from her tone.

"You know the answer."

"Well, if you'd listened to me then. 'As thee send, return to thee, good or ill, by rule of three....'"

"Stop quoting me the primer, Lili! By the gods' teeth, I've been a wizard for a thousand years. I've heard the rule of three a time or two."

"Well, then, you should have known what would happen if you let that man hold Luccan's cardinal name. With the things he'd already done, nothing could have stopped ruin from falling on his fool, stubborn head."

"You're wrong, child. I shouldn't have known. One can't know what will happen inside another soul." He stopped. It was hard enough, he decided, to defend himself against self-reproach. *By Behl's curly whiskers, I don't have to answer to my great-great-great niece.*

"What if—"

“Drop it, Lili.” Thurlock leaned into his hands again and started to massage his temples.

“Take some aspirin.”

“Aspirin?”

“For the headache. Uncle Thurlock, I’m Luccan’s mother. I know what’s best for him, and I know him. He’ll be fine in the Vortices. You can give him his other names to help.”

“I can give him the third, as soon as he asks for it. If he shows a single clear indicator that he’s ready to grow into his title, I can give him that, too. The second name, he’ll probably remember on his own—it was never a secret. If he doesn’t, you can give it to him when the time comes, since it came from you anyway. His cardinal name remains a problem, and as you’re well aware, it’s the one that counts.”

“I thought you said there’s a way you can call it back from the wind? And, you said some people remember it on their own.”

“There is a way, but I don’t know what it is. And some people do, but he hasn’t. I asked.”

“You’ve been working on this for thirty years.”

“No, dear, I have not.” He let his hands fall from his face and let his words fall quiet. “I’ve been divining Portals and surfing Naught trying to find where the Witch-Mortaine beached your son’s craft, while at the same time trying to keep the Sunlands from falling apart. How much time for research do you think that left?”

Lili narrowed her eyes, and though Thurlock had never considered green a hot color, at that moment, he half expected her irises to burst into flame. “Let me talk to him. I’ll remind him who he is.”

“No, Lili.” Thurlock spoke firmly despite his weariness. “He’ll want to believe anything we can tell him about his past, especially you, since you’re his mother.” He resisted the urge to add *poor child*. “He’ll convince himself that he remembers. A false memory, or even a vague one, will serve him no better in the Vortices than no memory at all.”

Thurlock slapped his open palm down on the table, emphasizing his next words. “True, clear desire of the heart, Liliana, that’s the only magic that works beyond the Portals, you know that. He has to have the real memories. Without his true name, it’s the only way. We’ll wait. We’ll give it time.”

“L’Aria went through.”

"L'Aria knows who she is. And for that matter, she didn't use the Vortices, not the way we do. She used her song."

"Bring him home. If Isa could banish him, surely the great Thurlock can get him back."

"First," he said, his voice scarcely louder than a whisper as he rose from his chair and began to pace, robes swishing, cheek twitching. "First, the power that the Witch-Mortaine employs is not available to me. Second, if it was, I would not partake. Third, although you might feel better, how will it help Luccan or Ethra if he comes home reduced once again to a blank slate?"

He stopped and turned to her, the muscles of his jaw working through his impatience. "When she banished him," he said, keeping his voice deliberately small, "he lost his identity because he never had it in the first place. That hasn't changed."

"I'm his mother." She'd risen to her feet too, and now she leaned toward the eye of M.E.R.L.I.N. Her features were set, and the words she hurled had barbs. "Since his father is dead, or at least gone, I alone decide for my son. He comes home now."

Adding together magical ability and political clout, Liliana amounted to one of the most powerful people in all of Ethra. Yet, Thurlock looked her in the eye and spoke with confidence. "In matters concerning Luccan, the authority is mine. The law is clear."

Liliana's jaw muscles tightened as she struggled for control. "I'll take it to the Council."

"I am the Council."

"You are one of the Council, as I am."

Thurlock simply pursed his lips and acknowledged her with the tiniest nod.

Without warning, she broke into sobs and sat again at her table. Thurlock could barely discern her words through her tears and the hands she held up to hide them. "He's my son, uncle, my only child."

Lili's threats hadn't touched him, but her tears did. Thurlock's ire fled, and his own voice grew thick. He reached across the table as if to reach into another world to take his niece's hand. "Liliana, dear, please don't cry. Be glad that we've found him."

"I am, of course," she said, dabbing the tears with a soft white handkerchief. "It's just… with him so close… it's harder. Can you understand?"

He ignored her question because no right answer could ever exist. “Maybe it will help a little,” he said, “if I tell you that I believe things will happen fast, now. I’m worried about what you say is going on there in the north, and every day here I discover some alarming development. Still, with reasonable luck, Luccan could be home within the month.”

He hesitated before conceding a final point. He didn’t want to give her future ammunition, but he longed to see her comforted. Sighing, he gave in. “And, if things here get to the point that your way seems the lesser risk, I’ll give him what information I can and try to bring him home.”

“Keep him safe.” Lili’s steady eyes demanded his pledge.

“I’ll do my best.”

After saying farewell, he broke the link, shut down the M.E.R.L.I.N., and addressed the silent room, echoing words spoken three years ago by a once-powerful man of Earth.

“My best,” he repeated, “but, Behlishan help me, *I don’t know if that’s enough.*”

Part Two:
Mystery, Magic, and Twists of Memory

CHAPTER EIGHT: THE DEMON QUEEN'S MIDNIGHT CARNIVAL

HENCH HAD not dreamed the return of the Black Blade. He'd proven that an hour ago when Isa's summons woke him from exhausted sleep, still clutching the knife to his chest.

This will change things, he'd thought then, but so far all remained the same.

He still limped; Isa still raged. She had ordered him out into the wild dark that hung in the ravine at night, and he'd gone. Now he crouched at the entrance to a shallow cave, melting into the shadows of cracked rocks and craggy oaks. Bile rose in his throat when he thought of the role he and the Blade were to play in tonight's ritual. Still, he waited in obedient silence for the witch to give him his cue.

The witch's new disciples came, twenty-seven of them from different corners of the night. Moonset had passed, and Hench almost laughed at the way they startled one another, coming out of the darkness in their black robes and cowls. They were ridiculous. But not everyone. One man stood tall and deep-chested, with hair so black it shone blue even in the night. He called himself Mordred Brede.

Isa, or the Demon Queen as she styled herself to these Earthborn acolytes, waited for them at the end of the clearing nearest Hench in the open. Her blue robes shone in the night, and a loose hood concealed her face. With her scavenger's features hidden, she looked regal. When her followers had gathered, she spoke. They listened, rapt.

"Disciples of the Demon Queen," she began and opened her arms in a theatrical flourish, fanning her draped sleeves wide like wings. "Tonight you who are chosen will receive your first revelation, partake of your first communion, and do your first service of obeisance."

She clapped her hands once, and the empty center of the clearing burst into blue flame. Twenty-six gasps sounded, and twenty-six black robes backed quickly away, broadening the circle around that center. Only Mordred remained calm and held his ground. The flames shot higher, obeying Isa's gesture, and then settled into the guise of a viper. Hissing blue breath, the burning serpent coiled at the disciples' feet.

Carnival tricks, Hench thought. *Earthborns are easily impressed.*

At her summons Hench came forth from the dark, a crippled mystery in a black cowl, and set a three-legged steel cauldron over the blue fire, flames cold enough to burn. He stepped quickly away, and the cauldron filled with clear viscous liquid. Isa's witch-fire chilled the summer air to stinging cold, and on the ground a ring of frost formed around the flames and then spread outward in a wave. Every toadstool, weed, and bug in its path shriveled, so that for a time the night was filled with snaps and pops and infinitesimal screams. Soon, the entire clearing was floored in frozen earth, silent.

Thin-winged insects hummed into the bright circle expecting heat, but froze in the icy air and fell away into the cold, bubbling cauldron. Bats plummeted, their wings cracked to ice, mammal screams frozen in their tiny throats. Spiders spun in on tethers of silk drawn to the smell of a thousand deaths, and found their own. The liquid went red, then black, and that was the color of the smoke that plumed up and out to form a dome of impenetrable sky.

The rite that followed was sophistry, no more than theater. Isa was playwright, director, and star. She worked her audience until they were marionettes, puppets on cruel, barbed strings. Her glass-tipped scourge writhed in her hand, and when she struck him, Hench's agony became the disciples' fear. They partook of that fear like a sacrament. They baptized themselves in delicious dread of the dark, bitter power they saw and foolishly thought they understood.

Hateful people with empty lives. Who else would have come? They coveted the power Isa showed them, too blind to see the illusion, a mask hiding something that would consume them. They gave themselves over, willing slaves.

Theatrics aside, Isa truly did possess dreadful magic. When the time was right, when the disciples' lust for power had risen to frenzy, she gave the night air the slightest magical tweak. A gesture, a whisper, a tiny twist in a single synapse in each of twenty-six brains, and she owned them. All but Mordred.

Then the show was over. Hench's chest tightened in dread. The witch would test her new slaves. Their part was small. The rite they would perform would be meaningless, darkly comical, if it were not for Hench and the Black Blade. Yet they would inflict real harm.

Still working the crowd, Isa changed the face she wore. She clasped her hands behind her back and paced like a concerned teacher, a professor contemplating commencement and students set loose to prove the worth of their lessons.

"I wish you well, but I will not stay. You must complete this ritual on your own, united. It is a test of your value as my disciples. I will leave my apprentice, Mordred, to observe and deal with any… problems. Hench, my thrall, will be the blood-letter. His knife is more than it seems. Trust that you do not want to meet that blade, so when the moment comes for your blood to flow, do not hesitate with your own dirks.

"Fare well in your service tonight."

She turned and walked to the edge of the clearing. The blue flames blazed skyward, then died away completely, a magician's trick but well performed. Hench stared along with the others at the spot where, an instant before, she had stood. In her place lay a yellow dog, the boy's dog, Isa had told him. The tools he would use were laid out beside the mongrel's limp form—rough twine, Black Blade, crystal chalice for blood.

He did as the witch directed. He made precise, perfect cuts, drew the dog's blood, and said the words that would bend the knife's magic to this purpose. He used the Black Blade this way even as it protested in his hands, and then he used its opposite magic to stop the blood and close the wound. He preserved the dog's life, but as Isa had required, he took possession of her soul.

After he finished, he sat at the edge of the clearing while the Earthborns completed their empty, hideous ritual, Mordred moving in their midst. Hench's eyes followed their dance, but he didn't see. He didn't hear their chant. The smell of their burning blood meant nothing. Every shred of his awareness fixed on two sensations—the dog's pain and the agony of the Blade.

Something in him broke. In the hour before dawn when some animals wake to hunger and move to hunt, he stumbled away, dragging his lame leg. He went as an animal goes, feral and deadly, to quell his hunger and slake his terrible thirst.

BORN A sacrifice, laid at first breath upon the consecrated ice of the Blue Floe in Ethra's far north, Isa was no stranger to pain. Unique among centuries of children born to that fate, she had clung to life in that heartless cold until Queen Hilgaardre, Mahl's high priestess, had intervened, taking her as heir. But Hilgaardre's heart harbored secrets, and in the end she'd sent Isa south mounted on Ahrion, the queen's moon-white winged mount, in the care of an old groom.

Years later Isa had forsaken the old man's kindness and the queen's ill-guided mercy and returned to the Ice-Lord, seeking access to his endless power—a path fraught every step with pain. She knew what to expect now from her Master's wrath. She had failed him before.

When she had banished the boy, she had not succeeded in separating him from the Key of Behliseth. A critical error. It would have made it so much easier to teach him hate, to shape his ambitions, to darken and subvert the power he would unleash when he claimed the Key and used it. And her spell had gone further awry—she had lost him in the Vortices. It had taken her three years to find him, and the infernal wizard had reached him first.

She had been punished, and punished again, and again, and each time it diminished her, damaged her until she had little life or power of her own left. She was Mahl's tool, his shadow, his servant. Serving him had become her only life, her only path to power or to the revenge she so desperately needed.

Now she had failed him again, lost the pathetic slave and his Knife. Mahl would punish her, and endure it she must. Endure it she would. That was one thing Isa knew how to do.

His touch inflicted agony, the infinite anguish of discrete cells dragged from their beds into the purposeful void of the Ice-Lord's maw. Yet in surviving his bitter attention, she had come to know Mahl more thoroughly, perhaps, than anyone ever had. His power was all-consuming, his form vast, but alone he could not tilt the scales that balanced the powers of gods.

He would not destroy her; he needed her mind, her voice, and her human hands. Once his shapeless fury over the lost slave was spent, she would offer another. Mordred Brede, an uncommon Earthborn ripe with magic and rotten with greed. She, the only living Witch-Mortaine, would mold him with her own hand. He would be a worthy weapon.

Then it would be time to take the boy, to bend, break, or crush him. One way or another, the power locked inside the Suth Chiell must be theirs.

CHAPTER NINE: THE BOY'S GOT MAGIC

THE SUN was still climbing and the grass was still wet with dew when Lucky ran across the field toward his shack the next morning. He felt a little guilty for having run off from Thurlock's house without saying anything to anyone. Last night, when Han offered to come with him this morning to get Maizie, he'd agreed. Maybe he'd been lulled by food and a warm bed, but last night he'd felt safe, and having Han go with him had seemed like a good idea.

And he'd still felt safe when he first woke up. The sash window had been open and the air in the room smelled fresh, and the morning light seemed pleasant, coming through the yellowed window shade soft and caramel colored. The bed felt soft too, and Lucky felt drowsy, cocooned in a patchwork quilt. Even though he knew he needed to go take care of Maizie, he was so comfortable he almost turned over and went back to sleep.

Last night, he'd decided to stay just because he felt so sweetly at home, cared for—a feeling he hadn't really had since Hank died. Han had taken him up the narrow stairs, showed him the room, and made sure he knew where to find what he might need. They'd talked in an easy, natural way that felt familiar even though he wasn't used to it. Before he left Han said, "Sweet dreams, lad," and the ordinary words had fallen over him like a spell.

When he woke to the summer morning, the charm remained. The room and the bed and the light seemed so normal Lucky almost felt guilty.

But then his brain cells woke up.

Who am I fooling? I spent the night in the house of an old man from another world who makes magic fire.

As if the bed itself were burning, Lucky bounded out of it, put on his clothes (laundered by Han), slid into his shoes (fixed by Han), and pulled his Key (strung on a chain by Han) over his neck. He put a leg out the window and stepped into the thick branches of a very old, conveniently placed maple. Pulling the other leg out behind him, he whispered, "I wish I was invisible," and descended. He hit the ground running, vaulted the fence, and beat feet down the road.

On the way to his shack, he pondered Thurlock's flames. Also Han's Mark, Hank's stories, the weird lady at the Quick-Shoppe, and of all things, the cat who stole his key.

If someone had been saying out loud the things he was thinking, he would have wanted to cover his ears like a child and say "la la la la la," very loudly. He decided to think about something else and when his stomach growled, food came instantly to mind. But that didn't prove to be a safe topic because he thought about the two burgers and paper sack full of fries he'd eaten last night, more than he'd ever eaten at one meal. Absolutely wonderful—but he remembered expecting Thurlock to conjure them like his flames.

"Luccan," the old man had said, "we do things the hard way unless we have a very good reason." Then he'd left to go buy the burgers, laughing all the way out the door, and Lucky was left to cope with the idea that for a moment, magic had seemed not only possible but normal.

Han bounded up the steps and burst through the side door, making an uncharacteristic amount of noise. Three paces took him through the big farm-style kitchen and around the corner to the stairway, where he began to ascend the steps three at a time. He stopped at the door to the room where Lucky had slept and listened, hoping his instincts were wrong.

Without knocking, he opened the door. He took one look and shouted, "Thurlock!"

"I'm right here," Thurlock said, and indeed he stood behind Han, no more than a foot away, shaking his head in disbelief.

"How could he have done it, sir? Your wards… my talent… and I've been watching his window since before dawn. How did he get past it all?"

The wizard snorted, and then he said, "Behl's sweet whiskers, man. It's obvious, isn't it?"

Han chewed his lip, but he didn't speak, and Thurlock supplied the answer himself.

"Magic, Han Shieth. The boy's got magic—rivers of it. Deep enough to drown him in a sea of trouble, and he hasn't even begun to learn to swim."

THROUGH FIVE or perhaps ten of the longest minutes in his life, Lucky waited for Maizie. He called over and over, whistled, went to the doorstep and rattled the kibble in her bowl. No raspy bark. No tail beating the brush, no bright eyes and sloppy tongue. No dog. He stepped onto the path that snaked through mesquite, around rocks, and under pines before it descended into the gorge, thinking that if Maizie was scared, she'd head for the ravine to find a place to hide.

While he jogged along the zigzag trail, dodging thorns, scaring up small birds, and leaping a sunning king snake, he tried to recall what Hank had taught him about tracking. At the time, he'd approached the lessons as a game, but now he hoped he remembered enough to use the skills. He slowed to scan the ground, and a few steps into the pines, he found a clear paw print in damp earth. He continued, sweeping his eyes side to side, checking the ground before putting a foot down every time. At intervals, he stopped and called out.

Any minute, he insisted to himself, *she'll come running.*

As the trail descended into the gorge the going got trickier, rough and steep. He concentrated on finding places for his hands and feet where the ground wouldn't crumble out from under him. Then, he heard a growl—vicious and close. His head snapped up. He saw, ten feet away and level with his gaze, two blood-rimmed brown eyes. Familiar brown eyes.

He couldn't believe at first that Maizie could ever look so dangerous, or would ever growl at him at all. He checked the dog's markings. There was the white half inch at the tip of her tail, the white "necklace" of fur half hidden in the gold, the pink freckle on her black nose. But that snarl, the bared teeth, and those bloodthirsty eyes, none of that belonged to the dog he loved.

She sprang at him suddenly, and he jumped without thinking or planning or even looking where he was going. When he landed, the shale cracked, and he tumbled down the rocky slope. He came to a hard stop, bashing his left shoulder against a black finger of basalt sticking up like a guardrail at the edge of a narrow shelf of rock. His left arm throbbed, scratched skin burned everywhere, and when he sat up, the world started to spin.

When it rolled to a stop, he was shocked to find that his legs dangled off the edge of the rock ledge, swinging in open air and pointing toward a long fall to the creek bed below. He scooted carefully away from the edge and put his back against the steep slope.

Maizie snarled again, the sound no less threatening, but farther away and coming from a different direction. Then the snarl broke, and she cried like a dog in pain. Although he couldn't understand how it had happened, he knew she had become dangerous; he remembered the way she'd lunged at him. But that cry was full of agony, and he loved her, and he couldn't bear to stand by and do nothing if she was in pain.

She needs me, he thought, and it sobered him. He reined his heart to a slow gallop, ordered his thoughts to line up single file so he could sort them out. With panic at bay, he focused on figuring out how to help Maizie, his best friend.

He scanned the slope above him in the direction of Maizie's cries. He searched the shadows behind boulders and scrub brush until he spotted her hidden under an overhanging ledge, further obscured by a manzanita shrub. A jerking movement had drawn his eye, a spasm of pain, he thought, but in the same moment she bared her teeth and snapped at the air in his direction, her eyes burning like twin fires.

Despite his good intentions, he had to resist a massive urge to run. He blew out a stiff breath and shoved his hair back off his face. After he bit back his fear and muddled through indecision, he found he had to swallow pride. He wrestled with it until Maizie howled as if someone had raked coals over her back, then he said three words that were at least as familiar on his tongue as ancient Greek.

"I need help."

He climbed out of the ravine and ran through the green shade under the pines. He ignored the blast of heat that assaulted him in the open field and raced for the phone booth outside the Quick-Shoppe—surely one of the very last in existence. His breath caught up with him while he dug in his pocket for quarters and the phone number Han had given him the night before, all the while cursing for never saving up enough money to get a cell phone.

Turning his back to the glare off the parked cars outside the booth, he laid the scrap of paper on the chrome shelf, took the bulky receiver off the hook, and punched in the number. *Han can help*, he was thinking. *Han will come. Han, Han, Han*.... It rolled through his brain like a chant.

Han picked up before Lucky heard a ring. "Luccan?"

"Han!"

"I'm coming, lad," Han said, not asking what Lucky wanted, where he was, or what was wrong. "Go back down into the ravine, but stay away from the dog." Han's voice came over the line clear and steady as rain on a lake, calming Lucky despite his astonishment. "Don't go to your shack; we don't know who else might be around. When I get there, we'll get Maizie. Hide. I'll find you."

Before he hung up, Han said, "I'll be there before you know it," and no sooner had Lucky settled down in the hollow between a boulder and a fallen pine than he saw the man's spit-shined boots approach.

"It's safe, lad," Han said. "Come on out."

Lucky surprised himself, and surely Han, by burying his face in Han's shoulder and clinging like duct tape. The quiet man hugged him back, patted his shoulder, and Lucky didn't cry, thank goodness, but the words "thank you" had trouble getting out.

"Certainly, Luccan. Let's go now." That was all Han said, but nothing could have been more reassuring.

The trek back to the place where Maizie had tried to hide was tough for Lucky, what with the burn of cuts and bruises and a heart beating fast from dread. Once they'd found her, Han climbed up the slope and squatted a few feet away, locking his eyes on hers. He kept still and quiet, but as she gazed back at him, the fire in her eyes cooled. Her growl died away, her hackles lay flat, and finally she sighed into sleep.

Lucky asked, "Will she be okay?"

Han hopped down to the ledge where Lucky waited before he answered. "I can't say for sure. I can't tell what's wrong."

Lucky had so many worries and questions he didn't know where to begin, and it must have shown.

Han rested his hand briefly on Lucky's arm. "Take it easy, lad," he comforted. "As I said, I don't know what's wrong, but I don't think it's rabies, or any disease. She's got a little cut on her leg, but it's healed, mostly, and not hurting her. No other injuries. So the—"

Panic waved giant red flags inches from Lucky's eyeballs, and he stopped listening. Han hadn't touched Maizie. He'd never gotten within three feet of her. Lucky's voice rose an octave or so in pitch as he said, "How do you know all that?"

The few seconds that passed while Han chewed his lip seemed like a month. Finally, he looked at Lucky sideways and said, "I have a way with animals?"

Lucky's eyebrows went up, but he said nothing.

Another silent month crept by, then Han shrugged. "All right, I can read their minds."

Lucky choked.

Han patted his back until the cough died to a raspy breath and said, "We'll talk about it later. Right now, let's get Maizie home."

CHAPTER TEN: MIND READING AND THE POWER OF WISHFUL THINKING

GOING BACK, Lucky and Han kept to the shelter of the pines. Once past Heart Lake at the west end of the ravine, they turned south to make an easy, gradual climb to the place where the wizard's unlikely house hung in a bony hollow of the dry-grass hills, some distance from the big, well-kept houses farther down the road. They only stopped twice to rest, and by the time they reached the leaning fence, Lucky's step had begun to falter. Sweat soaked the back of Han's shirt, but despite his ungainly four-legged burden, he remained strong.

To Lucky's surprise, they didn't go around to Thurlock's front steps, where Lemon Martinez eyed them from the porch rail. "Thurlock isn't home," Han said and carried Maizie around to a little house in the back corner of the yard, a building Lucky hadn't even noticed yesterday. It sported a neat coat of white paint, a clean-swept porch, and windows that winked with half-drawn shades.

Inside Han's "quarters," as he called them, Lucky found a sparse, cool, clean space, free of frills. Solid, just like the man who occupied them. Although he suspected he should feel suspicious—these people weren't normal—a blanket of security dropped over Lucky as soon as the door thunked shut behind him. He followed Han through the small front room, with its one recliner, to the bedroom, where the spread draped so neatly that every fringe hung just so. They ducked through a low door in the back wall and entered a shed with cloudy windows and a floor of hard-packed dirt.

The enclosure smelled of new-sawn wood and harbored a pen fashioned from two-by-fours and chicken wire. There, on a bed of clean straw, Han at last laid Maizie down. He knelt to examine her and sent Lucky to get blankets from the bedroom closet. She barely woke up while Han got her settled and gave her a dose of liquid from a brown bottle.

Han turned to Lucky and pledged to do his best to get her well. “That’s not an empty promise,” he said. “I really am good with animals.” His smile seemed kind but possibly a little sheepish, and though Lucky’s thanks were sincere, the words rekindled the question he’d left smoldering in the back of his mind while they took care of Maizie.

Before he could speak, though, Han said, “Lunch,” and led the way to his tiny kitchen. He gestured for Lucky to sit at one of the two chairs at the pine-board table and went to scrub his hands. Soaping up, he said, “Now’s a good time to ask your questions, lad.”

Lucky opened his mouth but then closed it to think. He watched Han take a loaf of white bread out of a rolltop breadbox and packets of meat and cheese out of his tiny, must-be-an-antique refrigerator, and then toss the loot onto the spotless cream tile of the countertop. He’d turned his back toward Lucky and seemed about as transparent as a brick wall.

He can read the animals’ minds, he said…. Lucky raised his hands to smooth back his sweat-damp hair. *So what about people? Can he—?*

“Yes, sometimes,” Han said. Suddenly. Without being asked. Startling Lucky and causing him to almost swallow his tongue.

After a coughing spell, he asked, “H-h-how did you know what I was thinking?”

“I don’t know *how* I do it, precisely. I was born with the talent, which is normal enough in Ethra, though not exactly common even there. When I was old enough to understand my gift, I worked at developing it.” He turned to face Lucky, a teasing smile in his eyes. “Think of it like this. Many people here in Earth can ride a bike, but only a few have the skills to do stunts.”

“What about you? How good are you?”

“If it were bike riding, I’d win all the competitions.”

Han tried to explain mind reading and Lucky tried to listen, but he didn’t exactly have an open mind on the subject.

“It’s just not right,” he said. “You’re invading everybody’s privacy.”

“That’s not how it works. I can’t just know everything you’re thinking.” Judging by the set of his shoulders and the way he smacked mayo onto the bread, he found the idea insulting.

“Listen,” he said. “Just like any inborn magic, it works two ways. The first way is self-protection, so if someone is close by, I hear what they think about me, which is not always pleasant. The second and stronger way my ability works is to protect others. If someone I have a connection with, like you, calls to me in their thoughts, I'll pick that up even from a distance, unless some other strong magic is in the way."

"The phone call?"

"Yes."

"Was there ever a phone call at all?"

"No."

Han turned his back again and continued to build their sliced ham sandwiches with the precision of an engineer. The activity must have worked out some mental kinks. By the time he turned back around, put their plates on the table, and took a seat across from Lucky, the set of his shoulders had softened and the kindness was back in his eyes.

He poured Lucky milk (white), drank his coffee (cold), and worried about why he couldn't figure out Maizie's ailments (aloud). He polished off two sandwiches in four bites—a feat Lucky admired but couldn't quite duplicate—and then sat back, scratched his T-shirted chest, and yawned.

Ridiculously normal for a mind reader.

Minutes later, Han disappeared into the bedroom, leaving Lucky at loose ends in the tiny house. Closing the door between them, Han said, "Lad, don't touch anything you don't fully understand."

So Lucky didn't touch the unstrung bow leaning in the corner by the redbrick hearth; runes were carved into it. And he didn't touch the arrows, some of which were fletched with feathers that had markings like the flame decals on street rods and stood in a quiver made of some kind of skin with big, shiny scales. A shield that hung on the wall had been made of similar skin—one huge scale, it looked like, with a mean-looking spike in the center that appeared to have grown there. Definitely not understanding that, Lucky left it alone. He didn't even think about touching the pale metal sword that also hung on the wall, or the scabbard—fashioned either from gold that looked like wood, or from wood that looked like gold.

To keep his hands from trouble, he did the dishes, but that didn't occupy much of his mind, so while he worked, he also thought. Of course, what he thought about doggedly, even after he ordered himself to stop, was the mind reader, Han. And the wizard Thurlock. And what had happened to Maizie, and.... *And why can't my life ever be normal?*

As he put the last of the silverware in the drainer, pulled the plug, and swished the cloth around the sink, Han came up behind him on silent footsteps and said, "Ah," apparently pleased.

That startled Lucky nearly out of his pants, but either Han didn't notice that Lucky was having respiratory failure, or he had faith that Lucky would recover on his own, because he went on talking as if Lucky wasn't clutching his chest and choking. "You did the dishes. Thoughtful. I can't think of the last time someone did a chore for me."

He grabbed his shirt off the back of the chair. "Thurlock is home," he said, pointing toward the door with a toss of his head. "Let's go talk to him about Maizie."

But before they covered half the distance across the yard, Thurlock came striding up, robes swirling in a tailwind, definitely scowling. Just in case that expression was directed at him, Lucky stood behind Han, where he felt a bit safer. But he needn't have worried; the old man ignored him altogether.

"We'd better talk, Han," Thurlock said. "I've got some important intelligence from home. Seems those killings up north were the tip of the iceberg, literally. Rumors are about drakes—blues, mind you—prowling into Sunlands territory on the heels of a creeping boreal freeze that's turned the whole Northern Marsh to frozen mud."

"What will…?" Han started to ask, but Lucky would never know what the question would have been, as Thurlock just kept talking.

"We've sent some relief supplies north, and we're bringing back some of the able-bodied to work the harvest so they can take wages and supplies home. Some of the basket weavers were thrilled at the prospect of a shipment of Rainbow Grass from the south coast. But—"

Thurlock stopped and looked into the west, where an inflated orange sun fell toward the needle-sharp peaks of the Ring. He pulled almost frantically at his beard and then suddenly swung his lion-mane head around to look directly at Han, eyes burning as if the sun had kindled them.

"It's the drakes, you see. The blues. The clans up north still remember the Northern Peril. For all that it happened two thousand years ago and most of Ethra thinks of it only as fireside legend, the Sooth Keepers still know it as history. The Clan leaders have fallen back on their old ways, now, to keep panic down."

"Sacrifice?"

The things Thurlock said seemed unreal to Lucky, like a fantasy movie. But Han's one-word question and the look on his face sent fear grating down Lucky's spine. *Sacrifice! What kind of world do they live in?*

Thurlock must have noticed his reaction. The wizard stopped short and leaned around Han to make eye contact with Lucky.

He tossed his hands up in a gesture of apology. "I'm forgetting that we have important things to think about right here," he said. "I'm sorry, Luccan. Did you find your dog? Is she all right?"

"Um, no sir…." Lucky trailed off, not sure where to go from there.

Han gave Lucky's shoulder a squeeze. "I'm worried, sir. The boy's dog is not all right. We were—"

A blue flash and a clap of thunder cut through Han's words, demanding attention.

"That's odd." Thurlock mused in scholarly fashion while heavy drops began to spatter off his spectacle lenses. He was looking up at a very large, very dark, mass that had gathered in the sky and now shadowed the hills to the north and west. "I don't remember seeing that cloud—"

Han ran back out from the cottage's covered stoop, where he and Lucky had already taken shelter, took hold of Thurlock's elbow, and tugged at him. "Perhaps, sir, you should wonder about it inside, out of the rain."

From under the low-peaked porch roof, Lucky watched the thunderhead roll in. Like a giant locomotive, it pulled a thick bank of clouds behind it, crushing the evening sun under its sparking wheels. No, it didn't seem normal. Not at all. He sucked in a breath of alarm and started to turn toward the door to Han's little house. But in that same breath, the rain stopped and the air went cold—so cold that Lucky's thoughts froze.

Forgetting his intention to run inside, he hunkered down, crossed his arms over the goose bumps prickling his chest, and started shivering hard. Lightning flashed again, this time kicking up a gust of wind that struck at Lucky hard enough to steal his breath.

A crackling sound assaulted his ears, and the metal Key sparked, flashed, and burned like a hot iron against the frigid skin of his chest. He ripped the chain over his head, dropped the Key to the worn boards of the stoop, and kicked it away, gagging on the stink of sulfur and what he guessed might be his own burnt flesh.

A horrible thought reared up in his mind, as clear and undeniable as the voice of a god. *It's here for me. Whatever it is, it's come for me!*

Han came back out the door bearing the sword and shield that had been hanging on the wall. "Luccan," he started, but Thurlock slammed out the door behind him and once again interrupted.

"Never mind, Han, go," he said. "I've got the boy." He stepped in front of Lucky, grasped him by the shoulders, pushed him back a single step, and then took a stand between Lucky and the storm. Holding on to Lucky's arm, he stooped for the discarded Key, all the while muttering strange words under his breath. When he stood up again, he said, "Here," his voice quiet but stronger, somehow, than the dry thunder or the wind. Lucky felt as if he'd just woken from a nightmare, but when the wizard dropped the Key over his head and put his hand over it, over Lucky's heart, Lucky instantly calmed, at least enough to hear.

"Come with me," the old wizard said.

Lucky anchored his eyes on the calm gray center of Thurlock's gaze. He nodded and took a step at the wizard's side. At that moment, thunder cracked so loud that the ground quaked and shivered. Lucky made a small sound and put his head down, covering it with his arms. But still, he heard Thurlock speak softly.

"It won't touch you, Luccan. Not while I'm here. Come now."

Lucky followed the wizard, clutching the sleeve of the man's gray robes like a lifeline.

Inside Thurlock's house, he relaxed the moment the oak door whisked quietly shut behind him. He grabbed hold of his Key; the familiar feel of it still offered comfort, and he felt certain that everything would be all right. As if from a distance, he watched Han and Thurlock go about the house doing purposeful things that didn't really seem to make sense.

Han strode to the door and swung it open, closing it again behind a frazzled, wet Lemon Martinez, who jumped to the top of the armchair and hung on like a bull rider as another wave of thunder rocked the room. Next Han made a circuit of the ground floor, securing windows and doors. Lucky still stood a few paces clear of the door, and Han didn't bother with instructions. Taking him by the arm, he pulled him to the foot of the stairs, took a deliberate place in front of him midway between the front door and the stairway, and turned to face the door.

He placed the sword's point on the floor in front of him and wrapped both hands on the hilt. He broadened his stance, and flexed his knees, and fixed his attention on the doorway. He'd strapped his shield to his left forearm, and the spike at its center protruded in front of him, as if set to impale an oncoming foe.

Light shimmered on the shield's iridescent disk, and sparks crackled over its surface like miniature lightning. The display of usually hidden force drew Lucky's attention, and he had a nagging feeling he was forgetting something.

But it wasn't until thunder crashed again outside that he remembered to feel afraid.

Thurlock had been standing in the dining room, looking off into the distance and speaking quietly to himself as if rehearsing a monologue. Now he moved to plant himself—quite precisely as if there were a stage mark—a few feet to Han's right. He began to sway and gesture like a Jedi master or someone practicing magical tai chi.

Lucky's eyes felt overworked, taking it all in. His heart thumped loud in his ears and he'd started to sweat, despite the way-too-cold-for-July air. It had grown too dark for the time of day too. Lucky realized, though he couldn't have explained why it made sense, that just as Thurlock and Han prepared their defenses, the storm prepared its assault.

The noise outside rumbled and rolled and cracked constantly, and beyond the windows thick mist tumbled in the wind, flashing with inner lightning. The notion entered Lucky's brain that they were inside the storm, that it had descended on the house and swallowed it whole. Or maybe the house had flown up into the black cloud's heart like Dorothy Gale on her way to Oz. Maybe if he went to the door and stepped out, he would fall a mile before slamming into the ground.

He looked again at Thurlock and found that the old man had changed. He'd grown so *very* tall, wide-shouldered and truly menacing. All of this—Han's weapons, the mounting storm, the mystery of who or what Thurlock really was—all of it added to Lucky's fright, speeding his heartbeat a notch higher.

Thurlock continued his strangely graceful dance, pointing his furled yellow umbrella here and there with his right hand, and all the while murmuring strange words, sending "s" and "th" sounds winging to every corner. A light began to build, a glow sheathing the umbrella and brightening until it shone like a miniature sun with the wizard's right hand at its center.

Lucky drew in his breath at the sight, and in precisely that instant thunder slammed like solid stone against all the walls of the house at once.

The chandelier's prisms rang against each other and the windows shook in their frames like prisoners rattling bars. Even the stones in the hearth shuffled loose in the dust of disintegrating mortar.

Lemon Martinez yowled, and the sound shredded what was left of Lucky's calm. By the time the thunderclap began to die away, his whole body thrummed with fear like a taut cable in a wind. Han, who yet stood rock-still, said, "Mr. Martinez," in a firm voice, and the cat settled onto his haunches, looking annoyed but managed.

"Luccan," Han said, "be calm, lad. The power behind this storm feeds on fear." He turned with confident grace to meet Lucky's eye and stood like a bulwark, the picture of unyielding strength. Encouraged, Lucky nodded and drew himself up to stand a little straighter, and when Han's mouth quirked into a tiny smile, he very nearly smiled back.

Maizie howled loud and high enough to be heard from Han's house, even through the storm, and despite his resolve not give in to fear, all the hairs on Lucky's arms stood up at once. Her howls grew wilder and soon they were the frenzied shrieks of a dog gone completely mad. Lucky's knees felt like they were melting. He looked at Han and the warrior spoke, but Lucky couldn't hear the words over the blood pulsing in his ears.

Thunder exploded again, this time somehow calling the light, slamming it down into Lucky, striking in the center of his forehead and exploding through his brain. For a time Lucky wasn't sure if his eyes were open or closed—all he could see was a sharp black afterimage on a blinding blue ground, like the negative image of photographed lightning. When that cleared, it was as though he saw everything with a brand new kind of eye.

Nothing remained unchanged. The span of time over which that vision held, perhaps a dozen breaths, could have been measured in seconds—Lucky knew that even while it was happening. But every heartbeat inside that moment stretched into a small eternity, every pulse lasted forever enough for him to see an unbelievable world, both wonderful and horrifying.

He saw faces roiling in the storm. Rotting, red-eyed things writhed in anguish, remains of things that were once alive. Caustic, nuclear eyes glowed in the faces of other creatures, things that had surely never been anything but the monstrous, fanged beings Lucky saw around him. Blue light snaked in under the door, and inside it Lucky saw the shape of a hooded, demon-eyed serpent.

It reared up to strike at the wizard, but Thurlock raised a shielding palm. “Avert,” he said, and a blaze of gold enveloped him, painfully bright. Thurlock stood at the core of that golden blaze, a pillar of pure light, more than a man. If he’d had wings, Lucky would have called him an angel.

The snaking blue light assaulted the golden armor around the wizard, testing it, and Thurlock’s umbrella swooshed out and clicked open. He held it at the end of his outstretched arm and spun on his heel, a full turn. Lucky saw the yellow fabric disk like a noon sun against deep night, but he also saw through the tool’s disguise and knew it wasn’t an umbrella at all—never had been.

It was a great staff. Six feet long or more, it had been crafted from golden wood and capped and shod with the same pale, alien metal as Han’s sword. Carved runes along its length shone golden, seeming to come forth at Thurlock’s Command, and streams of silver-white power ran through the wood like blood through veins. At that moment, Lucky would have bet both feet that the wood breathed and throbbed to the ancient beat of the wizard’s heart.

The blue light-serpent drew back, hissing as if angry or perhaps afraid of the wizard. It coiled near the door… and then shattered. Billions of shards and splinters flew outward like fractured glass. Thurlock had become a vision of pulsing, golden force, and Lucky feared him as much as he feared the unfathomable power of the storm that assaulted him. The two forces fought, and the house filled with sound and light and movement, and soon Lucky lost even the sense of what was up and what was down. A gust of wind came from nowhere, seemingly born inside the room, and swept him back a step.

Then Han spoke, his voice soothing and still soft, but strong and heartening. Lucky locked his eyes on the warrior.

Even with Lucky’s altered vision, Han looked the same. He was a man, no more, except that he burned with a steady light like a lone candle in a fortress holding off the dark. He spun his sword before him, and the pale blade echoed the wizard’s bright staff. The shards of deathly blue light, still hissing like the demon serpent they had been, flew into the spinning blade and shrieked like things with living pain. They recoiled and crashed back against the walls and windows and then into the path of the wizard’s staff, where they blew apart and vanished.

Lucky felt it all wash over him like so much deadly, overwhelming force. He could barely breathe. He wanted to run—would have, if he'd been able.

All the while, though sweat poured down his temples, Han stayed strong as oak, solid and calm. "Luccan," he said again, unhurried despite his labors. "Don't give in. You have strength you don't know about. Try to find it. *Resist.*" It seemed like good advice to Lucky, but he couldn't follow it. He was stuck in some kind of hellish limbo. He didn't know whether to trust his eyes, or whether he *wanted* to believe them.

If this isn't real, I'm crazy. If it is real, the world is a hundred zillion times too scary.

He stood in the middle of a living nightmare. He thought it would never stop.

Then, suddenly, it did.

Maizie let go a howl that shrieked above all the other noises, neither shrill nor deep but piercing everything. It stopped with the sound of glass shattering in the night in the direction of Han's cottage. Next, silence fell, and dark—everywhere, as thick and black as dirt from a grave.

The only things Lucky could see through that blackness were a flickering of wizard flame in the hearth, no bigger than a struck match, and an almost invisible white-gold sheath over the wizard's right hand. The silence weighed down every effort at thought; the only sound Lucky heard was the faint whistle of his own wary breath. Biting cold raked against his skin and wrapped around him like dead hands, locking down his muscles so tight he couldn't even shiver.

He jumped at the sudden crash of something heavy hitting the front door hard enough to send a crack snapping through the oak. Immediately that was followed by a whining, snarling growl from the porch. Light returned, and at the same time Lucky said, "Maizie!" Not fully believing he'd found the power to move, he ran for the door.

Thurlock and Han were stunned for about a millionth of a second, and then in unison they yelled, "Luccan, no!"

But Lucky wasn't listening. Maizie was outside the door, and she was hurt, again or still, and he was going to help her. Thurlock had raised his staff, and Han had already started toward Lucky, but it wasn't without cause that folks who knew Lucky from the streets of Valley City sometimes referred to him as "the blur."

He was fast. He was already there. He threw the door to the wizard's house wide open, and immediately saw his mistake.

Maizie snarled and bared her teeth. Her eyes blazed. She bunched her muscles, ready to leap for his throat. Ten feet behind her stood a familiar tall, gaunt woman in blue robes, eyes blazing with that same cold color, and she laughed. "Yes," she said. "Yes, dear boy, come out to play."

With his altered sight, he could see she was but a shadow of life, human in form but wasted and eternally hungry. Where her heart should have been darkness swirled, as if drilling away her soul. That blackness was the presence at the heart of the storm, the thing that wanted him, and he felt its malice like a bellyful of ice.

An image of stars leapt to Lucky's mind, galaxies burning hot at their core, spinning off streams of heat and clusters of light. If that black, spinning wind that stood in place of the woman's soul resembled anything, that was it, but it was all backward. It spiraled inward, sucking light and heat into its blackness, and Lucky understood that if it touched him, he would fall into it and never stop.

And it was cold. And it was less alive than death. But it was living, anyway, and coming closer.

Maizie sprang at Lucky, and so did Han. Han won, plowing into boy and dog at the same time. The impact sent Maizie flying back out the door and Lucky sliding sideways, not stopping until he slammed into a leg of the dining room table, whereupon he heard a snap that he hoped was not a rib. Thurlock shouted, "Head!" and Han ducked his, just in time to avoid being hit by the wizard's giant fireball as it rocketed out the door. The flaming sphere of magic zinged straight into the witch's face and knocked her back at least thirty feet, and the wizard spelled the door shut.

But not before a man came in.

The stranger might have believed himself a wizard too. Or something. He muttered ugly-sounding words and flicked his hands about. If he was a wizard, he seemed rather dark, but that could have been because of the black robe and the curly blue-black hair sticking out at the edges of the cowl.

Han and Thurlock both looked at him, then at each other. Han raised his eyebrows inquiringly toward the wizard, who shrugged in response. Han grabbed the man, easily pinning his arms behind his back.

"Throw him out, Han. It's time for some good rain."

"Sir," Han said, with obvious concern, "are you up to that?"

"Piece of cake. Besides, listen to them out there." He put a hand behind his ear, and Han tilted his head to listen too, but the man he held cackled noisily, interfering.

Han shook him, gave him a barbed look, and said, "Shut up, man—"

"Mordred Brede."

"Whatever. I'm trying to hear." Apparently Han did something that caused discomfort, because the man grunted and did shut up, and then Lucky heard too. Outside, almost but not quite lost in the wind, a thousand voices yelped and cried and hissed and moaned, chains rattled, ropes creaked, fog horns blew, ships' bells rang, and he could have sworn something kept saying, "Boo."

"You see what I mean," Thurlock said. "There's so many of the blasted things. It would take us all night to get rid of them any other way."

Han nodded, then lowered his shoulder and, with a grunt, heaved the black-robed man off the ground. Thurlock waved the door open and Han dumped his living load outside before the wizard waved it shut again. Another thunk rattled the oak, and a muffled "Ouch" came from the porch, followed by cussing in plain English.

Thurlock raised his eyes and his arms and his staff and said, "Behlishan? Thurlock here. If you would please?" Rain poured immediately, pattering against roof and shingle, and all the other sounds ceased. The shadows fled from the window, wizard flames surged in the hearth, and Han reached out a hand to help Lucky stand.

Over the wizard's head, stretched like a rainbow from palm to palm, arced a golden light so beautiful Lucky could neither bear to look at it nor to turn away. It dispersed on the wizard's breath and settled down into the corners and crannies of the old house, driving out the last of the shadows, a comfort to follow the storm. Lucky leaned into Han, seeking strength the way a child will after a bad dream.

But the wizard stood alone, sinking at the knees as if about to fall. His voice was low and rough and gravelly. "I need to reset the wards," he said, wobbling. "I could use some support."

In shock, Lucky came near the wizard and saw him unimaginably old, frail, and thin, with parchment skin and blood pumping blue through tortuous veins at his temples. Lucky feared for himself and for Thurlock. But more than that, he wanted to help. With every sense he searched, wanting to find some small thing to give back to this man who had—in protecting him—so obviously given too much.

He started to say, "There's nothing I can do," but pain flared in his skull, and he realized those words would have been a lie.

He took a long, slow breath, cornering some wild, neglected thing inside himself, and knowing suddenly that it had always been there, waiting to be tamed. At first he didn't recognize his own voice, so deep, so near that of a man. "I wish," he began, but he didn't know how to finish. This wish would make a difference. What should it be?

Finally, he said, "Safe."

Thurlock lifted his crinkled face and smiled, surprised. "Well," he said, "it's done, then. Isn't it?"

Lucky barely heard. As he'd spoken his wish, a fist of heat had formed at his solar plexus, then unfurled and pulsed out with his words, leaving him hollow, sick, and dizzy.

"Han," he croaked, and the warrior's stalwart hands caught him. Swirling stars, then silent dark, then nothing.

CHAPTER ELEVEN:
NO REST FOR THE WIZARDLY

TWO HOURS after the storm, Thurlock sat at the table under the blazing chandelier, wearing an old gray robe, with a well-used purple blanket draped over his shoulders. His hair sprang out in a chaos of sweat-stiffened curls. Han, stepping into the room from the stairwell, felt relieved to see the old man no longer trembled.

Thurlock pushed away the remains of his chicken soup and toast and asked after Luccan. It started a series of little conversations stuck together like beads on a string. While Han cleared the table, they discussed plans to go to Luccan's shack to retrieve his belongings.

"And while we're on the subject, Han, what exactly is he using for pajamas?"

"Yours, sir, of course. He was reluctant, but I assured him that wizard's pajamas won't cause permanent damage, and that you're happy to share."

Thurlock snorted. "It's not as though you have any pajamas to loan."

"I knew you'd understand, sir."

"Fine," Thurlock backed down. "Get the boy's clothes while you're there at his shack, and the Amber Knife."

As Han started washing up, Thurlock's tone turned grave. "I can't go with you and the boy tomorrow. I'll be going home. Again."

"Sir, with all this back and forth you're going to wear out the Portal," Han said, which was absurd. Portals could be collapsed or lost. They could drift or invert, back up or kink, even freeze or overheat. Nobody had ever worn one out.

"Lili wants me to assure the Clan Leaders we'll clear up the problem with those cursed blue ice-drakes."

"So they'll stop the sacrifices."

A silver curl had fallen across Thurlock's face. He blew it away. "We like to believe we've changed since the Peril, but most Ethrans are just as superstitious now. She fears that if panic brings back Blood Ways in the north, others will follow suit. If she's bending her neck to ask for my help…."

"It's serious."

"Precisely."

"And you can scold L'Aria, while you're there. Put the fear of the wizard in her."

"The girl's been sassing the Lady Grace, if you can believe that."

Han smiled as he lit the burner under an old copper kettle. "You'll have tea in a bit."

"Extra sugar."

"Extra sugar, what, sir?"

"Please. Extra sugar, please. After the Clans I'll go to Nedhra City, do a bit of research in the University Archives. *Willock's World Windings*, in particular."

Han's hand halted a half inch from a box of Lemon Sunrise tea. Willock was a name so infamous in the Sunlands, it had become synonymous with foul temper. *She's really got her Willock on today*, a student might say of a sharp-tongued schoolteacher. Or a parent would warn: *Don't you get all Willock with me, young man!*

Han asked, "Aren't those scrolls cursed?"

Thurlock clucked his tongue. "Nonsense. People are afraid to read them for fear of being thought grouchy—guilt by association. Even if information could be cursed, Willock couldn't have done it. As a wizard, he was a charlatan. Had about as much magic as you've got in your big toe."

Han tried and failed to think of an intelligent response to that.

Thurlock continued, "Fool that he was, though, he was observant, downright brilliant on astral influences and time flux…." He drifted off, gazing beyond the dark M.E.R.L.I.N. "What else did you and the boy talk about?"

"I explained that, though unpleasant, recoil is expected after powering up and releasing a spell."

"Did he seem to understand?"

Han stepped into the dining room to look Thurlock in the eye. "He looked at me as though I'd grown three heads." The wizard laughed heartily. "But," Han added, "it was you that scared him the most."

"Because of my awesome power, or because he saw me looking my age?" Thurlock wiggled his eyebrows, and his toothy grin was comical.

Han smiled at the clowning but didn't laugh. "You scared me too, sir. You seemed… drained."

Thurlock sighed and gathered his soft purple blanket closer. He rose from the table, joints popping. "It's because we're here, in this world. Behl is distant. Simple things like wizard fire and parlor tricks remain easy, but calling so much light against such a foe, drawing down the rain, that kind of magic never comes cheap. Here in Earth, I had to spend enormous sums of energy to do it. But I'm all right," he said and collapsed into an armchair, groaning. "Spry as a kitten." Raising his voice over the kettle's whistle, he said, "About Luccan, he'll master it in good time."

Lemon-scented steam bathed Han's face as he poured hot water over the teabag. "Lessons, sir? I should think it will be better once he's taught to focus his power through his tools."

"You're right. He'd learn best by starting at the beginning just like anyone else. Considering everything, though, there won't be any lessons just now. His tools are tied up with his identity; it would be dangerous to use the one without the other." He scratched roughly at his beard as if to roust a pest. "And because he is Suth Chiell, if he does put the two together…. Well, you saw what happened with the Key."

Han slapped his forehead. "I can't believe I'd forgotten that, sir. I didn't even salve the burn."

"No need for salve; it may leave a mark, but the injury will already have healed." Thurlock leaned sideways, eyeing Han in the kitchen. "He needed protection in that storm, and he got it. The Key of Behliseth burned him, but I'd wager my kneecaps it saved him from worse."

Han brought Thurlock his sweet tea and joined him by the fire.

Thurlock sipped, smiled his thanks, and then grew somber. "Am I right in assuming that you used all your skills to examine Maizie this afternoon?"

"Of course."

"Then you know what was done to her."

"I don't, sir. I've told you that," Han said, and though he wondered what the wizard was getting at, he jumped at the opportunity to talk about his frustration. "It was as if her thoughts had been coated with something slippery. And I don't know why my talent failed. It's never happened before."

"Yes it has."

"No. I mean—"

"I know what you mean, and yes it has. Your talent failed in exactly this same way before."

Han's face wrinkled with puzzlement. "When?"

"Two hundred odd years ago? You were seventeen. You'd always dug into your brother's mind as easily as your own. Suddenly, every time you tried, he sent you a clear 'no,' but you convinced yourself you didn't hear it."

"I remember," Han said, keeping his tone calm despite a blaze of anger. The old man knew very well that if there was one subject that was always a sore one for Han, his older brother was it. He resented the old man bringing it up. "This isn't the same," he said, picking at a loose thread in the chair's upholstery, sullen like the seventeen-year-old he'd been.

Thurlock nagged, "Don't pick at that, Han, you'll make it worse." Han chuckled, and a smile flickered over the wizard's face. "It wasn't a question, my friend. You know what's wrong with that dog. I saw Maizie for two seconds while she was leaping for Luccan's throat in a power storm, a thousand things going on, and I'm not a mind reader. Yet I saw clearly what had been done.

"There's one magic with that profile, Han. One person with that signature. You know them both."

Han knew Thurlock too, and it was plain that his patience had about fled. Yet he persisted. "Sir, you're not suggesting—"

Thurlock slapped a hand down on the chair's arm. "Behl's whiskers, I'm not suggesting anything. I'm telling you to admit to yourself the simple truth."

"So if I don't say what you want to hear, what will you do, use a Command on me?"

"Don't insult me, Han! Can I compel even you if need be? Yes! Will I if I must? Yes, again. This is far too important for me to allow you to hide from the truth." He paused to draw a breath and blow it out. The red that had suffused his face faded. In a quieter tone, he said. "I rather hope you'll face this on your own. Less painful in the long run."

After a heavy pause, Han's voice came out half-strangled. "Sir, it's not possible." He closed his eyes and let his shoulders fall, his sigh an admission of truth. "Okay, it is."

Silence followed, and Thurlock's voice scarcely broke it. "Would you like some coffee, Han?"

"Yes," he said, and though he felt drowned in weariness, he added, "I'll make some."

"No. You sit, for once. I'll see to it."

Han looked up in surprise. Thurlock's eyes twinkled mischief. He wagged a crooked finger, and a glass pot full of steaming, aromatic brown liquid hovered before him. Another twitch brought a mug gliding from the kitchen, and a wave directed the pot to pour. It topped off the brew just below the mug's thick brim and then went off to the kitchen while the cup came over to Han, who took it in two hands and laughed. "Sir, you shouldn't have."

"I had a good reason for that magic," Thurlock said and grinned. "A friend in need of something to smile about. Besides, parlor tricks don't take any more out of me than a flight of stairs—less, probably."

Han blew on the hot liquid and sipped. The billowing steam and familiar bitter taste offered comfort. "I wasn't lying," he said, "not deliberately. I didn't want to see it. I still don't." He shook his head. "What is it about the idea that… that Lohen Chiell is back… alive… that he's done this to Luccan's dog—why am I so desperate to deny it?" The question would have been rhetorical if he had posed it to anyone but the wizard.

"No mystery, Han," Thurlock said. "And no great failing. He's your elder brother. You don't want to see him as someone who could work dark magic at all, never mind harm Luccan. You want always to remember him as that brave young man who saved you from worse than death when you were helpless."

Han sipped his coffee, still wonderfully hot, and watched the flames dance in the hearth. It wasn't until he turned and met Thurlock's eyes with his own steady gaze that the wizard spoke again.

"Nothing your brother is now," he said, "or ever will be, will change what he was in the past. You don't have to relinquish your right to love him."

SILENCE BLANKETED the house as Lucky stumbled down the stairs, half-awake. The stairwell was as dark as a gravestone's shadow, but moonlight draped the archway at its end. The glowing arc framed a monster with hair standing out in silver-limned coils like a twisted halo.

When Lucky caught sight of that giant, he gasped in sudden, wide-awake terror. Shuffling backward up the stairs, he stumbled, but instead of crashing to the bottom, he was pulled up short in that nightmare's iron grip.

"You're all right, Luccan," Thurlock said, setting him upright.

Lucky's knees melted, and he sat down on the nearest step to recover. A moment later, he said, "I had a dream." His own voice astonished him. He hadn't intended to say anything.

"I'll listen, if you'd like to tell me," Thurlock said.

"Yes, sir," he answered, surprising himself again.

Truthfully, Thurlock scared Lucky. Scared him even when it wasn't the dark of night. Yet the old man had spoken softly then, and once Lucky's imagination had settled down, the stairwell seemed warm, small, safe. With robes whispering and stair treads creaking, Thurlock eased his long-legged frame down to sit three steps down from Lucky and turned his head to hear, perhaps kind, perhaps concerned.

"I dreamed I was a little boy," Lucky said. "I dreamed of having a father."

For a moment, Thurlock said nothing, and Lucky heard the house creak as if leaning in to listen. "Was it a bad dream?" the old man asked. "Were you afraid?"

"No, I wasn't scared. We were playing some kind of game, I think." Lucky tried to remember the pictures in the dream, but nothing much came to him except a feeling of being protected and happy. He recalled his own childish giggle and a husky laugh from deep in his father's chest. "It was a good dream, I guess."

"But you're troubled by it."

"It's just that I never dream about having a father." Lucky's words rushed out and echoed in the stairwell, striking him, on their return, as peculiar. "I dream about my mother—at least a woman I think is my mother—all the time." But the truth was, Lucky never thought about his father even when he was awake. In three years it hadn't crossed his mind to wonder about the man except in rare times when someone had asked, and then he'd only felt mildly curious.

How odd that seemed now, and incredibly painful. A wave of grief swept over Lucky, as if his emotions were trying to make up in one swoop for having forgotten about the man. For an awful second he felt the press of tears. He shoved his hair back ruthlessly and whispered, "I don't understand."

Lucky heard Thurlock stirring in the shadows, heard the rasp as he chafed his beard and a sound like bellows as the big man filled his lungs and then sighed. "I don't understand, either, Luccan." His hand fell on Lucky's ankle and gave it a friendly squeeze.

"But I believe," he said, "that it must be a good thing that you dream of him now. To lose your father was a sad event in any case. To have lost even the memory of him…."

Seconds trickled by, and then Thurlock cleared his throat. "But then, knowing what you've forgotten may be a step toward remembering. That's the bright side, if there is one."

"Wow," Lucky said, unable to bite back sarcasm. "Really, thanks." Thurlock made a funny noise, and Lucky's cheeks burned. Ashamed of his rudeness and afraid of its consequences, he'd mumbled, "Sorry, sir," before he realized the wizard was laughing.

"Oh, don't fret, Luccan. You're right. A rather dimwitted response, I'd say, coming from a wizard as old as stone." His low laugh rumbled again, and then he said, "I'll tell you what. To make up for that stellar wisdom, ask me one good question, and I'll do my best to answer it well. A 'why' question, I'd suggest. I'm told wizards are especially good at those."

Lucky pondered and shunned a hundred questions, and then it struck him. There was only one thing to ask, here in the close safety of night. "Why can't you just tell me, Thurlock?" he asked. "Why can't you tell me the things that you know, that I've forgotten?"

"Excellent. Like all the best questions, that one has a simple answer. Here it is: I want you to get home safe. I'll explain," he said and scooted up the intervening steps.

Lucky made room on the stair, and they sat side by side, facing the veil of moonlight. The wizard's warmth felt solid and welcome.

"You see," Thurlock said, "there are a few ways for us to get from here to Ethra, but it's complicated, because Ethra and Earth occupy more or less the same space. And then too, there are other worlds, other times, other possibilities." He stopped talking, scratched his beard, shook his head, and made a noise that sounded like "Umph."

Lucky hoped a more coherent explanation would follow.

"I suppose that sounds pretty strange," Thurlock said, and Lucky narrowly avoided responding with the ever-useful term, *duh*. "For now, perhaps we'd best leave it at that. What I want to make clear is that the ways to get home aren't like boarding a train or driving a car. They're the strongest magic we Ethrans know, and yet, at the same time, not magical in the least."

"Wait," Lucky said, scratching vigorously at his scalp. "What?"

Thurlock chuckled. "Sounds convoluted, doesn't it? It isn't really, but I invariably find describing and explaining problematic—thus I'm a wizard and not a scientist." Lucky felt another squeeze on the ankle and found it curiously comforting. "Let's try this," Thurlock ventured. "It's not possible for a person to travel from world to world if they have no magic in them. But magic, as we usually define it, doesn't work at all on the way."

"Just tell me," Lucky exclaimed. "What does work?"

The wizard's voice carried a teasing smile. "It's simple, Luccan," he said. "You only have to know who you are and where you want to go."

HAN STUMBLED in through the front door, thinking about a figure of speech Earthborns use—*the wee hours of the morning*. The present hour must be the most "wee" of all, he thought. He rarely got so tired that he woke up groggy at any hour, but last night had been an exception. By evening's end he'd been asleep on his feet. He'd fallen into bed and resolved not to get up before daybreak, no matter what.

Except in the unlikely event of emergency. Such as, apparently, this.

He flipped a switch and the chandelier lit up just as Thurlock tripped off the bottom stair into the living room. Though muted, the light shone too bright for bleary eyes, and both men brought an arm up as a shield. After their eyes began to adjust, they stood on opposite sides of the room and blinked sleep-deprived looks at each other.

"A call," Thurlock said.

"Yeah."

"An emergency."

"Uh-huh." Han hitched up the too-large pajamas he wore and, keeping the legs off the floor, shuffled to the kitchen. He ran tap water into a cup for a quick and lazy version of Thurlock's tea. For himself, he poured cold coffee from the wizard's magic pot. He stuck both cups in the microwave.

"The boy's okay," Thurlock announced, standing in the kitchen doorway. He leaned on his umbrella and hugged a frayed orange terrycloth robe around his middle. "And," he added, demonstrating keen powers of observation, "you've stolen my pajamas again."

"Borrowed," Han said over the microwave's final beep. In brighter moments he thought of the appliance as a little miracle of Earth-made kitchen technology. Now he muttered curses, poking at it blindly in an effort to open the door.

"Put a shirt on, Han."

Picking up a hoody off a hook by the door, Han replied, "You're just afraid if you have to look at my muscular torso, you'll want to jump me."

Thurlock laughed. It was an old joke between them, only not always funny. They both knew Han had pined after Thurlock for the entire two hundred years they'd worked together. And they both knew Thurlock wasn't likely to be interested, the only real lover he'd ever had having been female.

"Not my cup of tea," Thurlock said. "Anyway, at my age, my cup of tea is an *actual* cup of tea."

Han said, "Coming right up," but was busy trying to unravel the confusion of his arms and the hoody's sleeves.

Thurlock watched him flounder for a while and then rolled his eyes. He said, "Han, you're a disaster of apocalyptic proportions begging to erupt. I'll get my own tea." Reaching for his cup, he said, "Whatever the problem is, it must be important or they wouldn't call from the Sisterhold in the middle of the night."

"It's morning, really."

"If you say so." In the dining room, Thurlock fumbled in a pocket of his bathrobe for his spectacles and then laid them on the table. Standing behind his chair, he pointed the golden tip of his umbrella at the M.E.R.L.I.N. "Receive." The device crackled, and the glass swirled with color, and then ordered itself into a scene. In a sunlit, spring green room in Ethra, the sisters Liliana and Rosishan stood side by side near a table of golden wood. The curtains puffed with morning breeze, the ancient pine floor shone with centuries of polish, and multicolored vases overflowed with blossoms.

"Ladies," Thurlock said, creaking into a bow.

"Yeah," said Han, holding up his PJs, drinking coffee, and bowing too.

"Oh," Liliana gasped. "What time is it there?"

Thurlock cleared his throat but didn't answer. He was attempting to clean his spectacles with the hem of his robe.

"Too bloody early in the morning," Han muttered. He swished coffee around in his mouth and, while scrunching his waistband to keep his pants up, suggested they be seated. He ignored the sisters' shocked expressions, believing them insincere. Chair legs scuffed over floors in both worlds.

Thurlock called the meeting to order, senatorial despite his orange garb. "Shall we proceed? You request formal Council, I take it, ladies?" Lili and Rose nodded. "And it can't wait for full Conclave?"

Rose muttered, "Obviously."

Or perhaps she only thought it.

"All right, then," Thurlock said. "Called to order, et cetera." He primed his voice with a gulp of tea, made a sour face—clearly having forgotten the sugar—and addressed his niece formally. "Lady Grace, Liliana, begin please."

Lili was all business and wore a prim expression to prove it, but she started with a digression, mentioning the storm. The shock waves from all the power set loose in that conflict had disrupted magic in Ethra. "For an hour or so we found even a simple charm impossible." She believed it boosted her argument that Luccan should come home, "ready or not."

"Save it, Lili," Thurlock said, ignoring the formalities. "For your sake, I hope this isn't the reason you disturbed my sleep." He put an elbow on the table and leaned his head against his fist.

Lili stuck her bottom jaw out and said, "Well, this is Council, where we vote, and my vote is—"

"We're wasting time," Thurlock said. "Let's assume everyone votes yes, even those who are absent. Now it's my turn, and I say, 'Overruled.' The nays are thus victorious, having absolutely creamed the opposition." He drained his cup of bitter tea and allowed a moment's silence. Then he spoke again, leaving sarcasm out. "That wasn't, I assume, the matter you wanted to bring to Council."

Lili took a rainbow-striped shawl from the back of the chair and pulled it across her shoulders. "It's about L'Aria," she said, puckering like she'd just eaten lemons whole. "The other day when she ran off, she apparently hiked up to Tiro's Eye to do some scrying."

At first, Han was surprised. Tiro's Eye was a seer's pond in the Greenwood, the forest that covered the northwestern Sunlands in Ethra. Though the pond was situated so that weather never disturbed its glassy surface, the slightest unrest of a nearby human spirit would mar its smoothness with ripples. Most seers never mastered the stillness it took to put the pond to use. *But perhaps it's to be expected,* he thought. L'Aria was, after all, the daughter of the being—only partly human—for whom the pond was named.

Thurlock said, "I'd wondered how soon she would figure out she could do that."

"Well, good for her," Lili said, and everyone else traded amused glances. "That's not the point, though. She says she's found Lohen Chiell; that he's alive, and he's there in Earth."

Thurlock said, "Well, if anyone could find him, it would be her. And she's right; he's here; he has the Black Blade and he's used it. He worked a possession on Luccan's dog, Maizie, set a nasty hex. She's raving mad, and whenever she sees Luccan, she goes for his jugular."

Liliana's face went so pale that her freckles seemed to float, so Thurlock hurried on. "Don't worry; he's in no danger now."

Han interjected, "You know, I didn't mention this before, what with one thing and another, but she may be less of a threat to Luccan than it seems. Except for last night, in the midst of the witch's worst, she's been fighting that curse." He stared at his hands, chewing his bottom lip and lost in thought.

"Explain," the wizard said, impatient.

"The hex drives her to attack Luccan. Something inside her refuses."

Thurlock reflected. "Perhaps the maker of that curse didn't have his whole heart in it."

Lili made a small noise of derision. "We'd be fools to believe that," she said and ignored the wizard's glare. "More likely the Blade itself resisted. It might have been fashioned with the magic of the void, and it's certainly deadly, but it was never meant for his kind of cruel—"

Thurlock held up a hand that effectively forestalled the remainder of Liliana's diatribe. "Perhaps we're trying to unlock a mystery that doesn't exist," he said. "Maybe the dog simply loves the boy." He smiled under arched brows, daring anyone to argue.

"All right, fine. Love, unexplained mystery, or blind luck, it doesn't matter. Right now, you said he's safe. That's what counts." Lili put the prim look that said "business" back on her face. "We were talking about L'Aria."

"We were talking about Lohen Chiell," Thurlock corrected.

"Both," said Rose.

Liliana let her fist fall against the wood with an annoyed thump. "L'Aria tells us that Lohen is disturbed. She thinks we should help him. She wants us to allow her to go to Earth to find him"

Rosishan spoke up. "And I say she should go."

"And I say, Rose, you are as mad as the girl."

"And I," Thurlock said, defusing the coming explosion, "am surprised that she asked permission. Rose, why do you agree she should do this?"

"You know how she is about Lohen, Thurlock. She's always insisted he wasn't guilty. Of anything." Rose sat back and ran both hands through her mane of shining black hair, exposing the spear of silver-gray over her left brow. "She's been devoted to him since she was a toddler."

"Old news," said Lili, drumming her fingers.

Han cringed, expecting Rose to lash out at her half sister. The two never harmonized on anything except the magic they worked together with their strange spiral wands.

Rosishan only shook her head. "To tell the truth," she said, "I think Lili's right. He's lost. No one can save him. But L'Aria's always had—"

"A mind of her own," Lili said.

"—a stabilizing effect on Lohen. He's never harmed her—he protects her. Maybe, she can disarm him, so to speak." Rose shot a look at her sister, knowing but not unkind. "She's more capable than Lili thinks. Her power doesn't equal her father's yet, but her song gets stronger every day. And she's sassy, but not bad. I say, let her do what she can."

They talked about it for a while, at both tables, back and forth. Then Rose said, "Lili votes no. I say yes. Han, what's your vote?"

After a long, uncomfortable moment, Han said, "I can't sort this out, Rose. He's my brother. It clouds my thinking. I'll defer to Thurlock."

Perhaps Rosishan had counted on Han's support, thinking their long friendship should guarantee it, because her world-renowned temper flared. She slammed a hand down and shouted, spitting daggers from her dark eyes. "You always defer to Thurlock."

Rose was probably the only person alive who could dependably cause Han to lose his temper, and now, by force of habit, he raised his own voice. "There you go again, pulling a Willock. And I'll be darned if it doesn't always turn out—"

"Bicker later, children." Thurlock's tone was exactly the one he had used to stop their fights when they'd both been six years old, and they went silent as quickly as they had then. "Rose," the wizard said, "you and L'Aria are right, in a way. She might be able to help him, and if she could bring him somehow back to his true self… well, we all know it would be a boon for Luccan and for Ethra.

"Yet," he continued, shifting his gaze to meet that of his niece, "Lili, you have my vote on this one, and I guess that means you have Han's as well. That's three to one."

He pushed his chair back from the table, signaling to all that he was about to close the meeting. Rose leaned forward as if to protest, but for the second time in the last half hour, Thurlock held up his hand. He said, "I'll be at the Sisterhold tomorrow—or I guess that's today. As for L'Aria, I'll tell her myself to stay put, not that she'll listen. If she decides to leave, all she needs is her own voice and a knee-deep pool of water. Still, if we can, let's try to give both of these young people a chance to survive to adulthood, shall we?"

IN THE dream, Hench stands under a wide blue sky, a breeze cooling his face. He sees a woman with golden hair and green eyes like jewels. She turns toward him, smiling; surprise sparks her eyes. "Do you hear him?" They watch a toddling boy with hair the dark red of cedar bark and skin like heartwood.

"Papa," the child says, his first word. He reaches, asking to be held, and Hench bends low to gather him up, long-forsaken smile tugging at the corners of his mouth.

"Wake, Lohen Chiell." Another voice speaks in the dream, a voice Hench has known all his life. He doesn't wake but the bright child vanishes, and Hench's lame hand grips only the knife. "Blade Keeper," the voice chides and then calls him again by his true name. "Lohen Chiell, did you believe me lost? My faith never failed. It was your oath that was broken."

Hench flies, then, to another place and time, another world. He sees mountains painted purple and umber with dawn, marching into gray distance. He stands, brown curls blowing wild in the bitter wind, at the rim of the never-fathomed canyon, Mardhral.

He listens, searches that wind, his last hope. He prays to hear in its moaning a single word, a name the loss of which is so painful he can bear it no longer. The name of the son he cannot reach, cannot find, cannot help. The name of the son he has betrayed.

The wind doesn't speak, and the crevasse yawns wide and black and bottomless at his feet. He heaves the Black Blade over the edge. As it falls, it catches a sunbeam and turns the brilliance back on him. The light pierces his eye and burns it to dust and fume. Still the wind is silent, and he throws himself after the Blade into the bottomless canyon.

In the dream, Lohen wishes the deed could be undone. In the dream, the knife falls into his hand, and they plunge together into darkness. The Blade speaks, in the dream, telling him how he might have his wish.

"Make right the last wrong you have done, so that we might begin again."

CHAPTER TWELVE:
A FINE TIME TO REBEL

THERE HAD been a wreck on Meridian. Red and blue lights flashed against wet midmorning clouds, and traffic was jammed to a stop. Lucky was about to suggest to Han that they get off the bus and walk. Though it would be a long trek through the rain from here to his shack, where they hoped to find Maizie and collect his things, walking would be better than being stuck on a bus between a bass-booming low-rider and a moving van. But then traffic unsnarled, the bus moved, and he relaxed into his seat.

He looked sideways at the man sitting next to him, took in his carefully placid features, his eyes, which at the moment seemed to avoid meeting Lucky's, and the muscles which, even at rest, proclaimed raw power. The cords of Han's jaw rippled, a tiny, repeated motion, and Lucky guessed that meant he wasn't truly tranquil. Like the wizard's umbrella, Han was more than he appeared.

With a note of challenge, Lucky said, "You're not a servant."

Han glanced at him, then looked away and chewed his lip for a moment. Quietly, he said, "Han Shieth is my name, but it's a title too. Han Rha-Behl Ah'Shieth; that's the long form, the old language. Rough translation: Wizard's Left Hand." He settled back into his seat and crossed his arms. "It refers to a warrior's shield side. I'm the wizard's shield."

"Wizard's Left Hand," Lucky whispered, liking the sound. Exciting, like knight of the Round Table, Cheyenne Dog Soldier, captain of the Starship Enterprise. "But what do you do?"

"Sometimes it's about fighting, but Thurlock doesn't need a bodyguard. Basically, I deal with things I can handle, so Thurlock is free to do things only he can do."

"Like in that storm, what you did with your sword?"

"Yes," Han said slowly, "like that." He turned to Lucky, grinning, and it changed everything about him. "More often, I make sure he remembers to eat, has clean clothes, and can find his socks."

Lucky couldn't help but smile back, and then for a time he could ask questions and talk easily. The first question followed on Han's joke about his work for Thurlock.

"But… you…. Are you and Thurlock…?

"Spit it out, lad!" Han laughed again. "No, I know what you're wanting to ask, and I don't even have to read your mind. Thurlock and I are not a couple."

Lucky thought he should probably be embarrassed for being nosy, but heck, if Han was giving out answers, he might as well keep asking. "But are you gay?"

"Hm." Han shook his head slightly, but apparently he wasn't saying no. "Well, I'm a man, and all the people I could be romantically attracted to are men. In Earth, that makes me gay. Thurlock is definitely not, though I will confess more than I should to you and say that I very much wish he was."

"So what about in Ethra? You wouldn't be gay in your own world?"

"In Ethra, we don't have a label like that. We're just people."

"So… nobody hates people like us… you in Ethra?" Lucky was thinking he wanted to go there pretty quick, if that was the case.

"I wish that were true. It isn't. It seems that everywhere *some* humans have a penchant for hatred."

"Oh."

"Don't look so sorrowful! Ethra's a wonderful world, and when you finally get home, you will love it."

"But I'm gay. Or maybe bi. Mostly gay."

"I know. It will be all right."

They rode in silence for a time, and Lucky's thoughts shifted to more pressing concerns. He asked about Maizie, about what was wrong with her.

"Possession," Han said. "That's the simplest word for it."

"Like… demons?"

Han explained. "Not demons, it's magic that possesses her, fills her mind with an idea, and forces her to act on it."

That seemed less hopeless.

He asked why Han had come with him, why not Thurlock, concluding, "I mean, Thurlock's the heavy, right?"

A perplexed look came over Han's face. "I'm a cream puff?"

"Sorry," Lucky said, face flaming with embarrassment.

"Thurlock had to be elsewhere for wizard work." The last two words seemed to deserve air quotes.

"Like?"

"Reading," Han said. "He went to a very large library." They laughed together and when they'd stopped, a friendly silence sat between them on the cracked cushion.

"I have other questions, Han, several serious ones."

"Start with one."

Lucky blurted, "Who am I?"

Han shook his head. "Try again, lad. You know I can't tell you that yet."

The bus lumbered forward and stopped again, and now the strobes from the accident scene bounced off the faded, rain-soaked walls of the old projects. Lucky hugged his bare arms against seeping chill, his ease gone. In the streets, a ragged man tipped up a bottle-shaped paper bag, and a skinny dog nosed under heaps of garbage. Lucky recalled the times he'd taken shelter in hidden corners of those crumbling buildings. So very many people hid behind those condemned walls, yet the nights he'd hidden there had been his loneliest.

On the bus, he leaned a bit toward Han. He rocked and tilted around corners and breathed exhaust, but instead of the engine's whine, he began to hear Han's words to him in the storm, repeated over and over. *"You have strength you don't know about."*

Breathless with fear, he asked, "Could I have stopped it?"

"No," Han answered, apparently not needing to ask what he meant.

"Could I have helped?"

"You did."

The next question, Lucky whispered. "Was it magic, Han, what I did at the end?"

"Yes, it was." Han spoke low and steady as always, but it seemed to Lucky that the words ricocheted through the bus like three cartoon bullets.

No, he insisted. *I did not do magic. I don't know any wizards or people with swords. It's a dream. No, it's a nightmare, but I'm going to wake up.*

His head began to throb. He gripped his elbows like life ropes and slid down in his seat. Han watched him, eyes narrowed. Suddenly the bus seemed to revolve, and on its third turn, Lucky croaked, "Han, I'm going to be sick."

Desperate to stop the wave of nausea, he resorted to old tricks. *Normal, normal*, he mentally chanted his calming mantra. *Normal, normal, normal....*

And if I could just wish things and make them true, like in the storm, why am I here? All the times I've wished—

Han answered Lucky's thought. "All powers have limits, lad. Yours too."

Lucky shoved his hands through his hair and scratched at his scalp, painful and vicious. *I just want to undo it. I wish I could go backward five days. I wish... I* wish *it would all go away.*

He said out loud, "I wish—"

Before he could say more, that he wanted to be left alone and never see Han and Thurlock or anything magic again, Han grabbed Lucky's arm hard enough that it hurt. Lucky flinched, and immediately Han loosened his grip, but his eyes burned, and his voice turned gruff—pleading and angry at the same time.

"Don't," he growled. "Don't say it." He looked straight into Lucky's eyes and dropped his voice to a hoarse whisper. "Be careful. Be very careful what you wish. Your wishes may not have unlimited power, but they aren't trivial. Don't play with them."

Han's warning lingered, taking up space on the seat between them, and VC Transit Sixty-six seemed all of a sudden a very crowded bus. The familiar landmarks of Twelfth and Main came into view: the Quick-Shoppe, Failsafe Bail Bonds, the rusty VW in the third curbside parking space. Normal, Lucky thought, and he was glad they'd be getting off. He reached for the buzzer.

Han touched Lucky's hand and whispered, "Wait."

It felt as though that touch communicated much more than the single word, and every nerve in Lucky's body jangled in response. Lucky froze.

He followed the direction of Han's gaze to the Quick-Shoppe parking lot, where the pavement crawled with strange people who milled about like bugs suddenly exposed by a kicked-up rock. Dressed in black, they hunched shoulders and lurked in shadows. Way in the back of the lot, alongside a windowless wall, under neon that flickered weak in the daylight, the Crown Victoria brooded.

"We won't get off the bus, Luccan," Han said. "I'll take you back to Thurlock's house."

Lucky watched the black-clad group wander aimlessly until the bus pulled away, and then he sat back in his seat. *Where were all these people before? How can the town suddenly be full of weird people in black? And why doesn't anybody else seem to care?* Then he remembered the awful power in last night's storm, and though he wasn't sure why, in his mind he connected this strange swarm of people with the tortured souls he'd seen then. He told himself, *Han is right, it isn't safe.*

Yet ice-cold energy rolled through his limbs as if someone had whipped his nerves into a froth, and it demanded release. Sitting still ceased to be an option. As the bus neared the First Street stop, he snapped upright. "I'm getting off the bus, Han, whether you like it or not."

Han reached past Lucky and pulled the buzzer.

FIVE MINUTES later, the rain had disappeared; summer sun again burned bright and strong. Standing with Han in a square of hot shade under a green canvas awning that smelled of grease, Lucky again tried to ignore the anxious twitch of his calf muscles. He pretended to blame the muggy heat and the sweat rolling down his ribs for the antsy way he felt.

Han seemed not to notice Lucky's distress, or the heat, or the noise of cars, trucks, and bicycles splashing through the sea of rainwater pooled around the clogged runoff drain.

"Go back to Thurlock's," the man said, his voice hard but not frantic. "I'll find Maizie, and I'll get your things."

"No."

"Lad, you've picked a fine time to rebel."

Lucky's thoughts had run far ahead of his ability to express them. *That's not it. But how can I explain? I can't help it. I have to move!*

Across the street, a motion caught his eye, people in black again, and he realized he wasn't safe anywhere on the streets. Though the least safe action he could think of was to separate from Han, he nevertheless started walking down First Street toward the ravine. It might have looked bold, but he shook inside.

He thought about the trail he'd have to take from here to get to his shack via the ravine. First Street dead-ended at an old mill yard, and that ended in a sharp drop to Black Creek. Poison oak crowded the forest that ran along the top of this part of the gorge, and snake holes riddled the area like swiss cheese. The slippery, almost vertical wall of the ravine offered the only passable trail, a fold in the basalt a few feet below the canyon rim—a hazardous venture, best not taken alone.

Han whistled, a single note, and in the midst of his worry and confusion, hope jumped up in Lucky's throat. He stopped walking and turned, and when Han caught up with him, he resisted the impulse—wherever it came from—to dash for the gorge.

Han spoke loudly over the rush of traffic. "Luccan, I've got three choices." He ticked them off on his fingers. "I can let you go alone. I can take you back by force. I can go with you. Each choice could have consequences I don't want to think about, much less name."

A Freightliner roared by on Main Street, accelerating through several low gears, and Han tugged at Lucky's elbow, urging him down First Street toward the old mill. A block and a half from Main, where the street's noise faded, he pulled Lucky around to face him. "You want to go into that ravine, or maybe you think you have to go. We can go together, but by all that's good, lad, you must abide by my terms."

"Thurlock would be…." Lucky let the words trail off; they felt defiant and disloyal. He finished the sentence silently. *He'd be mad if you let me go alone.*

"Thurlock might be mad," said Han, "that I let you go at all. But the terms aren't about that. They're about safety, possibly about staying alive. Here they are: One, stick with me close. Two, if we get separated, go back to Thurlock's. Three, if trouble comes, do what I tell you to do, no matter what you see, hear, or feel. Agreed?"

Lucky did agree. It seemed a fair trade for having the strong man at his side, but Han's warnings and ground rules had set his heart galloping again. Part of him wanted to say *Never mind, run away*, and he feared that if he opened his mouth, the words would blurt themselves out. He shut his lips and nodded.

Lucky felt Han's eyes burning through his skull. He started to look at his feet to escape the painful scrutiny, but Han said, "No." So, he summoned his resolve, raised his eyes to Han's, and held them there.

Finally Han nodded. "Good enough, let's go."

Past the mill yard, a mound of gray-black basalt guarded the entrance to Black Creek Ravine, smooth and round like the helmeted head of some enormous watchman. A single pine towered at each side of the stone hill, marines at attention, sentinels bracing the gate.

Feverish sun beat down, soaking up remnants of rain like a hot rag. All around, not even a whisper of a breeze disturbed dandelion or dust. But a phantom wind rushed through that gate, and beyond it the air over Black Creek writhed, smoky with twisting plumes of alien-seeming mist, gray and black and electric blue.

Lucky's brain screamed *That's not normal. Go back!* But in the same instant his feet broke for the gate and ran, pounding the earth so fast his steps beat into a single long sound. He heard Han shouting as if from far away, and he should have cared, he knew that, but he couldn't stop and he couldn't slow down or even make himself swerve. He felt like a fish, hooked and hauled on a taut line.

The stone mound was eight feet high, but Lucky leapt and landed only two footfalls before he flew over the summit. He was still airborne when the world cracked around him like a silent sonic boom. Before that concussion, he could hear Han shouting, see the sun and taste its heat. After, he was alone in a blue-gray, soundless world, and the sun's orb had stopped in the sky, black and cold.

Sound rushed in as hard wind squalled from the east, blasting Lucky with sand and hurling pebbles. He raised an arm to shield his eyes from the blinding grit, but he still couldn't see. He came down too hard, too fast on the crevice in the rock that formed the trail, and his feet stopped there, but the rest of him didn't. His arms reeled in open air. He was about to plunge a hundred yawning feet to the hungering rocks below.

A great bird swooped in with a shrill cry. Its wings spanned twice Lucky's height or more, and its black feathers shimmered every color against the dark sun. Lucky teetered, seized by fear that he would fall, or that he wouldn't and the predator would pluck him off the slope and carry him away to feed its young. The raptor flew closer until Lucky could see himself reflected in its bright black eye, and its wings thrust air against him with enough force to counter the wind. He regained his balance.

Then the strong east wind stopped as suddenly as held breath. For that quiet moment, Lucky's fear and shock abated, and he could hear himself think. Sensibly. Smart thoughts.

This is crazy. I'm going back.

He pivoted instantly to make good on that pledge, but the east wind snarled anew and seemed to throw itself at him with such force that it propelled him westward along the trail. Hunched against the blast, shielding his eyes, he fought but he was losing ground. Driven back step by step, he put out enormous effort just to land each footfall solid on the trail and not over its deadly edge.

In the throes of the struggle, he stumbled on a quiet place inside his mind. He wondered what had become of Han, wished the man was there to help. Eventually Han appeared some distance back on the trail. Again, as in the storm in Thurlock's house, he shone like a candle against darkness, but this time the flame sputtered and flashed in the wind. He struggled but never faltered, and when he drew close enough, he reached out.

Just as Lucky was about to grab hold, the ground shook so hard it felt as though the world would crack wide open. With no time to adjust his stance and nothing to catch on to, Lucky toppled and started to slide. He tried to hug the stone, clawed at it, but it was silky smooth and offered nothing to grasp. A long way down, loosened stones splashed into the creek. The sound conjured pictures, news photos, grainy images of Hank George fallen. Shattered. Killed.

For a moment, Lucky's right foot hung unanchored in empty air, his left shoe jammed into a tiny crack in the stone. Then that shelf gave, and there was nothing left to halt his slide. He knew he would die. As he slipped slowly down the stone, he grew calm, thinking farewells. *I wish I'd had a chance to say good-bye to Maizie.... I really should have told Thurlock thank you for letting me borrow his pajama pants....*

Han slapped a rough grip on his wrist.

Rude interruption, Lucky thought, but he regained his senses quickly. With immense gratitude he latched his other hand around Han's wrist.

"Hang on, Luccan," Han coaxed.

But the ground rolled again, and stones rained down on them from above and the wind thundered, slapping at them over and over, striking impossibly hard. They couldn't win. They couldn't prevail against such relentless force. Lucky decided to let go, sure that if he didn't, he would pull Han down with him.

He heard a growl and looked up to where Han knelt awkwardly on the narrow path, struggling for purchase. The man's eyes were shut tight against the wind, which had stung them to tears. Salt had left tracks on his brown cheeks, the only softness in a hard, angry scowl. Suddenly, the copper eyes snapped open and locked on Lucky's. "*No!*" Han shouted. "No! Don't let go. Remember the terms, Luccan—you gave your word."

Han's grip couldn't possibly get tighter, but it did, until Lucky expected bones to break.

"This is trouble, right? And I'm telling you what to do. Hold on. Don't you dare let go."

So Lucky held on, and when Han flattened himself in the crevice, dug his elbows into the rock, and told him to tighten his arms and shoulder, he did his best to make them rigid. Han had enormous strength in his arms, but they needed leverage, and it just wasn't there. Every time Han tried to pull Lucky up, Han started to slip down. Lucky grew certain that though Han's sweaty fingers might not fail, his own eventually would.

"Gods," Han rasped. "Gods help us, I can't…."

Out of the opaque sky the bird appeared again, big and black and loud, and stretched its talons toward Lucky's back.

And it grabbed him by the seat of the pants.

And Han tugged, and the bird thrust upward, and Lucky's feet and knees indulged in frantic, bug-like scrabbling. The next thing he knew, he was laid out flat along the rock-fold footpath, definitely not crying.

Han lay flat on the rock too, head to head with Lucky, one hand still gripping Lucky's arm. After a few minutes, even though the ground still felt a little shaky, both of them breathed slower, and Lucky felt the heat of overexertion fade to the chill of emotional shock. Han sat up and silently helped Lucky do the same. He had composed himself considerably, setting his face into its habitual, between-smiles, stoic mask.

Using his hand as a visor to shield his eyes from the leaden glare, Han scanned the skies. After a minute or so, he dropped the hand and stared straight ahead, doing some serious lip chewing. More time passed in the same fashion, and then Han turned his head slightly and squinted at Lucky out of the corner of his eye.

"Tell me, Luccan," he said, "do you know that bird?"

Lucky still shook, but he was pretty sure the ground had stopped. He answered Han with a shrug, a shake of his head, and a wobbly smile, concentrating on fortifying his knees to stand. Once he felt secure in the upright position, he asked, "Was that an earthquake for everyone, or did it happen just for us?"

Han opined that the quake and the wind and even the strange, dark sun had indeed been conjured for them. "Although," he said, "we won't know for sure until it doesn't show up on the five o'clock news." He smiled, and Lucky finally stopped quivering.

But then Han stepped back to study Lucky's condition, and his face lost all traces of humor.

Dark red globules of blood seeped through the dust that coated Lucky from head to toe. On his left side, which had taken the brunt of the abuse, patches of color showed at elbow and knee and on top of his foot. Judging from the pain behind his ear, Lucky figured that was probably bloody too.

Han's voice sounded hoarse. "By the gods' gray whiskers, lad, your hands…."

Flexing them open and closed to show Han, he answered, "They're fine, see?" They hurt, but it didn't matter. What were bruises and shredded skin, compared to the gaping wound in his conscience? *It was my fault. I should have listened. I almost got us killed.*

"I'll go back," he said, searching for a way to soothe his guilt. "I'll go back to Thurlock's, if you think I should."

Han squeezed Lucky's least-scraped shoulder. "No point in going back now. We're halfway there, and if there's more trouble headed our way, I'd bet Thurlock's pajamas it'll find us regardless of which direction we're headed." He pointed west with a bob of his chin, toward Lucky's shack. "Let's stick together and… let's just go."

Lucky followed blindly, and despite Han's assurances that it wasn't his fault, guilt and remorse grew heavier with every step. He blamed himself for what had already happened; he worried about what would happen next and blamed himself for that too. The more he dwelled on it, the bigger it got, until he felt like he rolled a giant red ball of shame and anxiety in front of him along the narrow trail.

Hoping to deflate it at least a little, he whispered, "I'm sorry." When Han didn't answer, he said it again, louder. "I'm really sorry."

Han stopped, pivoted, and crossed his arms. "I heard you the first time," he said. "Honestly, I heard you before you said it. I'll say this because it's true and you need to know it. What's happening here is not your fault. Got that?"

Han stood poker faced, staring, and Lucky didn't know what to say, so he nodded.

"Good." Han nodded back. "Now I'll say this because it's even truer, and you need to know it even more. Letting guilt run away with your brain and your courage between its big yellow teeth never does any good, lad. You might need those things."

They hiked the tortuous trail for half an hour and advanced maybe a half mile west as the crow flies. Overhead, a steel gray sky gathered up the sun's heat and pressed it down on them like a crusher, squeezing sweat from every pore. The trail broadened to a yard-wide, not-quite-flat shelf of loose red soil and crumbling shale.

Laboring behind Han, Lucky kept his eyes on the man's straight back and sure stride. By force of will he kept his head high and his shoulders unbent, struggling to emulate the self-mastery of the man he followed.

Han's words had stung, but they'd rung true, and now Lucky's twin habits, honesty and mule-headed tenacity, asserted themselves. He might not manage quick-witted and brave, but he could at least avoid dull and chicken-livered. To that end, he let the salt-sweat trickling in his wounds clear his head and soldiered on.

Han's step slowed as the trail flattened and passed into a corridor leading through a grove of ancient myrtle trees. Waxy leaves turned the light and even the ground amongst gnarled roots emerald and silver. Protected here by a bend in the gorge from the winds that often stunted their species to shrubs, the myrtles had achieved their towering eighty-foot potential, and overhead their branches stretched across the road to clasp hands with kin. Through their million laced fingers peeked a clear sky, free of the day's iron haze, blue and dazzling.

Lucky drew up next to Han, and they stepped into the grove together. As Lucky crossed that threshold, he remembered how it felt, just two days ago, the first time he'd entered the wizard's house. Magic abided here, too—Lucky recognized it. Though not the kind that could be cast with a spell or summoned with a staff. Pure magic, here, life and light. For Lucky, and he guessed probably for Han too, it conjured a half mile or so of blessed respite.

The instant they began to trod the leaf-padded ground, a breeze whispered the sweet-bay scent to Lucky's nostrils. "I've been here before," he said softly, remembering that the grove sat almost exactly opposite Hank's cabin across the ravine. On rare days when the wind blew out of the south, the scent of this sanctuary would come with it over the creek, and Hank would sit on his porch, close his eyes, and drink it in. Sometimes the scent drew them, and they came around to this side just for the joy of being in the midst of the trees.

Lucky lifted an arm to point. "There's a spring over there, back in the trees," he told Han, "and the water's good—sweet and cold."

Han met his eyes, and Lucky saw something in the glance—appraisal, or perhaps appreciation. Han returned Lucky's smile and said, "We'll stop."

The niche was a short jaunt from the path, but those few strides plunged them into deep, cool shade. The water bubbled, astonishingly, from a cleft in a freestanding stone, smooth basalt and almost spherical. From its underground roots, the rock swelled as high as Lucky's shoulders.

Below the spring's egress, the rock wore green moss like a scraggly beard, and it bathed its round foot in a clear, leaf-littered pool. Lucky and Han followed suit, leaving Lucky's worn shoes standing in the shadow of Han's still-shining boots.

They laughed at nothing in particular and made trivial comments about how good the place felt. They rinsed their hands and took turns cupping them under the bubbling flow to slake thirst that suddenly seemed to Lucky as vast as the Mojave Desert. Then Han splashed his face, shook his hair loose and retied it, padded a few steps away and, to Lucky's astonishment, lay down full length on the aromatic ground and slept.

By the time Lucky had soaked off the caked blood and dust, he felt perhaps a year or two older and wiser and a great deal more human. He waded out of the pool and sat on the ground to don his shoes. For the first time he caught sight of the pale, slender knife strapped to the inside of Han's boot. He stared at it with a shudder of premonition, and when he raised his eyes, he found Han standing near, watching him.

"I'm a warrior, Luccan. I'm never without a weapon."

Lucky nodded and finished putting on his shoes. He looked back only once as they left the shady niche behind. The sweet-scented gallery looked as bright, pure, and good as on the way in, but Lucky's heart weighed him down. "You'll use it," he said. "You'll use the knife before the day is over, won't you, Han?"

"It seems likely," Han said, and there was no joy in his voice at all.

CHAPTER THIRTEEN: STONE KNIVES, TWINS, AND STRANGERS

LUCKY AND Han came to a place where the rocky path turned to muck beneath their feet, and there they stopped. They couldn't see the sun anymore, but behind dense, gray clouds Lucky could feel the hidden heat source arcing west. He remembered the cool green of the myrtle grove with longing.

At the edge of the grove's shade, just before they left the myrtles behind, Han had stopped and offered Lucky a choice. "I don't think our enemy will come to this place," he'd said, "not yet. You'll be safe, if you want to wait while I go on."

Lucky had declined, and he knew he'd made the right choice. He had Maizie to think about. And it was his life being torn up, so to speak, for new construction. He wanted to have some small say in the end result. He couldn't do that if he stayed behind lollygagging in the shade and let Han do everything for him.

They stood on the edge of a broad oval of flat land where the rock shelf that had been a narrow footpath widened out to create a bowl colonized by centuries of wayward soil, seed, and rain. To Lucky's left a wall of smooth stone pushed out to make Black Creek bend its elbow, far below. The rock pushed up into a lip two feet higher than the ground and then descended in palisades, a frozen waterfall of stone.

The last time Lucky had seen the place, it had been a green meadow dotted with sweet peas and daisies. He'd come here with Hank George to hear stories and picnic on smoked fish, saltines, and Coca-Cola. In the afternoon, they'd napped in the sparse shade beneath gnarly, aged red elders.

Now, more than a year later, the elderberries had ripened to the color of blood. The green grass had been churned to black muck. The sky sagged, dimmed charcoal gray and heavy with the smells of sulfur, ash, and rot. The wind had stilled, but now the earth gave rise to frail, cold gusts that teased at littered papers and rags. Near Lucky's foot, a square of white shifted in the restless air, weighted on one kinked corner by a rune-embossed coin from another world. He bent to retrieve it and found his most treasured photograph, a Polaroid of him laughing with Hank. The faces had half peeled away.

A deep voice called out from the center of the field. The man who spoke wore a black cloak and a cowl pulled back to reveal coarse, curly black hair, pale skin and paler lips, and a heavy blue-black shadow where his beard had started to sprout. His smile only made him look morbid. His eyes, like black coals, emitted an icy gleam.

"At last," he said. "You're here. We've been waiting."

At the word *we*, Lucky noticed another man standing ten yards from the one who spoke. They looked identical, except for the slack-jawed expression on the second man's face and the fact that he held a captive. He grinned, but all the while kept a tight grip on the rope that wrapped his prisoner's neck and held a hood of black fabric over her face.

"Perhaps you remember me," the first man said, drawing out the last word as if it was very important. "I am Mordred Brede. Boff, here—" He gestured with a snap of his fingers. "—is my brother, as you no doubt guessed."

"We're twins!" Boff's gleeful exclamation earned him a rock to the kneecap, aimed expertly by his perhaps not-so-loving brother.

"As you also doubtless see," Mordred went on, "Boff is stupid but strong. Unfortunately," he addressed Han, "Boff has this girl at his mercy. Our employer, the Witch-Mortaine Isa, thinks you might know her." He let the suspense hang for a few seconds, then snapped, "Show him, Boff."

While Boff worked the hood free of the rope, Mordred turned to Lucky with feigned sadness. "All I have, though, is a silly stone knife."

Boff revealed the girl's face, or at least her eyes and nose, since the rest was hidden behind a gag.

Mordred held up the Amber Blade.

Han sucked in a startled breath. "L'Aria."

L'Aria flipped her sable hair free of the rope, eyes blazing. She strained so hard against the cord that tied her wrists that the muscles along her neck stood out.

Lucky registered the girl and her saucy attitude. And her serious danger. But his eyes locked onto the amber in Mordred's hands. He said, "My knife." The amber glimmered in his eyes as if bright sun shone through. He could almost hear the stone call his name.

But what about the girl?

He came to a decision all at once, priorities clear, and charged like a bull, bent head aimed for Boff's ribs. Beside him, Han broke at the same instant, running at Mordred, extracting that nine-inch, pale metal blade from his boot while on the fly.

Lucky had covered half the twenty-yard distance when a half dozen people wearing black cloaks popped out of the shadows and blocked his way. He pushed and kicked, swung fists and elbows, but they moved like robots and acted like they didn't feel a thing.

They had him hemmed in, but he tore an arm free and on momentum smacked his fist into someone's jaw. The unintended blow knocked the man it hit into the woman behind him and sent them both sprawling. The success surprised Lucky, but he wasted no time taking advantage of the breach it left in the enemy line. With balled fists he dove through and prepared to assault the mountain of a man called Boff.

"Luccan, stop!" Han's order rang with authority, and Lucky slammed to a halt so sudden his shoes left skids in the mud.

Han's charge on Mordred had been a ruse. He ducked around Mordred's defensive crouch, whirled toward Boff, and—still running—raised his blade. It spun in flight, whispered past Lucky's face, and severed Boff's rope, slicing clean through and setting L'Aria free.

Lucky had no time to think about how such things were not supposed to happen in real life. The Black Cloaks were back on their feet, and they crowded around L'Aria while she tried to work her wrists loose. Lucky wanted to help, but he took a clout on the head, and for seconds the world went dark and silent.

When daylight and sound returned, L'Aria had tugged off the hood and tossed it aside. Lucky reached her just as the five still-conscious Black Cloaks started kicking and throwing punches. Soon, Lucky and L'Aria stood back-to-back, surrounded by a gang with hands as cold as zombie flesh and eyes like glass.

When Boff finally registered that the rope he held was attached to nothing, he roared and began to throw fists about like a blind madman. L'Aria and Lucky twisted and dodged and managed to miss being hit most of the time. But Boff wasn't really aiming, and the people in black acted like they didn't know they should duck. Before long, three of them had gone down under the friendly fire of Boff's fists.

Mordred entered the fray, yelling his brother's name and cursing nonstop. He took hold of L'Aria's hair, yanked her head back, and raised his fist to haul the hilt of the Amber Knife down on her face.

Lucky felt completely confused by his drive to protect this girl, but he focused on doing something about it.

The something he came up with was to dive at L'Aria, taking her down to the muddy ground beneath him. She survived the crush with only a squelching noise, and Lucky rolled quickly away. Lying on his back, he saw Boff stumble over L'Aria's legs and come crashing toward them both like a slain giant. Instinctively, he brought his feet up to take the brunt of the man's weight, expecting a two-hundred-plus-pound disaster.

It never came.

Mordred must have seen that with L'Aria out of the way, his brother's curly head would take the blow from the knife hilt, but he didn't stop. If anything, he drove the hit home with a little added force. On impact, Boff's head made a sound like a thumped melon. His nose crunched when it struck the ground before the rest of his skull. He went completely still, but his breath rippled the blood from his nostrils like wind on a tiny red lake—proof of life.

Lucky and L'Aria scrambled to their feet, L'Aria spitting mud, and their opponents charged. In the scuffle that followed, Lucky gave out as good as he got, slapping, kicking, and punching. L'Aria did a little punching too, but when an attacker came straight at her face-to-face, she stiffened, leaned toward him and…

Started singing!

The Black Cloaks seemed a bit dull to begin with, as if their own brains weren't in charge. Though L'Aria's song seemed to leave them even more confounded.

Now and then during the fight, the black hoods covering their attackers' heads moved out of the way, and Lucky caught a glimpse of Mordred and Han.

Han had retrieved his metal blade, and Mordred had the amber. They'd squared off, ten feet apart. Mordred crouched on wide-planted feet and rocked like a Sumo wrestler, but Han moved more like a butterfly, or a bee, or a middleweight champ. He danced around his opponent, jabbing and stinging and luring him farther away from Lucky and L'Aria.

Finally, seeming to flounder, Mordred backed off, holding one meaty hand to his bloodied cheek. He hawked and spat, and as soon as he had enough breath, he bellowed, "Set the creature free!" To Lucky's horror, a familiar snarl followed the shout, and Maizie bounded across the ruined green, teeth bared, hackles up, eyes beaded on him.

Fortunately, most of the Black Cloaks had been dropped, dazed or confused by then, but it didn't look like that mattered so much now. Lucky had about seven seconds before Maizie would get to him, and he had no idea what to do with it.

L'Aria's voice crept out into heavy, damp air over the field. High-pitched. Really high-pitched. Maizie slowed, stumbled, dropped her head and shook it, but then caught sight of Lucky again and came on. L'Aria's song trailed off.

Lucky shot a desperate look at Han.

Just as they made eye contact, a high-low hum halfway between the sound of power lines and microphone feedback pulsed across the field. Maizie froze and then backed off. All heads swiveled toward the elder trees near the cliff, where the sound came from. A barrel-chested man with a ruined left arm, a twisted left leg, and an impossibly fast rolling gait shot out from the brush.

He held his right hand high, gripping a stone knife by the blade. The raised hilt seemed to draw light from the hidden sun and then return it in a thin crystal beam.

Lucky thought *That knife.... It's like mine. Exactly like mine, except black.*

The stranger spoke and indigo fire shot from the blade he carried. The thin ray of light raked over the field and locked onto Maizie's eyes. She spun around and a low, panting growl sounded deep in her chest. The man spoke again and jerked the knife back. As if tied to it, Maizie jerked sideways on stiffened legs, and then she followed it toward the cliff, snapping at air the whole time.

As she neared the meadow's edge, she broke into a run, and then suddenly leapt to clear the upthrust stone of the palisades. Her howl fell through emptiness toward the creek. The splash that ended it echoed in Lucky's brain, sounding like the word *dead*.

The light fell back into the stone dagger's hilt and silenced it. The stranger retreated but kept his eyes locked on Han, whose stare in turn followed him. He edged into the shadows under the trees.

Though Lucky would have sworn Han had forgotten everything but the crippled stranger, in that instant he backed hard into Mordred, crouched down, and reached up to grab Mordred's head. One hand pushed against the bigger man's stubbly chin, and the other twisted a hank of black hair at the back of his skull, applying sideways torque. He rolled, pulling Mordred over with him.

The heavier man hit the ground hard, flat on his back, and took a second blow as Han slammed his own body down. Han kept rolling and sprang up while Mordred still struggled to reinflate his lungs. He stopped, metal blade balanced in his hand, poised in a fighter's crouch, waiting.

Lucky waited too and sensed L'Aria beside him doing likewise. Both of them watched the men fighting so intensely that they almost didn't notice when four new Black Cloaks came out of the trees. One of them held a choke chain. Lucky seethed, thinking they'd been using that on Maizie. The anger gave him enough energy to duck as the man swung it at his head, and then Lucky rushed in to tackle him.

Unpleasant surprise—the Black Cloak didn't fall. Lucky did, though, after he bounced off the guy's muscles. These four Black Cloaks acted like they ran under their own power. Instead of fighting like zombies, they fought like they meant it. Lucky rolled to his feet just in time for the next swing of the chain to connect with his temple, a glancing blow, but hard enough to make him cross-eyed. Then he heard a loud smack, and L'Aria grunted in pain.

She yelled, "Lohen Chiell, help me!"

The lame man who had slowed down to stare at Han had almost disappeared beyond the edge of the field. When L'Aria shouted, he pivoted and stormed back across the mucked-up grass. As he came near where L'Aria fought, he lowered his head, roared, and rolled in like Neptune on a tidal wave, throwing punches with his mean right fist. Ribs crunched, small bones cracked, and bad guys fell like broke-winged flies.

The man—Lohen Chiell, apparently—took some blows too. Lucky could see red spots that would be bruises, a bite mark, and bloody knuckles. The man didn't seem to notice. He stepped over to L'Aria, wrapped his good arm around her, and crouched down to hoist her over his shoulder.

When he straightened and steadied himself, he and Lucky stood eye to eye. He said, "Luccan."

Lucky's guts gripped in pure fear, and before he could think about why, he reacted, raining fists on the stranger's head for all he was worth.

The man stood stock-still under the assault for a moment, trying to talk but not fighting back. Then he shook his head, spun around, and stalked away.

Some yards off, he set L'Aria on her feet and snarled out a few gruff-sounding words, hooking the thumb of his right hand toward the creek. L'Aria's fists settled on her hips, and she leaned in like a harpy preparing to lay on a good scold, but before she could speak, the man narrowed his one seeing eye and growled, "Go!" She spun around, dark sheet of hair flaring out behind her, and then marched toward the cliff.

Lucky almost set his feet in motion to run after her, but one of the Black Cloaks formerly confused by L'Aria's song stood in his way. Lucky pivoted to face him, and in the process cracked him in the nose with an elbow, accidental, but effective. When he turned around again, he looked for L'Aria. She stood on the stone lip at the edge of the cliff. Before Lucky could move, she leapt and was gone.

Lohen Chiell still stood only a few yards from Luccan, and after L'Aria jumped, he cast a glance back over his shoulder. Lucky gave him the best glare he could muster. The stranger holstered the Blade at his belt and moved toward the cliff, his limp more pronounced, looking suddenly weary.

With no one left to fight, Lucky's supply of adrenaline dried up, and he sank to the grass. Ten yards away, Han and Mordred continued to struggle. Mordred's elbow struck Han's left brow with a crack, bone on bone. It split the skin over Han's eye, but he managed to land the kick he'd aimed at Mordred's knee. When the leg collapsed, the beefy man landed facedown in the mud. Han twisted Mordred's knife arm straight up behind his back, pinning the other arm on the ground under his boot.

With one hand freed, Han swiped away the blood that was already trickling into his eye. He held tight to Mordred but stared at Lohen Chiell as he limped by at just that moment. Lohen Chiell flung the look back at Han. Something, a challenge, Lucky thought, glinted in his dark eye like steel.

Taking advantage of Han's divided attention, Mordred squirmed with sudden energy until he got his feet under him to stand. Han jerked against the meaty arm he still held, and Mordred's shoulder popped loud enough for Lucky to hear it twenty yards away. The sorcerer howled in pain, but somehow kept hold of the Amber Blade. He shoved his weight against Han, knocking him off-balance, and then he snaked around to lock his undamaged arm around Han's neck.

Lucky scrambled to his feet, thinking he'd rush in and try to help, but the battle cry of Han Shieth curdled his blood and stopped him in his tracks.

It froze Mordred too, and even Lohen Chiell stopped and turned to watch before he followed Maizie and L'Aria over the cliff.

Han twisted, spun like a top, and slammed an elbow into Mordred's ribs. Still in the spin, he jabbed two knuckles of his other hand into the cluster of nerves under Mordred's jaw. A measured blow, but it left his opponent blind with pain. Mordred reeled backward, stumbled, and went down.

His head smacked against the ridge of stone atop the palisades. He was knocked out instantly, but his arm swung up and over with the momentum of the fall, and the Amber Blade flew from his grasp. The Knife arced over the ravine and tumbled, singing, through sudden blue sky and into the depths of Black Creek.

The strange twins were both out cold. All the others had fled. Han caught his breath and walked over to where Lucky waited, half in shock. He looked him up and down with hard eyes, turned him around, checking cuts and bruises.

He asked gruffly, "Are you all right?"

Lucky could only nod, too overwhelmed to trust his voice.

Han swiped the blood from his own face with the back of his arm. He stared at Mordred for a long minute.

"Help me with this," he said.

They dragged Mordred across the field and laid him next to Boff. Han turned both brothers onto their side—Boff almost gently, less so for Mordred.

"Han," Lucky asked, "why are you doing that?"

"So they don't choke on their own spit."

Startled by Han's growl, Lucky's eyes went wide, and without thinking he took a step back.

Han turned his eyes away, and though his voice quieted, there was no softness in it. "Go home," he said. "Go to Thurlock's."

"But I can help—"

"Go."

Lucky's eyes followed Han as he took off his boots and placed them carefully, side by side, on a rock. He stripped off his shirt and hung it over the boots. Then, like Maizie and L'Aria and the man she'd called Lohen Chiell, he leapt from the cliff into Black Creek's pools.

CHAPTER FOURTEEN: THE WIZARD'S QUESTION

ON THE way back to Thurlock's, Lucky ran into the Langdon brothers. For some reason, as if the day hadn't already been evil enough, they saw him from across the street and took out after him. Maybe the crazy woman from the other day had told them some kind of lie, but whatever the reason, they chased him past houses and churches and playgrounds and car lots, blocks and blocks before he finally escaped by diving under a rusty fender in a vacant lot. He was almost grateful; here at least was a threat he understood. But he ended up so exhausted, he considered staying in the corroded shelter until he either felt stronger or died.

He closed his eyes, but pictures of Han and Maizie and even L'Aria seemed to be tacked to the backs of his eyelids. *The wizard*, he kept thinking, *get to the wizard*, and though he wasn't sure what he really meant, he rolled out from under cover, stood, and started his long shamble to the foothills. Instantly, the sky blackened and opened wide, and Lucky trudged the entire way in a downpour that he felt certain must be setting a record for world's longest cloudburst.

By the time he reached Thurlock's back stoop, his hair clung to his head like thick red-brown plaster. His shirt hung in shreds. Mud, grass, rust, and blood painted him in broad strokes from head to toe. He raised his hand to knock, but the door swung wide with Thurlock looming on the other side of it. Without a word, the wizard pulled Lucky out of the rain and onto the bare floor of the mud porch.

Lucky stood there, shell-shocked.

Thurlock stood next to him, scratching his beard. "I'm not very good at this sort of thing," he said. "Han's usually the one that takes care of people." He pursed his lips, and then, seeming to make a decision, pointed a finger to the floor at Lucky's feet, conjuring a thick, shaggy rug. Lucky automatically began to wipe mud from his bare soles, not stopping until Thurlock said, "That's enough, boy. Be still."

The old man dropped his spectacles in an inside pocket of his robes and palmed his tired eyes. "Where are your shoes?"

Lucky didn't answer.

"Okay, then, we'll try another question. What happened?"

Lucky sighed, pushed his hair back, and said, "Han sent me home."

Thurlock raised his right eyebrow and shot him a curious look before leading him into the dim kitchen.

The last time Lucky had been in the kitchen, with Han that very morning, it had been a cheerful place smelling of cinnamon. Now it seemed dark and hollow and dank as a cave, and he had a feeling creepy things were hiding in the corners. It didn't feel normal. Nothing felt normal.

There's no such thing as normal.

Lucky began to tremble.

Thurlock sighed again, gathered Lucky under his arm, and ushered him into the bathroom. He started the water in the shower and adjusted the temperature. "You stink, Luccan," he said, and pulled the door shut on his way out. "Wash."

Under the hot water, Lucky's scrapes and scratches burned, but the heat soothed him and the soap smelled good. He stayed until the water went cold. When he stepped from the shower, all the events of that day fell on his shoulders like a lead shirt.

His brain felt swollen with painful thoughts that didn't make sense. Try as he might to straighten them into some kind of order, he couldn't. He wrapped himself in two fluffy towels and sank down to sit on the side of the tub, head hanging from hunched shoulders. Water ran into his eyes, and he wiped it away over and over again.

Thurlock knocked on the door and passed him clean sweats and a T-shirt. Lucky recovered enough to dress and to wonder halfheartedly whose clothes he was putting on. When he came out of the bathroom, he saw the wizard seated in his favorite armchair near the unlit hearth, but he didn't go to sit beside him. Instead, he plunked down on a hard chair in the dining room, laid his head on the table in the glow of the chandelier, and slept.

His own shout woke him. "Wait!" He panted as if he'd been running. He looked around the room and saw nothing in particular. Nevertheless, he was afraid of everything he saw. And what he didn't see, too.

Thurlock put a hand on his shoulder. "Let's go up to the tower," he said. "We'll be more comfortable." He started up the stairs, and Lucky followed, shuffling close on the wizard's heels because at this juncture being afraid of Thurlock was more bearable than being afraid of everything else.

At the top of the stairs, yellow light streamed under the tower room door like sunshine. Thurlock fumbled with the doorknob and muttered words Lucky didn't recognize, and nothing happened. The wizard heaved a sigh, rolled his eyes, and thumped the door with the palm of his hand, and the door creaked open. Lucky walked through, the door shut behind him with a firecracker bang, and a six-month ration of adrenaline flooded his bloodstream.

Then he saw the window.

"Oh," he said.

Framed in a west-facing window, brilliant sunshine blazed. All the other windows in the tower—which was round from inside out, though it was square from outside in—all the other windows framed rain falling in sheets from blustery skies.

"Don't worry about that," the wizard said, indicating the odd aperture with a wave. "I often get the most out of every little sun break through that window. The light is welcome, at a time like this, don't you agree? And rest easy about enemies and things. This room is never where it seems to be, so it always makes a poor target."

Not where it seems to be? "Where is it, then, sir?"

"It's just Thurlock, Luccan, please. Before long you'll be sounding like Han; sir this, sir that. I appreciate the respect, but it's not required from you, not appropriate." A heavy-legged oval table stood against the wall to Lucky's right. Thurlock pulled out a chair at the end of it and gently pushed him toward it. "Sit, please," he said, so Lucky did.

A fireplace occupied the west wall—a smaller version of the stone bulwark downstairs. Thurlock flicked his right hand and it blazed. He puttered about, humming and fussing with a black, lidded pot. He filled it at a small, possibly fossilized sink and then hung it from a hook in the fireplace.

Lucky felt confused.

"Instant cocoa," Thurlock announced, displaying a packet as if it were the Nobel Peace Prize. "Wonderful invention—one of the things I'll miss about Earth." He turned over two mugs. "Join me?"

"Yes, please," Lucky said, although just a few days ago he would not have wanted anything a known wizard had to offer. For a time after Thurlock plunked down the steaming cups, there was no talk, only crackling flames, and quite a lot of blowing, stirring, and slurping. The chocolate tasted sweet, and the square of sunlight had softened to a comforting glow, and Lucky began to relax.

"So," the wizard ventured, leaning back in his chair apparently to get a better view of Lucky's condition. "I'm no doctor, but I can help if you have injuries that need attention. Is there anything still bleeding?"

Lucky shook his head.

"Anything feel broken?"

"No, sir."

"No terrible headache, don't feel dizzy when you stand up? Not sick at your stom—"

"No!" Surprised by his own impatience, Lucky quieted his tone. "No, sir, I'm fine. It's only more bruises and scratches. They'll go away."

Thurlock smiled and shrugged. "I'm sorry. Han would have known without asking." His eyes twinkled, and he seemed then so human, so ordinary, that for a moment Lucky forgot his worries and just liked the old man.

Seconds later, Thurlock straightened the lapels of his wizard's robes, donned his spectacles, and aimed a serious gaze over the gold rims. "If I had been here today," he said, quiet and businesslike, "I might have known what was happening when it happened, but I've been away. Please, if you can, tell me."

Lucky didn't answer right away, didn't even think about the question. He focused instead on the unwizardly drip of chocolate in the old man's beard. But when he looked up and met Thurlock's gray eyes, he found them as calming as sunlit seas.

He began to recite, attempting to navigate a sensible course through the day's events. He spoke at length, but his tale emerged neither coherent nor complete. He answered a few questions along the way—especially about the big black bird, and about the myrtle grove—but mostly he stopped, backtracked, and started again until, at long last, he got to the end.

"Han was… I think he was mad at me. He didn't smile, not even his eyes."

Thurlock shook his head. "He wasn't mad at you."

Lucky shrugged. "I had promised, so I did what he'd told me. I came here."

"I'm glad you did."

Lucky leaned over his still-steaming chocolate, relieved that Thurlock let silence fall around them. After a time, he asked questions of his own. "Will I see Maizie again? Will she ever be all right?"

"It's not impossible."

"What about Han? Will he come back?"

Thurlock nodded. "Certainly."

Other questions hounded him, but just thinking them through left him exhausted, so he dropped his sore head in his battered hands and only asked, "Why?"

Thurlock gave no response but sat eyeing Lucky, tugging at a stiff strand of gray beard. He grunted, suddenly, and pursed his lips. He reached over and patted Lucky's hand. "Let it be, for now, Luccan. Drink your chocolate. Rest. There are always questions, and almost always another time will come for asking." He turned away to gaze into the hearth.

The wizard's tower was filled with ordinary things: a narrow four-poster bed; a ragged quilt and a bedside rug, both checked in purple and gold; fragrant tea and tiny oranges; books and a Rubik's cube; and jigsaw puzzles, lots of them, their boxes piled high and leaning against a credenza.

The place also harbored things that did not seem ordinary at all. Stacks of yellowed scrolls crowded into cubbies. Strange instruments occupied corners and counters. Mystifying implements sat side by side with luridly painted decks of cards. Shelves were crammed with bottles of powders and liquids of every color, small rocks, and desiccated insects, and every sort of wizard's whatnot. And, of course, the wizard himself.

A portrait of Lucky's mother hung on the west wall in a plain oak frame.

Lucky knew it was his mother, without doubt. The golden curls, the smile, and the green eyes, all of which he'd dreamed about on Midsummer morning. *Like mine, those eyes.* And he'd dreamed about them again just moments ago while sleeping off his terror beneath the chandelier.

He and his mother had been laughing, in that dream, and then his mother had smiled sadly and called him by his name. Next, though, she'd spoken unfamiliar words, "Suth Chiell," and a flock of invisible voices had repeated after her. An icy darkness chock-full of scary sounds had come howling in, just as it had in the Midsummer morning dream. But, in today's dream, his mother had put a hand on her hip, stomped her foot, and rolled her eyes.

"Not again," she'd said. "I don't believe this."

Lucky had shouted, "Mom, I don't understand."

Her green eyes had flashed, and her tone had become vexed. "Ask Thurlock," she'd said. Then she'd pivoted and stomped away, muttering under her breath.

"Thurlock?"

"Luccan?"

"I dreamed about my mother. Just a while ago. She said ask you."

"Did she now?"

"She stomped her foot and yelled, 'Ask Thurlock.'" He laughed to hear himself say it, and the wizard did too, and then they both lifted their mugs of cocoa, newly refilled, and drank. Lucky spilled a drop and looked around the table for napkins, but he didn't find any. "She really did say that," he said. And then, since he'd gotten started, he kept talking. "I've dreamed of her before, but I always thought it was imagination. She's beautiful."

"Yes." Thurlock scratched at his beard and discovered the drying chocolate lodged there. He got up to rummage in a drawer and came back with a handful of napkins from a taco stand. He put them down on the table, apparently forgetting about his beard, but he did offer one to Lucky.

Lucky took it and dabbed tidily at his spilled drop. "You know my mother."

"Yes."

"Will you tell me about her?"

"Perhaps."

"Now?"

"Soon."

"That's her." Lucky pointed at the portrait, amazed that he felt so calm.

Thurlock beamed a smile at him, clapped him on the shoulder, and said, "It is."

"She called my name—Luccan." Thurlock watched Lucky over the top of his cup as he sipped, ignoring the steamed-up spectacles at the end of his nose. Lucky went on. “She said another name too,” he said, just remembering. “Eli? No. El… Elieth.”

Thurlock nodded calmly, but color shaded his cheeks. “That’s right,” he said. “In Ethra, it’s what we would call your milk-name, the name a mother gives her child at birth.”

“Then she said, ‘Suth Chiell.’ What does it mean?”

Thurlock put his mug down and took a deep breath. His eyes narrowed, and his brow furrowed, intense, until suddenly a smile broke out. “Now that,” he said, “is the crux of the matter. It’s the wizard’s eternal question. What does it mean?”

He waved at the parchments and books. “Nine-tenths of a wizard’s work is learning, studying, taking in the facts. But the part that matters is putting all the factors together and figuring out, or guessing, most of the time, what they mean.” He pursed his lips, bobbed his head, as if conceding a point. “And then, yes, you’ve also got to decide what to do about it.”

He walked over to a cluster of parchment rolls and plucked one from the center of the stack. “I’ve seen some odd things, recently,” he said as he took a seat. “And I’ve been alarmed. We already knew that we were in a precarious position, Luccan, but now I realize we have a tougher opponent than any I’d imagined.”

Thurlock went silent again, rolling the parchment out inch by inch. Lucky could see round charts with lines connecting dots of various sizes, and he deduced that they were star charts. He stayed quiet, trying to be respectful, but he became convinced Thurlock had forgotten him. So, following up on the wizard’s last words, he asked, “Who?”

“Not who, my boy,” Thurlock said, snatching the spectacles off his nose. He pointed them at Lucky and said, “Not who, what. It’s time, Luccan. Time is against us. The day we met, summer solstice happened in Earth and Ethra at precisely the same moment, an extremely rare occurrence. We knew it was important, and we were right. We found you.

“But I hadn’t understood how profound a change would follow. I now see that these two worlds have begun to unfold in patterns precisely opposite one another. Look, look here.” He unrolled the parchment a bit more and held it out.

“You see? Ethra last night, on this side, the view from latitudinal and longitudinal coordinates matching the location of this tower in Earth. Sagittarius is shooting at the scorpion, as he should. On this side, here in

Earth last night, the view from this tower. Sagittarius, on my oath, is shooting at his own hindquarters. Outrageous! And there's more… moons, anomalies, fluctuations. I can't explain it all now, but you get the idea."

Truthfully, Lucky didn't get the idea at all, though he did understand that star clusters didn't, as a rule, shoot at their hindquarters. He opened his mouth to make a joke about it, but the wizard's expression had changed to just plain worry.

"I've been around a while," he said, and Lucky had to listen close to hear the soft words over the sound of drumming rain. "I've not seen anything like it. And I can't find any record anywhere, here or at home, that anyone else has witnessed such a thing, either. Not even old Willock." He paused to drain the last of his cocoa, dribbling a spot on his robes.

"Willock?"

"But I've done my job as well as I can," he said, "and I think I know what it means. In a nutshell… the long and the short of it… to cut to the heart of the matter—"

"Thurlock, get to the point." Lucky covered his mouth, abashed and afraid of Thurlock's reaction, but the old man laughed.

"Well said, my boy. The point is this: The roads between Earth and Ethra have endured longer than history can tell. But now, things change. Our twin worlds pull against each other like frightened horses linked in the harness. I haven't learned why, but what it means, Luccan, is that our window of opportunity to get you home safe is smaller than anyone knew. We are nearly out of time."

Having voiced that ominous concern, he rose and stowed the parchment away, calm and seemingly cheerful. "As to what you dreamed," he said, "and what that means…. Simply put, it means you have a memory. And that's a start, isn't it? Certainly, it's more than we had before."

Part Three: Revelations

CHAPTER FIFTEEN: WHO IS HE AND HOW DOES HE KNOW MY NAME?

AFTER THREE cups of cocoa, all the little oranges in the basket, and a plateful of bite-sized cookies shaped like leaves and filled with maple crème, Lucky was more tired than hungry. He thanked the wizard, watched while Thurlock slammed a palm into the stuck door to let him out, and then tramped down three flights of stairs to the little room he'd come at some point to think of as his.

Exhausted, but sick with the memory of the morning, he tried to sleep and fought it at the same time, afraid to find out what images shared his bunk in dreamland. But the sun coming through the window warmed him, and the maple tree cast shadow-leaves on the wall, and somewhere in its branches a couple of birds warbled. He did sleep, surprised himself by awaking refreshed after only a couple of hours. Even more surprising, he stepped out of his bedroom and nearly ran into Thurlock on the landing just outside his door.

"Ah," the wizard said. "Good, you're awake. That's a nice coincidence. I've a chore for you."

"Chore?"

"Yes, a chore. You can pretend you're a normal teenager, for the moment. Clean the attic."

Of course, "normal" was as good as a magic word to Lucky. He liked the idea, but he felt a "you're not my boss" rise up in his throat, anyway. He opened his mouth to say it, looked up to meet the wizard's steely gaze… and changed his mind. Rebellion might be normal for a teen, but he wasn't ready to risk it with this particular old man.

Instead, he asked, "There's an attic?"

"There is now. Upstairs, just off the third step from the top." Thurlock rattled off a set of instructions and then started down the stairs, calling the last few words over his shoulder, "And if you find anything you want, keep it."

Lucky folded himself through the half-sized door and found a room that could better be described as a hidey-hole. The gabled ceiling hung too low for Lucky to stand, even at its peak, and if he stretched his arms out he could almost touch the walls on either side. Wide gaps in the siding let in striped light from the sun outside, along with a crop of spiders and bugs that skittered out of sight when Lucky pulled the chain to light up the single glaring bulb.

The cubby begged investigation, chock-full of crates, bins, boxes, and one paper sack. All wore a deceptive coat of ancient dust, as if they and the attic had been there forever.

He worked a full hour, sweating and sneezing and sorting things out the way Thurlock had instructed. It was a task calling for organization, and he was happy to do it. He had a penchant for order. In a weird kind of way, the chore made sense, which hadn't been true of anything for three days.

He started with a row of four small chests made of dark wood, each with a rounded top and fitted with a golden hasp and hinge. The first three were empty; the fourth held small paintings so precisely rendered that he at first thought they were photographs. One pictured, recognizably, a younger Han. Two were of Lucky's mother. One depicted a little girl with a turned-up nose who reminded him of L'Aria. That made him think about the fight that afternoon, but he pushed that thought away. Still, he chose to keep that picture along with the others, setting them all in front of the door so he wouldn't forget to take them out when the job was done.

"Make a pile," the wizard had instructed, "of things you can identify but don't remember." That pile grew into a tall mound, a veritable tower built of everything from baby clothes to tennis rackets, horseshoes to flower pots.

Another instruction: "Make another pile of things about which you can't even begin to guess." In the end, that group held only four objects. The strangest was a conglomeration of gears and pulleys and bells in a glass housing that reminded Lucky unpleasantly of Thurlock's brain-teasing clock.

There was also supposed be a pile for "things you remember from your childhood but don't want." As Lucky could have predicted had Thurlock asked, no such pile developed.

Finished with the sorting, Lucky stood up as straight as the ceiling would let him, wiped sweaty hands on dusty sweats, and surveyed the results. His collection of keepers held only the portraits and one additional item, the thing that had been hidden in the brown paper sack. Lucky bent to pick it up and closed his hand around soft red-and-yellow plaid fabric.

He *didn't* remember the blanket. He had no idea why he thought he might—or why the object made him smile.

Later, as he sat in the wing chair in the wizard's living room with the red plaid spread on his lap, that was what he mused on. He ran his fingers over the silk binding around the edges, and it seemed to smooth out his troubled thoughts too. The chandelier rang soft tones in the almost-still air. Lemon lay curled on a corner of the blanket, purring. Even the tick of Thurlock's clock seemed lazy. If Lucky hadn't been so baffled by his mysterious fondness for the blanket, he might have fallen asleep.

The front door opened with a shocking rush, and Han came streaming in along with the late afternoon sun. The creek or the rain had washed him clean of blood and grime, and he'd tethered his hair back into an almost perfect queue. Only the gash over his eyebrow, some cuts and bruises, and a swollen right hand testified to the day's trials.

He spotted Lucky and asked, "You're okay, lad?" When Lucky nodded, Han smiled. "Good." Perhaps his step lacked some of its usual spring, but he took the stairs three at a time to Thurlock's tower.

Lucky wanted to follow, but a little voice told him to mind his own business.

"But this is my business." He said it out loud. "This is all my business."

He started up the stairs toward the wizard's tower, but he stopped on the third step from the top—where the attic door had been an hour ago—because, unbelievably, he could hear Thurlock and Han arguing in the tower. He knew eavesdropping was sort of despicable. Worse, for Lucky, it was dishonest—his stomach hurt just thinking of it. But… he felt he *had* to know, so he crouched into the shadows, consciously wished himself quiet, and settled in to listen.

Their voices gradually got louder, bit by bit, and then suddenly Thurlock's voice boomed, causing Lucky's innards to leap skyward in panic—and cutting off Han's voice altogether.

"Han Shieth! I've told you already, I do not hold you responsible for that mess at the ravine, nor am I upset that you didn't force Luccan to come home instead of going down there. I have every faith in the decisions you made. Now—"

A sharp crack punctuated his speech, and Lucky pictured his big hand smacking the table.

"—stop apologizing, before I do get perturbed!"

Complete silence followed, and Lucky kept every muscle still, lest the stairs creak. He didn't even breathe until it became unavoidable, and then he plugged his left nostril, which tended to whistle rather loudly. He heard shuffling and clanking inside the tower room, and then the rising sound of water filling cups. He unplugged his nostril and caught a scent of chocolate wafting by.

More quietly but still loud enough for Lucky to hear, Thurlock said, "And no, to answer your question, I haven't yet decided how or what or how much to tell the boy about Lohen Chiell."

"He has a right—"

"I know that."

"It might help—"

"I know that, too."

A long silence followed that sharp exchange, filled only with tiny slurping sounds. "So," Thurlock asked, no-nonsense, "he drew the Blade, set it humming… and then the dog ran? Tell me what you saw, exactly. Had he come with the witch's people?"

Lucky had a hard time imagining Han so disturbed that he would pace; yet he found himself tracking the man's voice back and forth across the room. He spoke quietly, and Lucky could only decipher the bits he uttered as he passed near the door. "…couldn't tell, sir… his mind was closed off… L'Aria as always… the look on his face… the dog is mad… can't read her thoughts at all—"

Silence.

Then Thurlock: "Luccan! Either come in or get away from the door."

As soon as Lucky finished choking, he got away from the door. No-brainer.

A short while later, Lucky lay on the bed he now thought of as his, feigning sleep. He hadn't seen Han after fleeing the stairs. Thurlock had knocked on Lucky's door, come in, glared for two minutes or nine thousand years, and swished out again, banging the door shut behind him.

Lucky tried to work up resentment, but he could only get angry with himself. He'd never had much practice at sulking, and it soon proved too boring to keep him awake. He drifted into a troubled sleep filled with stone knives, twins, and strangers.

THE INTERRUPTION caused by Lucky's eavesdropping had broken the tension between Han and Thurlock. As they passed on the stairs outside Lucky's door, Han said, "I'm starving."

He went to the kitchen and started a roast in the microwave. "I just love this thing," he said. He assembled a pie and stuck it in the oven, peeled potatoes into a pot of water, set biscuit dough to rise in the bowl, snapped green beans into a colander to be ready for steaming at the last minute.

Carrying two glasses of tea, he went out to the front porch, where he knew he would find Thurlock in the rocker, watching the shadows change as the sun began to fall.

"Sir," Han said, handing Thurlock a glass and sinking into the vacant chair at his right.

"You must have been reading my mind," the wizard said, and they both smiled. "But since I can't read yours, tell me. You never found it?"

"The Amber Knife?"

"I assume that's what you were after when you dove into the creek."

"I found no trace, not even a tingle of the Blade's magic."

"L'Aria's doing, perhaps. She didn't have it on her when she got home to the Sisterhold, or Lili would have known, but she could have hidden it on the way. Given enough water, her magic nearly equals her father's, aside from Tiro's ability to shape-shift."

"She stays in human skin, but she may as well be in otter fur." Han held his cold glass up to the cut on his brow. "It's convenient, the way they travel. They can go anywhere, if there's a river. Or even a pond."

"They're called 'Tir' for a reason. It's the old language, but roughly it means 'river song.' But they can only travel by water in Earth or Ethra, between these two worlds. I think their magic is the only kind that has survived from before these two worlds split. Some people think it's what binds these worlds together, as well."

"Power like that…."

"Tiro holds great power, surely, and L'Aria's likely will grow as she grows. But it's limited, for practical purposes. They can create Portals in water. They can tinker with an unprotected mind or heart, since so much of what makes up living beings is water. Tiro can change shape. As you know, of course, no one else in Ethra can do that. But no parlor tricks for either of them, no household spells, no wizardry, and they can't read minds, either. Still, I wonder how Isa's people managed to capture her."

"We were lucky to find her."

"And luck can't be counted on."

"Did Lili and Rose tell her to stay home, once she got there?"

Thurlock rolled his eyes and snorted. "Oh yes, they told her. About five minutes before she left again."

HAN RAPPED on Lucky's door. "Wake up, lad, and wash. Feast in five minutes."

In the dining room, the chandelier blazed even though summer daylight still stretched in through the west window. The old round table beneath the fixture seemed to sag under the weight of platters and bowls and baskets of food.

Lucky asked, "Is it a holiday?"

"It's just Han," Thurlock said, rolling his eyes. "You can always tell when he's had a rough day; he gets hungry. So he produces more food than we could eat in a week."

Lucky didn't mind. He smelled beef and gravy and biscuits. His stomach growled, gearing up for the pleasant task of consuming his share.

When Han finally had the table fully loaded, he sat across from Lucky and pushed a platter of roast beef under his nose. "You handled yourself well in the ravine today."

It took Lucky a full minute to realize there was no *but*, *however*, or *although* attached to the end of Han's sentence. He beamed at the unexpected praise, and then blushed and thanked Han for the compliment before digging in. He ate steadily for a while, trying to fill up what felt like a vast uncharted territory under his ribs. When he paused briefly with an empty mouth, he asked, "L'Aria…?"

"Home," Han said, also squeezing in words between bites. "She's safe, in Ethra."

Lucky was confused about how that might be true, and swallowed a bite early preparing to ask, but just then Thurlock looked at him sideways and said, "She mentioned that she thought you were rather gallant."

Embarrassed, Lucky stuffed a biscuit in his mouth and moved on to other questions.

Han said, "What? She has a crush on him?"

"I think she might be a bit smitten," Thurlock said. "Which is good, considering the prophecy."

Lucky wanted to ask his tablemates to back up and explain, but he couldn't get a word in.

"Not going to happen, I think," Han said. "But I won't assume. Anyway, the prophecy just says they'll unite, not marry."

"Oh!" Thurlock looked genuinely surprised—his fork stalled halfway to his mouth with a load of green beans. "Han, I believe you've hit on something. You may turn into a wizard yet!"

"No, thank you."

"Don't talk with your mouth full," Thurlock said. "But seriously—we've all been assuming. Everyone who had reason to consider that prophecy. Yet, you're right. Unity is not the same as marriage."

"Yeah, just ask my sister-in-law."

"Han, we'll steer clear of that subject while Luccan's around."

Finally Lucky could take no more. "Please! Stop talking about me like I'm not here! And if you're talking about some prophecy, and it involves me, maybe you could explain it."

"Not now," said Thurlock, and then added, "Sorry.

"Have another biscuit." Han held out the basket.

If Lucky had been thinking, he would have refused on principle, but his taste buds definitely wanted the biscuit, and they overruled his brain. He was still troubled, though. Instead of trying to get the two men to tell him what they were talking about, he decided to ask questions they might answer. He asked, "What about Maizie?"

"We don't know," Thurlock answered.

"My knife?"

"Missing," Han said, and then, preempting further questions, "and by the time I got back to the field, Mordred and his poor brother were gone, and no one else was around either."

Lucky became thoughtful, and aside from the scrape of silverware and polite requests to pass the pepper or the butter or the beans, they ate in silence for some time. Han seemed focused wholly on his plate, but Lucky could feel the wizard's eyes on him. He tried to ignore it, but when Thurlock cleared his throat and placed his fork at the edge of his plate, Lucky stopped eating too.

Thurlock said, "You have more questions."

It was true; Lucky did have more he wanted to ask, although these were questions that made him nervous. He took a huge gulp of water to wash down the beef and drown his nerves. He decided to start with generalities. "What is that black stuff?"

"Black stuff?"

"I don't know how to describe it… smoke? I saw it in the ravine today, and I saw it before, during the storm here, in your house."

Han raised his eyebrows, nodded vigorously to Thurlock. "It's just like I said, sir. He *sees*. Didn't I tell you?" He shook pepper over his potatoes and gravy with self-satisfied emphasis.

"All right, so you told me. How would I have known?" Thurlock stopped to sneeze, and then said through a wad of purple hanky, "You're the mind reader."

"And I'll wager he sees a lot more than that. He's got the Sight. And no, frankly, I've had very little success reading his mind except when he's calling me. He's blocking it already, I'm sure of it."

"With no training?"

"I'm as amazed as you, but he seems to be—"

"I seem to be what? What sight? You're doing it again, talking about me like I'm not here!" The house became very silent at Lucky's words, and then Thurlock and Han stumbled over each other trying to apologize.

"We're used to being alone," Han finally explained. "The Sight," he said. "You could probably describe it better than me. What you want to know is where it comes from, whether you can control it, and what you're seeing when it's working. Am I right?" He waited for Lucky's nod.

"It's a talent, like my thought reading. You can learn to call it up, to refine it, and to shut it down. As to what you're seeing…." Han paused for thoughtful lip chewing. "You're looking beneath what's usually visible, like lifting a veil, seeing the nature of things." He shrugged and flashed a brief smile. "Maybe Thurlock can tell you more."

"No, that was well said. But Luccan, you asked about the 'black stuff.'"

"I did, sir."

"Not sir, to you, just Thurlock." He sat back in his chair, pulling at his beard, and then launched into a discourse explaining what Lucky saw as "black stuff" in terms of Earth science, which he hoped Lucky would better understand.

But when the wizard had finished comparing the ghostly, swirly substance to a black hole with a personality that could break itself into pieces, appear in many places at once, and act through others' minds and bodies, and then concluded by saying it was really a god whose name was Mahl, Lucky just sat staring.

Han got up and brought back a huge, sugar-dusted apple pie. He hummed as he quarried them each a huge slab.

Lucky couldn't think of any way to ask for more information about the black-hole-god-thing-Mahl that wouldn't involve the word *evil*, which sounded far too melodramatic. So when Thurlock asked if he had more questions, he decided to ask the one that had lodged itself in his brain the moment he'd first lain eyes on the subject, that afternoon in the ravine.

"That man," he said, "Lohen Chiell. Who is he, and how does he know my name?"

No one answered, unless the sadness in Han's eyes or the concern in Thurlock's could be taken as reply. Lucky opened his mouth to repeat the question and insist on an answer, but the words froze in his throat when a howl of canine bloodlust shattered the peace.

Lucky jumped up and flew to the wide front window, where he got a clear view of scarlet-rimmed eyes and slavering jaws. Although he imagined teeth ripping his throat, he shot toward the door to rush to Maizie's aid—again. This time the wizard clamped an iron hand on his arm, holding him back, and Han flew past them, headed outside.

An instant later, the Black Blade's song—the strange sound Lucky'd heard in the ravine—hummed through the yard. As abruptly as Maizie's howls had started, they ceased. Her claws scratched against the boards of the porch, and Lucky heard her heavy breathing as she ran toward the road.

The blade's hum faded into the dusk.

Lucky turned away from the window and started up the stairs to go to his room, completely disheartened. Maizie had fled, and with her the time for questions.

CHAPTER SIXTEEN: A LESSON FROM OPHIUCHUS'S SERPENT

AS COZY as Lucky felt wrapped in his new/old plaid blanket, as grateful as his bones were to be snuggled up warm and relaxed, his eyes wouldn't close. He lay awake in the normal bed in the ordinary moonlit room on the second floor of Thurlock's house for what seemed like forever. Thoughts rushed by, drained away, hit the uptake, and ran again, like water in a recycling fountain.

He kept replaying the scene at the table, and he couldn't stop thinking about that last question, the one he hadn't asked again after Maizie had come and gone. Who was that man? He racked his brain, trying to think of a time when they'd met before that day, some way to explain why the man would know him—and even know his real name.

And, in case that didn't disturb him enough, he thought about what Thurlock had said in his tower. Crazy things that never should have been spoken in a room bright with sunlight and smelling of oranges and chocolate. "Time is against us… shorter than we knew." The words echoed back and forth in Lucky's skull—left brain, right brain, left, right—always getting scrambled in the middle but meaning the same frightening thing on every repetition.

He flopped onto his stomach, irritated. *How am I supposed to sleep with that going on in my head?* He flipped onto one side, and then back onto the other, but no matter which way he twisted, his brain cells refused to leave off playing Ping-Pong with worries about time and stars, and Maizie gone mad, and the Key of Behliseth, and a sassy girl some people apparently thought he should *marry*, and stone knives, and muscled-up twins, and a bunch of other stuff that didn't really make sense.

"And," Lucky added out loud, "a scarred man with one eye who had one of the knives, carried off the girl, controlled Maizie, seemed to know Han, and called me Luccan….

"So much for sleep," he finished. He rolled out of bed, hopped around until he managed to untangle himself from the sheets, hiked up Thurlock's pajamas, and left the room.

He went to seek the wizard's counsel, but that required getting to his door. At the uppermost landing of the stairs, Lucky found his way blocked by a small mountain glowing in silver light shining from above. He stood wondering whether to go around or climb over until he realized the whistling wind was only Thurlock's slow breathing, and the mountain was only the wizard's robe-covered knees. In the small space of the landing, Thurlock lay on his back with his knees drawn up and his hands clasped over his chest.

"Welcome."

The wizard's voice was quiet, but as always it filled the entire space between Lucky's ears. Startled off-balance, Lucky teetered on the very edge of the top step, listing dangerously backward. Not seeming to hurry at all, Thurlock reached out a hand and latched on to the cloth of Lucky's borrowed pajamas at the knee. It steadied Lucky until he regained his balance.

"Welcome," the wizard said again, "to my observatory."

Lucky peered up into the space he was sure had been occupied by an ordinary, boring ceiling the last time he was there. He saw a wide circular glass dome and behind it a sheet of star-filled midnight, so brilliant and close that Lucky reached up a hand, half expecting to pluck stars like picking berries. "Thurlock," he asked, "what are you doing?"

"I'm stargazing, of course."

"All this weird stuff going on and you're staring at the sky." It wasn't until every one of those sarcastic words had escaped his mouth that Lucky remembered he was talking to a wizard who could broil him with a thought. And he'd never thought of himself as rude, anyway. He mumbled, "Sorry."

Thurlock let silence hang between them in the dark, but when finally he spoke, his words seemed formed around a smile. "I learn a lot this way. Sometimes things that will be important begin in the heavens. At other times heavenly bodies shed new light on old puzzles or open our eyes to new possibilities." He shifted to one side of the landing, making room. "Would you care to join me?"

Lucky breathed, wiped his sweating palms on his borrowed pajamas, and stepped over Thurlock's middle to the space the wizard had cleared for him on the floor. Lowering himself to sit, he asked, "How do you know what's important in all those lights?"

Thurlock shook with quiet laughter. "You do have a way of asking the right questions, young man. That's the problem with stargazing, exactly."

Lucky shoved his hair out of his eyes and then spread himself on the floor alongside Thurlock. He felt like a dwarf next to the wizard and foolish for having attempted to chastise him.

He asked, "Why am I acting so strange lately?" He didn't explain. He figured the wizard would know what he meant.

"That," Thurlock said, "is another right question." After a pause during which Lucky heard him rasping at his beard, he went on. "Probably, it has several right answers. You are fifteen, first of all, and people do act in ways that defy explanation around that age."

Without thinking, Lucky clicked his tongue, dismissing that idea as rubbish.

"Though typically," Thurlock went on, "they refuse to admit it." He raised his arms to put his hands behind his head, in the process smacking Lucky with an elbow. "Sorry. Close quarters, eh?"

After he settled back again, he said, "Also, it's been a shock—all that's happened to you in the last few days." In a sudden rush of movement, he thrust a twisted finger at the heavens. "There. Do you see it?"

Lucky had looked at that spot before the wizard pointed. A burst of light had caught his eye, followed by a cluster of falling traces like fading fireworks. "Meteor shower."

"So it would seem, Luccan, but"—he came down hard on that word and repeated it—"but, there are no meteor showers to be seen in that part of the sky at this time of year. Look at the sky around the bursting lights. There is the constellation Sagittarius to one side, Scorpio to the other, and Ophiuchus, the Serpent Holder, standing above. Where those falling stars are, up until just seconds ago, Ophiuchus's foot was there. It's as though the Scorpion stung him with its tail and smashed the foot to bits."

"Wait… Thurlock, is this for real? I mean, stars don't do that, right?"

"Well no, of course not. Or maybe. I suppose it depends on how you look at it."

Lucky snorted, deciding he wasn't likely to get a straight answer. "Well, then, what does it mean?"

"Hm. That's more to the point, but I haven't a clue. I would guess, though, that the Serpent Holder feels about like you do, like your feet have been knocked from under you. It'll be interesting to see whether he keeps his balance and keeps the snake under control.

"And then too," Thurlock said as the light show faded, "there have been spells."

"Spells?"

"Yes, of course. That woman you've seen a few times, the unattractive one, her name is Isa. She's a witch. Quite a powerful one at the moment. She's done a crafty job with her spells, these past days, and I suspect that has influenced your behavior."

"I never thought it was for real."

"What?"

"Evil witches."

"Oh, there are evil witches all right, though certainly not all witches are evil. Your mother—since you've remembered her a little, I think I can tell you this—your mother is a wonderful witch. Her name, by the way, is Liliana."

Thinking about his mother reminded Lucky of his dream, the one he'd had that afternoon when he'd slept off his terror under the chandelier. "Elieth, you said it's another name? Is Suth Chiell my last name, then?"

"No, no. It's a title. We don't use last names in Ethra the way they are used in most places here in Earth. But, on your mother's side, if it's of interest to you, your family name is Ol'Karrigh, the same as mine."

"What about on my father's side?"

"On your father's side," the wizard said softly, "you are a descendant of the Drakhonic family line, like Han."

Lucky lay silently beside the old man for so long that his eyelids half closed and Thurlock's long, steady breaths almost lulled him into sleep. Then something flashed in the sky, a brilliant light cutting across the handle of one of the Dippers. "Is that a satellite, do you think?"

"Hmm," Thurlock considered, tilting his head. "That, or possibly a dragon."

Lucky laughed before he realized it wasn't a joke. "You mean… are dragons real?"

"In some worlds."

"Ethra?" Lucky hadn't said the word before, and it felt both strange and familiar on his tongue. Thurlock grunted in a way that seemed affirmative, and Lucky asked, "Do they breathe fire?"

"The green ones do," Thurlock said, "quite a lot of it. And they're the biggest, too, about the size of City Hall."

Lucky just barely stopped himself from asking if they hoarded treasure and had jewel-encrusted underbellies. He was getting off track. "Sometime, will you tell me more?"

"Sometime, but that isn't what you came up here to talk about. What would you ask next?"

"I must have other names."

"Why do you say that?"

"You asked me, that first night, if I remembered any more of them. Plural."

Thurlock laughed and raised two hands to shoo away a thickening silver mist that had gathered in the hall. "Stardust," he explained. "Useful, but it's a nuisance for visibility." He wiped his hands on his knees, causing his robes to glitter. "Not much gets by you, does it, my boy? You're right, you have more names. The third is Perdhro. It was passed on to you from your mother's mother's father, I believe."

"Luccan Elieth Perdhro? That's my whole name?"

"No."

"What else."

"I don't know, more is the pity."

Though he knew no one could see it in the dark, Lucky rolled his eyes at that answer. Then he scratched roughly at his scalp, considering his choices. He could either try to figure out what to ask to get the wizard to explain his answer, or just let the whole thing go. As tired as Lucky was, the choice made itself. That line of questioning had reached a dead end.

Pointing up as another light streaked across the sky, Lucky asked, "Dragon?"

"Jet."

"It's a title, you said."

"Jet?"

"Suth Chiell. What… what exactly is a Suth Chiell?"

"I'll show you," Thurlock answered. "Scoot up." He did so himself, propping his back against the wall. When Lucky sat beside him, the wizard pointed his right index finger toward the far wall, and a square of light appeared there, as if from a projector. Color swirled and then composed itself into a picture, a full-length portrait.

"There," Thurlock said. "There's a Suth Chiell right there. Lustrex was his name, poor man."

The man looked old-fashioned and a bit stuffy, to Lucky's mind, but on his head he wore a burnished circlet of pale metal, with a flashing jewel set in the center. Lucky's eyebrows shot up when he saw that the Suth Chiell Lustrex also wore a Key around his neck, either the same one Lucky had or another just like it. And Lucky's knife, the amber one, was sheathed at his belt. Many questions and observations vied for Lucky's tongue just then, but in the end he said, "I don't have a crown like that." He felt silly to have said it, but Thurlock didn't laugh.

"Yet," the wizard said.

"Uh… can't you tell me what this Suth Chiell thing is all about?"

"I could. No reason why I couldn't. But before I do you'd better be sure you really want to know. No," he said, then stopped to wave a hand at the portrait, which promptly disappeared. He lay back down flat in the starlight. "No," he continued. "Don't get all upset because I said that. I can practically feel you rolling your eyes.

"The thing is, Luccan, the more you know about what it means to be Suth Chiell, the more you will feel compelled by your nature to live up to the responsibilities. The requirements of the office are both grave and great, for many people will come to depend on you. To do those duties honorably and well, you must have strong faith in the truths of your own heart.

"Before you ask me to tell you more, ask yourself, are you ready, truly, to live up to that? Are you prepared to examine your heart at every turn and act, for the welfare of others, on what you find there?"

Lucky had it in mind to say, *I wouldn't have asked if I didn't want the answer.* But his native caution flashed warning signs, and he took a lesson from Han, biting his lip to stop the words. *I'm not*, he admitted, startled at the truth of it. *I'm not ready. I can't even take care of myself now that the world's gone whacky. How could I possibly take on responsibilities that are "grave and great"?*

"No." He couldn't hear himself over the pounding of his heart, but he must have said it aloud. Thurlock relaxed beside him and gave him a familiar, comforting squeeze on the ankle.

Lucky lay down and let his thoughts drift until the floor began to get noticeably harder, at which point he thought about leaving for the soft bed in his room on the second floor of Thurlock's house.

"He's your father, Luccan."

"What," Lucky said, reaching up to finger the jewel in his nonexistent crown, "Lustrex?"

Thurlock snorted as if he thought the question was more ridiculous than the rest of the conversation. "No, not Lustrex. Lohen Chiell. You asked who he was and how he knew your name."

Lucky's eyes burned suddenly, and he wondered if he could be allergic to stardust. Once he could safely speak, he tried to ask everything at once. "What does he…? Why did he…? Where… Thurlock?"

"Easy, Luccan. I'll tell you a little. I wish I could believe it would make you happy. It won't, but you'll want to know, and as Han—may Behl bless his scolding tongue—reminded me, you have a right to the information. Here, get up. Come sit with me. Nobody wants to hear these kinds of things lying down."

The wizard stood, snapped his fingers, and the stars went out. The door to the tower room swung open before them and the lamps flamed to welcome them. Lucky followed Thurlock to the small space before the hearth, and when the old man dropped into one of the chairs, he took the other. He felt so at home, for once, that without thinking he tucked his bare feet up on the seat cushion.

Thurlock wagged a finger, and rainbow flames crackled in the hearth, but even the warmth in the wizard's voice didn't stop the chill that raced down Lucky's spine upon hearing his first few words.

"The truth is, Luccan, your father left you a long time ago. You were very small—four, maybe five years old the last time he came home for any meaningful length of time. He was a troubled man, had been for years, and he fell into some bad ways. We thought…. This will be hard to hear," he said and reached a hand across the intervening space to squeeze Lucky's shoulder. "We thought he had killed himself."

Lucky drew in a breath that shook audibly. He wasn't sure why those words punched him in the stomach, but it hurt. Some people had tried to say the same about Hank George. That had nothing to do with Lucky's father, but somehow it did.

He was grateful for Thurlock's silence. He needed a moment to think. He tried to remember everything about the man he'd seen in the ravine that day. He saw his hand wrapped around the Knife, his scars, his blind eye. He heard the man say his name. What did that expression on his misshapen face mean?

"Your father has always been a dangerous man, Luccan. He hasn't always been mean, or bad, or on the wrong side. But he's always been dangerous."

Lucky recalled Lohen Chiell's dragging left leg, and at the same time the way he'd fought through the Black Cloaks, and the incredible ease with which he'd hefted L'Aria over his shoulder. The wizard's words sunk in.

"And he remains dangerous, withered limbs and all."

Lucky swallowed. "Thurlock, should I be afraid of him?"

"The fact is, I don't yet know."

The silence that followed did not separate Lucky from Thurlock. If anything, Lucky felt himself draw, in spirit, closer to the old man. He'd asked his questions; he'd received answers. He didn't like what he'd heard, but that didn't seem as important as he would have guessed.

They sat in the comfort of the wizard's room long enough for Lucky to feel at peace.

The chimes of Thurlock's clock on the mantel downstairs rose through the chimney, striking twelve. "Ah," the wizard said, yawning, "it's already tomorrow. How do you feel now, young man?"

"Sleepy," Lucky answered, surprised by it. He rose, flashed a smile, and headed out the tower room door, mumbling thanks and good night.

Words followed him on the stairs, whisper-soft but close and clear.

"Spells and stars," the wizard said. "Lost fathers, and being fifteen—those things are reasons, Luccan, never excuses. Ophiuchus has lost a foot, but I expect him to keep a firm hold on his serpent. You've lost many of the things a young person usually leans on, yet I expect you to find your balance. Act carefully, be wise, and trust your heart to know your friends. Even more than others, Suth Chiell, you cannot afford poor choices."

CHAPTER SEVENTEEN: A FAREWELL CUP FOR UNCLE HAN

LUCKY STOOD at his bedroom window, listening to the faint shuffling sounds the wizard made in his tower three stories up and wondering if there was something he should be doing. Across the yard, Han's little white house gleamed under a blue sky that felt impossible. Lucky pushed up on the window, and it readily opened wide. He took it for a sign, slid out, and made his way down the maple.

Han's front door swung open before he knocked. Han stood square-shouldered in the flat yellow light of late morning, his unstrung bow resting in his hands. Behind him, sword and shield glittered from the wall.

"You don't have to knock," he said. "Just come in."

"I thought it would be locked."

"It's always locked," Han laughed. "But you can always come in anyway."

He must have seen Lucky's eyes steal to the bow in his hands. "Tell me, lad," he said, eyebrows arched, "as far as you remember, have you ever shot a bow?"

Not much later, they gathered up arrows and filled a small pack with apples, cheese, and canteens of water for breakfast. Han showed Lucky how to position the quiver at his shoulder for easy reach and dropped in a bundle of yellow arrows with bright pink feathers.

"It's so you can find them easily," he said.

Lucky pointed to the other arrows, the ones with feathers patterned like fire. "What about these?"

"They're flame arrows. When they strike their target, they ignite, and they burn much hotter and stronger than ordinary fire. The birds who give the feathers are rare, and the arrows have to be enchanted one at a time by a wizard. Usually apprentices do it, but the three with golden shafts and feathers were done by Thurlock. We never use flamers for practice."

Han led him to a small valley just over the hill from Thurlock's place, where a streamlet flashed in the sun. The grass was as green as the banks of Black Creek. The sky stretched shoulder to shoulder, a wide blue field with one woolly cloud grazing near the horizon.

Lucky stopped in his tracks. *It's too beautiful.* "How could a day like this happen, right now?"

Han seemed to know what he meant. "Sometimes, it's coincidence," he said. "There might be an hour of quiet in the middle of a battle, a week of peace in a year-long war." He glanced up to where Thurlock's tower loomed against the blue sky, chewing his bottom lip.

"I suspect this is different, though. I'd bet Thurlock's clock the old man bought us a little time so we can rest. Or maybe to keep us out of his hair. Either way, it probably cost him dear." His eyes dropped sideways to meet Lucky's, full of his sudden smile, and he gave Lucky's shoulder a squeeze. "It won't last, but we'd be ingrates if we didn't enjoy it while we had the chance."

When Han showed him how to string the bow, Lucky thought *Simple enough.* But when he tried to do it, he discovered he had three feet and two left hands. Han stopped him, patient, but perhaps teasing just a little. "To start with," he said, "you've got your feet backward. This one goes behind the bow, that one in front, so you can bend it toward you. Equally important, you've got to hook the string to the bottom end before you start."

It was humbling.

But once Lucky had managed stringing the bow, practice draws went well, and Han said, "You're stronger than you look, lad." The praise patched Lucky's pride, and he smiled even after his first arrow fell from the string and bounced off his toe.

They followed the stream's green twists down through the foothills, away from people and houses and roads. They took turns shooting at long-abandoned wasp hives and bird nests, a few rotting hay rolls, hollow logs, and once a cracked blue bucket. Han always made his shot in a single fluid motion, "Look, draw, release." And he never missed.

Thurlock's tower stayed in view, a constant reminder, but they were clear of its shadow, and they didn't talk about trouble at all until late afternoon. They retrieved arrows, and Han congratulated Lucky.

"Look," he said, "you've got a nice grouping here. It means you're consistent. That's good, because then you know what to fix." Shouldering the bow, he said, "We'll work on that next time. For now we'd best get back. If I keep you out here any longer, the wizard will likely skin me alive."

Lucky stopped abruptly, staring at Thurlock's square-eyed tower.

Han stopped too, and turned to him with one eyebrow cocked. "Figure of speech, lad."

"It's not that," Lucky said, running two hands through his hair. "It's just… everything's so crazy."

Kindness and sorrow mingled in Han's voice. "It is," he said, "and I expect it will get crazier."

AFTER DINNER, Han went back to his own little house alone. With no lights on, the tile in his neat, tiny kitchen shone with a slow gleam reflecting a half-moon sky. Han leaned a hip against the counter, looking out the open window into the summer night and fingering the runes marking his bow. The touch took him back to his youth, and the memory of woodsmoke tickled his nose.

"You've made a beautiful bow," Lohen had said. "Let's not take chances. Burn the runes in, instead of carving; it will keep the fibers strong." He could still feel Lohen's rough hand fall on his shoulder. "You're going to be a powerful man, Han. You'll need a worthy weapon."

The memory had remained fresh; he relived it with the first arrow he nocked every time he used the bow. That time with his brother had been a rare day. Like today with Luccan. Respite in troubled times.

He leaned on the tiles of his countertop to gaze up at Thurlock's tower, all its windows ablaze as the wizard doggedly pursued answers to impossible questions far into the night. Suddenly, in the dark patch above the roof's peak, silvery lights burst and then blossomed like faraway fireworks. "Falling stars," Han said, trying out the words Thurlock had told him Earthborns used to describe the phenomenon. "Though scientifically," the old man had explained, "they're meteors."

"No." Han shook his head and then named them as Ethrans always did. "Wizard's tears."

Thurlock had not slept more than a few hours in three days. He hadn't left his tower all day except once to fetch a book and once to quiz Luccan on the progress of his memory, which had taken little time and left the lad nervous and the wizard disappointed. Han had left trays laden with sweet tea and the old man's favorite foods—even maple bars—by Thurlock's closed door. When he picked them up again hours later, cold and untouched, he worried.

Now, Han filled a tall amber glass with water from his kitchen tap. He drank deeply, washing down his anxiety. *I'll find out soon enough what's troubling the old man.* He put the glass down and started to turn, but glanced across the yard to the tower one last time. From the wizard's high window, a square of paper drifted down like an autumn leaf, and then came to rest in the grass afloat on moonlit dew.

By the time Han crossed the yard to pick it up, his sandaled feet were wet and cold. "Come upstairs, Han," the message read. "Now. We need to talk." Han raised his eyebrows, reflecting on the wizard's penchant for the theatrical.

Since Han had last seen it the previous day, Thurlock had transformed his tower into a fire hazard. Ancient Ethran charts papered the walls, many now spotted yellow with sticky notes. The wizard adored sticky notes. He'd also developed a fondness for broad-tipped markers in rainbow hues, which explained the feast of color amongst the heaps of paper crowding floor, table, and every flat surface.

Books five inches thick perched where they could, open to dog-eared, underlined pages. Hovering over a few of these tomes, golden lights with no visible source of energy or support scanned the print, placing an arrow here, a question mark there, turning the pages as if with a wet finger. None of what he saw was new to Han. He'd just never seen so much of it at one time. "What's happened, sir?"

Thurlock's spectacles hung at the very end of his nose, and he looked over their tops at Han. "Nothing new has happened at all." He walked over to the table and riffled around, digging to the bottom of the centermost heap. He extracted a page, paced back and forth along the only clear path in the floor three times, then put the paper on the table unexamined and laid his glasses atop it. He palmed his eyes, sad or weary or both. "Sit down," he said.

Han did so—and waited.

Thurlock opened his mouth several times as if to speak but only cleared his throat. Finally he rolled his eyes, reached a magically gloved hand into the fire, and hefted the kettle to pour water over the instant cocoa in two cups. Taking a seat before the hearth, he asked, "Luccan's okay?"

Han knew that wasn't the question the wizard had been building up to, and he almost said so but thought better of it. Relaxing into the other armchair, he crossed an ankle over the opposite knee and took a thumb to a scuff on his sandal. "He seems fine, had a quiet day." He took the cup Thurlock offered, meeting his eyes. "Thank you," he said, referring to more than cocoa. "I think he's starting to trust me."

"An uncle's just reward." Thurlock smiled gently.

Han matched the smile with a sad one of his own. "I suppose; but he still doesn't remember?"

"Getting close, I think," Thurlock answered.

Han asked, "Did you see what he brought out of the attic?"

"No, I was working. I meant to ask—"

"That old blanket he had when he was a baby—the red plaid."

This time Thurlock smiled thoroughly enough to crinkle his eyes.

Han grinned back. "He took it with him to bed!" In his mind's eye, he could still see a copper-toned two-year-old trailing that same blanket everywhere he toddled.

Soon the smiles slipped off both their faces. In the golden light, Han felt Thurlock's gaze on him, and he decided to make things easier. "Do you want me to leave tonight, sir?"

Thurlock snapped his fingers at each of the magical lights around the room, killing all the flames but one. In shadow, the wizard's face looked somber. "Morning will be soon enough, my friend," he said. "Come an hour before dawn, if you would. We'll share a Farewell Cup?"

BY THE time Han left Thurlock's tower, time had crept close to midnight. He yawned as he started down the stairs. Busy mulling over all Thurlock had said, the creak of a footstep on the stairs startled him. He looked up and froze, his own foot halfway between one riser and the next. For a painful moment he mistook the shadowed face looking up from the landing for his brother's, so similar was its shape.

Until Luccan spoke. "You're going to leave."

Han stood mute, blinking.

Luccan said it again. "You're leaving."

"Yes," Han answered, but he didn't try to explain everything Thurlock had told him before he'd left the tower room—about time compressing in some places and stretching in others, wormholes in the fabric of the worlds, reversing poles, shrinking Vortices, and uncertain endings. He didn't understand it, anyway.

He did understand that Black Creek Ravine had become a deadly place, and that someone had to go there and do what could be done about it, but he didn't say that, either. He didn't explain that he remained the only someone who might do the job. He didn't tell his nephew that, having chosen long ago, he couldn't be anything but Han Shieth, Wizard's Left Hand, now that need had arisen.

He especially didn't tell Luccan that the wizard had plans for him, too.

He only said, "It's important, lad."

Luccan's whisper quivered. "Don't go."

Han caught his lip between his teeth, afraid to try to speak.

"Or let me go with you."

Han had no answer.

Luccan looked at him for a long time, his young face growing hard, his dry eyes gleaming in the blade of moonlight that slashed the stairwell. Han remained silent and still until Luccan turned and closed the door of his room firmly between them. They hadn't said farewell.

TWO HOURS before dawn, a cool spear of moonlight pierced Han's eyes and woke him from a dream of dragons, swords, and drums. He sat up sweating, gaze darting to the corners of his familiar room, furnished only with the bed and a single stand, which held a small chest and a green-glass reading lamp. In accord with habit, Han had left the white walls free of decoration save for a crest above the light switch, three inches high and five across. A flame eagle.

Wrought of sun-metal, its fiery breath curled over its head like a wreath. A shock of arrows rode in the grip of its talons, and its wings were spread. The tip-most flight feathers each ended in a blade. This was the crest of Behlishan's Guard, the premier infantry of Ethra's Sunlands. Among them, Han had become the most premier of all. He'd chosen a warrior's path at nineteen, quite young by Ethran standards. From his point of view it had been easy to choose, and since then he'd never doubted, never once answered a call to arms with reluctance or regret.

Until last night, no one had ever asked him not to go.

Han shook away the troubling memory of his midnight encounter with Luccan and set about his preparations.

Dawn was barely a hint in the east when he stepped into Thurlock's room, but hearth and candle gave sufficient light to see that Thurlock had restored the tower to order. Han knew the wizard had seen to the cleanup for his sake.

In his honor, Thurlock had closed his books and stacked them, rolled his charts and tied them, gathered his papers and bound them in portfolios with neatly penned titles. Han valued order, and because the wizard valued him, he'd spelled the windows spotless, chased dust from the mantel, made the bed, buffed the floor, and laid straight the rugs beside his bed and hearth. Han loved beauty and color, so Thurlock's flames threw sparks that bloomed into lilies and roses; red, orange, and gold to mirror the blossoms filling the green vase centered on the table.

Beside the vase dwelled two earthenware cups without handle or stem and a slender bottle half-filled with the amber liquid known as Shahna's Gold, elixir of the Farewell Cup.

Warriors and wizards of Ethra did not take the Farewell Cup lightly. By tradition, it cleared the mind and shored up the heart for battle. By tradition, it assured that friends would be united when the fighting was done. By tradition, any cause would be thwarted if the Farewell Cup was shared by hearts not allied in peace and united in purpose.

Thus, when Thurlock stood in crisp robes, silver hair newly tied, and asked if he should pour, Han said, "Not just yet, sir. Please, sit with me by the fire?"

Han had things he would like to say, but they would be fruitless, he knew. Why tell Thurlock he didn't want to go? Why say that leaving Luccan, after the boy had pleaded with him to stay, was just too hard? He couldn't beg to be excused.

He'd come knowing that, fit for the mission. His hair was tight in a topknot; a sun-metal band protected his brow. He wore the uniform of Behlishan's Guard: kilted sun-cloth tunic over breeches banded under the knee; sash and belt of dragonhide fitted to secure weapons, provisions, and kit; shin-strapped sandals of pliable, durable, northern sealskin.

He sat in Thurlock's armchair and sank his teeth into his lip, said nothing, and tried to think of the greater good, to bring his heart into harmony with the needs of the moment, and with the wizard—who wasn't to blame.

In the end, after a silence so long the sun passed through dawn and on to the breakfast hour, Thurlock said, "You are the only one I can send. You won't be abandoning the boy, Han Shieth."

"Do you think he will come to understand that, sir?"

"I hope so."

Han got up suddenly and—for lack of a meaningful destination—went to the door and let Lemon Martinez in to curl up on the hearthstones. "It's getting late, sir," he said. "Orders?"

Thurlock let out a sigh heavy enough to jostle his magic flames. "Do what you can to hobble the witch," he said. "Try to disable whatever tools she's got on the loose in that ravine. The things I've discovered in my studies these last few days.... I believe she knows these things. Her window of opportunity is closing too, and she's desperate."

The wizard stood and began to pace in the small space before the hearth, curving around Han, who stood motionless in his path. "As long as she thought she had plenty of time, she would have done what she could to keep him alive as long as possible. The longer he would live under her control, the more of his strength she could steal, and the more effectively she could utilize it. But now...."

He stopped, pivoting to meet Han's eyes, standing silent until his swaying robes fell still. "She'll make a move, soon. If she takes him and can't subvert him quickly, she'll use faster means to extract what power she can from him. In that case, he won't long survive."

Their eyes remained locked for a long moment. Then Han nodded, and Thurlock turned to sag against the mantel. "I'll do what I can to prepare Luccan, and I'll try... I'll take him home. I'll come back and join you here as soon as I can.

"Meanwhile, try to find the Blades. Help the dog, for kindness sake, if you find her and you can." The old man paused, and his eyes softened. "And, whatever it might mean at this point, you'll have to deal with your brother."

A SOLITARY bird sang outside Lucky's window, but he lingered on a gold-lit island midway between sleep and wakefulness. Red-and-yellow plaid lay close to his face, blurring in his half-open eyes, and the fabric's softness soothed his cheek. With two hands he clutched the blanket by its silk-bound edge. He let his eyes close again, and in that instant he saw other hands clutching that same shiny binding.

There had been four strong hands holding four corners, lifting the blanket to toss a small boy—screaming with delight—toward the sun. The colors of the plaid swirled around young Luccan as he'd fallen laughing back onto the brushed wool, then he'd flown again into the joy of blue sky. The two men had laughed with him, and the sound had echoed from distant cliffs.

Lucky sat up in his bed in Thurlock's house, scarcely breathing. He hugged the blanket tight to his chest and closed his eyes, afraid to lose the picture in his mind. He was awake; it was not a dream, now; it was a memory.

Four brown hands had held the blanket, two men. One man was his father, but that face he couldn't see. The other face belonged to his uncle, Han Shieth.

Blanket flying behind him like the cape of a low-budget superhero, Lucky crashed up the stairs. He lifted his fist to bang on the wizard's door, but it swung open at his first touch, and he tripped on the leg of his pajamas—the wizard's pajamas—and fell through. On his way to the floor, his vision swept past Han's sword and bow leaning against the wall, and as he picked himself up, he saw Han, warrior-clad and rock-strong. An unfamiliar pride welled in his chest. He let it explode in a shout.

"Uncle Han!"

For once, he must have taken both men by surprise, for they stood in front of the magic fire, staring at him.

Thurlock's open mouth shut itself and then spread into a first-rate smile.

Han's smile played over his lips, cautious. He almost whispered, "You remember, lad?"

Lucky said, quieter, "Uncle Han...." He took a step toward the man, but before he could take another, Han reached him and wrapped him in a hug a bear would have envied.

Thurlock said, light in his voice, "Be careful, Han, you'll break him," and Lucky secretly agreed. Han only pulled the surprised wizard inside the hug too.

Lucky started to feel like sandwich meat, and said, "Mmmmmppphh." Han let go, laughing, and for a while they all stood at loose ends in front of the fire. Lucky folded and unfolded his blanket, the cat looked daggers at Lucky and swatted at the cloth, and Han smiled and bobbed his head. Thurlock scratched his beard, mumbling, "Good, very good indeed."

The silence almost felt permanent, until Lucky said, "You're leaving now, Uncle Han."

"I am, but believe, lad, this isn't good-bye."

Thurlock said, "It's necessary, Luccan."

Lucky pushed his hair back, then crossed his arms over his chest and took a firm stance much like Han's. He said, "Be careful." Both men seemed to breathe easier.

Han gave Lucky a nod and a smile. "I'll do my best."

"Join us," the wizard said, "for the Farewell Cup," and he told Lucky the story of Shahna, a warrior woman from the mists of Ethra's past, and the liquid gold that had sealed her oath to the flame eagle.

"And so," he finished, "we take a cup of Gold together, at partings like these. It's tradition."

Lucky stepped up to join in the toast, and Thurlock conjured a third earthenware cup. He poured and passed out the drinks. He had lifted his own cup and seemed about to say something more, something profound, but Han interrupted.

"Don't you think it might be a little… fiery… for him, sir?"

"Oh! Well, yes. Sorry." He tapped the side of Luccan's cup and smiled. "All taken care of," he said. "No stronger than apple juice."

The wizard's toast didn't seem so profound after all. "Here's to a good end," he said.

Lucky agreed heartily with the sentiment, but found that even without its flame, Shahna's Gold tasted bittersweet.

CHAPTER EIGHTEEN: A YOUNG PERSON'S GUIDE TO MAKING SENSE OF IT

AT BREAKFAST, Lucky and Thurlock occupied opposite ends of the dining table and between the two of them polished off six maple bars, two cinnamon rolls, and a half gallon of chocolate milk. Lucky chuckled, thinking *By the time Han comes back we'll both be round, toothless, and stuck in the doors trying to get out for groceries.*

He grinned at the image until Thurlock shattered it. "Brush your teeth," the wizard said, leaning around the chandelier. "Then clean the basement."

Lucky was not unwilling, though for the sake of form he wrinkled his brow and protested as if Thurlock had told him to break all his own toes. Teen angst, Lucky realized, came naturally when living with an adult who assigned chores. Truthfully, he hoped the basement would be like the attic. Maybe he would find some kind of touchstone, something else like the plaid blanket.

The cellar door opened like a vault from a raised concrete frame hidden in the pansies behind a mulberry bush. At the bottom of a flight of narrow stone steps, he found a cavernous space so still he could hear the dust settle. The bare bulb overhead lent a shimmer to the falling particles but otherwise illuminated only four quarry-stone walls, a dirt floor aged as hard as concrete, and the goose bumps prickling Lucky's arms.

Other than dust and air, the space held only a few underfed spiders and a horrendous amount of dirt. Lucky ignored the spiders and attacked the dirt with broom, mop, vigor, and determination, but the effort was doomed. If Lucky swept, the dirt went airborne, then precipitated; if he mopped, it clumped, then dried. He tried wishing it clean, but nothing changed even a tiny bit.

He gave up and sat in the corner to think about Han's departure earlier that day.

Han had said Lucky could walk with him, "To the top of the first hill, no farther." When they'd reached the hilltop, Lucky had stood next to him, knee-deep in gray-green grass, saying nothing until a hot, harsh wind blew from the east and stung his eyes. Then he'd asked, "Will you be gone long?"

Han had shrugged. "Not if I can help it." Chewing his lip, he'd glanced up to where the windows of the wizard's tower winked in the sun. He seemed, for once, at a loss for what to say, but then he caught Lucky's eye. "Remember, I have all of Thurlock's pajamas in my chest of drawers. Don't bother asking him if you need clean ones."

Lucky rolled his eyes, a skill he was getting better at.

Han smiled and stepped away.

"Wait!" Lucky had fidgeted, trying to find words. "Han… uncle… I'm sorry. If I could remember home, we could all go there, and you wouldn't have to do this."

Han had stepped back near Lucky, taken his drooping shoulders in his hands, and given them a small shake. "None of this is your fault," he'd said, the gold in his eyes blazing. "And, if you can go home now, I'll be glad because you'll be safe… safer, but there will still be things that have to be done here, and I'll still be the one to stay and do them."

Brief hours later, Lucky sat in the cellar's dust, sneezing, sniffing, and wiping his nose with a neat square of tissue he took from his pocket, wishing he hadn't started thinking about Han. He'd prefer not to think about anything at all; everything in his world had turned strange. Scratching his head angrily, he spoke loud enough to shake dust clouds from the walls. "I just wish I could make sense of it—any of it."

Instantly, Lucky felt a small explosion in his belly. Though he didn't remember passing out, he came to with an aching head and dust coating his eyelashes. His hand, he found, held a miniature book. The title glittered in the dim light, embossed in gilt runes. Though the runes looked as strange as ever, and though Lucky could not account for the sudden knowledge, he knew exactly what they meant.

"*The Revelations Regarding the Suth Chiell in the Last Days of the Mark of the Sun*," he read aloud. He lifted the book to the light to make out the smaller, English print below that. "*A Young Person's Guide to Making Sense of It*."

He read it again, twice. He cracked the book open and popped it shut. His heart had turned to butterflies, and his hands shook. Dare he believe he was holding the answers in his hands? What if he didn't like what he read?

I'll have to take the chance. A shiver ran through him as he opened the book to the first yellowed, onionskin page. *Perhaps tonight I'll be home.*

Yeah, right.

On the first page, in small, plain English typeface, were the words, "In darkest night dwells brightest light." On the second page, "When friends cry, the loyal fly." These were not revelations; they were proverbs—or maybe fortunes from Chinese cookies. Some of them had a nice ring. Lucky especially liked the sound of, "When hope fails, love sails." Still, if they meant anything at all, Lucky had no clue what it might be, and they didn't strike him as momentous. He flipped through the pages, shaking his head, disappointed.

Until he got to the end. The last two facing pages were certainly cryptic, yes. But important. The hints were not subtle.

When Lucky opened to those pages, a choir of voices accompanied by a full symphony orchestra burst forth in a hyper-angelic crescendo. If that wasn't enough, the bold, black typeface was aflame, burning the words into the page as if pressed with a hot iron brand.

"Like Bonanza," Lucky said, remembering Hank's smile every time the reruns came on TV with the Ponderosa brand burning through the map. The flaming words in the book seemed to suggest something like, "See, this can't be all bad."

And, once he'd read the messages, he realized it wasn't bad, not at all. At the top of the second-to-the-last page, the words read, "The broken lamp may yet shield the flame." Lucky didn't know what it meant, but it seemed strong, hopeful, reassuring. Like a parent tucking in a dreaming child, unseen and barely sensed, but a comfort all the same. Lucky breathed deep and, for the moment that fit inside that breath, felt safe.

Halfway down that same page, still-smoking letters read, "A Gateway may be hidden, but never truly closed."

Whatever that means.

As soon as Lucky finished that thought, an asterisk flashed next to the words, and another down at the bottom of the page, followed by this footnote in fine print: "Some scholars, notably Willock III, have argued that this passage refers to the fabled Suth Chiell's Gateway of premodern times." Lucky still had no clue what the words meant, but they seemed to hold out some kind of promise, and his mood continued to rise.

The last words in the book, scrawled large on the final page, were speaking directly to Lucky. Or so he surmised, since he was the Suth Chiell who'd conjured the book. "Though all other hopes should fail," he read aloud, "Suth Chiell, you will prevail."

Feeling the prediction reinforce his backbone, he lifted his eyebrows. "Okay, then," he said in that on-again, off-again deep voice—a man's voice that was starting to sound familiar.

He admitted that it was hard to give full faith to a prediction that burned itself onto a page in a book he'd wished into his hands while cleaning a cellar that didn't exist beneath a wizard's house.

Still, he saw no reason to quibble.

THE GOLDEN globe-shaped handle of Thurlock's umbrella flamed in the sunlight, sparking return flashes from the chandelier's prisms. Thurlock picked it up from the table and let it thump the floor in time with his right foot as he paced behind the table, robes chasing him like a worried dog at his heels. Lemon sat with his back turned, snapping his tail against the floor, clearly disturbed by the wizard's unease.

"Uncle," Liliana said from the M.E.R.L.I.N., "can't you be still? You're making me seasick." She did look ill. Her hair looked brassy, her eyes heavy, and her complexion nearly as pale as snow against the azure wall of her dressing room.

His pacing wasn't causing all that, but he stopped anyway, leaning on the windowsill. He wished he could escape his troubles by climbing out. "Liliana," he said, "I'm worried, more worried than a wizard should ever be."

He came back to stand where he could meet his niece's gaze but, struck by the realization that her capacities were stretched thinner even than his own, he clamped his mouth shut. He'd been on the verge of confiding all his concerns. Now he wondered if it might be better to tell her nothing at all. But she'd be anxious to hear about Luccan, and she had a right to know about Lohen.

"I've sent Han into the ravine," he told her. "I'm not certain what else he'll meet, but I know he'll have to deal with his brother." Thurlock started to pace again. "I've never seen Han so unsure."

Lili ignored the remark about Han's state of mind. "What do you mean, 'deal with' Lohen?"

"Good question. I don't know the answer." Truthfully, Lohen's actions in the ravine, the day he'd charged in on Maizie's heels and then flown to L'Aria's rescue, bewildered Thurlock. He hadn't tried to hurt Luccan or engage Han directly, but Han had said he wasn't 100 percent certain whether Lohen had been part of Mordred's bunch.

"You know Lohen better than anyone, Lili. What do you think he'll do now?"

"When I married him, I never imagined I would say this, but—" Her voice caught in her throat, and she looked away, breathing deeply for a long thirty seconds. When she spoke again, her voice had cleared, and only the white handkerchief she clutched and crumpled told how hard the words came. "Lohen has been troubled and at least a little insane as long as I've known him, but it's different now. He's too far gone."

Her voice fell to a whisper, as if she passed a death sentence. "He's past redemption. Whatever he does next, it won't be good."

Thurlock stroked his beard, as if smoothing its kinks would straighten his thoughts as well. "Lili," he began and then stopped, looking out the window and absently fingering the roundness of his umbrella handle. It began to glow and hum, the disguised staff so much a part of Thurlock that his distress called its magic to the ready.

"Put it down, uncle."

He didn't put it down, but he stilled his fingers and concentrated on thinking as clearly as he could about the threat of Lohen Chiell. *Am I certain*, he asked himself, *that he means harm, that he is, as Lili says, not redeemable? If so, I can stop him, easily enough.* But, in plain words, stopping him meant killing him, and everything that defined Thurlock as a wizard and as a man rebelled.

Liliana broke into his thoughts. "He's beyond hope."

Thurlock raised his gray eyes, steadier now, more certain. "We don't know that."

"He's done horrible things, uncle."

"Some, yes, but not half so many or so horrible as the storytellers make out." He rose from his chair and went to the window again, thumping his umbrella beside him like a cane. "I think that ending up in the service of the witch was the last thing he would have wanted."

"He joined up with her, didn't he?" A bitter laugh punctuated her words.

Thurlock whirled around to face her. "Willingly? You feel sure of that?"

It was less a question than a rebuke. Lili's eyes sparked but she stayed silent, waiting.

Focused on something far off, Thurlock pulled the tie from his hair and shook it out, a silver halo. "A thousand years is a long time to be alive, niece. It gives one a lot of opportunity for mistakes." He fixed his gaze unflinching on Lili's eyes. "The last thing Lohen did that we all knew about was jump into Mardhral Canyon—meaning, I'm sure, to take his own life. Do you know what he did just before that?"

Lili shook her head, mute.

"I do," Thurlock said. "He came to me and asked to join this very mission, to help find Luccan. I couldn't bring myself to trust him. That, I think now, was one of the worst blunders I have ever made."

"Uncle—"

"Hear me out!" Thurlock's face flushed with the heat of impatience. "This is not easy for me to admit, even to myself. As I said, it was a mistake. Yes, bitterness and anger had taken him, but I should have looked deeper." He shook his head in regret. "At the least I should have taken the opportunity to keep him close, where I might have prevented him from doing more harm."

"You couldn't have—"

"I could have, and I should have, but I did not, and he jumped." He worked his jaws around a bitter taste. "While we all thought him dead, I could almost live with it. I told myself that it was better, that his misery was over, that Luccan and Ethra and all of us were safer." His let his eyelids fall closed in a bid for control. When he looked up, only the unstoppable twitch of the tic beneath his eye could have betrayed his remorse.

"Uncle," Liliana pleaded. "He's lost."

"No," he said but then hedged. "Maybe."

"Maybe!" Liliana's wide eyes and shocked tone said clearly she thought his mind had snapped at last.

"Yes," he said—with a bit of sauce. "Yes, maybe, as in perhaps, as in I'm not sure. I've recalled what Han said when I debriefed him about the ravine, about the moment when Lohen called Luccan by his name. He said that his brother's face 'shone as if with hope.'"

Liliana stood silent, twirling a long, golden lock around her forefinger, then sat again at her dressing table, laid her arms on the wood, and rested her head there. After some time, she pushed herself up. "Good day, then, uncle," she said with no trace of emotion. "Keep me posted."

"Wait, child. There's something I want you to do."

With a tired look and a heavy sigh, Lili turned back to Thurlock.

"Talk to your son," the wizard said. "Tomorrow, I'll try to bring him home."

CHAPTER NINETEEN: A STORY OF BROTHERS WITH BLADES

THE JUNE sun was only more punishment to Lohen. He trod the heart of the ravine, the banks of Black Creek, blind to its beauty. The rainbow-flanked fish, the golden lilies, the sun-caught red of a dragonfly—they were no more than a trial to be borne, like the sucking black mud beneath his feet. Anger turned everything ugly, blazed back at the sun from his eye. He hated the rushing demands of rage, but he'd lost all hope that he could stop it.

He had tried. In the chill dawn mist, he'd built a lively fire between the sheltering cedar and the singing creek. The slow healing of his limbs, surely wrought by the Black Blade's touch, had given him hope that his heart could be healed too. That the wrong he'd done could be redeemed. He'd trembled with fear that this slender thread of hope would snap if he tested it, but he'd thought of Luccan and resolved to act.

He'd cleansed the Blade in the flames, bathed in the cold creek, sent up a smoke of cedar and herbs to clear his mind, doing everything he knew to make sure this magic would be unpolluted. "I never meant to hurt my son," he'd said, swearing "by Behl's Light," though it had been so long since that name had passed his lips that the shock of it hurt. He'd repeated the oath until his throat had gone dry.

This would be his last chance at even a small measure of mental peace. This would be his only chance to help his son, the boy whose first word had been "Papa," the boy who'd grown now to the size of a man.

"Make right the last wrong," the Blade had instructed in his dream.

He'd called Maizie, using the magic's hold one last time to compel the dog's obedience. Then, finding a surprise of relief at the kindness of it, he set about doing what must be done, so that he might, as the Blade had promised, begin again. Hours had washed by since he'd countered the hex and released Maizie. He'd set her free, yet she'd followed on his heels every step he took, her eyes alight with devotion.

Nothing else had changed.

In the past few days, Lohen had become stronger, but his face remained a scarred mask; his left eye socket remained an empty pit. The scab where his soul had once tethered still itched and burned deep inside, and his hard-fisted heart still pounded his breastbone demanding, if not justice, at least revenge.

His mind still circled, searching for a word, that single name that might render him worthy once again to be called *Papa*. That secret stayed hidden but a memory surfaced, a memory he'd held submerged for two centuries, the memory of what a soul blacker than his had done.

The stream spoke as it hissed over rocks and choked in the shallows, and the rasping taunt bit into him like a surgeon's saw, slicing bone with every stroke. He tried to shut his ears against the story he heard in the rushing water, the story he hated most. The story of his life, of the day he'd lost his youth, his home, and his hope. The day hate had dug its seed into his heart.

LOHEN SMELLED smoke, striding down the hill toward home. He'd visited Nedhra City, fifty miles from the family's stead. In addition to news and letters for his parents, he carried a gift for his brother's twelfth birthday—a sling that could be wound tight to toss stones an incredible distance. Perfect for a boy who liked both weapons and mechanical things. Lohen looked forward to seeing Han smile when he put it in his hands.

The smoke disturbed his happy thoughts. It didn't have the flavor of a cooking fire or the pungency of the smokes used for curing meat or fish. It was the wrong time of year for the fields to be burned off, and the smell seemed wrong, anyway, dirty—or contaminated. He stopped when he rounded the bend and had a clear view of his parents' stead.

And then he started running.

When he got there, remnants still burned, but only low ridges where the walls of the house had stood, huddled pieces of resistant furniture, and in one place a blazing doorframe leading on both sides to nothing.

The first corpse he saw, as he stood with the heat of flames and coals on his face, was his uncle, an old man whose skill with horses had taken him to work in the far north long ago, and whose devotion to an orphaned girl had reaped him no reward of love. Abandoned in old age, he'd come to stay with his sister's family, bringing a kind face, a sad smile, and grand stories of winged horses and starry northern skies.

He'd not simply been killed, nor had Lohen's mother and father. Everywhere he looked, Lohen saw evidence of torture. He couldn't bear seeing it, but he couldn't look away. He stood, not moving or thinking, until night crept in and the flames around him hissed into silence.

Mindless, Lohen turned and took a step back toward the road, and that was when he heard a faint sound. He followed the breathy cry and found Han hidden in a holly thicket, hugging his knees and sobbing. At first Lohen was only glad, relieved to see him alive. Then the truth dawned, and he fell to his knees, the wind knocked from his lungs by a horrifying new thought.

Han Shieth had seen his family murdered.

Lohen struggled to choke back nausea and pulled Han out of the shelter, shielding him from the holly that tore at his own skin. Ignoring the stink of vomit, he carried Han to the brook where they had fished and played, and where the remains of their parents and uncle were mercifully hidden from sight.

It seemed to Lohen that the stream should run hot with ash, black with filth, or red with blood, but it was cool and clean. In moonlit summer stillness, Lohen bathed his brother's face, cleansed and soothed the fist he must have bitten to keep from screaming, and let Ethra's sweet water wash him clean.

When he'd done all he could, he sat with his back against a willow and held Han under the crook of his muscled arm. He sang their mother's songs in a low, steady voice until Han slept, and then he kept singing until, against all odds, the sun came up.

BY AFTERNOON, glazed with sweat from hot summer sun, Han made the summit of a rocky, thistle-grown ridge to find Lohen in plain sight at the bottom of the descending slope. Unbelievably, Lohen kneeled at Black Creek's edge, choking on sobs and slamming his hands into the rough, pebbled ground again and again. Han's heart rose to his throat when he saw his brother's pain, and without thinking he called out to him.

Lohen leapt to his feet and whirled to face him, grief translated instantly to rage, eye blazing a challenge. He moved swiftly, crashing through thin ranks of trees to claim possession of a level clearing just inside the forest that studded the slope like a rough crust. Feet planted wide, he lifted the Black Blade in an arc over his head and with a word transformed that implement into its alter ego, the Sword of Light.

Han would have to fight, but reluctance born of old love and new pity gripped him like barbed wire shackles. If his life was all he stood to lose, he might have left his sword sheathed and met his brother's blade with bared neck. But the stakes were far higher, and when the wizard had said, "Deal with your brother," he'd made a claim on duty and a warrior's honor.

Before descending the slope, Han laid aside his bow, quiver, and pack, hiding them out of the way of the path. He strapped on his shield and adjusted his knife in the sheath bound to his leg. Then he clipped the two-inch-wide sun-metal circlet on his head, slipping it over the crown piece that made it a fair helmet. All of that took him only seconds.

Finally, he loosened his sword and whispered its name: "Chiell Shan." Child of Light, that meant, and for all that it carried death on its shoulders, Han knew it had always fought for Behlishan. Forged of sun-metal, an alloy with no Earth-made match, the strong, light blade never went brittle though sharpened to an edge so fine it almost could not be seen. It had drawn its first blood in battle over five hundred years ago. Han's grandfather had carried it to war, his great-grandfather before that.

The legendary weapon had rested over the mantelpiece in Han's childhood home. Thurlock had plucked it from the ashes after the fire when Han was twelve and presented it to him when he'd started weapons training at fifteen. The wizard had told him the sword's stories and its name. "Never," Thurlock had said, "use this blade with hatred or vengeance."

When he stepped into the clearing and drew his weapon, it felt good in his hand and the metal rang out a call to duty. Yet even that music, a warrior's song, could not subdue his whispering hope that he and his brother might find another way.

Han stood upslope from Lohen, and that should have given him an advantage. He was stronger, less damaged, and more practiced. His sword had been crafted with magic at the forge, and he knew the weapon better than he knew his own hand. The odds, it would seem, should be in his favor.

But Lohen had put the sinking sun at his back and in Han's eyes. Though shorter in stature, Lohen had always been brawny and tough. Most of what Han knew about fighting, he'd learned first from Lohen. A hunter, not a warrior, yet all of Ethra renowned him for his skill with the blade. And his weapon was not made with magic; it was made of magic. No part of Han was fool enough to think this fight would be easily won.

"Han Shieth," Lohen said when they faced off, his tone casual as though they met for coffee.

"Brother," Han answered, the word sticking in his throat.

Lohen whispered, and indigo light flared along his Blade, pulsing from hilt to tip. The sword looked solid, one instant gleaming like polished iron, the next like blue steel. The light was real; the steel and iron weren't. It didn't matter. Real or illusion, the sword could kill.

Lohen's first savage swing came overhand, meant to cleave bone. Han dropped into a defensive crouch, gripped his sword with two hands, and raised it from his shoulder, sliding Lohen's strike off the flat of his blade. Lohen struck next at Han's left flank, but Han pivoted and blocked with his shield. Shifting his grip, he reversed his sword and smashed the pommel into Lohen's face like an iron fist, crushing skin over bone beneath the empty eye socket. He'd bought a moment to breathe.

Lohen stepped back and swiped his hand over the gash. He glanced at the scarlet smear on his fingers, the red of it like flame, like rage. Then he brought the fight in earnest. Han continued to meet Lohen's ever-faster slashes and thrusts with shield and blade. Once he even knocked away his brother's sword with the back of his hand. He hit the flat of the blade, but still the edge nicked his knuckle, and Lohen pressed harder, seizing advantage from Han's pain.

But Han held back. He danced away from Lohen, parried his powerful moves, feinted but never tried to drive his sword home.

He couldn't win the way he was fighting, and he knew it. *If an opponent means to kill, and one does naught but defend, the defender will certainly die.* Those words made up the Warriors' First-Learned Premise. As Han pivoted and ducked and danced his defense, the axiom sang through his mind, always in the voice of the man who'd taught it to him—Lohen.

They battled on, Lohen without the protection of a shield, but also unencumbered by it. The Black Blade fell as heavy as a two-hander but handled as light as a rapier, and Lohen wielded it with great speed.

By the time Han began to slow, anyone with less skill and strength would have long since been slain. Yet, with Han dripping sweat, his chest heaving, the moment came when his reaction lagged a fraction of a second. He raised his shield in time to take the blow but stumbled back, off-balance. Lohen saw advantage and bulled in aiming a two-handed thrust.

He veered at the last second, bellowing as if in agony, and threw the Black Blade down into the churned mud and trampled grass at his feet. His head hung down, brown curls flung wild, like a man tied to a stake. His shoulders heaved as if racked by sobs, yet he made no sound.

He lifted his face and screamed, "Kill me!"

The words were so thick with venom and pain that it took seconds for Han to understand.

Lohen snarled again, vicious and impatient, "Kill me now." He turned away, body bent around some wound Han hadn't given him and couldn't see. Over his own labored breath, Han barely heard the next quiet words at all.

"Han, I want to die."

Han stood, sandals rooted in slick mud, searching but finding nothing to say. His silence seemed to anger Lohen all over again, and he hauled himself around to face Han, his look both defiant and pleading. Han shook his head, more bewildered than he'd ever been.

Lohen might have taken the motion as refusal or contempt. "Fight, then," he spat, picking up the Black Blade. "You came to do the wizard's dirty work? Do your job." Transformed, possessed of absurd calm, he flicked his wrist to bring forth once more the sword of steel blue light. "Here is where one of us will die."

"I don't want to fight," Han said.

"Liar! You love to fight, love your weapons, love to win. Do you think I don't remember you, warrior child? You live to fight." He laughed, low and easy, lifting his sword to the ready. "Let me tell you, little brother. This is the battle you've been preparing for all your life. I am the enemy you've been trained to kill." He stopped, half smiling. "Do your best. You might win, eh?"

He crouched, blade held just above shoulder height in front of him, and taunted, "Live by the sword, die by the sword, they say. But you can't do both, Han. Choose."

Han didn't move.

The seconds grew long. Lohen grew impatient, and when he moved his dance was amazing, beautiful, impossible with his weak leg. He bobbed, spun, quick-stepped side to side; he feinted, thrust, slashed, always a split second ahead of Han. He mounted a textbook attack, staged a master's demonstration. Impressive, but not pressing, and Han realized Lohen no longer fought to kill.

Han kept centered to his brother's sparring, dodged and parried. He thought he knew Lohen's mind and decided to try to beat him at his own game. Words punctuated with the clang and clash of swords, he said, "It's true, Lohen, Thurlock sent me to deal with you. You know why. But—" He broke off to dance around a stone. "—maybe there's another way."

Lohen screamed, "Fight, curse you," and then blitzed Han, once again in deadly sincerity. They clashed until they both bled from dozens of cuts. The smell of fresh blood and salt sweat made Han want to retch, but he fought on, defending—always defending—searching for that centered calm that had won him many a battle. It wouldn't come, the Warrior Mind. He cared too much.

Lohen lifted a sleeve to wipe watery blood off his brow. With an offhand tilt of his head, he said, "You think I won't kill you? I'll plow you into the ground unless you kill me first, brother." Suddenly, his face lit up with satisfaction, like a child who'd figured out the one taunt that would goad his playmate every time. Scorn saturated his words like poison.

"But you're not my brother, are you? You're the wizard's creation; Thurlock's tool. My mother and father wouldn't even recognize you."

"Fury," the wizard had taught Han, "is as likely to kill you as your foe," and Han had taken that tenet to heart. He never gave anger a place in a fight. But when he heard Lohen's taunt, he succumbed at once to rushing, mind-stealing, hurricane rage.

He attacked viciously, and for the next five minutes didn't care if he died. He didn't think about Luccan or Ethra or Earth. He didn't consider duty or honor, or remember anything sweet and good or precious or loved. He wanted only to punish his brother for those words.

Breathing in gasps, words pierced by the crashing blades, Han shot bitterness at the man who had once been his moon and sun. "Don't," he snarled. "Don't talk about our parents. Don't dare call them into this. I was there! I watched them scream while their skin smoked. I watched them die." Landing an arm-shocking blow against Lohen's blade, he let his voice fall into a deadly, cold rebuke. "Don't call them down to watch us betray them."

Lohen's face warped with emotion, but his flagging fight surged. Even half-crippled, with the Black Blade he almost matched Han's wrath and their grandfather's sword. Words flashed between them as sharp as blows, and they crossed into territory they'd never before trod.

We should have said these things long ago, Han thought, and the wave of rage crested and broke.

Lohen backed away, his voice came breathy and low. "Yes, you saw. I didn't. I was too late." He planted his sword point and leaned on the light as if it were steel. Something like a sob broke from his heaving chest. But he pulled air back into his lungs, roared, and came at Han like a mad wolf.

No more words; breath couldn't be wasted. Attention couldn't be spared; strength mustn't be squandered. Han at last found calm. In perfect rhythm he struck, blocked, slashed, danced, thrust, shielded, struck again, and again, and again. Lohen listed to the left, his weak limbs failing. He stumbled.

With Lohen's defenses wide open, Han rushed in hell-bent to deal a final blow, but as his brother had done, he pulled his blade wide a split second before impact.

He'd thrown so much force behind the swing that when he turned it, he was wrenched around. His foot slid in the ooze, and he went down. The mud grabbed his sword, tore it from his grasp as he fell backward. The base of his skull struck stone. He sprawled under a spinning, black-edged sky.

The sound Lohen Chiell made, running at Han, could have been a scream or a war cry. Hearing it, Han believed he would die, and he had more time than he would have expected for regrets. He pushed them away, squinted in concentration, and refused the encroaching blackness.

He would wait; he would know when the sword struck.

AFTER THE fight with Han, Lohen had fled like a hit-and-run driver, leaving his brother unconscious and bleeding in the muck of the battleground. He'd stumbled over the treacherous ground, letting Maizie lead. She'd broken a trail through briars and thorns and night.

Now, hours later, she led him back to where Han still lay in the muck, silent as death, flies buzzing his wounds.

Lohen laid a hand on his brother's chest, felt his heart beating strong, and stood up in sudden surprise at the wave of relief that washed over him. He roughed Maizie's fur, looked into her calm black eyes, and said, "Thank you, dog."

He kindled a fire, brought water, moistened Han's lips, and cleansed the cuts and bruises. In moonlight, he killed two brindle-furred rabbits with Han's bow and sent Maizie through the grass to retrieve them. He roasted the meat over orange coals, let Maizie eat what fell in the fire, and set the rest aside to stay warm for Han.

While stars stood still overhead, dripping seconds out one at a time, he fed the fire's small appetite and stood vigil. All the while he knew that none of this caretaking and nothing he could do would change what he'd become in his brother's eyes. *He won't want to see me*, he warned himself. *Not now, not ever.*

Past midnight, Han stirred and the pattern of his breathing changed from semiconscious to ordinary sleep. Lohen smoothed Han's hair in parting, whispered farewell, and left to wander again across the remains of night.

CHAPTER TWENTY: PLANS AND CONTINGENCIES

LUCKY GAVE up all pretense of cleaning the basement. He sat on the hard dirt, absently brushing at crawly things and studying the little book he'd wished into his hands. He was tracing his fingers over the embossed golden runes on the cover when Thurlock came down to the basement and laid an enormous hand on his shoulder.

"There's someone waiting to talk to you, young man."

For the first time in three years, using the M.E.R.L.I.N. planted in the wizard's dining room wall, Lucky spoke to his mother. He didn't care that they spoke from separate worlds, that he couldn't touch her hand, or smell her hair, or feel her warmth. It made no difference that they found little to say. Every minute was perfect. Cloud nine.

"I miss you, Mom," he said after a long silence.

"I know, son." The love and longing in her eyes was so patent that Lucky felt she might drink him up, but it wasn't a bad feeling.

She introduced him to a sturdy, dark-eyed woman. "This is your Aunt Rose."

He smiled, but before he could make a polite reply, she shooed the smiling woman away. Then she started dishing out advice.

She told him to trust Thurlock, to be careful, to work hard and always do his best. He should be polite, brush thc back teeth too, and never run with his shoelaces undone. Early to bed was good. Chocolate milk for breakfast was not.

"And come home," she said. "Come home safe and soon."

Lucky didn't listen too close. When he'd first seen her face, the sun had come up in his heart, and the whole time they talked, he was pretty sure he'd never be cold or lonely again.

But when the magical window went blank, he immediately felt like a bug trapped in the porch light after someone cut the switch. He could still crawl around in the dark, but he couldn't find any way out.

Later that evening, the big house stood dark and quiet, and it seemed emptier than the absence of one man should have made it. Thurlock sat with Lucky on the porch until night spilled its ink over the long summer twilight. Clouds walled off the stars. It would be hours before moonrise. Out beyond the reach of light from lamps and windows, the whole night wore mourner's black.

Lucky and Thurlock retreated indoors and sat at the table under the dim chandelier, swatting occasionally at a party of flies searching the sticky table for sustenance.

Lucky flung a question at Thurlock like throwing down a gauntlet. "Why now?"

The wizard arched his brows and frowned.

"Why did you have me talk to my mother now?"

Thurlock scratched his beard before he answered, his half smile making him seem unsure. "It seemed like the right time," he said. "I thought… hoped it might help."

"Well," Lucky said, "it made things worse."

Days of struggle, of unbelievable happenings, towering fear, and dreadful possibilities all fell on him and pinned his courage to the floor like a moth in a landslide. Hope slipped away. *I'll never make it home, Han will never come back, and I'll die before my time due to the effects of chocolate milk for breakfast.*

Lucky wanted to sleep. He wanted to forget everything, possibly forever, and the only thing that kept him from heading immediately to his safe, soft bed was hunger.

"Pizza," the wizard announced.

The pizza driver's knock surprised Lucky—he'd come to think of Thurlock's house as a place that wouldn't appear on any map—but he let it go without comment, and they ate in silence, companionable but not exactly friendly. The intimacy of their late night conversations in the stairwell had evaporated.

While they cleared away the trash and crumbs of dinner, Lucky tried a couple of questions about his magical book.

"Yes," Thurlock said, thumbing the pages. "They're prophecies."

But when Lucky asked for their meaning, Thurlock said one could never tell.

"They're not riddles, exactly; the meaning comes clear, eventually, but until that happens, they're rather open-ended. One can only watch and wait."

Lucky started up the stairs with the wizard's heavy footfalls clumping behind him. He paused at his bedroom door, not feeling charitable, but not wanting to be rude. "Good night, sir," he said.

"Not sir," the wizard said. "It's just Thurlock, to you." His eyes sparked with humor, and they both smiled. "Good night to you as well," he continued, "but before you sleep there's something I'd like you to do.

"Gather in your mind thoughts of Ethra. The small things you've remembered, what we've told you, the little you've seen these last days, and even the places of your dreams. Keep your mother in your thoughts and practice building a picture of her face behind your eyelids. Will you do that?"

Confused, Lucky hesitated. "Yes.... Yes, I will. But, why?"

"You'll need those thoughts for the trip home." He smoothed Lucky's flopping hair back for him, turned, and continued up the stairs. "I'll wake you. We'll depart at 3:00 a.m."

WHEN THURLOCK woke him a little before three in the morning, Lucky was surprised he'd slept, and still more surprised that he now felt rested and calm. He dressed quickly and rolled Thurlock's pajamas, his magic book, and the pictures he'd found in the attic tightly inside his blanket. He stuffed that bundle in his ragged backpack and headed for the stairs, doubling back for the Key of Behliseth. After slinging the Key on its chain around his neck, he went down to meet Thurlock in the dining room, as instructed.

His stomach growled. He hoped for another sweet breakfast before departure, but before he could even speak, the wizard rolled his eyes, mumbled, "Not hungry," and suddenly Lucky wasn't.

The wizard tilted his head toward the hall. "Restroom?"

"Huh?"

"Behl save me," Thurlock said, "from teenagers at three in the morning." He slid his hand over his eyes and tried again, enunciating clearly. "Rest. Room. Do you need to use it?"

When Lucky came back, Thurlock had just finished a cup of tea, and he said, "Better now. Sorry for the impatience, my boy, I'm not a morning person." He produced a maple bar from a pocket in his robes and handed it to Lucky, saying "Quickly, now." Lucky downed it in three heroic bites.

"Did you do as I asked last night? Rehearse your memories?"

"I did." Lucky considered adding *the best I could*, but he wasn't given time.

"Fine, let's go. Give me your hand."

Lucky held up his left, and Thurlock wrapped it around the staff, which had been stripped of its umbrella disguise. He placed his own hand over Lucky's, sheltering it completely, and then gave stern instructions.

"Hold firm, it will help you through the Portal. But beware. Once we're in the Vortices you may lose awareness of the staff, my hand, and even your own body."

A shiver Lucky could not stop rattled him from soles to crown, and the wizard abruptly stopped speaking. After a moment, he cleared his throat and spoke in a softer voice, reassuring. "I won't let go, boy. I'll be with you; I'll help guide you. But Luccan—" He paused until Lucky met his eyes. "—you must *want* to get there. You must want to go *home*. Do you?"

Lucky swallowed, said, "Yes," and hoped dearly that it was true.

HURTLING THROUGH the Vortices at greater than the speed of light feels exactly like floating in nothing at a complete standstill. But humans, confronted with the absence of tangible reality, have an odd habit of making one up.

Thurlock knew the strange sensations well, the prickle of cold air that wasn't really there moving over flesh that had lost its substance, vistas from a roadside that existed only in the mind, calls of birds from remembered treetops, the scent of imagined grasses, and the rustle of a ghost breeze.

Fellow travelers, beyond the Portals, would usually feel about as substantial as a new idea. If they'd traveled a lot and had a grip on where they wanted to go, they might feel as solid as a well-pondered theory. Thurlock had learned to expect such ghostly company.

But Luccan faded to less than a wisp of a dream.

They had stepped up to the M.E.R.L.I.N. and through the Portal, and in a wink that slender, all-important strand of person slipped out of Thurlock's grasp. Struck by fear, anger, and blinding self-doubt, Thurlock nearly also lost track of himself. He had to struggle to keep from being strewn piecemeal to the farthest corners of Naught.

His staff helped. Magic was useless in the Vortices, but there was so much of Thurlock in the wood and metal, after all these years, that he could use it as an anchor. He felt like a tattered flag, but he gathered his intentions and reached his destination in one piece, only slightly askew.

He made landfall in Ethra in a rolled-up position that would have been convenient for close examination of his kneecaps. It wasn't altogether bad, for it allowed his metal-capped staff to precede him. That, along with the thickness of his nearly petrified skull, protected him when he hurtled out of the Portal and bumped to a stop in a cave-like niche in an outcrop of feldspar—his intended destination. Home Port.

"Behl's fiery whiskers," he said, but he silently gave thanks that he'd arrived at night, when the Ethran countryside slumbered. Anyone could access Home Port, since it lay not more than a hundred yards from Sisterhold Manor and right off the road. In daylight a crowd often gathered; after dark, no crowd. He didn't have to defend his dignity, field questions, or explain his scowl.

Convinced of solitude and preoccupied with unkinking his spine and shaking out his robes, the sound of a soft, baritone chuckle startled him. He whirled toward the orchard shadows that surrounded the Port, sparks ready at his fingertips.

"Hold, wizard!" The voice sounded deep and light at the same time, rich with laughter flowing just beneath the surface. Despite the apparent youth of the compact man who stepped forward, his half smile and lively eyes bore witness to a love of life that, through loneliness and every kind of tragedy, had endured uncounted ages.

Thurlock's grim face softened to a smile. "Tiro! I can't begin to tell you how good it is to see you." He embraced the dark, rough-clad man. Hope made seeing his friend even more joyous. Perhaps his appearance at this particular time boded well for Luccan and the outcome of the peril in Earth.

"Aye, Thurlock, well met, though I wish it was in untroubled times." Tiro's old-fashioned, formal diction took nothing from either the warmth or the urgency behind his words. "I was hoping to see the Suth Chiell emerge from the Portal in your wake. I'd hoped also that you would bring my daughter, or at least word of her safety."

"I'm sorry."

Tiro stepped back into the trees, and Thurlock followed, knowing the reclusive changeling would be more comfortable where they wouldn't be seen should anyone pass on the road. They sat together on an old log, the remains of an ancient cottonwood that had fallen decades ago alongside Orchard Creek. The stream, sifting over its sandy bed, sang gently of ease. Fireflies lazed among reeds on the opposite bank. An owl made its usual inquiry, a calm and dignified, "Who?"

"I am afraid for L'Aria, wizard."

Thurlock shook his head. Tiro's words in the midst of the peaceful night chilled him to the marrow. His own steady voice surprised him. "You couldn't persuade her to stay home?"

"As you might expect, she gave me no opportunity. She well knows how and when to avoid me." Tiro said it with an indulgent smile, but it didn't erase the worry from his eyes. "And what news of Luccan?"

"I failed," Thurlock said. He clenched his jaw tight until he could speak without his fears rushing out, then he continued. "I couldn't hold on to him in the Vortices. He slipped away."

"Back to Earth?"

Thurlock scratched his beard, considering. "I think so. Yes, very likely back to Earth."

Beside him, Tiro sighed and ran his hands through the mane of dark hair that stood out from his head in soft bristles. "I've brought something."

He stood and walked to a spot among the reeds and willows lining the creek's bank, then shouldered two large, fur-clad waterskins. Dropping them by Thurlock's feet, he said, "From Kindled Springs. Might it help?"

"Certainly it will. Thank you."

Water from Kindled Springs refreshed body, mind, and soul like no other food or drink known to Ethra. Many speculated, but no one knew whether magic produced that quality, or if the flame that eternally skimmed its surface somehow changed the water.

For an ordinary human—even a powerful, skilled wizard—to reach the Springs took days of traveling mountain terrain and then more days through a maze of caves. Once there, a person could easily die in the attempt to fetch the water, either from breathing the gases in the cavern, or while attempting to pass through the scorching flames.

Waterways led to the Springs in a much more direct line, but it required the ability to stay submerged through long tunnels beyond the capacity of ordinary lungs. Tiro, shifting shape and swimming as a king of otters, could make that trip and fetch the water without ever surfacing in the dangerous cavern.

"I wish I could offer more of it," Tiro said, a slight smile touching his eyes, "but this was all I could tow back through the tunnels."

Thurlock knew the journey couldn't have been easy, even for Tiro. He laid a hand on the smaller man's vest-clad shoulder. "This will be enough," he said. "It may well save the day."

"Fare well, this mission," Tiro said, and then he waded into the shadowed stream and vanished from sight.

LIGHTS BURNED in all the downstairs windows of Sisterhold Manor, though the summer dawn would be waiting in the wings for another hour. It seemed likely the household hadn't slept at all, awaiting Luccan's return.

Thurlock mounted the steps to the veranda, lifted the brass-stag striker, knocked three times, and went in.

The furniture and the polished floor shone in the glow of candles and lamps. A long table groaned under the makings of a feast. Platters piled with fruits, baskets spilling sweet rolls and spice cakes, griddlecakes waiting for butter and syrup; milk, juice, coffee, tea, and even a small keg of golden ale. From the kitchen came the clank and clatter of pans, the sizzle of meats on the fire, and a tapestry of smells that set Thurlock's stomach clamoring for attention.

But Liliana, Rosishan, and a handful of others stood silent, facing Thurlock with their reactions etched on their faces. Surprise. Disappointment. Fear.

"I'm sorry," he said, scowling to hide self-doubt and forestall questions. "Luccan isn't with me."

He tightened his grip on his staff and his confidence and made no further apology. He regretted the new, heightened fear Liliana must have for her son, but this wasn't the time for bickering, blame, or *I-told-you-so.*

He needed speed. He'd formulated a contingency plan to address this situation before he'd ever stepped across the Portal with Luccan in tow.

With Tiro's gift, the plan had more chance of succeeding, but L'Aria's danger added to his concerns. No certainties; even magic can't guarantee success, but the quicker his plan could be put in motion, the better the chances.

He spoke quietly, not wanting to cause panic. "Lili, Rose, I'd like a private word in the library." He stopped to survey the crowd and settled his gaze on a tall woman with laconic eyes who seemed to melt into the walls a few feet away. "Please join us, Gerania.

"The rest of you, a feast awaits, and we'll have angry cooks if it goes unappreciated. It's a tough assignment, but perhaps you'll give eating it your best effort?"

Thurlock smiled, and it seemed to brighten what had become a gloomy room. A few chuckles answered him, and people shuffled away. Thurlock made for the stairs in the back of the spacious hall, the three women following close.

Small leather sandals pounded across the floor, and two high-pitched voices called, "Mama, wait!"

The little girls with dun-colored heads looked a lot like Gerania. Thurlock spoke up before their mother could answer. "Trista, Glayda, two of my favorite and shortest neighbors." He went down on a knee to wrap one long arm around the both of them as they rushed in for a giggling hug.

"Girls, listen, we four adults are going upstairs to the library to talk, and talking always makes me thirsty. And, the smell of all that food is making me hungry. Would you sneak a tray of rolls—sweet rolls, mind you—and a pot of tea from the kitchen and bring them up to us? I'll owe you a favor."

The girls, whose eyes had flown wide at the promise of being owed a favor by the great wizard, rushed off in a flurry of ribbon-tied braids and flowered skirts. Despite his worries, Thurlock smiled.

The smell of leather, dust, and ink greeted Thurlock as he walked into the library. He breathed a little easier, surrounded by books and scrolls. Chair legs whispered over the carpeted floor as everyone took a seat at a round table in the center of the room. Lili took her spiral Spring Wand out of a deep pocket of her gown and tapped the chandelier over their heads, setting it ablaze.

Thurlock met Lili's green-gold eyes and laid his hand over hers on the table. "Niece, I've done some probing, and I believe Luccan isn't lost."

Lili's look brightened a bit, hope crossing swords with fear and anger.

Thurlock took a deep breath and forged on. "He's returned to Earth, which is better than Naught, but yes, he is in grave danger there."

"I'm going to him, uncle! Don't try to stop me this time—"

"Yes," Thurlock interjected. "Yes, Lili, I will need you now to help with the situation in Earth, and Rose as well."

When the blank look faded from Lili's face, Thurlock knew his words had sunk in. He told them all what he'd guessed about Luccan's situation, and Han's. They asked a few questions and he answered when he could. When they were as up-to-date as he could make them, he sat back, smoothing his untidy beard as if it would help order his thoughts.

He nodded toward Gerania and asked, "How long before day breaks here?"

The second-in-command of Behlishan's Guard, ranking officer in Han's absence, had a reputation for impeccable precision belied by a lackadaisical manner. "Fifty-three minutes," she drawled, "and uh, twelve… no, ten seconds, sir."

"That's not much time. Let's get down to specifics. Lili, how many of the Mounted Guard do we have that can make it through the Portals with us, with their mounts?"

Lili shook her head. "Not many, at the moment."

Thurlock waited for more, but it was Rose who explained.

"We've sent troops north, as you suggested, trying to hold down the disturbances. Last week—my idea, I'm afraid—we doubled the size of the mission when we got reports of ice-drakes—"

"Winged blue salamanders," Thurlock corrected.

"That's right, sir, ice-drakes. Some incidents involved wights and glacier wolves too. We had four reports in a day."

Seconds ticked by.

"What is it, Rose? Please, drop the other shoe."

"We don't know where they are, sir."

"The salamanders?"

"Those too, but I meant the troops. They're not killed, so the seers tell us, but no one can find them."

"I see…," Thurlock said, tugging at his beard. Suddenly he nodded, perched his spectacles on his nose, and peered over the rims at each of the women. "It's Isa's work," he said. "A trick. She's brilliant at times. But then, if she were incredibly stupid she wouldn't be the Witch-Mortaine, would she?

"Come to think on it, though, it makes little difference. We need speed, I think, not numbers. Southport is the only Portal within fifty miles big enough for horses, and even there we can only travel through a few at a time."

"What about at the other end?"

"I don't think that will be as much of a problem, Lili. There's a very large natural Portal in the ravine that will work fine as long as we can emerge in the cavern proper, and not the caves behind it. It's manageable."

They discussed how many soldiers to take and finally settled on six, all professionals, members of an elite squad of the Mounted Guard known as Shana's Rangers. Liliana commanded the Rangers, and she trusted her troops.

"Rose," Thurlock said, "I want you to get in touch with Ghriffon. I'll feel much better if we have a few eagles with us."

A light knock announced the two little girls, come with a well-cozied teapot, sweet rolls, and smiles that were not shy at all.

Thurlock thanked them for saving him from starvation.

When they'd off-loaded their goods, Gerania straightened braids, dusted skirts, and tied a loose sandal. "Go eat, girls, and then you can play, but don't have any fun." They giggled all the way out the door, obviously used to their mother's teasing. Everyone smiled, but faces went grim once more when the children had gone.

Nabbing a cinnamon sweet roll and a cup of tea, Thurlock continued laying out the plans. "Gerania, you'll have the Regular Mounted here to support Behlishan's Guard."

"That'll help, sir. We'll be spreading the troops pretty thin covering the Sisterhold, Nedhra City, and the Portals."

Swallowing the last of the roll, Thurlock wiped crumbs from his beard. "It will be enough," he said. "The real battle will be happening in that awful ravine, which is certainly not what or where it seems in the first place, and is completely skewed now that Isa's planted her cursed tower at the east end."

Gerania, who had less experience of the Witch-Mortaine than the others, shook her head. "What about the people, sir, the Earthborns? They tolerate her evildoing?"

Thurlock shook his head, arched his brows, chewed. Mouth empty, he answered. "If there's anything Isa has become very skilled at, it's concealing her presence and the damage it does. She has that tower so well hidden I had trouble pinning it down myself. And, of course, she's managed to twist some Earthborn minds." He paused to shake his head, tired and disgusted. "Anyway, you're in charge here, Gerania, and you can put together a search party to go north. We three and the six Rangers will head for Earth. Rose, let's pray Ghriffon still likes you. We'll need those eagles."

He paused to wash his third roll down with tea, then pushed his chair back. "Now, if I'm not mistaken it's nearly dawn."

"Just under nineteen minutes, sir," Gerania offered.

"I've got to get to the Oakridge. Meet me at Southport in two hours."

Rose objected. "That's not enough time."

Lili shot back her reply wearing a scowl. "It's too much time, when my son is in harm's way every passing minute."

"I'm sorry, Rose, Lili is right this time, and in fact it's worse than that."

The women all looked back at him with questions in their eyes.

"You see," Thurlock said, "the balance is disturbed, and growing more so, thanks to the Ice-Lord Mahl. Time is… perhaps 'wobbling' is the word. It can't be counted on at all."

CHAPTER TWENTY-ONE: MORDRED BREDE

ISA SAT at the glass worktable in her chamber, surrounded by potions and powders and horrid things pickled in brine. Pale blue fire lit the room beyond, sending tints and shadows to dance over her pallid hands. Exhausted, she raised a steel chalice to her cracked lips with shaking hands.

She had delivered Mordred to Mahl, as she had promised. Time had been short, so rather than drag him along the usual twisting path to sorcery, she'd sustained him with her own tainted blood and drilled him nonstop. When he'd learned enough Dark Chant, when he'd gained the skills necessary to stifle and bend the mind of a preconditioned mob, then she judged him ready to meet his Master.

She'd nurtured Mordred's cold heart, fed his quest for dark knowledge, bequeathed to him the core of her morbid sorceries. All that remained was to give him power. That he would get from the Ice-Lord, just as she had long ago.

For the last hour, she'd watched him writhe while the Master possessed him, infected him with the power of the void, the essence of Naught. As it ended, his tortured body arched painfully and collapsed, falling hard on the stone floor. A long, smoky breath escaped his lungs. Then, for a moment, nothing… until a gasp started him breathing again.

His eyes had been as deep and richly black as raven stones. Now, he looked back at her from discs of blue ice, shallow, pale eyes that mirrored her own.

"Mordred," she called.

Mahl had forced him, she knew, to the very brink of death. When she beckoned, he struggled to stand, but couldn't. In the end he crawled, a show of obedience she was pleased to see. If he had not obeyed, if he had thought to challenge her, she would have had to destroy him, and then all the energy she'd spent on him would have bought her nothing but Mahl's wrath.

"You've done well," she told him. "You will be rewarded." She offered him her chalice, with the remains of her fortifying potion.

Trembling, he took the cup. "Thank you, Witch-Mortaine. I'm honored." He raised the cup and swallowed, and after a moment his breathing slowed.

"Rise, now," she said, knowing the potency of the brew she'd given him. "Listen."

She set Mordred over her followers as captain and put most of her resources at his disposal, assigning him the task of taking Luccan. "Alive if you can," she told him. "I'd prefer for him to die later, after I've made use of him. Apply all of your tricks and powers. Use our black-cloaked slaves. Let the boy think he'll die. He'll run blind, right into your trap."

Mordred smiled, a cruel expression.

"If the girl gets in the way, kill her if it pleases you."

"Yes," he answered slowly, clearly savoring the prospect.

"Just don't forget, apprentice, which child is your prime target."

His feet fell heavy, rattling the stone as he left her chamber.

As for Thurlock, Isa thought, *if that old trickster shows up, he's mine*.

HOME. LUCKY thought that single word over and over, clenched it in the folds of his mind as hungrily as a wolf clamps a rabbit in its jaws.

Home. That was where he was going. The wizard had told him so. "I won't let go…."

But he was alone now. He'd lost Thurlock. And if it was home he was heading toward, he seemed to be taking a long time to get there. He struggled to hold that home in Ethra in his mind as Thurlock had instructed, but too many people he cared about remained in Earth. They popped up in his thoughts like bubbles, one after another.

He remembered Lohen first, which seemed odd, and then Han and Maizie and the shack. That had also been home, where he and Maizie had lived—walked in the pines and played by the creek. He'd played by the creek with Hank George too, and Henry.

He became aware of something soft and smooth, but powerful, brushing against him. Great wings beat noisily and seemed to whip a wind into the empty space. Lucky breathed deep and smelled sage, cedar, woodsmoke, perking coffee, and birthday candles burning on maple syrup pancakes.

He slammed to a stop. In the dark. Making full-body contact with rock.

He used his hands to examine the space around him. Rock below, packed earth above and on the sides.

He recognized the sounds outside and guessed where he had landed. Nettle Brook babbled off to his left, tumbling down into Black Creek, which hummed a deeper note down below. As regular as a ticking clock, one stone clunked and slid in the middle of the brook, perched right at the edge but never falling. It had floated there at least as long as Lucky had been in Earth.

His fingers clamped around a familiar object, a G.I. Joe he'd left in this "foxhole" two and a half years ago, when he'd still thought of himself on some days as a child. Yes, he knew this place. He laughed, relieved to be alive and not stuck in nowhere—or wherever he'd gone after stepping through the M.E.R.L.I.N.

Reaching his arms out past his head to the den's entrance, he found the root he knew would be hanging there. He pulled himself out, climbed to the ridge, and headed up to Hank's familiar front door.

The log house was dark and cold, and once Lucky had lit the hurricane lamp on the mantel, he saw dust balled so thick in the corners he expected it to sprout legs and whiskers and skitter away. He shrugged off his pack, amazed that it had come through the journey intact. He took out the little portraits and studied them briefly, one by one, and then he dropped the blanket over his shoulders, both actions done in an effort to ward the wintry chill—which he was at a loss to explain, in July.

The blanket helped, but Lucky still shivered.

Layers. He still had clothes there in Hank's house, if they'd fit, but he looked at the dark doorways to other rooms and quailed at the idea of going through them. He rifled through his pack, found the wizard's pajamas, and pulled them over his jeans. At last he was warmed.

The firewood he'd carried in, the kindling he'd split, and even the newspaper Hank had read on the morning of his death were all still neatly stacked by the river-rock fireplace. Lucky was no Thurlock—he couldn't make magic flames, and he had only one match to light the fire. So as he struck it and held it against the tinder, he added a fervent wish. He wasn't sure if it was the wish that did the trick, but the fire blazed, and he held up a fist in victory.

For a while, he didn't think. He just stood in front of the fire, wrapped in red plaid and wizard's pajamas, absorbing heat and light and growing hungry.

When he heard the first thunk from Hank's hand drum, which still hung next to the mirror above the mantel, he didn't think the noise was odd. The warming skin would often "talk," as Hank would say, as it grew taut over the drum's bones. Lucky felt glad to hear it, and he caught himself thinking *I've missed you*, as if the drum was an old friend.

But it wasn't at all usual for the drum to keep talking in a rhythm matching exactly the pattern of Hank's song. Lucky thought, *ghost*, but he didn't believe it until the drum began to shine like a small sun forging through night. Fascinated, he stared at that white luminous hide so hard that he saw it happen, witnessed the moment when the standing bear, painted there in red and black, began to dance.

"You need sleep," Lucky told himself, tearing his eyes away, "or food, or heavy medication."

He pushed his hair back from his face, shrugged away the dread slinking up his spine, and even forced a laugh. But when his gaze swept past the dim-lit room behind him in the mirror, his eyes grew wide and he forgot to breathe.

The face in the mirror hid in shadow, but Lucky could read the smile. Cold fled before a landslide of pure relief, and he wondered why he'd thought the log house empty. The light was on in the kitchen and the herbed stew Lucky could hear bubbling on the stove filled the air with a steamy, savory promise of a full-bellied good night.

The stew smelled like Hank's, but the man in the mirror wasn't Hank George. Lucky knew that. Hank was dead.

Lucky turned, smiling. "Henry, I—"

But the room was deserted.

The drum rumbled like thunder and dropped off its nail to land, silenced and dull, in the dust at Lucky's feet. A warning.

He took a fortifying look at the picture of his mother, stripped off the wizard's pajamas, and stuffed them both in his backpack. He looked around one last time in the golden light of the fire, doused the lamp, and turned to leave.

Sudden frost blighted the room. Every calorie of heat fled so abruptly that the mirror cracked. The imagined glow of the kitchen bulb and the soul-nourishing smells of food vanished completely, replaced by the bleak, hard smells of ice and carbon vapor. The empty house teemed with life, or with its terrible opposite. Ghosts, monsters, living dead.

"The Sight," Han had said. *"You can learn to call it up, to refine it, and to shut it down."*

Lucky shut his eyes again and concentrated on remembering the steady beat of Hank's drum, drawing his racing heart down into its strong rhythm. He started for the door, not needing eyes to know the way. A draft of ordinary night air whispered over him, rattling the frost-coated strands of his hair. The spirit sounds stilled. The breeze brought in the brook's chatter and predawn's tentative birdcalls.

Lucky sighed, relieved. He'd reached the door, and a summer day was ready to come alive.

He opened his eyes, and they widened in shock. Mordred Brede blocked the exit. Outside, a swarm of black-cloaked followers held torches to wall and post and eave, setting Hank's house aflame.

"I've a car waiting," Mordred said and seized Lucky's arm in a titan's grip. "Come on out now, Luccan. I wouldn't want you to burn."

Part Four:
When All Others Fail

CHAPTER TWENTY-TWO: IN THE LIGHT OF A NEW DAY

HAN FORCED his crusted eyelids apart a fraction but then squeezed them shut against the million stars that blazed back. Their brilliance hurt, and the constellations confused him.

Those are the wrong stars....

I'm camping in the Greenwood with Lohen, and he keeps me safe....

No, I've been dreaming....

He opened his eyes again. *I'm not a boy; this isn't Ethra. It's been a lifetime since we camped in the Greenwood. And it was Lohen I was fighting when I fell.*

As Lohen had taught him, Han lay still, trying to get his bearings, to discover what might be nearby, waiting for him to move. He felt the shadows of treetops waving against the graying east—dawn hovered near. The creek muttered downhill from him, and behind him he sensed the solidity of the looming rock slope. He smelled, as expected, grass, dew, mud, pine, river moss, and, faintly, even fish. He also smelled, *not* as expected, campfire ash and roasted meat.

He let his eyes close again, wondering if those surprising aromas lingered from his dream. A heavy shoe fell, not far away, crushing grass; then another step and another, closer.

Han waited, and when the time was right snaked out an arm, grabbed a thick ankle, lifted it, and gave it a twist, laying his assailant facedown in the dirt. In seconds he was on the man and had a knee jammed into his kidney. He twisted both his assailant's arms up against the shoulder blades and clenched the big man's stubbly chin in a rock-hard grip.

The predawn sky bore down on Han, heavy as lead. Sweat ran in his eyes, tinted with yesterday's blood, and they burned like flame. His breath sheared through flared nostrils. He bit his lip bloody in clenched teeth and raged, silent and nearly mindless, at the man he held pinned in a high-torque wrestler's grip. A slight movement with one hand, a half-inch twist, would snap the man's neck.

For half a minute, it was all Han could do to keep that hand still. Almost too late, an old voice in his mind cut through the rage and made itself heard. "The least degree of force," it insisted.

He shuddered, released a rattling breath, relaxed his hold but kept it secure, and struggled to clear his mind. The man on the ground tried to talk. The light had grown, and Han saw his captive's face. Thinking he recognized the man, he said, "Mordred?"

"Nggoo Mmmfff."

To Han's surprise, a whimper followed. What's more, in the inch of skin showing between dark eye and wiry beard, gleaming in the gray light, were runnels of tears. Han let up a little more on the chin. "What did you say?"

"Boff," the man said, but he was also thinking about Han, and Han heard those thoughts loud and clear in his own mind.

Scary man, like Mord.

Han didn't mind being scary when a situation called for it, but he didn't want to be like Mord. "I'm going to let you up, Boff. Please don't run and don't fight." He helped him to his feet, watched him wipe his dripping nose on his sleeve, walked him to a rock, and told him to sit. He didn't seem likely to move, he and the rock appearing equally inert.

Han took a deep breath, shrugged the tension out of his shoulders, and tried to decide what to ask first. "Where's Mordred, Boff?"

"He killed me."

"He killed you?"

Boff was a man of few words, but by aiming his questions carefully, Han gleaned some key facts. Mordred had pushed his brother off a cliff. Boff had missed the rocks and fallen into the creek.

And L'Aria had pulled him out.

"Behl's Whiskers," Han said, borrowing the wizard's epithet. He said it again after Boff told him who he'd seen making the fire and shooting the rabbits that roasted in the coals.

Then Boff screwed his face into a pout and volunteered, "You killed me."

Han, thankful to have avoided switching occupations from warrior to murderer, apologized. By way of making amends, he passed half a roasted rabbit to Boff. The big, childlike man tore into it, eyes wide with joy.

Han smiled, but after his first careful bite, he joined his guest in ripping meat off bone in glorious abandon. They finished the first rabbit, then the second. Han sighed and cleaned the grease off his face, hands, and arms to the elbows with a bunch of grass.

His cuts and bruises had been washed. Looking around, he found that his things had been fetched and brought down to this little camp. His waterskin had been filled, and his tunic had been rinsed and laid over the top of a juniper scrub to dry. His bow and quiver leaned against a boulder beside his sword, which had been cleansed of blood and polished to a shine.

Lohen. It had been Lohen who had done these things. He'd come back, tended Han's wounds, hunted and cooked his food. Sometime soon, Han would have to think about that.

But now is not the time. The sun is climbing, and I've still got a job to do.

THE SUN flashed off Black Creek a hundred feet below, blazing into Lohen Chiell's grit-scratched eye. A grouchy crow mumbled in the shadows, and jays shrilled from the treetops. The scents of hot pine and shale dust thickened the air. Weary, Lohen prayed for an hour of silent dark or even cloud cover and a slingshot to shut the scavengers up.

He'd climbed slowly, cutting diagonally up the slope of the gorge for the last half hour, though not mindful of any purpose. His legs had begun to ache with effort, yet he'd kept on, step after step, following Maizie, who'd been his guide through dark morning, comfortless dawn, and hours under a sun hot enough to wring sweat from stones.

West of Isa's blue tower and east of the clearing where by now, he prayed, his brother would have awakened and enjoyed his rabbit, he came upon the Myrtle Grove. He marveled that in all the days he'd wandered this canyon, on the witch's errands and then lately on his own, he'd never seen this stand of ancient trees. But there was more to Black Creek Ravine than met the eye; the place harbored secrets in every shadow. Why should this one surprise him?

A hint of green-laden breeze, barely cool, blew over the myrtles and rattled their papery leaves, carrying their sweet-sharp scent and promising refreshment. Maizie trod the path into the tunnel of cooled, dim shade, and as Lohen followed, just for a moment he felt as though he'd walked out of Earth and into Ethra.

He chuckled, realizing how unlikely such a thing was. *Although, where there's a wizard like Thurlock and a witch like Isa involved, one can never be too sure that anything truly is where it seems to be.*

Deep inside the grove, Maizie led him away from the road and then stopped beside a pool where clear water bubbled out of a globe of black rock. He dunked his head in the freshet, hoping the cold would dull the ache between his ears. Sitting back on his heels, he slicked water off his hair and tried to quench his burning eye, pressing a wet hand against the lid.

He was looking for the energy to stand when Maizie bounded back from her brief exploration in the brush and nudged him under the arm with her big, bony nose. In his exhausted state, it was enough to knock him flat. Sprawled and muddy, his only defense was to raise an arm, shielding his face from her pink, slopping tongue.

He decided he was too worn out to get to his feet and instead scooted out of the mud like an upside-down inchworm. He had to stop, breathless and laughing at himself, glad no one could see his ungraceful effort. When he recovered, he slid back until he found a hollow in the thick leaf mold, a place that felt ready to receive him, as if someone else had lain there recently, with him in mind.

"Dog," he said, "watch over me. I have to sleep." He expected slumber to drop like a stage curtain. Instead, the backs of his eyelids flickered in video replay of the last sixteen hours blow-by-blow.

The fight with Han, his flight, and his return to his brother's side. The pain of having to leave before Han opened his eyes for fear of the hatred he would see in them. After, he'd roamed the dark ravine, following Maizie's lead through the remains of night and too far into morning, not stopping for food or sleep or even to rest his blistered feet.

Now, in the cool of the grove, his eye began to burn again, and he blinked away the salt gathered in its corners. He sighed, turning the tail of it into a yawn. "Watch over me, dog," he said once more. Blessedly cool in the shadow of green leaves, darkness fell behind his lids at last like a benediction.

Minutes later he heard singing, a distinctive song, a singular, unmistakable chiming voice.

L'Aria.

This strange, magical girl had loved him since she toddled. Sometimes, for Lohen, it was a bloody nuisance.

Unable to keep exasperation from his voice, Lohen asked her before he even opened his eyes, "Why are you here, Spitfire? I'm sure your aunts told you to stay home after your last adventure?" He opened his eyes then and saw her throw her head back in laughter, a gesture that lived up to her nickname.

L'Aria answered the second question first. "They told me not to cross the Portals, and I didn't. If there's water, I don't need a Portal. I have my song. And what I'm doing here is finding you, because it's important."

Her saucy tone and lopsided features brimmed with defiance, but Lohen was way past wanting to argue. His eyelids hung so heavy he wished that if he must keep them open, he could tack them up with glue. No reply seemed worth the effort. He spent the last of his energy to sit up, tossed his wild hair out of his eye, and waited to hear what L'Aria deemed so urgent.

"Your son needs you," she said.

"Oh," Lohen responded. He gave the word no emphasis and said nothing further.

"I have the Amber Knife." She said more but didn't offer to explain how that came about, and Lohen didn't ask because he knew he would wish he hadn't. What mattered was that she wanted to hand it over to him.

She also had the woven-reed pouch she'd given Luccan on his twelfth birthday, filled with old coins—the same pouch and coins that had been among the things that disappeared with Luccan three years ago. Lohen watched her shake them out into the pool, using the last one to anchor the pouch atop the stone globe. What she did with the coins at the spring seemed the sort of thing any young girl might do, but Lohen did wonder how she came to have them.

He also wondered what would prompt L'Aria to want to put Luccan's knife into his hands. Lohen was a traitor and a madman—a murderer, most Ethrans believed. And L'Aria surely knew all about that. The thought crossed Lohen's mind that perhaps, by some unimaginable means, this unique, troublesome but innocent girl had fallen under the Witch-Mortaine's influence.

But when he looked into her well-deep black eyes, he knew Isa hadn't touched her. There was no evil there. Weary as he was, his eye flew wide with surprise at what he did find in her gaze. Something he'd not seen in human eyes for many years. Something more magical than any Blade or Staff, curse or spell or song.

Trust. L'Aria had chosen to believe in him.

Absently, Lohen rubbed at his left hand, still damaged, though healing since the Black Blade's return. He wondered what part of him was whole and good enough to deserve L'Aria's faith. *But how can I refuse what she asks when she looks at me like that?* He took the Amber Knife, and he tucked it, safely sheathed, into his belt opposite the Black Blade.

"I know you'll do what's right," L'Aria said, hand on her hip. "You don't know, Thurlock doesn't know, but I do. You will."

Overpowered by fatigue, Lohen shook his head and sank back into the soft fragrance of rich soil and fallen myrtle leaves. The breeze didn't touch the ground, but he heard it sighing through the trees' crowns. It whispered syllables, like a remembrance of the Gods' Breath, Behlis Ethra's fair dawn wind.

"Go home now," he told L'Aria, having found himself once again on the sweet edge of sleep. He cut her protest short, touching the Black Blade once to remind her that, though her aunts couldn't make her stay, he could make her go. And it might be unpleasant if he did.

"Fine, then," she said, pouting, and she waded into the pool. Lohen had to smile, watching her disappear beneath the surface. He hoped she would go home where she might be safe, but he was under no illusion that her obedience was a sure thing. Fading at last toward dreams, he let that thought go, along with all others but one.

Please, Lohen begged the wind, *whisper to me my son's lost name.*

BY THE time Han rose and prepared himself to move, warrior-clad and armed, the sun had moved well past noon. He put his tardy start down to having been injured, but he admitted he'd been reluctant to go searching for new trouble. Now, he stood at the edge of the clearing and called his thoughts to order.

All right, first things first, he started, and for some reason it reminded him of Luccan.

At the same instant, his nephew's mental call for help slammed into his brain, full of fear and fight and an image of Mordred Brede shoving Luccan to the floor in the back of Isa's big white Ford. In seconds, Han shouldered his bow and his pack and hooked his quiver at his belt, preparing to run to Luccan's aid.

He headed east to Isa's keep, the only place Mordred would take his captive. Chills and heat, fear and anger battled in him at the thought of Luccan held at the nonexistent mercy of the Witch-Mortaine.

WHEN LOHEN woke up to the touch of Maizie's wet nose, the sun was spinning down through thin clouds toward the western peaks. White rays sliced into the heart of the grove between the trunks of the sheltering myrtles, their touch on Lohen's skin like cold steel.

He gazed toward the east, squinting as if he might peer through magic veils and miles of trees and rocks.

Maizie whuffed, seeming anxious to be on the move.

Lohen nodded and scratched her ears. "You're right," he said. "It's time to go. We'll find something to eat on the way."

She set off through the trees, and he let her lead, but this time he knew where she would take him. And he knew what he had to do. He took a last deep breath of the grove's sweet air and whispered to the wind what he'd come at last to understand.

"My son," he said. "My son needs me."

CHAPTER TWENTY-THREE: LET AUNTIE ISA TAKE CARE OF YOU

LUCKY REMEMBERED the icy touch of Mordred's hands as he shoved him into the Crown Vic, but he didn't remember the ride. It was almost as if it hadn't happened, as if he'd fallen into the car outside Hank's, and fallen out in this damp corner of stone and dust, alone and cold.

He'd sleep if he could, but his eyes refused to close on the blue light seeping from the walls, though it stung them like sleet. No sounds reached his ears except a faint echo of his pulse and, high above, a distant howl like the ghosts of long-dead wolves. His lungs rebelled at every breath of rancid air, and his stomach was so empty it made a fist. He had with him the clothes he wore and nothing else—no red blanket or wizard's pajamas to block the creeping chill, no small portraits to warm his heart.

He had no way to know how long he'd been curled in that corner hugging his knees. It felt like such a long time that everything that had ever gone before was lost. And if by chance it was night now, he was sure it was going to stay night forever.

A moment of comfort did come, a small golden light and a fluttering like tiny wings against his chest. Lucky looked for the source and found the Key of Behliseth humming at the end of its chain. It felt like finding home, and he cupped both hands around it. For that small moment, he felt warmed.

Then a door Lucky had not before seen slammed open. He dropped the Key behind his shirt to keep it secret. Two women and two men entered the room, all with whitish hair, pinkish pale skin, and lightless indigo eyes. They dressed alike in short tunics and loose trousers of a cloth that seemed sometimes white, sometimes blue. Their torches sputtered and cracked with blue flame, yet their eyes stayed dim.

Crowding around Lucky in his corner, they started in kicking and beating him, never uttering a word, never showing any emotion—which made them seem all the more vicious. They hit him so many times that his muscles cramped and every square inch of his flesh burned like frostbite. But it was their frigid breath, like poison gas, that laid him out flat.

Lucky imagined his brain slowly coating with ice. It was hard to think about anything but heat, and after a while he forgot even to defend himself. That was when two of his attackers dug their fingers into his hair and dragged him out the door and down a dark, slanting corridor, the other two following behind.

At first it was a relief when they left him alone on an ice-slicked cobbled floor in the center of a vast circular dungeon. But the only light in that place fell from a single bright dot of open sky so high it seemed miles away, and horrible sounds came through the dark from everywhere around Lucky, begging terrifying explanations. Immense breath rattled, something squished and slimed, teeth chomped and crunched. Closer now, but still coming from above, the same ghostly wolves still howled their hunger.

Lucky huddled in his fears for minutes or hours or forever, wishing for anything but dark. When a door opened in a distant, shadowed wall, he at first welcomed the burst of blue light. His relief died immediately as the Witch-Mortaine Isa strode in, chrome blue robes shining like a housefly's carapace, chilling eyes wicked with hate. The four servants who had dragged him from his cell carried the hem of her robe, bowing so low Lucky was amazed they could walk.

Together, they spoke in hollow, apathetic tones. "Fall on your knees before the Demon Queen."

Lucky just stood there, thinking how stupid that sounded and shaking in fear. Isa pointed at him with a claw-like finger, and his legs started to fold under him in obedience. He fought it, struggling to stay on his feet and muttering over and over, "No."

The witch started talking—at least Lucky assumed the sounds were words—and her slaves picked up the refrain as if they were having some kind of monstrous sing-along. The sounds invaded his brain, so ugly he felt them crawling through its folds like worms and bugs, until at last the chant broke off. Once again Isa jabbed a sharp finger at Lucky's face. Shrouded in sudden pain, he dropped. His knees hit the stones.

"Ah," Isa said, "that's better. I see you're not so unreasonable after all, Luccan." Looking down her long nose at him, practically drooling contempt, she said, "Come, dear angry boy. Let Auntie Isa take care of you."

It was a magical Command, like Thurlock's, but mean-spirited and steeped in evil magic. Something like air filling a balloon unfolded Lucky from the floor and stood him on his feet. Something like wires moved his arms and legs and pulled him toward a breezeway that wound upward along the keep's blue-glass walls, its inside edge kissing open space. Lucky clambered up the steep ramp, following the witch in mindless obedience.

Torches mounted in steel brackets along the way stained the walls and stone ramp with splashes of sickly, luminous blue. The flames burned cold, stealing Lucky's body heat as he passed, and the walls wore a hard coat of frost. He stayed as far from them as possible, avoiding their icy touch even though that meant treading inches from the deadly drop into the tower's central well, an open space so deep it seemed to have no floor.

At last they stopped, having climbed for so long that Lucky imagined he'd find himself eye to eye with the pinnacles of Death of the Gods if he could look out. They stood on a narrow landing, he and the four pale people waiting silent and still, until a steel panel slid open at Isa's Command.

They filed into a chamber shaped something like a slice of pie with the tip cut off. Large, but not cavernous like the vast round hall he'd just come from.

White marble slabs tiled the floor, and on a broad stone platform at the back of the room, thirteen pole-mounted torches flared and hissed. Their fire lent only icy light, but a pit near the center of the chamber held a brazier crackling with orange flames. Without a single thought, Lucky flew toward that bright, hot blaze like a moonstruck moth.

Isa stood at the front of the room on a platform of blue stone. To each side of her, a steel column supported colorless candles burning blue and throwing shadows in flickering waves. Beneath them Isa seemed to grow taller and more terrible, and Lucky heard again in his mind the words, *Demon Queen.* He turned away, but the witch's stare prickled at the back of his neck.

He remained silent but for his shivering breath. Uneasy with Isa at his back, he pivoted to face her and then moved to put the orange flames between them. For comfort and courage, he leaned as close as he dared to the heat, but it wasn't nearly enough to cut the tower's arctic chill.

Isa stared at him unblinking, lids half-lowered, and Lucky felt as though he was being measured, or perhaps recorded.

Finally, as she turned to leave, she instructed her slaves. "I've things to attend, a nuisance at our doors, I'm told. See to the boy's comforts. Find a way to warm him. He's frail; he won't survive the cold. I want him alive, for a while. Keep him that way." She slithered out of the room dragging a cold wind in her wake.

Cold slave hands pushed Lucky back to sit on a heavy black cloak they had taken from a niche in the wall and laid on the floor near the brazier. They placed another cloak over him, and he was dully grateful. He hardly noticed the rank stench wafting from the fabric.

Someone pushed a cup at him, and he wrapped his hands around the heat. The dark liquid steamed, clouding Lucky's eyes, and he didn't resist when told to drink it. After he swallowed, warmth spread to his toes and a bag of lint enveloped his brain. He didn't like the fuzzy feeling, yet he felt relieved when he stopped shivering. He stared at the bright flame in the brazier and, for no reason he could name, he took it as a promise.

As long as it burns I'll be all right.

ISA LEFT her four Ethran servants to tend the boy until she could return and summoned her recent Earthborn recruits. She gathered them in the vast circular sanctum, the better to show them their insignificance, to inflame their need to serve the Demon Queen. She preferred dimness and shadow, but weaker, ordinary eyes needed light. With a dark word and a flick of thin, sharp fingers, she set a ring of torches burning behind them, blue and cold.

She stood tall in the center of the space, robed as always in blue. Acolytes surrounded her, all Earthborn and easily enslaved by magic. They numbered fifty-two, and huddled in kneeling quadrants of thirteen each. Not as many as she would have liked, but a fair number considering the limitations of time.

Mordred waited in the dark outside the circle, bearing a small stone dagger and a mirrored tray holding four large crystal goblets. Each cup contained a potion brewed of red elder, skullcap, bindweed, and rue. As Isa had taught him, Mordred had, in each cup, drowned a wolf spider and weighted it with moonstone and jet. The final ingredient, the one that would bind them to Mordred, and through him to her and to Mahl, would be added later, in ritual sacrifice.

Having earlier cast a glamour to mellow her voice and visage, Isa lifted her draped arms and bade the supplicants raise their eyes. She began to speak, preaching with a rhythm and flow designed to mesmerize. As eyes glazed in the audience, she blended her words into Dark Chant, low and guttural, sending shadows into their hearts to bleed them of heat.

The last syllables of the spell echoed into the vastness of the sanctum. From the slaves, no sound, no movement.

"Mordred," she called, and all heads turned to follow him as he came forward, placed the tray at her feet, and went to one knee. He turned the knife and offered it. She took it and then pulled him to his feet, raising his hand to present him to the gathering.

"Here is your captain," she said. All bowed their heads, and a slow smile of satisfaction twisted Mordred's face. His eyes glittered in anticipation of new power.

After a moment, Isa instructed the Earthborns to stand in their places. "As is proper, your captain will fortify you with his own strength, through his own sacrifice.

"Behold his gift."

He knelt again before her, and she drew the knife three inches down each of his forearms, turning the knife to slide under the skin and increase the flow of blood. The smile didn't leave his face. He uttered no sound. He held his arms over the tray and let his blood, dark with the taint of Mahl, fall into the cups drip by drip.

Quietly, Isa said, "Sufficient."

Mordred stood, bearing the tray, and waited while she instructed the supplicants.

Isa had named a leader for each quadrant of thirteen, a person with some small portion of magic underlying their greed. To each of these four, while his tarnished blood still flowed down his arms, Mordred entrusted a crystal goblet. They did not drink first, but passed the cup each among their twelve.

When all the others had partaken, the leaders took the cups again and drank, draining every drop of potion until stone and spider fell upon their pallid lips, a sorcerer's kiss.

CLOUDS, DARK as coal against the three-quarter moon, swirled and sparked around the blue tower's spiked peak. Han lingered just inside a narrow strip of forest, a bony claw of the pine barren that edged Isa's domain. The mat of needles at his feet was still green and pungent, but the gray branches overhead had been laid bare. The ghost forest testified to the witch's stock-in-trade. Death.

Stripped trees supplied sparse cover, but with silence and the almost magical camouflage of his sun-cloth tunic and cloak, Han hoped to avoid watchful eyes from Isa's lair. He chewed his lip. Tender though the flesh was after his fight with Lohen, indulging the habit helped him think. He focused all his senses on finding any flaw in the witch's stronghold, which thrust from Earth to sky a hundred yards away, but a hopeless distance across her empty moat's abyss.

Han blew a hard breath out his nostrils and followed it with a growl low in his throat. Dismay and frustration that had been mounting since dawn drove his heart to beat hard and fast, and irritation hammered at his temples. Search as he might using every skill he possessed, he could neither see nor imagine any way to sneak, break, or fake his way into the witch's tower.

And what would I do if I could get in? Seize the witch's keep by my lonesome?

But he knew he wasn't alone—not completely. Thoughts emanated from four familiar minds somewhere close by: L'Aria (which shouldn't surprise him), Boff (whom he'd left behind hours ago), Maizie (which seemed somehow expected), and (most astounding) Lemon Martinez. Han looked away from the tower and caught sight of them almost at once. He laughed—they seemed so unlikely, standing together on the blighted ground, craning their necks at the tower.

But it wasn't so funny, really. Han shook his head, thinking that though he felt happy to see them, their presence complicated his dilemma. He would hold himself responsible for them. He couldn't help it—that was his nature. Immediately his mind treated him to imaginings of a thousand threats that could make it impossible for him to keep them safe.

He put that future problem from his mind and followed their collective gaze, again searching the sheer walls of the tower up to where they met the clouds. Sharp as his eyes were, he found only glass, steel, more glass, and more steel. He kept his thoughts to himself, wondering what in the name of the wizard's pajamas they were all gawking at, why they were there in the first place, and what in Behl's blazes he was supposed to do with them.

His memory helpfully supplied the wizard's voice chiming in with a frequently given scolding. *"Han, some things remain beyond your control."* Han grimaced, enjoying the thought like heartburn, but bowed to the inevitable. He stepped out of the dead pines to greet what would surely be his own little strike force. The strangest, teensiest, most mix-and-match army ever to do battle.

As he approached, L'Aria looked at him and pointed up. He followed her finger's direction. Finally, he saw, and it stopped him cold.

Lohen Chiell.

He had ascended the tower despite its sheer walls, climbed so high he seemed no bigger than a fly. He struggled now along a narrow crow's walk with only a thin steel rail glinting between him and the wind-whipped clouds.

"How did he get up there?"

L'Aria quirked one side of her mouth and shrugged.

Han watched as Lohen tugged a hatch open against the wind and disappeared into the tower. The hatch slammed shut with a report like a gunshot. A chill shivered down Han's spine. It had nothing to do with weather.

CHAPTER TWENTY-FOUR: AND THE WITCH IS GLAD

LUCKY BECAME aware of a beautiful light shining golden all around him and dancing with the rhythm of his heart. A smooth road of rich earth lay before him, lined with fragrant trees and roadside pastures studded with wildflowers. He traced the spiraling lilt of a robin's song. He feasted his eyes on morning. At the end of the road, like a beacon of all that is right and good, stood Lucky's mother, arms spread in welcome.

Then he heard the sound of the steel door sliding back; he felt the change in the room when the witch stepped in. When his eyes flew open, Liliana vanished along with the promise of sunshine and the golden road. Pale hands snatched away the cloak that had warmed him. Groggy and afraid, Lucky chafed at the goose bumps on his bare arms. The servants bowed, foreheads to the floor, one of them shoving Lucky on the way down, trying to make him bow too. He steeled his spine and got to his feet instead.

Isa planted her feet wide, directly in front of him. In her hands she held a many-tailed scourge unlike any weapon Lucky had ever seen or imagined. Its glass-tipped lashes squirmed as if alive. Lucky worked up his sluggish courage, tore his gaze from the terrifying weapon, and raised them to meet Isa's glowing orbs.

She stared back at him but spoke to her slaves. "I have called three cairnwights with their wolves from the wolf-hold to replace you here. You four shall proceed to the nether gate. The enemy at our doors—"

She broke off, making a strangled coughing sound, and some seconds passed before Lucky realized she wasn't choking, but laughing. After a time, she caught her breath and resumed her instructions. "Where was I? Oh yes, the enemy at our gates (chuckle) is motley and ridiculous (snort), but battles are by nature unpredictable (sigh)." Directing her gaze with her words to the four pale slaves, she finished, "So, heed my commandment. If the war drums die, raise the gate. Let the ice-drake fly."

For the first time, Lucky thought he saw a sign of life in the servants' faces—eyes widened in fear. Still, they filed obediently out the door, and Isa turned her attention to Lucky.

She smiled, though Lucky was not sure that was the right word for what happened to her face. Then she waved a hand at the brazier, extinguishing the warm orange flames. To Lucky she said, "Do your best to hold up in the cold. Glacier wolves can't abide heat and neither can the cairnwights who keep them, and they are useful to me."

With the flame doused, Lucky felt as though his last friend had died, and having nothing much left between him and the cold, he shivered hard enough to hurt.

Isa spun on her slipper-clad heel and leaned her weapon against the wall, as if disarming for truce talks. Horribly, the whip continued to writhe and clatter and hiss out black smokes, standing in its corner.

She said, "We should get to know one another, boy. You have no way to know this, yet, but you stand to gain a great deal by virtue of my acquaintance."

As she spoke her tone sweetened, but Lucky felt sure it was part of her magic. He didn't know how to hold off the spell she cast with her voice, but he struggled, trying his best to do it anyway. He didn't find out whether it had worked, because just then the steel door at the front of the chamber slid open again.

"Enter," Isa said without looking behind her. "Take guard positions."

The beings that filed in—cairnwights, apparently—appeared almost human, but they had no hair and translucent skin like parchment. Black veins webbed what Lucky could see of their arms, legs, and faces, pulsing through the pale skin. They wore sleeveless short robes, belted at the waist with thin steel chains. Their eyes and robes shimmered, a blue so pale and cold it held not even a memory of sun.

The wolves resembled large Afghan hounds at first glance. White shaggy hair. Curled-up tails, noses too long for their faces. Their limbs were long and their bodies narrow—the same aerodynamic shape as a greyhound.

Definitely, though, they wouldn't have made good pets. They snarled through rows of razor-like teeth, double sets of gleaming two-inch canines. Their lips and noses were the only places not shrouded in pale fur; the bare skin there was colorless. Lucky could almost see through it. Their eyes pearled ghost white except for the pupils, dart-sharp and burning red.

As they crossed the room, the wights' flat feet slapped the marble floor, but the wolves' paws clicked and scraped, sporting claws like hooked knives.

The cairnwights controlled the wolves with whistled commands, two beasts to each wight. They stationed themselves and their animals around the room, so that every eye was trained on Lucky.

"Luccan," Isa said, "pay them no mind."

Lucky thought that would be a tough order to follow even if he wanted to. But she went on speaking, and she seemed to draw closer even though she was still standing in the same place on the platform at the front of the room. It became harder and harder for Lucky to resist her mesmerizing voice.

It felt like her magic strangled his thoughts, clamping down tighter and tighter. It hurt, but Lucky bent over his knees and clutched his fists to his chest, determined to hold on to his mind. Just when he thought he might break, the Key of Behliseth pulsed under his hands, a tiny throb next to the crazed beat of his heart, and he wished he could put all of himself inside it. He couldn't, but behind his eyelids he saw the golden light again, and the road with his mother waiting at the end of it.

"Mom," he croaked. "Help me."

"Stupid boy," Isa snapped. "Your mommy isn't here." Her voice changed again, becoming a demon's growl. Hearing it grate against his ears was agonizing. Lucky cringed, dreading her next words, but they didn't come.

Instead, another voice spoke, deep and masculine. "No, Isa, his mother isn't here, but I am."

The cairnwights seemed to stand even more still. The wolves growled, but so low it was hard to hear. Isa spun toward a small door at the side of the room, and Lucky's eyes followed.

Lohen Chiell.

Surprise broke Isa's concentration, and Lucky's pain lifted. His mind cleared. The trouble, now that he could think, was that a hundred thoughts shot to the surface all at once, and close on their heels came a hundred fears.

"He's always been dangerous," Thurlock had said.

My father.... Lucky tried the sound of the words in his mind. *My father, Lohen Chiell.* The concept itself seemed foreign. As far as he could remember, this man had spoken only one word to him—"Luccan"—and that in the midst of a brawl in Black Creek Ravine.

Now Isa honed her voice to an edge so sharp Lucky wondered if it might draw blood, but she wasn't speaking to him. All her attention went to Lohen Chiell.

"You dare to stand before me? Perhaps you expect me to protect you from the wizard?" She snorted a rude laugh and shook her head as if disbelieving. "Slave, if you hope to draw breath for another minute, you'd best bow low, and you'd best bring me something that will buy your life."

Lohen didn't smile, but something flickered in his one seeing eye that seemed part humor and part threat. Very quietly, he said, "My knees are tired of floors. As to what I bring, perhaps it's death."

Lucky had no context in which to fit those words, and his mind raced. *What does he mean, he brings death? Whose death?* He hoped the man—he couldn't think *my father* just yet—he hoped Lohen meant to kill the witch, though he doubted anyone could accomplish that. Except perhaps Thurlock.

Lohen advanced straight toward Lucky. In his right hand he carried the stone blade Lucky had seen at the ravine, the Black twin to his own Amber. And amazingly, that Knife, the Amber, hung in a sheath on Lohen's belt. His left hand rested on its hilt. Lohen didn't look at Lucky, but the scowl on his face scared him anyway.

Lucky turned to face him. He didn't see a father. He didn't see a rescuer. He saw a scarred, hard-muscled, rough-talking man brandishing knives and threatening death. He saw a man who had "always been dangerous," just steps away now and coming closer, with the Amber Knife and the Black Blade—both certainly deadly—in his hands.

Fright rode in fast and fierce, and Lucky forgot about wights and wolves; he even forgot about the witch. Every cell he owned was riveted on the man alleged to be his father.

Lucky panicked, and he saw no way out, no place to run, so he attacked.

"Luccan," Lohen said, "son," but Lucky could hardly hear it. His blood was rushing loud in his ears like liquid fear. He stormed at Lohen, hailing punches with all his strength.

Surprised, Lohen let the Black Blade clatter to the floor and seized Lucky's hands. "Luccan, wait."

Lohen's voice sounded choked, and Lucky twisted around to see his face. Tears trailed over Lohen's scarred cheek from a brown eye that seemed familiar and far too gentle for a madman.

But now Lucky was caught up in the fight body and soul, too caught up to stop and wonder what the man's tears might mean. He focused instead on the advantage they might give him. He jerked his arms free and fought for all he was worth. Just like that day in the ravine, Lohen tried to stop him but never hit back.

All at once, that fact sank in. Surely Lohen could have done harm, but he didn't even try. The tears, the gentle eye, the way Lohen nearly choked every time he said, "Luccan." Lucky added up the bits of information like two plus two plus two, and he finally got it. Jolted to his senses, he stopped his fists.

I've made a mistake about this man, a bad mistake—

Across the room Isa leaned on the steel candelabra, her smile both cruel and smug.

And, Lucky finished his thought, *the witch is glad I did.*

CHAPTER TWENTY-FIVE: WOLVES, WIGHTS, AND HEROES

FAINT SOUNDS had begun to escape the tower—calls, orders, footsteps echoing against the cold walls. Han and his unusual troupe took cover amidst a hill-sized stack of boulders and twisted deadwood. They remained within yards of the empty moat that surrounded the tower, but shielded from the wind and the tower's blue glare.

A horn shrieked from inside the witch's keep.

Peering between stones, Han watched a sally port open where nothing but blank glass had been before. Mordred, protected behind a shield-curtain visible as blue light, a force field in Earthborn terms, stepped out onto a granite ledge. Two young women rolled a huge drum past the sorcerer and into a niche in the tower's glowing wall. A young man followed, cradling a huge battle horn.

The deep voice of the drum began to beat a cadence. His upraised hands crackling with power, Mordred began to chant. He conjured a ghostly construct, a thin gray mist that arced fifty yards across the moat. Particles appeared within the cloud and started to swarm like excited gnats. They multiplied, clustered, and then condensed to form a bridge. In the crossed light of moon and glowing tower, it gleamed as black and slick as demon's blood.

Hope, like a tiny balloon, quickened Han's heart. He pictured the conflict to come, remembered the clumsy, bewitched slaves in the ravine a few days ago. He drew Chiell Shan with his right hand, drew the sun-metal knife with his left, and drew a breath to send L'Aria and the others back into the pines to find better cover. Only two or three Black Cloaks could come off the bridge at a time. He could hold them off alone, at least for a while.

But instead of Black Cloaks, a cairnwight emerged, followed by six more, each handling a pair of glacier wolves.

Han turned to survey his volunteers and saw L'Aria climbing toward the top of the mound. When she reached the summit, she started to sing.

Han had little magic of his own, but he could, at least, see it. The girl's chiming song flowed shining over the rocky ground in waves. *Interference*, he thought, something to mix up Mordred's spells and befuddle some minds.

Boff stepped out from the rocks, picked up a stone the size of a skull, and hurled it across the moat. It didn't break through Mordred's shield, but the sorcerer flinched. Boff threw another stone, and another….

L'Aria's song and Boff's stones would at least add up to a fine thorn in Mordred's side.

But the wolves, with two-inch fangs and razor claws, had no need of Mordred's attention.

They were by no means invincible, Han knew, but they were tough. The wights were the weaker link in the partnership, carrying only hobbles and short crystal knives. They had frail bodies, even compared to humans—their distant kin. At home in the Ice-fields, the wolves helped the wights hunt and in return received shelter and food in the harshest seasons. In battle, wolves served as shields and weapons and took payment in enemy blood.

But the narrow bridge meant only one pair of wolves could confront Han at a time. The best bet would be to stop them there.

"Piece of cake," Han said, but the sarcasm tasted sour. He swallowed it as the first wolf team neared the end of the bridge, then he dashed out from behind the rocks and came at the wight and its wolves from the side. With a two-handed sweep of Chiell Shan, he slashed through a wolf's neck before it could dodge and dropped it where it stood.

The cairnwight stumbled over its slain charge, and Han brought Chiell Shan down in an overhand strike that laid the wight's pale skin open from ear to hipbone. It fell, bloody arm collapsing beneath it, and knocked the next wight in line back into the ranks.

Han spun quickly to meet the slain wolf's battle mate, a fury of claws and teeth. The beast danced side to side, and Han also danced, using moves so well practiced they'd become instinct. He twisted away as the wolf leapt for his throat. Claws raked his shoulder, but he landed a bone-cleaving blow to the creature's head. It fell in a heap.

Defending, buying time to assist their comrade and move the dead beasts, the wights stationed two teams of wolves in a snarling half circle at the end of the bridge.

Boff moved in closer and targeted them with his stones. Han couldn't see Lemon Martinez, who could easily have been napping, but Maizie lunged and snapped just close enough to the enemy creatures to harass and distract them. L'Aria's song had no noticeable effect on the wights, but to Han's surprise, it clearly unsettled the wolves, making it a bit more difficult for their handlers to maintain control.

With his three comrades keeping them confused, Han had time to step back, switch weapons, and fire three arrows.

Another wight fell and both its wolves.

They'd made a dent, Han thought, and apparently it set the enemy back. The remaining five wights whistled their wolves into an orderly retreat. Giving chase would be suicide; the bridge would probably disappear underfoot. Han considered spending more arrows, but he didn't have many, and he had a gut feeling the real battle hadn't yet begun.

"Well," he muttered, "we've got a reprieve, anyway." He strode back to the rocky hill, signaling the others to follow into the shelter of the boulders. Lemon was already there.

Han took stock. No injuries yet, aside from his own. That was good. His little squad seemed in good spirits. *Perhaps too good*, he thought. *They don't understand what's yet to come.*

He imagined his nephew locked in the tower, facing the witch alone. The thought made his heart skip. And in that moment, he let himself admit a painful truth. *I'm not going to be able to get inside. I can't help him.*

The image of Lohen disappearing through the hatch into the tower popped into his mind. He thought about the previous day, felt Lohen's light-sword bite into his skin as they fought. But then, he all but tasted the roasted rabbit Lohen had left afterward.

"My brother," Han asked L'Aria. "Whose side is he on?"

She looked at him with the most level look he'd ever seen her wear. "He'll do what's right," she said.

Han wanted to believe her. But he couldn't let himself feel relieved because, where Lohen was concerned, Han had little faith left. *By all the gods, let's pray that "Lucky" is more than a name. What happened just now out here....*

Trying to clear his mind and do his job, as he saw it, Han said to the group, "We gained a bit, but that was mostly luck."

"Not *all* luck, Han." L'Aria stood in the shadows of the stone shelter with fists clenched at her sides, clearly angry at Han's assessment.

Han flashed a smile, marveling that she remained defiant even at a time like this. “You’re right, Spit,” he said gently. “Your song helped. But from now on I want you to stay back here. Sing your magic from out of sight.”

She sighed, “I can’t.”

Not sass, for once, an honest statement. Han asked, “Explain?”

“My magic’s not strong. I’m not like my father.”

The admission clearly pained her. “You’re young,” Han said. “Your magic will grow.”

L’Aria half smiled but otherwise ignored the reassurance. “I can already do a lot with water,” she said. “Move it, stop it, use it to make a Portal for myself. But other stuff… not so much. I can confuse people a little and make them feel like they’re swimming against the current, so to speak. But if I can’t see the target, I can’t focus my song. The magic sort of… drifts away.”

While she spoke, she’d torn a shred from the hem of her skirt and poured a bit of water on it from Han’s canteen. Then she approached Han, said, “I hope this won’t hurt,” and began to dab at the wound on Han’s shoulder, humming while she worked.

Surprised at her action and at how much it soothed the icy pain, Han closed his eyes for a second and let go a tense breath. “Thanks,” he said, meeting her eyes again.

Despite her kind touch and apologetic tone, determined fire still burned in L’Aria’s dark eyes, and Han understood that it had cost her pride to admit her limitations. She’d done so only because she truly wanted to help as much as she could.

“Okay.” Han nodded. “Do what you’ve been doing. They… the witch… that sorcerer… whoever’s in charge over there, they haven’t had time to train archers so I wouldn’t worry about that. But watch for stones and things being thrown your way. I’ll have Lemon stay with you. He can be pretty mean—”

The cat growled. Han didn’t interpret. It wasn’t fit for L’Aria’s ears.

“—or distract someone until I can get to you.”

“She saved me,” Boff said. “I’ll help.”

“Good,” Han said to the man. “Thanks. And Maizie,” he said, giving the dog a good scratch, “will do well as guard at the base of the hill where you’re singing.”

Having settled their plans for defense as best he could, Han rationed out half his remaining supply of water—not enough, but no one complained. He cinched his essentially empty pack and stowed it in the rocks. "It won't be long before we'll have to fight again," he said to the others. "Stay here until then, rest if you can. I'm going out."

"They'll see you," L'Aria said, saucy but concerned too.

"Likely they won't. I've got skills and sun-cloth. But you stay here," he repeated. "When it's time, I'll signal."

Moments later, he stood more or less concealed inside the margins of the ruined forest. He narrowed his eyes against the tower's glare, scanning. Nothing moved but the evil wind, a frigid blast that could not be natural in the summer night. He stooped to yank up a handful of dead grass and began to clean his sword, scraping away half-frozen blood. Gory, sticky, and it stank.

"Now this," he said quietly, "is fun." He chuckled, but there was a bitter edge to it. This break in the fighting had already lasted longer than he'd expected. He needed a real plan, he needed it now, and he had no idea where to start.

In the glow from the tower, he peered through the night that had fallen over the forest, searching amongst the ghostly trees. Sarcasm agreed with his mood, so he continued. "What? Do I think I'm going to find a strategy tied to a branch? Perhaps a battle plan will fall from the sky."

Something did fall from the sky at precisely that moment—not a battle plan but something huge and black. It had wings, it smelled like a birdcage, and it settled neatly to the ground ten feet away amidst a flurry of black feathers.

Han lifted his sword, ready to lunge but stopped when the giant winged thing became a man. Tall, dark, all lean muscle, wearing black jeans and a T-shirt, holding both hands in the air, and saying, "Don't shoot."

Han looked at his sword. "Shoot?"

"Slash, thrust, whatever." The man dropped his hands to his long black hair and rebanded his ponytail, then smiled and held out a brown hand. "Henry George, Hank's nephew, if that means anything to you."

"I've heard of you, yes," Han said. Cordially, he returned Henry's smile.

But the smile vanished instantly, as did Henry's, when they shook hands. Pain flared in Han's undamaged shoulder, burning as if the Mark of the Sun that had been there all his life was just then being branded into it. When he met Henry's eyes he found his own surprise and pain mirrored there. Han remembered what Hank George had told Luccan about the Mark of the Others.

"My nephew is the last."

The pain vanished when they pulled their hands apart. Each shrugged his shoulder and cleared his throat, but neither said a word about what had just happened. After a time, Henry's slow smile found its way back. "I'm pleased to make your acquaintance," he said.

"Likewise," Han said, and then he realized he'd felt something else too, just at the moment they touched—another kind of connection. And something inside let go in that instant; whatever it was that had made Thurlock the never-to-be-requited love of his last two hundred years, it faded. This new thing felt like hope—but it had come at such a hopeless moment.

Han shook his head slightly, knowing he needed to focus on here and now. He sat on his boulder and gestured to another, as if inviting Henry into his parlor. Then he asked Henry for his tale and listened while he told it.

Henry had been at home in his city apartment, sitting at the table with a cup of coffee….

"Suddenly, I was struck by a bolt of fear about my Uncle Hank. It didn't make sense; Hank's dead. Still, I couldn't shake it. I flew up to uncle's place, but the worst thing I found there was dust mites."

"But you're a changeling?"

"You mean a shape-shifter?"

"That's strong magic."

"Oh, not so much. It's a talent I was born with, like my grandfather. I practiced a lot, so I got pretty good at it." He smiled. "It came in handy when I was in the army."

With a twinge of hope, Han asked, "You're a warrior, then?"

Henry shook his head and waved a hand. "Just plain Henry." He crossed his arms and chafed his biceps. "It's warmer in the sky than it is down here. Strange weather for June. Gives me goose bumps."

Not goose, Han thought. "What kind of bird?"

"Condor, basically a big vulture. I'm a little bigger than most, twelve-foot wingspan. Prettier than most, too, if I might say so myself."

Han smiled a little, agreeing silently, and huddled into his cloak. "You followed Lucky here?"

"No. I had to get back to work, I'm a firefighter, when I'm not a bird, and I had duty for the next couple days. I got back to Hank's at daybreak this morning, just in time to see his house burning. Heck of a note. I got that taken care of but it set me back hours. Eventually, though, I decided to do a little recon, and flew out this way, just now caught sight of that blue tower."

"You can see it?"

"I can't now." He swiveled his head this way and that, reminding Han of a bird looking for a meal. "But I could see it fine when I was wearing feathers. Strange. Like magic?" He arched his brows to make it a question.

"Yes," Han said.

"Thought so," Henry said, nodding, and then continued. "Anyway, I don't have a good feeling about that place, and I'm thinking Lucky must be inside. I saw a bit of your fight. How can I help?"

Han opened his mouth to speak but then snapped it shut and stared. Suddenly, he laughed. *He's not Thurlock*, he thought, *but he's one more fighter than we had before.*

Han decided to give Henry a down-and-dirty briefing while he had the chance. "Here's what you should know," he said. "There's a sorcerer, goes by the name of Mordred. He's powerful, but he's new at the job, and his boss has given him a bite that he can barely get his teeth around—"

Throom, throom, throom….

The sudden thunder of the northern drum shook the last dead pine needles to the ground and jolted Han to his feet. The horn blasted from within the keep, answered by the yaps and snarls of wolves and muffled footsteps.

Han cinched up his belts and secured his bow on his back. The quiver at his hip still held a handful of plain arrows and five flamers—including three made by Thurlock. Shield in place, sword in hand, he turned to signal L'Aria and the others, but they'd already come out. They didn't look prepared, but they did look stubborn. Han smiled, but his fondness was laced with fear.

The time for briefings and explanations had fled, though, so he took Henry by the elbow and met his eyes. "If you want to help, help Lucky," Han said. "Just fight for all you're worth."

The sally port gaped open, and Mordred emerged. Safe behind his force field, he conjured the black bridge anew. This time when the buzzing mist the sorcerer brought forth clotted solid, the bridge split into two spans. Han sighed, wishing he could split himself too.

Then Mordred's chant got louder and the drumbeat got faster. Black-cloaked Earthborns, moving jerkily like puppets on strings, began to quick march across the bridge. On the parallel span, five cairnwights kept pace. Their wolves slathered, bloodlust strong in their eyes.

Han sent an arrow through the neck of the lead wight, and the creature fell to its knees and toppled to the bridge deck. Instantly, the loose wolves lunged, all teeth and gleaming claws, turning their bloodlust on their own pack mates, even tearing into the wight's corpse. The other cairnwights' luminous eyes, normally placid, flashed alarm.

Taking in the wolves' behavior, Han knew it wasn't right. He nocked his next arrow while he tried to figure it out. *Glacier wolves are pack animals; their survival depends on loyalty. Why would they turn on each other?* A flash of insight came as he drew back his bow for the second shot.

It's the magic.

The ravine was swimming in it: the massive power Isa expended to maintain her presence in Earth, to hold her blue tower there—or at least make it seem to be there—and yet keep it hidden from the world at large; the spells and enchantments she'd laid on her Earthborn servants; Mordred's steady chant to direct those slaves and hold the bridges. Add to that L'Aria's song, probably Henry's thing, and maybe even Han's small skills.

It's driving the beasts mad.

Even so, the wights demonstrated amazing skill. They whistled and gestured in perfect coordination, their pale forms liquid shadows against the blue light of the witch's stronghold, like dancers moving to some fantastical, hypnotic song. By the time Han gave himself a mental shake and loosed the second arrow, the wights had begun to bring the half-crazed beasts into order.

But the second arrow flew true and took a cairnwight through the lung. This time the newly orphaned wolves rushed at Han. He barely had time to stumble back, shoulder his bow, and tear Chiell Shan from its sheath. Arm and blade outstretched, he swept it in a wide arc. He connected with nothing more solid than the tip of an ear, but for a split second he kept the snarling beasts at bay. The maneuver bought him just enough time to shift his stance and gather his strength.

Without discipline, the keeperless wolves flung themselves at Han with unchecked energy. He used it against them, letting one impale itself on his thrusting sword and seconds later slicing open the belly of the second.

But his moves had been desperate; his success, at least in part, had been luck. His timing lagged a thin shade behind his intentions, and the cairnwights seized their moment. Keeping their fragile selves out of Chiell Shan's reach, they played two teams of wolves against him at once in a deadly, teasing rhythm. Feint, dodge, stalk, lunge. One beast and then another.

Han could never predict where the next wolf would strike or exactly when. He was forced over and over again to defend on one side and leave the other exposed. Like a castle besieged, he inflicted small damage where he could. Doomed, he supposed, to fail in the end, he fought even harder, determined to take his last chance to cripple the power these creatures served.

Claws slashed his right leg, and it burned and ached as though immersed in dry ice. Han noted the injury, took it into account, shifted his weight, and altered his moves to allow for it. But he didn't retreat. He thought of Luccan, the wizard's laugh, the warm golden shine of Behlis Ethra's springtime, and… yes, the shape-shifter Henry's agreeable brown eyes. Things he treasured.

He found what he needed then—the Warrior Mind. He began to fight with cold purpose. His moves felt to him like slow, smooth motion, though his weapon flashed lightning fast. He didn't gain the upper hand in the fight, but he held on and whittled away at the wolves' numbers.

A true captain—even in combat, even in pain—as he fought he gave a corner of his mind to how his troops, such as they were, fared. A stolen glance, the sound of a cry or footsteps, now and again a shred of someone's thought.

The Condor landed, transformed, and pulled a mean-looking club from the hands of a black-cloaked corpse. Positioning himself at the end of the second bridge span, Henry took on the enemy two by two as they stepped off the bridge. Many fell; blood soaked the ground.

Most of those who slipped by didn't make it ten feet before they met the sharp end of Maizie's madness. Maybe the same magic-sickness that had affected the wolves got to her too. Whatever the reason, the driven rage she had previously turned on Lucky swelled again. This time, she turned it on the enemy.

The few Black Cloaks who made it past the dog's teeth headed for the hill of stones where L'Aria sang and Lemon, unmoving but for his flicking tail, feigned indifference. Han wondered why Mordred would direct so much energy toward L'Aria. Perhaps he wanted to silence her magic, lighten his load. But Han couldn't help but think the sorcerer's motive might be something more twisted.

But the would-be assassins couldn't match Boff's strength. He planted himself in their path and blocked their way with hammering fists and unshakeable determination. L'Aria's song flowed on unbroken.

Fierce pride in his comrades swelled Han's heart. It gave him strength, but it also fed his fears. His soldiers fought hard. Brave, resourceful, and strong, they amazed him, and he was grateful. But they were so few, so unready for this mortal struggle.

L'Aria's voice grew hoarse. Maizie's tongue lolled and dripped as she panted between attacks. A stone slipped from Boff's bloody grasp. Henry swiped stinging sweat from his eyes. And, even the Warrior Mind can't hold a body up forever; the claw marks in Han's shoulder burned more, not less, as time passed, and his injured leg became a slow, heavy burden.

And as long as the drum would beat, as long as Mordred would chant, the bridges would hold and Isa's slaves would march across.

Mordred is the key.

Han knew he must find some way to deal with the sorcerer, but he could think of nothing that didn't require more strength, more speed, and undeniably more magic than he could hope to find.

A laugh escaped him. Gallows humor. *Why*, he asked himself, *are wizards never around when you need them?*

Courting resentment for Thurlock's absence, Han stumbled heavily out of a desperate two-handed slash. He took down the attacking wolf, the blade slipping through the skin of its throat like a knife through cream, but his momentum took him too far. He landed heavily on his injured leg and went down.

Total, he had killed four wights and eight wolves. Three teams of the creatures remained.

And, Han thought, *I'm finished.*

MOST OF the Ethran Mounted Guard joining the expedition to Earth had already gathered in the hall on the lower floor of the Sisterhold. Most of the others present at the feast counted among those who needed to know the plans. Lili and Gerania headed down the main stairs to deliver the news and set things in motion.

Rose went up, rather than down, to the small, thatched belfry, where she would blow her eagle-whistle to send its piercing note off to ride the winds. The call, as always, would be answered within minutes by one of Ethra's colorful, horse-sized flame eagles.

Thurlock took the back stairs. Down one flight past the armory, another past basement workrooms, and down a long ramp into cellars carved from rock and dirt and shored up with rough-cut timbers. Thurlock, who long ago had been imprisoned in a dungeon built in much the same manner, fought off a chill of fear and whispered to himself, "You won't be trapped, you old fool."

He kept up the self-talk as he continued through a long corridor lit by glowing stones. He passed by all the doors, turned three times at intersections, came to a blank wall, knocked it with his staff, and fell through the trap door that appeared beneath his feet. He landed on his feet, hard and stiff-legged.

"Behl's hairy teeth," he growled, "I am getting too old for that." He headed for the back wall, thinking longingly of Earth devices such as escalators, elevators, and convenience stores. He ducked hanging bundles of herbs, feathers, and sundry whatnots. He dodged tables, benches, barrels, and a central brick chimney over a fire pit, complete with cauldron on an iron hook. He banged his knee, stubbed his toe, and got dust in his eye.

He blew more dust off a shelf holding various glass vessels and coughed vigorously while attempting to sort through the goods. Finally he selected three vials, all with brassbound corks—two large, one small, all tempered for heat, frost, and light, and pretreated with an infusion of cracked-shield lichen and creeping sandwort.

He went back the way he had come, complaining, "All that trouble for three empty bottles," and dashed out the back door. His long strides ate up the distance to the Oakridge, and he arrived with about five minutes to spare until dawn. Just enough time to let his horse know he needed her.

West of the ridge, rolling pasturelands lay cradled between the twin ranges of the Sister Hills. Somewhere in the miles of grass, Sherah, Thurlock's famous silver-gray mare, awaited his call. Thurlock stuck two fingers in the corners of his mouth, just as his cousin Thorland had taught him when he was seven years old, and sounded a loud, sharp whistle. He smiled, just as proud of that whistle as he had been on the day he first mastered it.

He turned to face east, and when a faint gray light began to shimmer at the world's edge, he raised his staff to the heavens. Just as the sun charged the horizon, blindingly bright, he shouted, "Behl-Eth Dahn," *Behl has given*. Chanting a repeating psalm, he called the light into his outstretched left hand.

Slowly the fire spread through him until he stood like a torch in the wind. He channeled Behl's light from his right hand, through his staff, and from there let it pour into the three vials.

When they were full he said, "Thanks," rather casually, then capped the bottles.

"Now, Behl, the wind?"

In much the same process but without the pyrotechnics, he gathered in the dawn wind, the Gods' Breath, and filled it with his own strength, goodness, and valor. As an afterthought he added in a little joie de vivre, and then with a magical word he locked that wind into the fibers of his shining staff.

"Done," he said, and then he climbed down to greet his waiting horse. "It's time, Sherah," he said. "Be swift."

THE INSTANT Lucky stopped fighting Lohen, Isa's loathsome voice echoed in whispers around the blue-lit chamber. "Luccan, you are lovely when you're angry. We may yet become friends." She laughed, and it chilled Lucky to the heart. She strode to the wall and hefted her weapon. "Alas, you didn't finish the job that needs doing. It's my turn."

To Lucky's right, Lohen dove into a roll, retrieved the Black Blade as he passed, and snapped to his feet lightning fast, smooth despite his stiff left leg.

"Stop him!" At Isa's Command, wights whistled and wolves moved. In a blink, all six beasts circled Lohen, a loose, snarling hoop of glittering teeth.

Lohen twisted the Black Blade in his hand, and a sword-shaped beam of indigo light sprang forth. It was an amazing thing to see, and at that moment Lohen seemed an amazing man. *My father!* Lucky tried the idea again and found it had begun to fit.

One of the wights whistled a short trill, and its wolves leapt. Lohen spun with the sword, dodging one and slashing the other with the magical blade. The sight of all that blood, scarlet even in the awful light, left Lucky startled sick. Before the slain wolf even hit the ground, the wight sounded a note and the other creature lunged again, snapping teeth.

Lohen turned his head slightly side to side, apparently to compensate for his one-eyed field of vision. He stood otherwise still as if unsure. But when the beast leapt, he moved just enough, just in time, shifting his blade to impale the wolf.

The sudden weight of the dead wolf tipped him off-balance, and he stumbled back. But he recovered, stepped sideways, and sliced the shoulder of another beast, shallow but damaging.

The cairnwights' stiff features remained unreadable, yet their surprise was almost tangible. They delayed an instant before giving the next command, and Lohen seized that shred of opportunity to slide inside the protecting wolves. He cut through a cairnwight's throat.

Lucky sensed the other two wights' alarm. The wolves seemed almost out of control now, crazy with bloodlust. Even the wounded wolf snapped and tried to lunge on three legs.

Then, with a sharp whistle, the wights set all the remaining wolves on Lohen at once. To Lucky it seemed as if the handlers had simply joined the wolves in their madness. Whatever the reason, that tactic changed things. The wolves no longer worked together, guided in a coordinated assault, and maybe that was what kept Lohen alive for the next few minutes. He spun and dodged, clearly with no time to do anything but react and defend himself, and when seconds had become long minutes, he'd only been able to kill one more beast.

Scratched and bitten in a dozen places, with every step he left a bloody print on the slick marble floor, an image Lucky couldn't shake from his mind, and his thoughts tumbled.

He's fighting alone, for his life....

For his life! Lucky's father had finally shown up and could very possibly die right before his eyes. That reality struck Lucky like a stone, and he balled up his fists. *I have to help.*

Isa must have sensed his resolve, somehow, and she roared, "No!" The magical Command latched onto Lucky like claw-fingers in a death grip. He couldn't move. "That's not to be, boy," she said. "I'm enjoying this sport!"

Lucky pulled against her magic with every ounce of strength he had. To his own surprise, he began to gain ground—he could almost move, and he could feel the witch's hold begin to weaken.

Isa screamed, "Stand, boy!"

Lucky's eyes and ears were chock-full of wolf snarls and hairy white wolf bodies and claws and teeth, all battering the man he now thought of automatically as *my father* into a corner. Panicked—and encouraged by his own slow progress—Lucky redoubled his efforts to break Isa's hold.

"I *will* teach you obedience, boy." The witch had her scourge in hand, and its many lashes writhed as she cocked her arm back for a blow. The weapon sliced through space, hissing as if in warning.

Lucky turned away at the last hair's-breadth instant and the blow struck across his back. Pain he couldn't have imagined until that moment blazed through the tendrils of every nerve. He heard a blood-curdling, terrified cry and then realized, *I'm the one screaming.*

The whip flashed upward in preparation for another strike, but Lucky hardened himself against it, dredging up every ounce of stubborn will. *I won't*, he vowed. *I won't scream like that again.* He held his breath, waiting for the scourge to whistle through the air, waiting for its cruel tails to rip his flesh.

"Not my son!" Lohen Chiell's bellow rang through the cold chamber like a battle cry. As if it powered him up, Lohen went as wild as the wolves. He slashed, cleaved, and thrust, killed one more wolf, and sliced a bloody gash down the length of a wight's back.

Each wight still commanded one wolf, but Lohen's mad rush left them startled, injured, and bewildered. They withdrew their beasts, stepping back toward the corners, away from Lohen.

Isa stared at Lohen Chiell, stunned, her mouth hanging open as if her jaw had come unhinged. But to Lucky, it looked like Lohen had spent what energy fury had lent him, and now he sagged, chest heaving and blood dripping from a hundred wounds. Isa, for her part, recovered her wits quickly and ordered the wights back to their task, now turning the threat of her scourge on them.

Lucky started toward Lohen again, still determined to help, but he was exhausted by hours of pain, effort, and terror. He stopped, dizzy, teetering on the edge of the now cold fire pit. But his movement had drawn Isa's attention, and she once again turned to strike him.

After a desperate struggle, Lohen took another wolf out. Then he stumbled across the chamber and rooted himself between Lucky and Isa's lash, spreading fatherly arms out like the shielding wings of an angel.

The whip came down on Lohen once, but then he pivoted, raising his light-blade. When the whip fell again, he slashed through its tails. The damaged weapon sizzled and flared like cut power lines, and the room clouded with stinking black smoke.

By then blood and sweat poured off Lohen like rain, his breath came hard, and his voice had been worn to a rag. Still he insisted, "You cannot have my son."

Isa fixed him with a stare, then turned her back and walked across the chamber. The surviving wolf, amazingly, was the one Lohen had wounded early on, and now blood loss had weakened it so much it could barely stand. Isa rasped a Command at the wights.

"Take that useless beast and get out."

Vicious scowl pasted in place, Isa turned to face Lohen and spoke very softly. "You stupid slave. Fool, you are, to think you've already suffered the worst that I can do." She muttered strange words and waved her hand in a quick gesture. Like spider legs, the severed tails of the whip grew back, glass-shard tips and all.

This time, when Isa snapped her weapon, she muttered a spell behind it, and it struck Lohen so hard that he slid across the floor. He put his arms under him to rise, but the witch struck again. Lohen's clothes were shredded, and blood beaded on his flayed skin.

Whatever parasite—fear, exhaustion, pain—whatever had held Lucky back, in that moment it lost its grip. Strength reared up inside him, part wish, part rage, part terror, maybe part compassion. Without thinking he set it loose, and it drove him in a headlong, roaring rush, straight at the witch.

Isa wheeled around to face him. For the tiniest moment, her ice blue eyes widened in shock or alarm. Then she raised the scourge as if to strike again, but stopped, looking at it as if considering whether it was truly the best tool for the job. She shook her head and laughed, her smile an ugly slash.

She raised her hands and began to chant.

She seemed to be calling down some awful power, turning the air between them thick and foul and drawing every last shred of warmth out from the stone and steel of the bloody chamber.

Lucky, stalled in his tracks by the weight of her magic, felt a warm comfort at his side and he knew it was Lohen before he looked. His father was bloody and bruised, but on his feet. When he took hold of Lucky's hand, his grip was sticky with blood but warm and strong and impossibly steady.

Turning Lucky's palm up, he slapped down the hilt of the Amber Knife. The two of them stood at the same height, and he met Lucky's eyes with a level gaze. "It's what I came here for, to give you what's yours. It's more than a knife, Luccan, more than amber."

Lucky's hand curled around that Blade as if it had its own mind, as if it had waited, biding time for the touch of this very stone.

"Luccan," Lohen said, calling Lucky's attention back. "It's dangerous; great magic always bears risk, and there's no time to teach you. But, if all else fails, and if luck is truly yours, this Blade can stop Isa."

The witch kept up her chant, the harsh sounds swelling and repeating in a tangled echo. A flash from the dais where she stood was followed by a grating sound, like a train braking to a stop on rusty rails. The massive spell she'd created, a hissing ball of blue flame and ropy black smokes, began to spin in her hands, looking like a mass of sparking electric eels trapped in translucent skin.

Lohen released a ragged breath and gulped another. He took hold of Lucky's arm and pulled him around so they were face-to-face. When he spoke, he sounded as if he believed the words would be his last. "Son," he said, "maybe you'll forgive me in the end."

The child inside Lucky demanded explanations, wanted to shout questions. *Who are you? Why did you leave me? Why come back now? But*, said a smarter voice, *now isn't the time.* He put kindness, not forgiveness and not love, but all the kindness he possessed into his eyes. "Papa," he said, his voice deep, like a man's.

Lohen nodded, showing Lucky a smile, small and sad but honest. Lucky pushed his hair back and locked eyes with his father, and then they turned together to face the witch.

"Lowly slave," Isa said to Lohen, the last echoes of her chant falling away. "You've caused nothing but grief since the day that Black Blade was returned. It ends now." Without even a blink of hesitation, she hurled the spell.

But the floor was bloody, and she slipped.

The spell flew off course, rocketing not toward Lohen, but toward Lucky. For an instant, the entire chamber held its breath. Isa froze with her pale brows arched, her mouth slack. Then she shouted, "Not the boy, I want him!"

Lohen stepped in front of Lucky, setting his feet wide and raising his magical sword into the path of the spell.

The explosion of clashing magic shook the tower to its foundations, knocking Lucky sideways with a force that felt like a speeding truck. Miraculously, when the initial shock passed, Lucky found he could move. He rolled to his knees and stared for a moment at his empty hands bleeding scarlet on the white marble floor, then he raised his head to see.

Death.

Carcasses of wolves, a wight's torn corpse, shapeless piles of debris stained with blood, both red and black.

And a scarred man in torn clothing, hand still clutching a black stone knife. *Broken lamp... shield the flame.* The words had comforted Lucky when he'd read them in his strange little book in Thurlock's basement. Now, they tore at his heart.

CHAPTER TWENTY-SIX:
BLACK HEARTS AND FLAMES

A BREATH of strange silence, and then an explosion cracked the sky around the tower's steel spire. The world shivered in Han's eyes as if about to dissolve and shook beneath him. The blue glare of the tower, for an immeasurable fraction of time, failed. Mordred's chant faltered; the drum skipped a beat. The bridge vanished, and the team of wight and wolves stationed at the span's end fell to their deaths in the deep emptiness of the moat.

Something had happened inside the tower!

In that moment even the wolves stalled, and Han scrambled for his sword and then for meager cover behind the root mass of an upturned tree. For a moment, his heart soared, lofted on hope like wings. His thoughts went immediately to Luccan, and he tried to shoot a thought-message past the tower's wavering magic. But in no more than a blink, a low sound like humming power lines arose and the eerie blue began to shine again.

The drummers beat the cadence of sorcery with fear-born fervor. Mordred's chant snaked on. Mordred's shield reformed and crackled as the sorcerer powered it once more to full strength. And Mordred's army, though tattered, fought again.

The sally port began to yawn open in the tower's wall.

More Black Cloaks, reinforcements.

More thralls to be thrown against Han and his allies. More pawns to the will of Mordred, himself a product of the witch and her evil lord. Han knew the man could only be stopped with a wizard's power.

Watching it begin again, Han's emotions traveled a dark road. Mordred, Isa, and the emptyhearted Lord of Ice—he hated them as he had never hated before. But worse, so bitter was he to be left here with little power and less hope that it was on the tip of his tongue to curse gods and wizards too. All of them.

But….

Perhaps by accident, his fingertips brushed the feathered arrows at his hip. As if the touch had tripped a switch, a memory tumbled forth.

Dawn. The sweet tang of Shahna's Gold on his tongue. Han had given Luccan's shoulder a squeeze and turned away to leave the wizard's tower.

"Wait," Thurlock had said.

Han stopped in the doorway.

"Remember, warrior. Flame will sometimes find a path where even your strength and skill cannot take you."

Cryptic, but now Han understood. All this time he'd spent bemoaning his lack of power, when the wizard's own magic had been riding his hip, waiting for him to set it loose.

"SIT UP!"

Isa spat the Command from across the death-littered room, and, without any contribution from his mind, Lucky's sore body tried to obey. Hands and feet slipped on stone slick with blood and sweat, and he finally stopped, exhausted, when he'd scrabbled onto knees and elbows. From that humiliating position, he stared at the Witch-Mortaine in disbelief.

Her skin hung loose, glimmering with graveyard sheen, a semblance of flesh that hardly covered her bones. The ice blue shield she'd thrown up just before the blast had protected her from the spell's worst impact, Lucky suspected, just as Lohen's intervention had protected Lucky. Still, to look at her, it was hard to believe she was strung together well enough to stand.

In fact, she wasn't. She leaned against the wall, and as Lucky watched, she began to tremble. She fixed him with a look that clearly dared him to say anything, and then she took a flask from a deep pocket of her blue-shine robes.

Steel, slender as two fingers, as long as a hand, the bottle was capped with a black plug bound on by thin red threads. In one motion the witch sliced through the bindings with a sharp thumbnail, popped the cork, and lifted it to her upraised, gaping mouth.

She didn't swallow, but rather sucked the smoky black substance into her lungs, looking at Lucky sideways the whole time. She inhaled for so long that he began to hope she would burst, but all she did was cap the bottle, hide it in her robes somewhere, and let her breath out real slow.

Something horrible happened then, something Lucky knew he would wish for the rest of his life he had never seen. Her eyes flickered. Her skin faded, or more accurately thinned, until Lucky could see through into the sick, blackened organs and veins within. And then Isa was gone, and a shadow, a kind of witch-shaped nothingness, took her place.

The whole weird transition happened in less time than it took Lucky to do a double take, and when it was over, he wondered if he'd really seen it. Because, by the time pure shock got knocked out by a giant wave of fear, she was back in her body.

As horrible as ever.

Laughing.

"Sit up," she yelled again and crossed the cavernous room in ten strides. She grabbed him by the shredded back of his shirt and dragged him to the nearest corner. "Sit," she repeated, but instead of putting magic in the words, she yanked him upright and drove the order home with a hard shake that slammed his head against the wall.

She brought out her steel bottle. "Perhaps you need a sip of my special tea to shore you up?"

He pasted his hands to the walls, ignoring the icy surface, willing himself to stay upright at all costs. He retched at the thought of that horrid… stuff… fuming into his body.

She chuckled. "I'll take that as a no. Now, don't move."

Lucky doubted that he could.

She walked to the center of the room, then pivoted, waving at each of the thirteen torches and killing the blue flames. She left the triplet candles burning on the platform, then stood beneath those eerie lights, one hand pressed against each of the steel pillars that held the candles aloft. For a long time she stayed there, silent and still, her tattered blue robes draped from her outstretched arms like wings on an angel's ruined corpse.

Lucky pulled his eyes away from her and looked again at his father. Lohen's body hadn't been torn or crushed. He'd simply gone still. Lucky tried to convince himself that he saw Lohen's chest moving up and down, very slightly. Then he shook his head hard enough to wake up its knocks and bruises.

He's dead, he told himself. *And I'm a fool. I never know when to quit hoping, quit believing.*

Suddenly, the smoldering anger Lucky always pretended wasn't there burned out of control. He stared at his father's brown, bloody, lifeless hands and demanded, *How could you do this? How could you leave me again?*

But in the fifteen short years of his life, Lucky had been left or lost a bunch of times. To be honest, his life had left him mad at everyone. He started mentally ticking off the list of who he harbored anger toward and why: *Hank, for dying. Henry, for letting me leave. Thurlock for losing me on the way. Han, for leaving me. My mother for not—*

Wait.

There stood the Witch-Mortaine, only yards away, hanging between supports as if suspended by her own evil. *She* was the cruel one, the dark one. *She* was the real, root cause of Lucky's trouble.

Once he put his mind to it, tacking all his hatred onto Isa came easy.

HAN'S MOMENT of enlightenment cost him dearly, for in the scant seconds he'd spent immersed in golden memory, blind to the blue-lit night, the last remaining team of wolves had crept up silently behind him. They'd launched themselves at him before he knew they were there. He whirled, swinging Chiell Shan two-handed in a desperate arc with the beasts in midleap.

He caught one wolf across the hindquarters and flank, and it fell to the side, where it scrabbled helplessly on the blood-slicked rock. The second wolf escaped the blade and leapt. Han stumbled backward off the rock and thought he was surely done, but it was the fall that saved him, because instead of tearing into his throat, the beast rocketed right over his head.

Han had curled up as he fell, so he avoided breaking his head on the rocks, but his back hit the ground hard. His breath rushed out, and try as he might, he couldn't suck a new one in. Han knew the wolf would return, but until Han could breathe, he couldn't move.

The sky went black overhead, and Han expected the worst, but the shadow was Henry in condor shape, coming to Han's aid. The great bird raked his talons across the wolf's belly and opened a pair of gashes, long and deep. The beast thrashed on the ground, howling in pain.

The Condor prepared to strike again and finish it, but pulled up suddenly and circled overhead. Han rolled to his feet but soon saw that this fight was over.

With movements so quick and small they were hard to follow, the last wight standing slit the throats of each of its wounded wolves. Each time, it covered the beasts' eyes with a gentle hand, and spoke—the only words Han had ever heard a wight utter. The pale, almost-human creature from the north of Ethra then reversed its slender dagger, held it with two hands, and plunged it into its own belly, twisting for a fatal cut.

Henry had already altered his course and flown to the hilltop, where a knot of Black Cloaks tried to get past Boff and Maizie to reach L'Aria, who hadn't stopped singing yet, though she sounded hoarse and strained. Han thought that with Henry's help the others could keep her safe, and he had another task, so he turned away, knowing he might not get another chance.

Stumbling, bleeding, and sweating, Han climbed again to take cover behind the huge spread of the upturned tree root. He drew three arrows from his quiver, two bearing rainbow flames, the third fletched in sun yellow and painted gold. He took aim beyond the shield curtain, beyond the heavy black of the sorcerer's robe, on a spot deep in the cold center of Mordred's heart. He loosed the first two arrows in rapid succession.

The first arrow sent a shiver of sparks through the shield. The next strike lit the whole force field with rainbow flame. He nocked the third arrow—Thurlock's golden work—to the bowstring. He drew it back, and set it loose.

Clarity.

A moment spaced within heartbeats, moving so slowly past Han's senses that it might have held a lifetime. The bowstring thrummed, and recoil punched his shoulder like a slow fist. All the light in the blue night drew close in to brighten a slender tube through which Han watched the wizard's arrow fly.

The sun-metal point shattered the shield and struck home. So tuned were Han's senses that he heard the black threads of the sorcerer's robe snap under the point, felt layers of skin stretch and tear. Finally, the dense, determined tissue of the sorcerer's black heart sucked the arrow in as if welcoming death, and exploded in a burst of golden heat.

Han watched Mordred's eyes widen, soften, even smile in surprise. Then, the animal smell of fear. No longer was Mordred a sorcerer, an enemy, a fiend. He was simply a man, someone's child. In striking him down, Han had done nothing evil, only a job that must be done. Yet for that instant he wished with every shred of his soul that he could take it back. The slow, stretched seconds snapped.

Wild night rushed Han from every direction, everything happening at once, none of it what he expected. Before Mordred's knees even crumpled, Boff shouted in dismay. He tensed, head to toe, and then ran onto the bridge holding his arms out as if to catch his brother or break his fall.

The port in the tower wall opened wide behind Mordred, and it seemed it would swallow him whole. But Mordred fell forward, not into the tower's heart, but into the abyss that held its roots. The black bridge vanished under Boff's feet, and Boff, too, plunged to his death.

In that instant Lemon screeched, a blood-curdling, alley-cat's yowl. L'Aria screamed a half beat later, ending her song in a cry so crammed with anger and fear that Han could taste it. He leapt from his perch to go to her aid, scanning the bloody battle yard on his way.

A few Black Cloaks ran for the pines. A few milled in confusion with no sorcerer to drive them. But some were fighting, and now they fought as if they meant it, as if they had just woken up to their own bitterness.

A dozen of them, led by a brutish blonde woman, swarmed over the mound toward L'Aria. Before Han had finished his first step, Lemon Martinez leapt, transformed into a snarling ball of claws and teeth. He sprang straight into the big woman's face, dug his front claws into her scalp, and slashed with the hind claws again and again.

She killed him, of course. She tore him from her face, dashed him to the rocks, and then stomped with her heavy boot until his tiny, secretly loyal heart split wide open. Her vengeance was blind; Lemon had shredded her eyes. And it was futile. L'Aria let go all of her youthful rage on the woman and pushed her back so hard that she fell, tripped up two of her followers, and landed broken on the rocks, spitted on her comrade's spear.

The other Black Cloaks came on, and L'Aria fought back, young hands curled into determined fists. Maizie reached her side and darted at the attackers, snapping and tearing their flesh. The Condor landed and transformed, and Henry used his long reach to take charge of the hill.

As Han reached the foot of the hill, he caught sight of L'Aria's face, bruised and bloody.

The truth struck home.

She'll die here. Why didn't I send her away?

A sound startled him out of his lament, a sound like the roar of wind in an ice-cave. Every motion ceased. Fear froze hearts good and evil alike and the battle stopped, posed like a museum tableau. Han knew the sound, and he forced his head to turn toward the tower, where the door gaped wide.

"Ice-drake," he said, and he couldn't suppress a shudder, both of fear and revulsion. In Han's opinion, ice-drakes, mutants made from dragons' eggs and foul magic, were Ethra's most abominable mistake. Their frigid breath killed with horrible efficiency, and everything was prey. And if dragons—mutant or not—could talk, the one thing they would never say is, "I'm not hungry."

The beast emerged and spread her majestic, glittering wings.

Most drakes were small and flawed, often flightless or blind, mistakes produced when bungling sorcerers mishandled the dark magic formulated to transform natural beasts into evil creatures.

But this was not just any ice-drake.

This drake was legend.

"Sahlamahn."

As Han whispered her name, scenes from stories his great-uncle had told him of this cruel, wondrous northern beast played out in his mind's eye. He heard again the cadence of the old man's voice, just as it had sounded when it fueled his childhood imaginings.

Sahlamahn, the first ice-drake ever transformed, and the only one ever to rise flawless. *Sahlamahn*, eerily beautiful while her cousins were horrid and clumsy. Sahlamahn outsized other blue drakes by half, and she had it all: flight, armor, claws, and breath that could freeze-dry blood still in the veins.

She bore no riders now and never had. She'd never done the bidding of anyone except the sorcerer, long since dead, whose evil had made her what she was.

So why will she do Isa's bidding now?

Clearly, Han wasn't the only who wasn't sure the drake would pick and choose her prey. A stream of the remaining black-cloaked figures broke for the trees, seeking cover. Han thought that wasn't a bad idea, but he saw Henry atop the hill, supporting the sagging L'Aria against his hip with one arm and pointing with the other.

Following that gesture, Han saw that the fleeing Earthborns had stopped in their tracks. What could have given them a scare to rival Sahlamahn? Then, on the high ridge just beyond the trees, Han saw what approached, and smiled.

Liliana, at the head of a mounted column that ranged along the ridge. Her steed, Aedanh, led easily, his gait proud, his hooves fleet. His coat shone like spun gold even in the tower's foul glow, and Lili and her mount both boasted the gilt and silver colors of the Sunlands. Just behind rode six of Shahna's Rangers, the Mounted Guard's elite, bedecked in burnished mail and the diamond patterned green of the Sisterhold, their horses' tails and manes streaming in a wind raised by speed.

Five flame eagles sailed the sky above them—massive birds plumed in white and crested black, saffron, and red. Rosishan rode upon their battle-wise king, Ghriffon. The wind lifted her cloak, flashing the stark red of the Eagle Alliance, the diamond green, and the bright-sewn rainbow symbols of Rose's own magic.

"On your left!" The shout came from the tail of the column of horse soldiers, accompanied by the ring of an extra set of hooves, falling fast and light. Again, the deep voice, "Passing on your left."

As the others moved aside to let the rider by, Han smiled. Relief threatened to flood his eyes. He'd stopped believing this moment would come.

Thurlock had arrived.

LUCKY SAT in his corner, vaulted in darkness, and glared at Isa, letting rebellion build like a mudflow behind a dam. *She's ignoring me*, he thought, *because she thinks I can't hurt her.*

His nostrils flared at the awareness of her casual disregard. He recalled his father's instruction. "This Blade can stop her." He sucked at his cheek, tasting blood. He'd lost his hold on the Amber Knife in the blast, but he spotted it now on the floor across the room, close to Isa.

I'm fast enough, Lucky decided. He tensed to spring.

But Isa heard something or somehow sensed his intention and pivoted to point a finger at Lucky. She conjured a fist-sized bullet of blue, crackling light and hurled it streaking through the fumes to stab through his skull. Instantly, he writhed in pain, unable to control his movements or the mewling sounds he made. A million or so years later when Isa dropped her hand, the torture stopped as suddenly as it had started.

"We'll try once more to have our talk," Isa said. "Before we do, let me compliment you. Defiance looks good on you. Or was it hate?" Her lips twitched, and she chortled in glee. "You gave me a little boost, and I do appreciate it. But we've things to do. Forget the Knife. Let it lie where it is."

She turned on a heel and began to pace, robes trailing. After a few passes, she stopped in front of Lucky. She locked her death blue gaze on his eyes, and her bloodless lips twisted in the most hateful smile Lucky could imagine. She held her hands out toward Lucky and slowly unfurled her fists. Something flowed out of them, some kind of magic that smelled like cheap wine and felt as thick and deadly sweet as molasses in a flytrap.

"Luccan," Isa said, her voice smoothed out. Speaking in hypnotic cadence, she continued, "I'm sorry about your father. I couldn't let him continue. I was afraid he would kill you."

"You lie, witch," Lucky said. "It was you who almost killed me." The words were bold, even brave under the circumstances, but to Lucky his voice sounded small and pointless, a lot like the last buzz of a dying insect.

"Luccan," she said again.

Lucky felt magic fall around him like chains.

"You've been misled. In no way do I desire your death. Quite the contrary, these regrettable events today were not my wish, not my doing. All I want is a chance to help you. I brought you here to show you your potential, the vast power you could choose to embrace." If Lucky's attempt at defiance had angered her, she kept it secret. Words oozed from her lips in sticky-sweet, hypnotic globs.

Lucky tried to stay strong, but he knew he was going under, sliding into her words, drowning in her lies.

Calling up all the strength he had left, he put his feet under him and stood. He gathered in the corners of his mind and focused as best he could, struggling to complete one thought: *I wish—*

Isa raised her voice, then, spinning her spell in a voice like thunder and diamonds. She held her hand up and her long fingers squirmed like spider legs. And just like that Lucky's mind was caught in her glittering web.

"No one has told you the whole truth about that Key you wear, have they, Luccan?"

Lucky lifted his hand, touched the Key where it rested beneath his torn shirt.

"No one has told you what that Key will unlock. They don't want you to know what you hold, what you are. They let out knowledge like fishing line, keeping you on the hook until they can reel you in. They make choices for you, and make you think you've done the choosing."

Threads made of words and magic clung to Lucky's brain, hung in the doorways of his mind, studded with treacherous beauty like wintry ropes coated with glittering frost.

She captured him, pulled her web tight, dropped her voice to a sly whisper.

"The truth is, Luccan, power is beautiful, and those that hold it need not apologize. And your power… your power could be endless. All people could be at your disposal. Their lives should belong to you. The power to make—and to unmake—is rightfully yours."

Lucky stared straight ahead, straight into the witch's eyes. He wanted to turn away, break free, disappear. He pictured himself charging the blue glass walls, head down like a bull, launching himself through in a burst of shards. But he couldn't move, couldn't even shift his weight, and in seconds those last self-made thoughts vanished.

"Luccan, I can help you," Isa said, promising the reward she'd twisted his mind to make him want. Her voice grew urgent, and she lowered herself to one knee. Eye to eye, she leaned so close that her cold breath ruffled the fine hairs on Lucky's lip. "I can give it all to you," she promised. "But one thing you must do first. You must remove a single obstacle; the one man who has the power to oppose you. You will have to kill him."

She fell silent, letting the words circle like buzzards before swooping in to strip the meat from Lucky's last resistance. "He is outside, fool enough to come to our keep, where the Lord Mahl has fortified every inch of stone and steel, and where his own master will surely never come."

Slowly, never breaking her gaze, she drew the slender flask from her robes once more. She held it up between them and flicked off the cap with a thumb, allowing the greasy smoke to billow out. When a tight, dense cloud had formed above the bottle, she blew a long, putrid breath into it, sending the haze swirling toward Lucky.

He didn't want to, but he couldn't help it. He breathed.

"Yes," Isa said. "That's good. The Essence will help you see, Luccan, make you strong for your task."

As cold flooded Lucky's lungs and became part of him, or he became part of it, she rose to her feet. Stepping over Lohen's body, picking her way through scattered debris, she went to the door. Before opening it, she stopped.

"Rest now," she said. "When I return, I'll lay your nemesis at your feet. We'll join together, Luccan. We'll rule the worlds, once Thurlock is dead."

CHAPTER TWENTY-SEVEN: SAHLAMAHN

SAHLAMAHN SWOOPED out from the tower, flying low and causing everyone on the battlefield to cringe. When she lifted away toward the dark, predawn sky, her wings catching the tower's glow and glinting like sapphires and ice, the collective relief seemed almost an audible sigh.

The Black Cloaks turned their attention back to the coming riders. A handful of the Earthborns broke for a getaway. Han let them go. The rest, to Han's amazement, seemed prepared to take a stand. No more than perhaps twelve remained. Even if they'd all been fresh and none tired or injured, they would have posed little threat to six Mounted Guard.

Thurlock sped past Ethrans and Earthborns alike, bent low over Sherah's mane. Even at night, the mare's silver coat flashed as they passed through shadows. Her hooves, shod with sun-metal, sparked with every stride.

Liliana passed the Earthborns by, too, a sweep of her sword pointing her soldiers to the tattered fight, such as it was. Han limped as quickly as he might to the base of the hill, and got there in time to grasp Sherah's bridle as she skidded to a stop. Aedanh crowded in, and Ghriffon perched on a boulder.

Only Thurlock dismounted. Time was short.

Han said, "Sir, the drake.... It's Sahlamahn. I've only two of your arrows left."

"Where's your shield, Han? We can use that."

Han opened his mouth to answer before he realized he didn't know. It had been struck from his arm in the fight, and he had no idea when or where.

Henry, who had propped the exhausted L'Aria on a boulder and stood aside from the Ethrans, panting and bleeding a little, spoke up. "I know where it is. Let me catch my breath and I'll fly for it."

"You're the Condor," Thurlock said, and though it wasn't a question he waited for Henry's nod before continuing. "Lest there be no time to say it later, sir, thank you for what you've done. But you're exhausted and injured." He stopped to look at L'Aria, Maizie, and Han. "All of you are. I've brought something that can help a little."

Thurlock called down one of the eagles, a she-bird named Fiera. At the wizard's direction, Henry told the bird where to find the shield. As Fiera flew to her task, Thurlock took a fur-covered waterskin from his saddle and stepped toward Han, the most seriously wounded.

Han shook his head and pointed to L'Aria.

The wizard nodded. "Yes," he said, "of course."

When all the others had received their share, Han poured a swallow on his tongue, and recognized it instantly.

He smiled at Thurlock. "You've seen Tiro."

Thurlock only smiled back.

Though the Kindled Springs water didn't heal Han's injuries, it helped him find strength in spite of them. Not a night's sleep, but at least as refreshing as a long nap.

"Lohen went in—"

Thurlock held up his palm. "It's no surprise."

"Lemon is—"

"Later," the wizard said. "Right now we've a blue salamander to deal with. You're okay to ride, and shoot?"

He acknowledged Han's answering nod, and then turned to Ghriffon. "We'll need you and your crew to help with the drake."

In reply, the Eagle King lifted his beak and blew a column of furious scarlet flame ten yards high into the night. Flame eagles and ice-drakes had a list of grievances between them centuries long. It took no convincing to get them to fight Sahlamahn.

With a few words—and some squeaks and head tilts that no one else save possibly Henry understood in the least—the wizard told the king what he'd planned. Then, while Han strapped on the shield Fiera had brought back to him, he lifted the protesting L'Aria onto Ghriffon's back behind her Aunt Rose. "You'll be safest here," he told her.

Thurlock then said something in Sherah's ear, mounted up, and reached out a hand to help Han up behind him.

"Lady Grace," he said, "and Rose. I'll need to go into the tower, so I have to cross the moat, and we may as well kill a drake with the same stone, so to speak. Can the two of you give us some ground to stand on?"

"Yes," Lili said.

Rose added, "Be quick, though. We're too far from home to keep that up for long."

"All speed, then," the wizard said, and looked to the sky. "Sahlamahn is on her way in to find breakfast. Let's begin."

The four riderless eagles took off, circled around, and got into position behind Sahlamahn. Staying carefully clear of her deadly breath, dodging her whipping tail, they drove her in like avian cowhands. Blasts of flame charred her scales and nudged her toward the moat as if it were a cattle chute.

On the ground, the six soldiers tidied up the last loose ends of battle with the Black Cloaks, rounding up the die-hards and offering them a single chance to flee into the pines. All but two took the deal, and the crew quickly subdued them.

Lili dismounted, handing Aedan's reins to one of the guard. "In case something happens," she said.

Ghriffon airlifted Rose to the ledge where Mordred had made his stand, left her there, and then perched on a higher ledge, wings half-spread for balance, while L'Aria clung to his neck.

Liliana and Rosishan, sister witches, began melodic chants that spanned the moat and echoed one off the other in ethereal counterpoint. Each sister held a Spring Wand, a slender coiling branch the length of a woman's forearm. Lili's was formed from a pale green bough, Rose's dusty red.

Small globes of light formed near their hands, then climbed the length of the wands one after the other, blossoming from the tip. In seconds, their voices entwined and grew strong, and a long garland of light-blooms roped from each wand. Then the witches swung their wands forward to point toward each other. Their magic met, spliced, and broadened into a bridge cobbled from stones of rainbow light.

Mounted behind Thurlock, Han felt curiously small, but under the circumstances he thought that was fine. Sherah's patience seemed thinner than either his or Thurlock's; she stamped and snorted, while they did their best to relax and still keep their seats. Everything was ready, and they'd said the few words needed to cement their plan. Now they only waited for the drake to be jockeyed into place.

Sahlamahn had other ideas, though, and made her move so fast that probably no one saw it coming; certainly not Han. His jaw dropped. He choked out, "Sir!" He pointed.

Thurlock said, "Oh," seeming just as surprised.

The drake had suddenly swooped straight up with a single push from her great wings, an aerobatic move even the eagles couldn't match. Their efforts to follow, fast as they were, looked placid next to her mercurial climb. In a flash she escaped the reach of their flames.

Sahlamahn repeated the swooping maneuver with ease again and again, each time falling into a slight curving drop, then rocketing upward. Soon she had risen so high that even the jewel glitter off her wings disappeared in the distant dark. Ice-drakes on the hunt liked to fly in the high, cold winds to give an added chill to the air in their auxiliary lungs, the ones they used to kill.

Thurlock said quietly, "Han, tell the witches to conserve their energy."

Han conveyed that to Rose by means of thought, and Rose signaled Lili. The sisters lowered their wands and the volume and speed of their melodic chants, but kept the glowing magic ready.

Sahlamahn returned in a nosedive, wings pinned flat to her sides. Falling bullet fast, she aimed for the cluster of soldiers and captives who had taken shelter in the trees. Thurlock reined Sherah around and signaled with his knees, and the mare dashed ahead full speed. When they were within range, he lifted his staff, but Sahlamahn flew fast and very close to her intended prey. The wizard couldn't set the full force of his magic on her without endangering the people he wanted to save.

He swung his staff out in front, holding it like a jousting knight, and sent a single white-hot blade of flames across the drake's path. She swerved, using the reverse thrust from a blast of super-cooled air and a tweak of her wings to power into a labored climb. It cost her speed and agility, but she froze both captive Earthborns and an Ethran soldier with just the edges of that breath.

The eagles had been circling overhead. Now they dove, but the Condor got there first. He flew straight toward the drake, coming at a right angle toward her long, toothy snout—a reckless move. Sahlamahn had expended much of her killing air, but a drake is never defenseless. She turned her head toward her bold assailant. Han, watching below from too far away to help, expected the Condor to freeze and fall like an iceberg—and if that happened he thought his heart would follow suit. But just in time, the black wings splayed and swiveled and propelled Henry upward an essential few feet.

Fly, Han mentally urged, *get away!* But Henry perched on the monster's head. Digging his talons into tough hide and curling his neck at an impossible angle, he pecked at Sahlamahn's white, dinner-plate-sized eye. She screeched, bucked, twisted in the air as vitreous fluid spewed out, and then she pushed into a desperate climb.

Henry hung on, scraping talons and beak wherever he could find something soft enough to scratch until she rolled so sharply that he lost his hold and tumbled down. He pulled himself up just short of the pines' spiky tops, then braked with his wings and descended into the branches.

Han scarcely had time for a sigh of relief.

The Condor's rogue attack held the drake close in and left her half-blind, unsure of her course without binary vision. It bought time, and now the eagles caught up. They flew as close as they safely could to her good eye, knowing she'd dodge away from their flames to protect it.

Ghriffon, though avoiding recklessness with L'Aria still clinging to his back, swept off from the tower's wall. Riding the air between Sahlamahn's vast wings, he raked his talons over the drake's back time and again, keeping her close to the ground. Bit by bit, they herded her closer to the tower until she flew over the moat. She dove, and the eagles let her go, pumping their wings to keep from being dragged down in her tailwind.

Thurlock once again lifted his golden staff. Sherah reared up and burst into full, flying stride.

"Hang on," Thurlock shouted. He and Han leaned toward Sherah's neck as she bunched her haunches and leapt. A true leap of faith, for when Sherah's hooves left the edge of earth, nothing spanned the moat beneath them but blue-lit air.

But the sisters had their magic in hand, and even as wizard and warrior sailed out into nothing, their linked magic hardened again into the rainbow bridge. Sherah came down nimble and sure on stones of light, her sun-metal-shod hooves blazing gold.

In the tower's cruel light, Sahlamahn's ice blue scales sparkled like diamond knives. Han had expected that she'd stay low in the moat, but instead she shot up suddenly, fifty yards to their right. Her sapphire wings raised a dark, steely wind. When she trumpeted, ragged fringes of her breath laced the wizard's beard with frost. Like a serpent, she curled into a tight, twisting turn, then flattened her wings against her flanks and bulleted into a deliberate dive, driving hard at Han and Thurlock.

Thurlock never flinched. He raised his voice over the howl of Sahlamahn's monster wind. "Shield!"

Han raised the dragonhide buckler, thrusting it toward the right as if that small disk would stave off the monster's onslaught. Thurlock pointed his staff toward her and spoke. A spinning ball of white light and concentrated power shot from the staff's sun-metal tip like lightning and passed through Han's shield. Fire blasted from the far side of it, a thundering flash of superheated, golden magic.

Sahlamahn's great, beautiful wings burst into gem-bright flames. Reeking smoke coiled from burning hide. In agony, she screamed and dove in a futile attempt to escape the blaze she carried in her flesh.

The sisters' magic beneath Sherah's hooves began to pulse and vibrate. The witches were near their limit. Thurlock swung his legs over Sherah's head and jumped to the bridge deck, tossing the reins to Han. "Trust Sherah," he called back over his shoulder and then ran, planted his staff, and vaulted onto the granite ledge at the tower's hidden door.

As Sahlamahn neared her next pass under the bridge, Han strove for calm. Thurlock had given him what he needed—two remaining sun-fletched flame arrows and a crippled dragon. It was up to him to finish her. He'd have one chance to do it.

The drake ducked to pass under the bridge. As Sherah struggled against the wind and the faltering magic to give him a steady seat, Han nocked the wizard's arrow and pulled the bowstring back into a full draw.

Sahlamahn's great head emerged beneath him. Chewing his lip mercilessly, he struggled to take aim on the tiny, moving target. There, just behind the drake's armored skull, just above the reticulated scales of her back, a sickle of pale, pulsing, unprotected flesh.

He fired.

He missed.

The arrow bounced off the drake's hard skull and fell unlit into the moat.

For an instant, the sisters' magic broke down. Sherah stumbled, but the witches made it solid again before she fell. The close call set Han's heart thumping. When the fright passed, he finally relaxed—and almost laughed.

Die later, fool, he told himself. *Right now, aim, fire, kill the drake before it's too late.*

He sensed the continuing strain on the magic that held them aloft over the moat, felt Sherah quiver as she wrestled with her instinct to flee before the road vanished. He watched his small target pull away until it became a tiny blip in his vision, an idea more than a sight.

Somehow, the distance, the difficulty of the shot, the impossibility of survival, made it easier. Nothing existed in any world except this single bowshot. With his mind, he rode the arrow as it flew.

The shaft ran fast and true and plunged deep into the beast's brain. Paralyzed, Sahlamahn began to plummet, wizard's flame wreathing her skull and bursting from her eyes, nostrils, and mouth.

"Behl-Eth Dahn," Han whispered, incapable of another thought.

Sherah moved, not ready to die now *or* later and not willing to let the wizard down. He'd entrusted Han to her care, and care she would—Han was aware of her annoyed thoughts even as he struggled to hang on. Trumpeting as if calling to the wind for aid, she muscled into a leap. She landed her hooves once just before the bridge vanished. With one more great push with her powerful hindquarters, she bounded to the safety of solid ground.

Han slumped out of the saddle and, hugging the mare's frothy neck, turned to face the tower. The wizard, gray robes shining, stood at the edge of the granite and looked back at him.

A smile. A wink. Thumbs up.

Han laughed, and Sherah whinnied softly. Only Han knew that she was laughing too.

Thurlock took a deep draft of the water from Kindled Springs, pivoted on his heel, and rapped his golden staff on Isa's door.

CHAPTER TWENTY-EIGHT: MANNATHA

THURLOCK. LUCKY heard the name, and even spoken in Isa's hollow voice it stirred his memory, chiseled bits from the ice that had encased his heart. The door to the chamber slid open, and the witch said the name again, but this time with a note of surprise, or perhaps alarm.

"You were perhaps not expecting me?" Thurlock's voice chimed into the chamber as mellow and rich as struck gold. The haze over Lucky's eyes thinned, and he saw the wizard framed in the dark doorway, staff gleaming with its own light.

"How did you get up here?" Isa sounded both angry and incredulous.

"I followed my nose, Isa. Unmistakable scent."

The cold in Lucky's bones still held him stiff, but the wizard's quip made him want to laugh and cry all at once. He did neither, but his voice scraped loose. "Thurlock."

The wizard responded with a businesslike nod. "Hello, Luccan."

Lucky's heart thumped.

"Luccan!" The witch cast his name at him on a growl, all wrapped up in power again. In the same moment, she drew from her robes the slender steel flask and sent it flying toward him with a jet of magic.

Lucky flinched, but it would have been too slow. Thurlock swung his staff like a bat and intercepted the missile. The flask shattered in a flash of light. The remains of the smoky black substance sizzled in the air and evaporated.

"Isa. Leave the boy alone."

Isa's reply hissed through the chamber. "You, Thurlock, have no power to Command in my tower and no power at all over me."

"But I do."

"You're a weakling, soft. Sentiment and self-doubt cripple you. You cannot prevail."

"It's true, I'll grant it. I'm but human, and I can't stand against you in your master's house. But I've brought along some things that might help."

Isa stared at him, a look so cold Lucky thought it might freeze fire. She spoke very softly.

"When I've finished my work here today, wizard, when I have given that child's power to Mahl…." She paused to gaze at Lucky. "You and your weakling god will be like ants at the feet of my Lord Mahl and…. Well, he'll be interested in the boy, but I'll… dispose, let's say. I'll dispose of *you* myself."

She thrust her hands overhead and screeched out sounds so foul they could only be a curse. Bringing her hands down in front of her like judgment, she jabbed all of her fingers toward the wizard, blue lightning streaking from their tips. The wizard's head jerked back, and then he stood frozen in place, glazed in icy flame.

All of the dark doubt the witch had tried to plant in Lucky withered away. He tried to stand, but the Essence had not yet let go of his limbs. They felt stiff and painfully cold. He wanted desperately to help the wizard, but beyond wishing it, he could do nothing. He finally managed to move his right hand a few inches and take hold of the Key of Behliseth.

Thurlock's hands tightened on his staff, and a thin white-gold shield expanded inch by inch to surround him, holding the blue force off him by the slimmest margin. His face contorted with effort and slowly, slowly he lowered his left hand to his robe and drew a heavy glass vial from a pocket. He opened his hand, and the vial clattered to floor, but it didn't shatter.

Against the force and weight of Isa's magic, he raised his staff knee-high and then brought the sun-metal tip crashing down on the vial. The glass disintegrated and light exploded, creating a sheet of golden flame that battled Isa's fire. Freed, Thurlock raised the staff again, higher this time, and held it with two hands low on the shaft. "By Behl's light and the Gods' Breath of the Sunlands," he thundered, "you will not have him!"

This time he brought the pommel down, striking the sun-metal globe against the blood-smeared marble floor with a loud *crack!* A wind rushed forth from it, a great undying gust that blew the wizard's robes and hair back and then circled him as if he, Thurlock, was the very heart of a whirlwind. With a broad sweep of his arms, he threw the staggering force of the wind toward the Witch-Mortaine.

The mighty wind quenched Isa's magic and hurled her against the hard, icy walls. Her skull crashed against the glass block. She remained standing until the wind let go. Then she slid to the floor and sat with her back propped crookedly against the wall of her fortress, glass blue eyes wide open and empty.

Thurlock's wind, smelling of new hay, salt breeze, and sunshine, had driven the last traces of Isa's smoky evil from Lucky's lungs. His mind cleared, warmth filled his chest and spread all the way to his toes and fingers. He still hurt just about everywhere, but at least his body felt like it belonged to him again.

Better yet, the witch was dead. He said, "Yes!"

But Thurlock, after stooping for a moment to catch his breath, had walked heavily over to Isa's body, and now he knelt beside her corpse, shaking his head slowly. He whispered something Lucky couldn't hear and then closed her eyelids with a gentle hand.

"I'm sorry, Isa," he said. "I wish it had been different."

Lucky gaped in disbelief. "You're sorry! Don't you want her dead?"

"My wants don't much matter at this point, do they?" Ire flashed in Thurlock's eyes, but he spoke calmly. "Since you asked, you should know. Isa wasn't always the creature you've seen. Once she was… I loved her, long ago."

Lucky started to object that it wasn't possible for Isa ever to have been someone who could be loved, but he shut his mouth when he read a warning in Thurlock's face.

"We'd better go," Thurlock said, back to business.

He might have said more, but again Lucky interrupted. "But we're safe now, aren't we? I mean, she's dead…."

"We are for the moment, but you forget, or perhaps you never knew, that Isa was but a servant, a tool. I have no doubt that her master can still make use—"

A thin wheeze and a weak cough came from across the chamber.

Lucky nearly tripped over his still-aching legs, trying to run toward what he had thought was his father's dead body.

"He's alive!"

Thurlock's huge strides got him there first. He knelt by Lohen and raised his head to ease his breathing. Two steps away, Lucky stopped, finding himself too anxious and afraid, too happy and angry, to move or even breathe.

Lohen's eye was open, glazed as if with fever, but not blind. He met the wizard's gaze. "The Gods' Breath," he rasped, and a flicker of a smile crossed his bloody lips. "I remember, wizard. I heard it in the wind. The Oakridge… my son…." The words trailed into a fit of coughing.

Thurlock waved Lucky closer. "Here, Luccan, help me. Hold his head up." From his robes he fished out a waterskin covered with fur; he uncapped it and held the spout to Lohen's mouth.

After a few drops had trickled past his lips, Lohen breathed easier. He nodded at Thurlock, and the wizard gave him more. He seemed to relax then, as if the pain eased, but he said, "I don't have much time."

Thurlock took hold of Lohen again and eased him back to rest, propped against his shoulder. "It's you he wants, Luccan. Come around where he can see you."

Lucky bent over Lohen, willing tears not to fall, wanting desperately to find words of reassurance.

"Son," Lohen breathed.

"You're going to be okay. We'll get you out of here and—"

"No!" Then, more gently, "No, son. I'll die."

Lucky swallowed a protest. "Papa."

That brought Lohen a smile. "Listen," he said between labored breaths, "Mannatha. It's who you are. Luccan Elieth Perdhro, Mannatha, Suth Chiell." He lifted a hand and smoothed Lucky's hair off his brow. Seconds later, he was gone.

Thurlock put a hand on Lucky's shoulder, and a long, silent moment went by. Just as it seemed Thurlock might speak, a strange, hollow laugh came from across the chamber….

Near the wall….

Where they'd left Isa's corpse.

The witch's broken remains still lay skewed crookedly against the wall, but her eyes had popped wide open. In life, the irises had been so pale Lucky had feared he might see through them, but now they'd gone blue-black and dull. And they never blinked. Her dead lips moved. Her voice erupted unlike that of any living human soul.

"You are impressive, Wizard Thurlock, certainly more durable than this pathetic witch presently at my service."

A foul voice, certainly foul, but it carried the accents, patterns, and closed-mouth vowels of a person highly educated at an English university. Lucky arched his brows and stepped back in open-mouthed shock.

"An idea strikes me," the voice continued. "Borrowing a phrase from this world, we might say my 'star is on the rise.' On the other hand, your master, that conniver Behl, is well past his day. Why don't you cut your losses, join up with me? You can live forever, second in power only to me. Quite an offer, eh, old boy? What do you say?"

Thurlock rolled his eyes. "I won't even grace that with an answer, you old fraud."

The thing laughed, in that restrained "huh, huh, huh" of the English upper crust, and Lucky's jaw dropped even farther. Then a shadow, a transparent yet solid blackness, oozed from Isa's body and hovered around her like a smothering cloud.

Lucky knew that blackness.

Mahl. The evil god Thurlock had tried to explain that night a million years ago over apple pie. Lucky wondered if he could will himself blind, turn off the Sight. But as horrible as it was to see a talking, dead witch possessed by an ultra badass shadow, he didn't dare look away.

"Well," the dead mouth said, "I had to try, you know. A matter of form. I must admit, old man, choosing you was the smartest move your boss Behlishan ever made. I say, though, what about a compromise? Give me the boy. I'll take him and let you live for now. Surely you won't miss him much—he's only a pup. You can train up another."

"As generous as that offer is," Thurlock answered, lips curled in sarcasm, "I refuse. Even if I was inclined to agree, which I am not, Luccan isn't mine to give."

"Well, then." The voice dropped to a whisper, in that instant gone deadly cold. "Let the games begin."

The shadow wrapped around the witch and raised her body to stand loosely on its dead feet. Then it swelled around her until it filled the chamber, straining the glass tower's seams and leaving only a shrinking circle of light where Lucky and Thurlock stood over Lohen's body.

The darkness flashed and crackled, bristled with bolts of blue fire. It started to swirl around the little circle of light, picking up speed until it whirled so fast Lucky felt dizzy. The noise of it shook the floor, cries and howls and crazy laughter. Thousands of tiny, tormented souls, that was what it sounded like, and all of them hungry.

The shadow deepened, intensified, and a wave of blue flame, low to the floor, rolled through it thundering like a freight train. As it passed over and through each of the dead wolves and wights littering the chamber, they started to move in a sick imitation of life.

Alien zombies. It seemed like the last straw.

Whatever grit Lucky had found in recent moments, whatever hope Thurlock's return had brought, whatever secret faith Lucky had nurtured that he might win free, it fled before this devil's carnival.

Raised like an unholy Lazarus, a cairnwight emitted a choked whistle. The other wight joined in, and the wolves howled. The beasts had turned blacker than night now, though in life they'd been white as snowfields. The ruby flames of their eyes had died. The only things that hadn't changed at all were the glistening teeth and steely claws.

The blue flame broke through the thin curtain of light and rolled toward Lohen's body.

"No!" Lucky shouted, throwing himself down to cover the corpse. "You can't have my father!"

But the blue fire crept on, and though it seemed to move at a snail's pace, Lucky had scarcely drawn another breath before he felt icy flames licking at the skin of his back. Hunched over Lohen, clutching the Key of Behliseth against his chest, he said it again, this time barely a whisper.

"No. You cannot have my father."

Maybe that was one of Lucky's potent wishes, or maybe it was because the Key of Behliseth was pressed between Lucky and his father. Perhaps there was another explanation. Whatever the cause, when the blue flame rolled through, Lohen wasn't raised. His remains vanished in a flurry of sparks, Black Blade and all, there one instant and gone the next.

Lucky lay on his back, drenched in pain, struggling to breathe and stay conscious.

Thurlock shouted, a huge sound with no words, and Lucky turned in time to see him crash his staff down on another vial. Again, light exploded. This time Thurlock spun in place and swept his staff in a circle, carrying along a fountain of gold-bright stars. The brilliance conquered the bits of shadow that had encroached and walled off the dark, enclosing Lucky and Thurlock in a cylinder of light.

But Thurlock wasn't done. He concentrated, worked so hard he began to sweat, chanted until from somewhere he raised a golden fire that engulfed his staff and the hand that held it. Then he lifted his face and said in a loud, clear voice, "Hold! I, Thurlock Ol'Karrigh, Rha-shi Behliseth,

Premier Wizard of the Ethran Sunlands, bind this light in balance against the void."

He drew his hand across the space, spouting flame, and emblazoned the golden wall with the runes—somehow familiar and known to Lucky—of his name. At once, the light-shield hardened. And the blackness outside of it, though it seethed and whispered, fell nearly still.

Thurlock leaned over his staff, dripping sweat and laboring to catch his breath. Glancing toward Lucky, he gestured, waving him closer. Lucky got to his feet, a painful process, and took two steps to stand by the wizard.

The old man pulled out the waterskin and passed it to him.

"Drink," he said.

Lucky took a short swallow and started to hand it back, but it was so good, so refreshing, that he brought it back to his lips for a good long draught. When he came up for air, he noticed the wizard—the tired, thirsty wizard—looking at him with brows raised.

"There's some left," Lucky said, passing the skin back. Thurlock tipped it up over his mouth, but only a few drops fell to his parched lips.

Chagrinned, Lucky said, "I'm sorry, sir… I, uh, I wasn't thinking."

"Oh, it's fine Luccan," Thurlock answered, and the twinkle of a smile gleamed in his eyes. "It's fine. I'm glad you drank it, and I'm glad it's done you some good. A few drops are plenty for me. I'm better already, and I need you to be strong."

"Me?"

"I'll need your help."

It was the last thing Lucky expected to hear. Hadn't the wizard come to rescue him? Flabbergasted, Lucky shook his head, pushed his hair out of his eyes, started to tremble.

Get a grip, Lucky, he thought.

"Luccan, listen. This can't last. This—" Thurlock broke off to wave a hand at the light-shield. "This is all I've got. I have no more vials of light, no more dawn wind stored in my staff. My strength isn't gone, but neither is it endless. And Behlishan, the god who can make me stronger, won't come. If you want to get out of here alive, you must help."

"Won't come? *Won't come!* What kind of god is that? That thing out there—" He jabbed a finger at the blackness beyond the shield. "—that's a god, isn't it? Mahl? Isn't that what you said? If that thing can be here, why not this… this Behl?"

"Please calm yourself," Thurlock said.

Lucky tried to loosen his clenched fist and jaw. But he turned away from the wizard's eyes.

"No Ethran god belongs in Earth." Thurlock said. "Mahl destroys Earth's balance just by being here. But he's always hungry, empty. That's what he is, a living void that can never be filled. He doesn't care a whit about balance. He feeds wherever he can.

"But, just as Mahl has his nature, Behl has his. He *is* balance. If he came here to Earth, it would only tilt the tables farther. He won't do it. He loves you; he is my greatest friend. But nothing will make him betray his nature."

Lucky heard. Brainwise, he understood. Heartwise, all that came through was *You're on your own, kid.*

Again.

But this time was different. All the times he'd felt alone before—even in the cave Hank called the Road Between, even when Hank died, and even, especially, here in the tower before his father or Thurlock showed up—always some secret part of him had believed that help would come.

Now, his mind strayed to Han, but he sensed nothing that might have been his uncle's presence, and that little twinkle of hope died before it was born. Thurlock would fail, was failing already. *And my father... dead and gone.*

"Luccan, you must help," Thurlock repeated.

Lucky glanced at him. Once again Thurlock had planted his staff squarely in front of him. The shadow outside had begun to quiver and bend, though the dead still stood unmoving, as if pickled in black formaldehyde. Thurlock worked hard to hold the light-shield firm a while longer.

Lucky wanted to say, *Stop. Forget it. What's the use?*

He stared at the spot where his father had lain in his final moments. Remembered how he looked in that moment of death. His features had relaxed, and despite the scars, Lucky had seen for the first time how alike they were.

Lohen had looked young. He'd looked peaceful. But even at his last breath, he'd gripped the Black Blade with two hands. Lucky thought of that knife's twin, the Amber, and his right palm began to itch for the weight of the hilt.

"This Blade can stop her," Lohen had said.

Could it?

It was about a yard beyond the wall of light, practically at the feet of the zombie witch. But the shadow didn't touch it. A bubble protected the Blade; shadow surrounded it but didn't make contact.

Maybe... maybe Mahl is afraid to touch it. If the Amber could stop the witch, maybe it can hurt him.

He gauged the distance. *I'm fast*, he thought. *I could get it.* But he'd have to go through the fires that battled at the barrier, both gold and blue. And then he'd have to go through the shadow. All the horrible things inside it would touch him.

What would happen to me?

But what did it matter? He might die, but he was pretty sure dead was the only way he'd ever make it out of this nightmare, anyway. He caught sight of the witch's face and felt his lips curl in a snarl. He thought nothing of it when she grinned in return.

He hated her, dead or alive, now as much as ever. All her malice was still there, all her selfish glee in the power to destroy. He wanted to slash her so bad he could feel the knife in his hands. It might be worth it, even if he died in the instant afterward.

"Luccan," the wizard said.

Lucky dove for the Knife. His right arm went through the curtains of flame.

Thurlock shouted "No!" He grabbed hold of Lucky's ankle and dragged him back, and at the same time swiped his staff through the breach. "Hold," he panted, and it almost sounded like he was pleading with the magic. "In Behl's name, hold."

"What did you do that for?"

"Luccan—"

"I wanted to kill her! Why did you stop me?"

The wizard seemed tired. He might have been nearing exhaustion. But when he shouted, there was enough power behind it to prickle Lucky's scalp.

"You cannot kill what is already dead!"

He had Lucky's full attention.

In a more normal tone, he said, "Your anger, your hate is a *gift* to Mahl. He feeds on it. He revels in it."

The hideous noises had started up again outside the wizard's circle. Horrible laughter, a deep, hollow sound doubled by the screech of the witch's dead larynx. Zombie wolves howled. Zombie wights whistled. Echoing voices from things hidden in shadow cried and moaned. Isa's empty voice started a chant. The living dead began to circle the chamber, like twisted children in a playground dance.

Gooseflesh prickled on Lucky's skin. It became clear: Thurlock could not keep the shadow and its creatures out forever. Mahl would win; he only needed to persist.

"I'm sorry that all of this has happened so quickly," Thurlock said, "and you're being asked to help though you've had no chance to learn how. It's patently unfair." A trace of his usual humor sparked in his gray eyes, but then it died.

"I can't fix that," he said. "The best I can do is to offer a few words and ask you to listen with your heart open."

Not too sure, Lucky only nodded.

Thurlock pursed his lips, as if concerned about the adequacy of that response, and then took a deep, resigned breath. "I cannot do this alone," he said.

"Then we're going to die, Thurlock." Even as Lucky spoke, he thought, *So much for listening with an open heart*, but he couldn't stop. "We're going to die, and that monster out there is going to win because I can't do it. I thought I could, but I was wrong. I can't. I'm sorry, but you're the wizard, not me."

"Yes," Thurlock said, patience sounding strained. "I'm a wizard, but Mahl is a *god*, and we're on his turf."

"It's hopeless, then—"

"Hush. Listen. Hate—that's his power source. Anger. Revenge. Those things make him strong. And when I say 'hate, anger, revenge,' I mean yours. It doesn't matter who you're hating—Isa, Mahl, me, even yourself—you're fortifying the very thing you want to destroy. Let it go, Luccan, before it's too late."

The words "too late" echoed.

Five yards away on all sides, a super-powerful light-and-life-sucking shadow full of dead things waxed more wicked strong with every second. Blue and white lightning bolts streaked through it a hundred times a minute. Ravaged faces grinned at Lucky; dead hands clawed at the wall between them. Zombie voices chanted and hissed; ghostly throats shrieked and howled.

The shield of golden light, the only thing holding it all back, had worn thin. Lucky felt Thurlock waiting for him.

I don't know what he wants me to do. Whatever it is, I can't do it.

"Luccan," Thurlock said softly. "Don't give up. Hold on to hope."

Lucky snorted. "My hope," he said, and thrust his burned hand out to point, "was that Knife."

"Luccan, the Knife is not the way." Thurlock's brisk tone drove the next words home. "We're out of time. Please, use what you've been given and take us home. This is *your* task. You have the key."

Oh… the Key. Lucky reached to the place where it hung at the end of its chain.

"Not that Key. That's part of it, but it's the key that lies beneath it—"

Wrong again, Lucky. Frustrated beyond hope, up to his neck in things he couldn't believe and problems he couldn't solve, he closed his ears, clammed up, and refused to think. But inside his silent shell, thoughts found him. Memories.

In his strange book: *Suth Chiell, you shall prevail.* A lie?

His father's dying words: *"Mannatha. It's who you are."*

Thurlock, speaking of a name given to Lucky that was lost, that even he, the wizard, didn't know: *"More is the pity."*

Mannatha, the name his father had found in the wizard's wind. That was the name the wizard had wanted. A secret name. A powerful name.

"Use what you've been given," Thurlock had implored.

Well... what exactly is that? Ever an orderly person, he started a mental list. To think, he pushed his hair out of his eyes; it hurt.

Make that number one, I've been given cuts, bruises, torn clothes, and a very painful burnt arm. Despite everything, he almost smiled. But that's not what the wizard meant.

What else? Speed.... Tools and power I don't understand.... Magic I can't control.... A new name....

But there was more, a gift wrapped inside his father's voice, tucked away in three small syllables. His father had died to give it to him, but he hadn't seen it then. Now it slammed into him like a punch in the gut.

His father had given back to him what the witch had stolen three years ago, the only thing Lucky had ever really forgotten.

He understood.

What was out there in the witch's chamber wasn't darkness, but emptiness. And what he could use against it, what he had been given, was the power to fill it up. With light, joy, laughter, even with tears. With life.

Mahl could *want*, but he couldn't *love*. He couldn't *hope*. For all his god-power, he could never decipher the human spirit. That was why he had needed Isa.

That's why he wants me.

Using Isa's corpse, he had her hands, but her soul, her humanity, had gone. Without that, he was blind to the heart. He would never guess that one person would fight or even die for another. He just didn't get it. That was the giant chink in his armor. Against Mahl, Lucky was armed to the teeth.

He had in his arsenal his mother's voice, her laughter, her breath brushing his cheek; Hank George beating his drum; Han's gentle words, "Take it easy, lad"; the taste of Thurlock's instant cocoa; the comfort of a lesson under the stars. Forever, he had the memory of his father saying, "Forgive me."

Love, brighter than a wizard's magic flames.

Hope, all the strands of it tied together.

Those were the things he had been given.

And a Key. "The one that lies beneath." With a small, surprised laugh, Lucky put his hand over the Key of Behliseth. Buried but alive under that bright metal, thumping a beat steady and strong, he found the true Key. Yes, the Key to magic, but also to powers greater and more mysterious.

"Luccan?"

Lucky jumped, startled by the wizard's voice. It had taken only seconds for him to wind through his thoughts, but time hadn't been standing still. The shadow had gained momentum. Evil screamed and howled out there, now, and the zombie witch and zombie creatures circled so fast they were almost running. The relentless dark magic had weakened the light-shield, forced it down and bent it over so that now all that protected them was a small, lit-up dome. And it was shrinking. Time was up.

"Now," Lucky said. He flashed the wizard a smile and took hold of the Key of Behliseth.

"I am Luccan Elieth Perdhro, Mannatha, Suth Chiell."

He spoke his names in a strong, steady voice, but when he finished he gasped in shock. His shoulders blazed.

Twisting his neck to see, he found that on his right shoulder a dark sun had erupted, the duplicate of Hank George's Mark of the Others; on his left burned its pale twin, the Ethran Mark of the Sun. The Marks spread like wildfire, central rays reaching toward each other.

When those beams joined over Lucky's heart and broached the Key of Behliseth, Lucky's bright magic was set free.

He wouldn't have known what to do next, but Thurlock guided Lucky's free hand to grasp his wizard's staff. Lucky closed his hand on the wood, and it felt exactly right. Twelve rays of light beamed from the sun-metal globe that topped the staff, in rainbow colors—all lively and warm, even the blues.

Without thinking about it first, Lucky held his other hand out and called the Amber Knife. *Thwack*, it hit his palm. In a gesture of victory he couldn't hold back, Lucky thrust that hand up, the Blade clenched in his fist stabbing skyward.

A pillar of white light blasted from the Knife's point and up through the roof of the dome. Around them, the great dark mass of the Ice-Lord Mahl fell away; the dead and undead thinned and dissolved to hazy mist.

For a slow-motion instant, Lucky locked his gaze on Thurlock's ancient, gray eyes.

"Together," the wizard said.

As one, they lifted the heavy staff and crashed it down. The stone floor vanished. Light sheeted from the heel of the staff and curved to form a glowing golden orb.

With Lucky and Thurlock safe inside, the magical sphere rocketed through the tower's spire like a shooting star.

Part Five: Finding Home

CHAPTER TWENTY-NINE: LUCCAN, LET GO!

LUCKY OPENED his eyes, thinking he must have passed out. He didn't know where he was or how he got there. Trying to work it out, he searched through the crazy events of the last twenty-four hours like so many hyperlinks: horrors.net, revelations.com, youcantbeserious.uk.co, and, all by itself on the imaginary webpage, magic.ru.

Yeah. No wonder his legs felt about as sturdy as a dishrag. One thing for sure, wherever his magic had taken him, he wasn't in Isa's tower anymore—too much light. Everywhere, 360 degrees. And it was all warm and golden. He liked it, but….

Where's the floor?

"Let go, Luccan." Thurlock sounded annoyed.

Lucky woke up the rest of the way and found that one of his sweaty hands clutched the wizard's staff, and the other had a death grip on the wizard's robes. He was standing so close that Thurlock's beard tickled his forehead and the smell of stale sweat was stealing his air. Far from pleasant, but still.

"If I let go, I'll fall."

"You won't." Apparently clinging fifteen-year-old people were not tops on Thurlock's list of favorite things. And the wizard was tired, looking older than stone again, though not nearly as bad as after the storm in his living room. But he seemed way more solid than… light. So Lucky argued.

"I will, too."

"Luccan, you'll be fine." Thurlock pried Lucky's fingers from his clothing and held him at arm's length. "Look," he said, "I'm standing, you're standing. We're not falling."

He's right, Lucky admitted. He breathed a little easier until two breaths later, when he suddenly remembered he had been holding the Key of Behliseth in his now-empty hand. He panicked. Then, patting at his chest like it was on fire, he found it on its chain around his neck.

Relieved and drained, he sank down to the… nothing and sat on it. "I thought it was over," he said and dropped his head into his hands.

Thurlock bent creaking joints one at a time, and then, when he was down far enough, sort of rolled sideways and ended up sitting. He sighed. Or maybe groaned.

"Have faith, Lucky."

The sound of the nickname, for some reason, helped. He gave Thurlock a weak smile. "You called me Lucky."

"It's one of your names, isn't it? And fairly apt, I'd say. That Hank George knew a thing or two."

Lucky nodded, pushed his hair out of his eyes, and swallowed hard. "Where are we? I mean… what is this… round—?"

Thurlock's exclamation cut the question short. "Look!"

Lucky's head jerked up, and his eyes flew wide. Straight out in front of them, slightly veiled by a skin of golden light, something loomed. Something that had five sides, stood in the middle of nothing, framed in stone, and hummed and vibrated like a turbine engine. Something for which, although he sorted through his entire vocabulary, Lucky could find no name.

A hole in the world.

The space inside it flashed, alternating black and white, faster and faster. Then it filled with steady light, so bright Lucky had to squeeze his eyes shut. A heartbeat later he opened them again and saw a universe slowly spinning toward a black center. He gaped, mesmerized.

The blackness grew. The bright dots around it could have been stars or sparks or even fireflies, spiraling inward to drain into the dark—which seemed as hungry as a black hole.

Gradually, it took on a new dimension. A membrane grew over the emptiness to cover it like a lens. That only made it seem deeper, darker, and more mysterious.

Like the wizard's eye.

Odd thought.

CHAPTER THIRTY:
THE TWIN STARS OF HOME

With a stomach-flipping jerk, the sphere of light in which Lucky and Thurlock rode began to move toward the spinning darkness. Energized with a wave of panic, Lucky grabbed the Key of Behliseth with one hand, the wizard's staff with the other, and sprang to his feet.

From nowhere the idea struck that this monstrous thing might be a Portal, though it bore no resemblance at all to the tame M.E.R.L.I.N. in the wizard's living room.

"Thurlock," Lucky said, voice quavering like an aged soprano. "Is that what I think it is?"

"If you think it's a Portal of Naught, then yes." Thurlock struggled to his feet with the help of his staff and Lucky's belatedly offered hand. Brushing invisible dust off his robes, he went on. "No fear, though, Luccan. Think of it as a road, or a gateway, perhaps."

Lucky's skin prickled head to toe. "A road," he said, treading with caution. "A gateway… to where?"

The wizard's eyes crinkled above his tattered beard, and he gently laughed. "Well," he said. "Not to answer a question with a question—I know how you hate that—but, where do you want to go?"

Worlds started to spin in Lucky's head. He felt the light-coach they traveled in stumble as if its power source threatened to fail, troubling his queasy stomach. "Can't we slow this thing down?"

The wizard leaned closer, the gathered wrinkles around his eyes spelling out concern. "I can't," he said, "but you probably can. This is your magic."

Lucky wanted to rebel against that idea one last time, but he said, "Okay," and to that simple admission the orb responded, slowing to a cosmic crawl. "Okay," he repeated and tried to think.

Where do I want to go? That depends. "Thurlock, what about Han?"

"Hmm, well." Thurlock tugged at his beard. "I left him outside Isa's tower not long ago, and he was all right. A bit worse for the wear, but he can deal with that, and he's quite resourceful, you know. He has little magic, but in a way that is his magic, if you get my drift. Why, once I saw him—"

"Thurlock, the point!"

"Oh, sorry. I'm back to my old habits, aren't I? The point is Han will be fine—"

"L'Aria?"

Thurlock smiled and raised his eyebrows. "She'll be fine, too. You aren't the only young person with gifts, you know."

Lucky thought he should feel better, hearing that, but he didn't. It wasn't that he didn't believe the wizard. Truthfully, he'd already known—somehow, sort of—that Han and L'Aria were both okay. He still worried about them, and Maizie, and a million other things, but that wasn't the trouble.

He pressed his palms against his eyes, trying to slow the whirling images in his head. Small improvement, though. When his mental chaos slowed, it settled into fearful visions of blood and death and evil. His stomach heaved.

"Thurlock," he whispered. "The things I've seen...."

The wizard went still and serious. His sea gray eyes rimmed with moisture, the muscle of his cheek twitched to the rhythm of old, secret pain. He reached out a hand and tweaked Lucky's hair out of his eyes.

"I'm sorry," the old man said.

Lucky looked back at him for a long time, steady. Finally he nodded. "Yeah."

The visions scattered, broken up by bits of remembered childhood. His mother, Han—his uncle, Thurlock, and even his father. And L'Aria; she'd been his friend, almost a sister. A winter kitchen, a flowering orchard, a summer swimming hole. Moments, pieces of time frozen like snapshots.

Beyond the wizard's threshold, Lucky had expected to find his way back to his childhood, but it couldn't be done. He knew that now. Three years and the last long week, crammed with things, people, terror, impossible events that had happened anyway, all of that hung between him and childhood like a curtain of stone.

So he straightened his shoulders, shoved his hair back, and set his sails instead for a bright star, a mirrored beacon that would always shine in twin places: one, his own heart, and another just beyond the horizon of the future. Together those lights made up a single destination, and Lucky knew what it was called.

He turned again to meet his friend's age-worn eyes. A smile crept onto his face.

"Home," he said. "Thurlock, I want to go home."

APPENDIX ONE:

OBSERVATIONS REGARDING CAPRICIOUS TIME STREAMS IN TWINNED WORLDS

—Willock III, in *Willock's World Windings* (Foreword)

THE PHENOMENON of twinned worlds is one that learned Ethrans have documented over many centuries. Indeed, the concept is rooted deep in the fabric of our most ancient oral traditions, and there has never been a time when Ethra did not recognize its twin, Earth, as occupying very similar, though not quite identical, universal coordinates. Interestingly, the population of Earth has only very recently begun to recognize and explore—via a philosophy of "scientific investigation"—the concept of parallel worlds, or dimensions of existence. While Ethrans have for millennia been utilizing the Portals of Naught to travel to Earth (as well as more spatially distant worlds), Earthborns have even now not admitted the possibility that any other world could in fact be co-located on the planet. Witness the quaint practice of naming the planet after their own world, and referring to places as "on" Earth, whereas any Ethran school child knows one can only speak of being "in" Earth, or "in" Ethra.

Twinned worlds indeed do exist elsewhere, and in fact a few worlds have been documented to share essentially identical space (on the same planets) with as many as seven additional worlds. It is theorized by some Ethran scholars and learned wizards that, indeed, all worlds bear the potential for multiples and will at some point develop siblings. (Thus we understand the foolish conceit of those who would call the planet upon which their world is anchored by the name of their world—or indeed by any name at all.) Regardless, however, of the prevalence of multiple closely aligned worlds, some aspects remain poorly understood. Not the least of these is the capricious nature of time as it relates to the processes underway in related worlds.

We, of course, know the behavior of time in Ethra and Earth more intimately than elsewhere in the universe, and I will confine my observations and postulations in this study to that which we know. We have well documented that time behaved in a very similar (if not identical) fashion for a long geological era after the worlds split due to a rift in the underlying creative process. However, as separation became more entrenched, we began to see time behave quite (if you'll forgive the term) capriciously. For most of the last millennium, Earth's time has proceeded at a much faster rate than experienced in Ethra. Some have proposed that circumstance as the reason Earth lost much of its understanding of manipulating matter through mental power, emotional strength, and alliance with divine beings—techniques we have come to call magic, or when more sophisticated, wizardry.

However, recent evidence shows that time cannot be counted upon to continue in this fashion. In fact, the difference in time speed between the twin worlds varies greatly, and recent observations hint at the fact that Ethran time is outpacing Earth time by a multiple of ten. The questions raised by these observations are many, and confounding, but may be of key importance if we are ever to regain a true relationship with our sibling world—a much sought after goal throughout some Ethran lands, notably, our own enlightened Sunlands.

In past experience, while Ethran travel to Earth has been undertaken by parties both large and small, Earth has been completely unable to deliberately traverse Naught and visit our world. Science in Earth may indeed be close to achieving this. While travel was one-sided, true shared study could not be safely achieved, and it is to our shame that we must admit unscrupulous Ethrans have all too frequently used our capability for nefarious purposes. Dare we hope that, at last, Earth can join us in mutual exchange?

This, as well as other mysteries of time, locale, and technology, is where my study has focused these past decades. In these volumes I humbly record my observations, possible conclusions, and my invitation for discourse and further scholarly investigation.

Humbly,
Willock III, Wizard of the First Order

APPENDIX TWO:

A BRIEF INTRODUCTORY HISTORY OF CIRQUE VALLEY AND VALLEY CITY, CALIFORNIA

Prepared for the Valley City Pioneers Association Millennium Commemoration
By Stu D. Baker, PhD
December 21, 1999

Valley City's history has been much influenced by topography. Most significantly, it is enclosed within a ring of volcanic hills, topped in places with more vulnerable pumice and even sedimentary shale or sandstone, but primarily composed of basalt and resistant to erosion. This range—now known as the Noose—is not arable, and except for a few homes in the foothills, has proven essentially uninhabitable for the human population. Marked by trails, in some cases worn by centuries of use into the rock itself, these peaks once provided subsistence hunting for the indigenous population and early settlers, yielding abundant small game, as well as a small subspecies of mule deer, now thought to be extinct. In the present day, the hills of the Noose are sparingly used for recreational purposes such as hiking or mountain cycling, but such exploitation is limited, as the area has been designated a wilderness preserve.

The historic effect of this ring of essentially untamable wilderness on the population of Valley City, which has spread to fill the entire Cirque Valley basin except for the rough terrain of Black Creek Ravine running through its center, has most significantly been isolation. Secondarily, it has contributed to a culture of respect for the vagaries of nature and the potential for harm thereby. A byproduct has been a reputation for a high prevalence of superstition among the populace, especially members of those families that have occupied the valley for several generations.

The first of these effects, isolation, is slowly being undone by technology. Roads have been blasted through the basalt and improved, over the years, to the point that there are now three easily traversed viaducts into the interior of the basin, usually open year-round. And, of course, the city's inhabitants enjoy the latest advances in satellite and cable broadcasting, computing, and Internet communications. There is a problem with cell phone technology in that signals traveling over certain areas of the Noose or across the central ravine are scrambled or lost, with a secondary result that traditional landline phone service continues in primary use, in homes and business as well as public coin-operated booths. Several technology enterprises and a team of researchers from Caltech are all working toward understanding and overcoming the cellular transmission anomaly, and most expect a solution in the near future.

In regard to the high degree of respect shown by Valley City's inhabitants for the potential for natural disaster (small and large), and to the propensity for superstition among the population, it must be said that the ravine mentioned above has been at least as influential as the presence of the Noose. Black Creek, which runs through the center of the ravine, is more correctly a river, but its source is a mystery. Interestingly the stream emerges from its underground presence just at the base of the twin basalt spires named Death of the Gods and runs west nearly to the opposite foothills. There, it descends in a steep cataract into Heart Lake, which then empties into Falls River, flowing in a southerly direction. Just within the foothills of the southwestern arc of the Noose, the river disappears underground again. While it almost certainly would make its way westward again to the Pacific, no one has ever located its terminus, confluence with another river, or coastal delta.

Although geological evidence shows that the ravine once channeled a much higher volume of water, the cut is a product of a split along two nearly parallel deep fault lines, which occurred an estimated 25,000 years ago, very recent in geological terms. Its width measures more than twenty miles in some places, less than five in others, and its floor elevation varies greatly, from twenty-eight feet below sea level at its lowest point near the very midpoint of the valley basin, and up to 246 feet above sea level near its eastern end. (The floor of the Cirque Valley basin itself lies essentially level at around 300 feet above sea level.) The part of the ravine that dips below sea level, astoundingly, has never been known to flood, though it is usually damp and in some places boggy. The reason it does not flood remains unknown, though it invites speculation and many theories have been advanced.

Chief among possible explanations is the idea that water drains away here to an underground reservoir that perhaps then feeds back into the underground portions of Black Creek and Falls River, or emerges as an underground spring feeding into Heart Lake. No evidence has been found for this draining, and it begs an obvious question: Why then does Black Creek itself not descend underground at that point? The theory persists in popularity, in the opinion of this writer, primarily because no sounder theory has yet been advanced.

Black Creek Ravine is lined in places with basalt palisades that stand like crowded pillars. The shelves where the columns have broken boast a thin covering of soil rooted and held in place with hardy pine, mesquite, or other brush. In other places the present day walls of the ravine are formed by piled up sediments, like snowdrifts against a fence, and the slopes, though still precipitous, ascend more gently, and can be traversed on foot. Some relatively wide level areas along the slopes have become meadows and glades, including a singularly successful stand of myrtle.

The soil of the ravine bottom, as one would expect, is rich and fertile, though never more than a few feet thick over the underlying rock. It is home to many species of flora and abundant wildlife, including a few smaller species or subspecies that have never been found elsewhere.

The area's more widespread mammal species are coyote, rabbit, various smaller rodents, and a recent population of feral domestic cats and dogs. The rock-strewn slopes are also home to desert tortoise, numerous snakes and lizards, and noteworthy insects and arachnids. The forest is of course home to many smaller bird species, most of which can be found throughout the greater region, and the grassier slopes and the creek's banks host *Lepidoptera* and small waterfowl. The higher crags and evergreens provide nesting territory for several species of hawks and owls, as well as golden eagle and, surprisingly, a small but persistent population of California condor.

The troublesome topography of Black Creek Ravine resisted efforts toward human exploitation during the first century of nonnative habitation of the valley. In 1963 the entire area was designated as Valley City Watershed Preserve. This was a precedent-setting move that has since been imitated by smaller cities around the United States, but it came as a result of disastrous failure of earlier attempts to utilize the rich resources of the ravine and its surrounds.

Black Creek and the deep ravine yielded heavily for trappers until the otter, mink, beaver, and bear nearly disappeared. Early families found the fishing fruitful and hunted the strangely placid deer they found in the mixed forest of the ravine. Settlers tried as well to mine the mineral-rich slopes and farm the level land immediately adjacent to the ravine on either side. Mines proved to be impractical, the technology of the time inadequate to the task of creating stable, workable tunnels. The rich soil at the edge of the ravine, however, produced abundantly when cultivated. Letters sent east by the earliest pioneers, preserved in the historical society's archives, hailed the valley as a utopia, a Promised Land, Eden itself.

Settlers were soon dispossessed of contentment and confidence. Repeatedly, unexplained events resulted in the death or disappearance of settlers, one alone, or in numbers. A few people blamed the native population, but the idea was proven false (though not before some lynch-style hangings had occurred). To read the firsthand accounts of these events and their aftereffects is even now hair-raising.

In addition to mining disasters, over the course of two decades the area experienced an onslaught of numerous wildfires, lightning strikes, and violent storms. A number of occurrences seem more difficult to explain. Trappers were found many miles east or west of their trap lines, dead or unconscious. Children swimming in Black Creek disappeared before the eyes of the parents and were never located. (This despite reportedly crystal-clear water, efforts to probe the bottom, and no evidence of underwater egress.) In one incident, an entire slope of the ravine shifted in the absence of quake or flood or other clear explanation, and three farmsteads disappeared. Only a few traces of the buildings were later recovered, while a few farms animals were found dead or dazed at a site on the opposite side of Black Creek. Of the estimated thirteen people present at the time on the steads, no trace was ever found.

Perhaps understandably, the population gradually abandoned the ravine, and the adjacent acreage now stands vacant in strips one to four miles wide on either side, running most of the length of the ravine up to the cataract of Westfall. In 1971, that acreage was added to Valley

City's protected watershed, and in 1973 a park was created at the western end of the ravine around Heart Lake. It has been free of unusual calamity.

The original inhabitants of Cirque Valley called themselves the Kotah'neh, and they remain the only group of people ever known to have successfully occupied Black Creek Ravine and the land near it. The remnant of this civilized, tribal nation is spread thinly now across the US and Canada, and some members live in other parts of the world. Those who remain with relatively pure lines of descent number fewer than fifty. Although it would seem that the number is likely to decline in the future, the Kotah'neh, like many indigenous peoples, have been remarkably successful at survival.

Although the Kotah'neh (commonly referred to in early accounts as Cirque Valley Indians) have substantially left Cirque Valley to the nonnatives who came to the area, by Kotah'neh standards, only recently in the mid-1800s, there remains a small core, members of a single family, who continue to inhabit the George cabin. The cabin stands in a wooded area of mostly pine wood on the north side of the flat land on the rim of Black Creek Ravine. It neither hugs the hills of the ring, nor perches close to the ravine's edge, its snug location providing a possible explanation for its ability to endure the ravages of time in an area known to be unstable.

The area from the twin spires of Death of the Gods to the old Martinez Road, on both sides of the river and the ravine, belongs to the Kotah'neh in perpetuity, but it is not an Indian reservation in the legal sense of the word. Kotah'neh ownership derives from a land deal they made with the once-influential Martinez family and the Township of Valley City in 1899. Their title is not conditional; there is no requirement that the Kotah'neh occupy the land or that they maintain tribal identity. It is, simply, theirs forever, as they claim it has always been. Interestingly, in the deal that led to this provision, it is acknowledged that the Kotah'neh ceded the remainder of Cirque Valley to the Township, which would support the idea that the nonnative inhabitants of the time acknowledged the tribe's ownership of the whole.

The earliest Euro-American pioneers, arriving in the summer of 1864, were ten families: Martinez, Salcedo, Walburg, Goldberg, Langdon, MacDougall, Moore, Usitalo, Brzezinski, and Kerrigan.

Many of these families remain in the populace today. Traces of their early work can be found everywhere, including homes, cultivated or pasture lands, and roads.

Many new families of settlers made the arduous trek over the Noose during the next four to five decades. After the turn of the century, population growth slowed and stabilized before accelerating again in the post-World War II years. The population has since remained at about 70,000 as counted in the last two national census years (1980, 1990). It is expected that growth will come slowly over the next century, owing chiefly, still, to the nature of the land itself.

LOU HOFFMANN, a mother and grandmother now, has carried on her love affair with books for more than half a century, and she hasn't even made a dent in the list of books she'd love to read—partly because the list keeps growing as more and more fascinating tales are told in written form. She reads factual things—books about physics and stars and fractal chaos, but when she wants truth, she looks for it in quality fiction. Through all that time she's written stories of her own, but she's come to be a published author only as a Johnny-come-lately. Lou loves other kinds of beauty as well, including music and silence, laughter and tears, youth and age, sunshine and storms, forests and fields, rivers and seas. Proud to be a bisexual woman, she's seen the world change and change back and change more in dozens of ways, and she has great hope for the freedom to love in the world the youth of today will create in the future.

You can find Lou on Facebook at https://www.facebook.com/lou.hoffmann or Twitter @Lou_Hoffmann.

The 7th of
LONDON
Beau Schemery

http://www.harmonyinkpress.com

Pretty Peg
meow!
Skye Allen

TRIANE'S SON RISING
AMY LANE
BITTER MOON SAGA
BOOK I

CPSIA information can be obtained
at www.ICGtesting.com
Printed in the USA
FFOW01n1534300914
7687FF